LIKE A CHARM

EDITED BY

KARIN SLAUGHTER

Also by KARIN SLAUGHTER

COP TOWN

Cop Town

THE WILL TRENT SERIES

Unseen

Busted

Criminal

Snatched

Fallen

Broken

Undone

Fractured

Triptych

THE GRANT COUNTY SERIES

Beyond Reach

Faithless

Indelible

A Faint Cold Fear

Kisscut

Blindsighted

OTHER WRITING

The Unremarkable Heart

Thorn in My Side

First Thrills, Vol 3

Martin Misunderstood

LIKE A CHARM

A Novel in Voices

WILLIAM MORROW
An Imprint of HarperCollins*Publishers*

A continuation of the copyright page appears on pages 377–378.

For information address HarperCollins Publishers, 195 Broadway, New York, NY 10007.

HarperCollins books may be purchased for educational, business, or sales promotional use. For information please e-mail the Special Markets Department at SPsales@harpercollins.com.

A hardcover edition of this book was published in 2004 by William Morrow, an imprint of HarperCollins Publishers.

FIRST WILLIAM MORROW PAPERBACK EDITION PUBLISHED 2005.
FIRST DARK ALLEY PAPERBACK EDITION PUBLISHED 2005.

Illustrations by Bill Burgess

Designed by Mia Risberg

The Library of Congress has catalogued the hardcover as follows:

Like a charm : a novel in voices / edited by Karin Slaughter.— 1st ed.
p. cm.
ISBN 0-06-058330-4 (alk. paper)
1. Detective and mystery stories, American. 2. Bracelets—Fiction.
3. Charms—Fiction. I. Slaughter, Karin, 1971–.

PS648.D4L55 2004
813'.6—dc22 2003067676

ISBN 978-0-06-058331-6 (pbk.)

15 16 17 18 19 OV/RRD 10 9 8 7 6 5 4 3 2

For Cathy,
who thought this was a great idea

CONTENTS

LIKE A CHARM

ROOTBOUND

Karin Slaughter

Blood Mountain, Georgia, 1803

Macon Orme was so hungry when he found the squirrel caught in the snare trap that he ate it with his bare hands. The hot rush of blood hitting his stomach was like poison, but he swallowed the fatty meat past the gag that wanted to come, the squirrel's razor-like claws cutting into the sides of his face as he gorged himself on the sweet meat of the creature's underbelly.

Satiated, he fell back against a rock, his breathing coming in pants, the lingering taste of the squirrel sticking in the back of his throat like molasses. His stomach made a churning sound, and he put his hand there as if to quiet it. He could feel the blood dripping down his chin and caught it with his sleeve, hoping the dark material of his shirt would not show the mark of his sin.

"I'm sorry," he said, an apology that would never be heard to the man who had set the snare.

Three days had passed since he had stood at the *poctaw,* the wishing circle of the Elawa. Hallucinations came easily with hunger, and when Macon closed his eyes he was sitting there again. He could smell the smoke from the fire, feel dark hair brushing against his bare arm. The woman had stood before him, half naked and gyrating in some dance that obviously had a religious meaning for her people but in Macon had only brought out burning lust. He squeezed his eyes shut, thinking about being inside her, feeling the gyrations firsthand. So many years had passed since he had lain with a woman without having to pay first. So many years had disappeared into the quagmire of his mountain existence. When he thought of her beneath him, his balls ached with anticipation, even as a cold winter wind snapped through the trees.

Macon stood because he had to. He felt a flash of guilt for breaking his self-imposed fast, but three days without nourishment was a lifetime to a man whose belly was all too familiar with the pains of hunger. Bad fortune had made him go without food before, but it seemed like every time he thought of the woman his body demanded more nourishment than it had ever needed before. If he did not want her so much, he would hate her.

As if they sensed his need, animals seemed to taunt him, running across his path, veering in and out of his line of sight. A deer stood in the forest, eyeing Macon carefully, as if searching his soul. A rabbit followed him for a mile at least, slowly hopping in Macon's footsteps, pausing now and then to clean its face. Most of his life had been spent trapping these beasts in the hundreds: laying snares and steel traps that cut so deep, sometimes there would be an amputated paw waiting instead of a full-size jackrabbit when he checked on his weekly rounds. Other times, he would see the teeth marks in the stubbed end of bone where they had gnawed off their own limb in order to free themselves. These were cunning animals, bent on survival. Macon gave them his respect because he saw in them something he saw in himself. He would survive.

Though he found himself of late wondering what this survival cost him. He had not seen a looking glass in many years, but often Macon would see his own reflection in a stream when he stopped for water. Age had descended harshly. White grew into his beard, and when he thought to comb his fingers through his hair, chunks would come out in his hand, the roots sticking up like tiny fragments of his youth.

There had been a time when vanity had been second nature to Macon Orme. He had oiled his hair and done it proper with the bone comb that had once belonged to his father. Saturdays he had bathed before the weekly dance, where he would hold the neighbor's daughter close to his chest, smell the musky scent of her, dream of pressing his hips into hers. Sundays he had worn a starched collar that chafed his neck, pants that showed a fine crease down the front. He had kept a watch in his pocket on a slender silver chain. Macon Orme had been a farmer, a man concerned with the passage of time. Then the Muscogee came and destroyed the farm. The Indians were merciless. They stole the horses and gave his mother such a fright that she grabbed her chest and fell dead to the ground. They razed the crops and what they could not carry away on horseback they burned. They took it all like it belonged to them.

Macon punched his fist into his thigh. Here he was, fifteen years later, making a fool of himself for some dark-skinned heathen; the same sort of heathen who had birthed the bastards who took his farm. That farm would have been Macon's inheritance. He would have had something to give the neighbor's daughter, something to lure her into letting him press his hips into hers for real. He would have given her a child—many children. They would have grown old together but for that day when everything had been taken away from him.

And yet he longed for the Indian woman in a way he had never known. He dreamed about her, tasted her in his sleep. Even before he had happened upon their camp three days ago, Macon had felt a tugging at his chest, as if a string had been looped around his heart and something—someone—was pulling him toward her. That last night before he found their small settlement, a powerful burning in his chest had awakened him and he had abandoned his camp and stumbled up the hill toward the woman without even knowing why.

She'd stood there at the peak, wind blowing her wild black hair. Fire of a color he had never seen spat up in front of her, the smoke climbing lazily into the night air. Macon inhaled, and the burning in his chest calmed with each deep breath. Peace came over him, and he crouched in front of the fire like a heathen and watched her dance.

"O-cho-wanee-ki," she sang, her voice husky and without any particular music. Her skin was as dark as pitch; hairless and smooth.

A gold chain trickled out either side of her fisted hand, and she held it over the fire, inches from the flame, so close that a sweat broke out over Macon's body just watching her. Slowly she let out the chain, mumbling incomprehensible names for the small charms attached to the bracelet.

"A-shownee," she said. Bear.

"Coskoo," she said. Monkey.

Six charms slid out of her hand, snaking closer and closer to the fire. Macon watched, his mouth open, smoke wafting into his lungs as a golden bear dangled over the flames. The detail was astounding, the creature almost lifelike as the flames licked up and down the side. He could see every part of the animal: the soft fur, the needle-thin claws, the pads of its one open paw as it stood on hind legs to strike. Macon leaned closer to the strange fire, hypnotized by the tiny red jewel at the center of the bear's chest.

Hours might have passed, but Macon did not notice. The woman danced in a circle around the fire in all her naked glory. She twirled and leaped until the moon hid behind the mountain-tops, and then she stopped as suddenly as it all had started, again dangling the bear out over the roaring fire. Her head jerked up suddenly, and she stared at him—right into him. Macon felt every muscle in his body tense, his bones aching from the pressure. He was panting; his head started to spin.

She chanted something under her breath, so low that even straining he could not hear her. Something flashed in the deep, dark black of her eyes and she held out her hand, the bracelet in her palm. Macon could see the charms, but his mind gave no name to any of them but the bear dangling at the end. This last charm she held swaying over the fire, so close her skin must have burned, yet she did not flinch.

The gold slowly melted and began to drip into the flames until all that was left was a teardrop-shaped lump of gold with the red stone in the center. As Macon watched, the woman took the bracelet, held it above her open mouth, and bit off what was left of the bear. It sizzled on her tongue, then her neck moved as she swallowed. All Macon could think was how good it would feel if she swallowed him.

As a trader, Macon had wandered all over these mountains. He knew the peaks and valleys like a man knows his own heart: the Coosa and the Tallapoosa, Licklog, Slaughter Gap. Paths had been cut into the ground by Macon's own two feet as he trapped and killed, skinned then traded the animals for comforts he would not otherwise have known: coffee, tobacco, shoes, women. Two skinny rabbits got him a cake of soap. A tender-eyed doe that happened into a snare brought a sturdy old rifle with good sites. Indian jewelry would get him a woman; a rabbit's paw or some other trinket would buy the lard and lavender mix the madam sold to ease the friction when they fucked. Macon knew all the tribes in the mountains, traded with them because he had to, more often than not getting the better part of the deal. He knew the Lower Creek wanted arms while the Cherokee wanted silk, and that it didn't matter because Jefferson was forcing the filthy bastards the hell out of there anyway.

Yet, that night, stumbling upon the woman, Macon was shocked to find a people he had never known. The Elawa weren't like the other Indians Macon had seen. There were no tepees or mounds or animal skins strewn about. The woman's solitary dance was nothing he had ever witnessed during tribal rites or war parties. They spoke no English and seemed uninterested in learning any. He was not even sure what they called themselves. "Elawa" had been a name of Macon's own design, borrowing from the Cherokee for "earth."

They were living out of shallow caves carved into the belly of the mountain, scraping up gold dust and smelting it into jewelry the likes of which Macon had never seen. The quality of their work was remarkable considering the meager tools they used: blunt instruments that seemed better suited to grinding flour than performing delicate deviations in heat-softened gold. The men toiled all day, their backs curved into permanent arcs as they held a round wooden platform between their feet, turning it this way and that with their toes as they created art that Macon knew would fetch significantly more up north.

Other things about them stood out. There were no useful animals around the compound—no horses or cows or even donkeys. Dogs had free reign of the site, but the people parted for them as if they required deference. The tribe flinched at the sight of the skins Macon offered to trade for their gold charms. Even when he brought out his better merchandise—deer, bear, chinchilla—they recoiled as if the death he held in his hands carried some kind of contagion.

After the woman had finished her dancing, a powerful-looking young man whom Macon took to be the chief came up the hill, his headdress riddled with solid black feathers, his body painted in animal designs: rabbit, snake, lion. Behind him was a gnarled old man who leaned on an even more gnarled walking stick. His eyes were cloudy white, like spoiled milk, his teeth as black as night. Red clay was smeared all over his body. Black dirt from the forest marked his naked genitals.

From the cotton pouch the man wore at his side, Macon guessed this was the medicine man, the healer of the tribe. He tried a smile, not wanting to get on the man's bad side, knowing instinctively that this was the most respected man in the group.

"Lapacha ko wanee," the old man snarled. He reached into his bag, pulled out a handful of black dirt, and threw it on the ground with disgust. Macon had no idea what it meant until the man spat on the lump of dirt three times in rapid succession.

It was a curse.

"Ha." Macon tried to laugh, saying the word instead of making the actual sound. Indians had cursed him all of his life. There was nothing this old dirt-covered coot could do to Macon that hadn't been done to him already.

The chief clapped his hands once, and the woman from the fire appeared. A crowd had formed, but they parted for her, and he understood that she was something special to them, something precious. She was dressed in a simple band of cloth around her waist, her bare breasts high, dark nipples taut enough to make him bite the tip of his tongue. The thin bracelet she had held over the fire was clasped around her wrist, the remaining charms tinkling as she moved.

She took Macon's hand and led him to one of the caves, showing him a root cellar. In it were several baskets of berries and roots taken from the forest and dried for the long winter. At the back of the cave in a sort of altar was a metal chest, animals of the hunt etched into the open top: a bear similar to the one from the fire reaching up to strike; a snake slithering along, fangs bared; a bird swooping down from a tree. Inside the chest was a mound of fresh earth. Macon stared at the dirt, his vision suddenly blurring. Was the dirt shaking? Was there a subtle vibration under his feet?

Without thinking, Macon moved forward, putting his hand in the cool earth. The moist darkness surrounded him. His eyes rolled back into his head and he saw visions: a man playing a musical instrument he had never seen, a woman dancing on the tips of her toes.

The visions snapped like a flash of lightning as the woman slapped his hand open, scattering the dirt. With her feet, she pressed the earth into the ground, mumbling something under her breath.

Macon tried to apologize, though he did not know why. "I didn't mean—"

Her piercing black eyes met his, and he felt paralyzed again, rooted to the earth. She walked toward him. Her body pressed into his, her mouth just inches away. He inhaled her, took in her breath. His mind reeled and he leaned back against the wall, intoxicated.

She followed him, grinding herself harder into him until his cock stood out and his hands were exploring every part of her. Currents of desire spread through his body as she palmed him with her hand. Her other hand explored his chest, fingers curling into the hair, stroking across his nipples until she felt the beating of his heart.

She stopped, her hand over his heart, a question in her eyes.

"Yes," he whispered, wanting her so badly his teeth ached in his head. "Yes," he breathed. She could have anything she wanted as long as she kept touching him.

Their mouths finally met and she sucked on his tongue, sucked his breath so that his lungs felt spent. Stars spun in front of his eyes and again his mind flashed on strange images: a key that wouldn't unlock any doors; a locket that held the secret to death; a kneeling angel who could not atone for any sins.

Then, just as suddenly, it was all gone. Macon found himself lying on the forest floor with nothing but the clothes on his back. No gun to hunt, no snares to set, no horse to carry him back to the woman. Though everything seemed familiar, he had no idea where he was. For three days, he traveled, judging his progress by the setting sun. At times he felt he was going in circles. Even the streams seemed to flow in the wrong direction. Nighttime, he fell asleep on the south bank, only to awaken the next morning on what seemed like the north. Three days of this passed. Three days of hunger, of longing, of misery.

Still, his heart told him that he was going in the right direction, the direction that would take him back to the caves, back to the woman. As the sun beat down on his neck and his belly grumbled with emptiness, he felt driven up the hills, certain that every footstep was taking him back to her. Even as the mountain stretched tall and wide before him, a crevasse splitting the middle, virgin water trickling from a warm place at the center, he thought only of her. He would lick his lips, wishing the rough chapped surface he felt under his tongue was her. Sometimes Macon would be so taken with the wanting of her that he would drop to the ground, his pants down around his boots, pulling at himself until he could not bear it. He would stroke himself raw with thoughts of her, and still, even as ropes of his seed saturated the earth, it was never enough.

Plans came to Macon. He would build a house to take her home to. They would have a bed of feathers and a real kitchen. A barn would house horses and cows. She would carry water from the stream to wash his clothes and cook his meals. He would farm again. They would grow their own food, food like she had shown him. Every night, he would fuck deep into her, making *her* scream from the pleasure of him. In return, she would give him children—sons; sons he would pass his farm on to, sons who could protect the land.

With each mile Macon walked in the forest, the woman grew more alive to him. Their life took shape as surely as the trees that grew in the forest. Everything about the woman had been seared into his memory: sight, smell, taste. He remembered the cave, the berries from the forest, the way she had pressed her body into his and let him breathe her breath. He understood everything she had told him without saying a word. The Elawa worshipped the birds in the sky and the animals in the woods. The gold charms they created were meant for worship, not trade. This was how they honored the beasts of the forest, and in return the forest gave them food, shelter, warmth. Without uttering a word, she had conveyed a lifetime to him. All she had to do was look into his eyes with that piercing black stare and she *was* him.

Behind him, a twig snapped. Macon spun around, but there was nothing there. He looked into the sky and saw a crow circling—or was it a buzzard? The animal's wingspan was enormous, enough to block the sun. Macon squinted, shielding his eyes with his hand, but the bird was gone.

Another twig snapped, and his heart jumped into his chest even though he saw nothing. He ran, tripping over a root that stuck up from the forest floor. Pain radiated from his twisted ankle. Facedown on the ground, he smelled the musky odor of darkness, of death. Underneath that, he smelled blood. He looked at his hands, shocked to see they were covered in blood. Was this from the squirrel? From the earth?

The ground vibrated against his belly. Behind him, the padding of four heavy paws shook the ground.

Macon scurried to stand, dirt kicking up in his wake as he stumbled deeper into the forest. The pain in his ankle was nothing as his mind reeled with possibilities. Something was chasing him; he heard the heavy gait of a large four-legged animal as it followed him through the forest. Was it a bear? A coyote? A lion?

His mouth opened, sucking in air; he tried to breathe as panic tightened around his chest. Macon chanced a look over his shoulder and stumbled again, this time catching himself before he fell. He heard something sigh behind him, and even as he ran Macon replayed the sound in his head, reproducing the sigh second by second, hoping for exhaustion, desperation, even pity. There was no denying the absence of all; whatever chased him was merely annoyed. Impatient. Stubborn. Hungry.

Another bird cawed in the distance, or was it the old medicine man with the blackened teeth? Macon's mind flashed on the healer, the three globs of spit on the dirt.

"Lapacha ko wanee."

I curse your seed.

Macon was so close to her. He could feel it, feel her wrapped around him in their feather bed. She would hold him inside of her, milk him, suck out his essence. The pleasures they gave each other every night would soothe away the pain and loneliness of his mountain existence. The Indian woman would give Macon what the other Indians had taken away. They would have their own family. Macon would hunt for them. Their sons would eat the meat and be strong. They would be safe from attack.

Was she calling him now? Was the woman saying his name?

He jerked around as a puff of air pricked up the hairs on the back of his neck. It was as if the animal was directly behind him. Chills ran through his body as Macon turned a complete circle, looking all around, trying to find his pursuer. His knees buckled and he caught himself against a tree. The bark was rough under his bloody hands. He looked at his fingers, the palms, the wrists . . . all smeared with blood. Whose blood?

"God damn you." Macon sucked his fingers as he cursed the forest. "God damn you to hell."

He forced himself to move, his injured ankle beating out a protest along with his pounding heart. Another step, then another . . . he felt as if his ankle was on fire. The heat was burning him up inside, a fever taking hold like a steel vice around his leg. In front of him Macon saw the house where they would live. Could he see the woman in the distance, making her way toward him? Was she looking at the forest floor as she walked, her hands already filled with herbs and berries?

Macon put his hand to his crotch even as he stumbled through the forest. His cock burned when he thought of the gnarled old medicine man, heard the vicious curse in his head.

"Lapacha ko wanee."

Dirty Indians and their dirty charms. That he could curse a man like Macon so easily when life itself was a curse. How else would anyone end up in this godforsaken mountain trying to live off this unforgiving land?

Up ahead! The house! It was *their* house! The yard was swept clean, chickens scratching at the packed dirt. A cowbell clanged and a dog barked, urging its master homeward. Tendrils of smoke came from the hole in the thatched roof. Macon ran toward it, but behind him his pursuer's gait matched his own, growing quicker, more impatient.

Another exhalation sounding so like "Macon" that he turned his head. He stopped short, his breath knocked out of him by some unseen force. Suddenly, he saw things not from within himself but from without and above. Macon stood there facing the woman. She was naked, the thick thatch of her pubis wet with the wanting of him. He moved for her but she pushed him back to the ground and stood over him. All he could do was look up, his body frozen, rootbound to the earth. The woman straddled him, tore his clothes away.

"Yes," he hissed as she impaled herself on him. He groaned, watching himself disappear inside of her again and again. As wet as she was, the tightness was almost unbearable. He heard crackling and rustling as the leaves around them circled into a spiral. The air grew thin and he struggled to breathe as his body began the spasm of release. He came so hard his teeth rattled, spit flying from his mouth. He reached out to touch her but her skin burned white hot, the blood on his hands boiling the flesh. Macon screamed from the pain even as pleasure convulsed through his body. The forest grew dark then finally black as his eyes rolled back in his head.

Spent, he could only lie there, his arms splayed to the side, angry welts festering on the tips of his fingers. Macon did not care. A startlingly clear calm washed over him, and he felt as much of the forest as he ever had; his body was one with the ground. Everything had sudden clarity: the creek gurgling in the background, the quiet noises of the forest, birds, insects, animals. He thought of his mother, the way she would wash her hair in the old iron tub and then sit by the fire, brushing it out as it dried. He thought of his father sitting in his chair, whittling a toy for the brother or sister Macon would never have.

Without warning, the air changed again, becoming thicker,

almost wet. Macon felt the brush of her skin, the silky hair on her legs mingling with his own. Slowly, she moved down, taking him into her mouth. Such was his tiredness that he could only lie there, eyes half shut, staring up at the sky. He was empty. There was nothing more he could give her.

He shuddered as she worked her tongue along his body, licking his stomach, chest and neck, then back down again. Like a dog with a bone, she lapped every inch of him with her silky, warm tongue as he lay there, faint from pleasure. He let out a small sigh even as the weight of her body grew, pressing him deeper into the ground. Macon felt the heat between them, the mingling of their hair, the soft scratch of her skin on his stomach as she leaned harder into him. He felt himself stirring again, throbbing from want. He arched his back, thrusting up into her, gasping as he opened his eyes to find the woman gone and a mighty black bear straddling him in her place.

He screamed in terror, his throat straining as if he had swallowed glass.

A mighty claw slashed across Macon's chest, tearing open the flesh. His brain exploded from the pain, his lungs lurching for air. Macon opened his mouth to scream again but the bear stilled him with a look, one paw resting lightly over Macon's heart. There was no question in her eyes this time, and Macon knew it then—she had come to collect on the awful bargain he had made in the cave.

"Yes," he had said. She could have anything she wanted as long as she kept touching him.

Without further hesitation, the bear reached into his chest, like a child reaching into a bag of candy. Macon's eyelids fluttered, and he saw his own heart glimmer in the sun as the bear offered it up to the heavens. Rays of light licked against the wet tissue like a burning flame. Blood dripped down the bear's arms and chest, splattering his hips, pooling at the joining point between them. The creature roared, and Macon saw the glint of a bracelet around the bear's surprisingly slender wrist just as she put Macon's still-beating heart into her open mouth and swallowed it whole.

VANITAS

Emma Donoghue

This afternoon I was so stone bored I wrote something on a scrap of paper and put it in a medicine bottle, sealed it up with the stub of a candle. I was sitting on the levee; I tossed the bottle as far as I could (since I throw better than girls should) and the Mississippi took it, lazily. If you got in a boat here by the Duparc-Locoul Plantation and didn't even row or raise a sail, the current would take you down fifty miles of slow curves to New Orleans in the end. That's if you didn't get tangled up in weed.

What I wrote on the scrap was *Au secours!* Then I put the date, *3 juillet 1839*. The Americans if drowning or in other trouble call out *help*, which doesn't capture the attention near as much, it's more like a little sound a puppy would make. The bottle was green glass with POISON down one side. I wonder who'll fish it out of the brown water, and what will that man or woman or child make of my message? Or will the medicine bottle float right through the city, out into the Gulf of Mexico, and my scribble go unread till the end of time?

It was a foolish message, and a childish thing to do. I know that; I'm fifteen, which is old enough that I know when I'm being a child. But I ask you, how's a girl to pass an afternoon as long and scalding as this one? I stare at the river in hopes of seeing a boat go by, or a black gum tree with muddy roots. A week ago I saw a blue heron swallow down a wriggling snake. Once in a while a boat will have a letter for us; a boy attaches it to the line of a very long fishing rod and flicks it over to our pier. I'm supposed to call a *nègre* to untie the letter and bring it in; Maman hates when I do it myself. She says I'm a *gâteur de nègres* like Papa, that we spoil them with soft handling. She always beats them when they steal things, which they call only *taking*.

I go up the pecan alley toward the Maison, and through the gate in the high fence that's meant to keep the animals out. Passersby always know a Creole house by the yellow and red, not like the glaring white American ones. Everything on our plantation is yellow and red—not just the houses but the stables, the hospital, and the seventy slave cabins that stretch back like a village for three miles, with their vegetable gardens and chicken pens.

I go in the Maison now, not because I want to, just to get away from the *bam-bam-bam* of the sun on the back of my neck. I step quietly past Tante Fanny's room, because if she hears me she might call me in for some more lessons. My parents are away in New Orleans doing business; they never bring me. I've never been anywhere, truth to tell. My brother Emile has been in the Lycée Militaire in Bordeaux for five years already, and when he graduates, Maman says perhaps we will all go on a voyage to France. By *all* I don't mean Tante Fanny, because she never leaves her room, nor her husband, Oncle Louis, who lives in New Orleans and does business for us, nor Oncle Flagy and Tante Marcelite, quiet sorts who prefer to stay here always and see to the *nègres*, the field ones and the house ones. It will be just Maman and Papa and I who go to meet Emile in France. Maman is the head of the *famille* ever since Grandmère Nannette Prud'Homme retired; we Creoles hand the reins to the smartest child, male or female (unlike the Americans, whose women are too feeble to run things).

But Maman never really wanted to oversee the family enterprise; she says if her brothers Louis and Flagy were more useful she and Papa could have gone back to *la belle* France and stayed there. And then I would have been born a French mademoiselle. *Creole* means born of French stock, here in Louisiana, but Maman prefers to call us French. She says France is like nowhere else in the world: it's all things gracious and fine and civilized, and no *sacrés nègres* about the place.

I pass Millie on the stairs. She's my maid and sleeps on the floor of my room but she has to help with everything else as well. She's one of Pa Philippe's children. He's very old (for a *nègre*), and has *VPD* branded on both cheeks from when he used to run away. That stands for *Veuve Prud'Homme Duparc*. It makes me shudder a little to look at the marks. Pa Philippe can whittle anything out of cypress with his little knife: spoons, needles, pipes. Since Maman started our breeding program we have more small *nègres* than we know what to do with, but Millie's the only one as old as me. "*Allô*, Millie," I say, and she says "Mam'zelle Aimée," and grins back but forgets to curtsy.

"Aimée" means "beloved." I've never liked it as a name. It seems it should belong to a different kind of girl.

Where I am bound today is the attic. Though it's hotter than the cellars, it's the one place nobody else goes. I can lie on the floor and chew my nails and fall into a sort of dream. But today the dust keeps making me sneeze. I'm restless, I can't settle. I try a trick my brother Emile once taught me, to make yourself faint. You breathe in and out very fast while you count to a hundred, then stand against the wall and press as hard as you can between your ribs. Today I do it twice, and I feel odd, but that's all; I've never managed to faint as girls do in novels.

I poke through some wooden boxes, but they hold nothing but old letters, tedious details of imports and taxes and engagements and deaths of people I've never heard of. At the back there's an old-fashioned sheepskin trunk—I've tried to open it before. Today I give it a real wrench and the top comes up. Ah, now here's something worth looking at. Real silk, I'd say, as yellow as butter, with layers of tulle underneath, and an embroidered girdle. The sleeves are huge and puffy, like sacks of rice. I slip off my dull blue frock and try it on over my shift. The skirt hovers, the sleeves bear me up so I seem to float over the splinters and dust of the floorboards. If only I had a looking glass up here. I know I'm short and homely, with a fat throat, and my hands and feet are too big, but in this sun-colored dress I feel halfway to beautiful. Grandmère Nannette, who lives in her Maison de Reprise across the yard and is descended from Louis XV's own physician, once said that like her I was *pas jolie* but at least we had our skin, *un teint de roses*. Maman turns furious if I go out without my sunhat or a parasol; she says if I get freckled like some Cajun farm girl how is she supposed to find me a good match? My stomach gets tight at the thought of a husband, but it won't happen before I'm sixteen, at least. I haven't even become a woman yet, Maman says, though I'm not sure what she means.

I dig in the trunk. A handful of books; the collected poetry of Lord Byron, and a novel by Victor Hugo called *Notre Dame de Paris*. More dresses—a light violet, a pale peach—and light shawls like spiders' webs, and, in a heavy traveling case, some strings of pearls, with rings rolled up in a piece of black velvet. The bottom of the case lifts up, and there I find the strangest thing. It must be from France. It's a sort of bracelet—a thin gold chain—with trinkets dangling from it. I've never seen such perfect little oddities. There's a tiny silver locket that refuses to open; a gold cross; a monkey (grimacing); a minute kneeling angel; a pair of ballet slippers. A tiny tower of some sort; a snake; a crouching tiger (I recognize his toothy roar from the encyclopedia); and a machine with miniature wheels that go round and round; I think this must be a locomotive, like we use to haul cane to our sugarmill. But the one I like best—I don't know why—is a gold key. It's so tiny, I can't imagine what door or drawer or box in the world it might open.

Through the window I see the shadows are getting longer; I must go down and show myself, or there'll be a fuss. I pack the dresses back into the trunk, but I can't bear to give up the bracelet. I manage to open its narrow catch and fasten the chain around my left arm above the elbow, where no one will see it under my sleeve. I mustn't show it off, but I'll know it's there; I can feel the little charms moving against my skin, pricking me.

"Vanitas," says Tante Fanny. "The Latin word for?"

"Vanity," I guess.

"A word with two meanings. Can you supply them?"

"A . . . a desire to be pretty or finely dressed," I begin.

She nods but corrects me: "Self-conceit. The holding of too high an opinion of one's beauty, charms, or talents. But it also means futility," she says, very crisp. "Worthlessness. What is done *in vain*. Vanitas paintings illustrate the vanity of all human wishes. Are you familiar with Ecclesiastes, chapter one, verse two?"

I hesitate. I scratch my arm through my sleeve, to feel the little gold charms.

My aunt purses her wide mouth. Though she is past fifty now, with the sallow look of someone who never sees the sun and always wears black, you can tell that she was once a beauty. *"Vanity of vanities, saith the Preacher, vanity of vanities,"* she quotes; *"all is vanity."*

That's Cousine Eliza on the wall behind her mother's chair, in dark oils. In the picture she looks much older than sixteen to me. She is sitting in a chair with something in her left hand—I think perhaps a handkerchief. Has she been crying? Her white dress has enormous sleeves, like clouds; above them, her shoulders slope prettily. Her face is creamy and perfectly oval, her eyes are dark, her hair is coiled on top of her head like a strange plum cake. Her lips are together; it's a perfect mouth, but it looks so sad. Why does she look so sad?

"In this print here," says Tante Fanny, tapping the portfolio in her lap with one long nail (I don't believe she ever cuts them), "what does the hourglass represent?"

I bend to look at it again. A grim man in seventeenth-century robes, his desk piled with objects. "Time?" I hazard.

"And the skull?"

"Death."

"*Très bien,* Aimée."

I was only eight when my uncle and aunt came back from France, with—among their copious baggage—Cousine Eliza in a lead coffin. She'd died of a fever. Papa came back from Paris right away, with the bad news, but the girl's parents stayed on till the end of the year, which I thought strange. I was not allowed to go to the funeral, though the cemetery of St. James is only ten miles upriver. After the funeral was the last time I saw my Oncle Louis. He's never come back to the plantation since, and for seven years Tante Fanny hasn't left her room. She's shut up like a saint; she spends hours kneeling at her little *prie-dieu,* clutching her beads, thumping her chest. Millie brings all her meals on trays, covered to keep off the rain or the flies. Tante Fanny also sews and writes to her old friends and relations in France and Germany. And, of course, she teaches me. Art and music, French literature and handwriting, religion and etiquette (or, as she calls it, *les convenances* and *comme il faut*). She can't supervise my piano practice, as the instrument is in the salon at the other end of the house, but she leaves her door open when I'm playing and strains her ears to catch my mistakes.

This morning instead of practicing I was up in the attic again, and I saw a ghost, or at least I thought I did. I'd taken all the dresses out of the old sheepskin trunk, to admire and hold against myself; I'd remembered to bring my hand mirror up from my bedroom, and if I held it at arm's length I could see myself from the waist up, at least. I danced like a gypsy, like the girl in *Notre Dame de Paris* whose beauty wins the heart of the hideous hunchback.

When I pulled out the last dress—a vast white one that crinkled like paper—what was revealed was a face. I think I cried out; I know I jumped away from the trunk. When I made myself go nearer, the face turned out to be made of something hard and white, like chalk. It was not a bust like the one downstairs of poor Marie Antoinette. This had no neck, no head; it was only the smooth, pitiless mask of a girl, lying among a jumble of silks.

I didn't recognize her at first; I can be slow. My heart was beating loudly in a sort of horror. Only when I'd sat for some time, staring at those pristine, lidded eyes, did I realize that the face was the same as the one in the portrait of Cousine Eliza and the white dress I was holding was the dress she wore in the painting. These were all her clothes that I was playing with, it came to me, and the little gold bracelet around my arm had to be hers too. I tried to take it off and return it to the trunk, but my fingers were so slippery I couldn't undo the catch. I wrenched at it, and there was a red line around my arm; the little charms spun.

Tante Fanny's room is stuffy; I can smell the breakfast tray that waits for Millie to take it away. "Tante Fanny," I say now, without preparation, "why does Cousine Eliza look so sad?"

My aunt's eyes widen violently. Her head snaps.

I hear my own words too late. What an idiot, to make it sound as if her ghost was in the room with us! "In the picture," I stammer. "I mean, in the picture, she looks sad."

Tante Fanny doesn't look around at the portrait. "She was dead," she says, rather hoarse.

This can't be right. I look past her. "But her eyes are open."

My aunt lets out a sharp sigh and snaps her book shut. "Do you know the meaning of the word *posthumous*?"

"Eh . . ."

"After death. The portrait was commissioned and painted in Paris in the months following my daughter's demise."

I stare at it again. But how? Did the painter prop her up somehow? She doesn't look dead, only sorrowful, in her enormous ice-white silk gown.

"Eliza did not model for it," my aunt goes on, as if explaining something to a cretin. "For the face, the artist worked from a death mask." She must see the confusion in my eyes. "A sculptor pastes wet plaster over the features of a corpse. When it hardens he uses it as a mold to make a perfect simulacrum of the face."

That's it. That's what scared me, up in the attic this morning: Eliza's death mask. When I look back at my aunt, there's been a metamorphosis. Tears are chasing down her papery cheeks. "Tante Fanny—"

"Enough," she says, her voice like mud. "Leave me."

I don't believe my cousin—my only cousin, the beautiful Eliza, just sixteen years old—died of a fever. Louisiana is a hellhole for fevers of all kinds—that's why my parents sent Emile away to Bordeaux. It's good for making money, but not for living: that's why Napoleon sold it so cheap to the Americans thirty-six years ago. So how could it have happened that Eliza grew up here on the Duparc-Locoul Plantation, safe and well, and on her trip to Paris—that pearly city, that apex of civilization—she succumbed to a fever? I won't believe it. It smells like a lie.

I'm up in the attic again, but this time I've brought the Bible. My brother Emile, before he went away to France, taught me how to tell fortunes with the Book and Key. In those days we used an ugly old key we'd found in the cellars, but now I have a better one; the little gold one that hangs on my bracelet. (Eliza's bracelet, I should say.) What you do is you open the Bible to the Song of Solomon, pick any verse you like, and read it aloud. If the key goes clockwise, it's saying yes to the verse, and vice versa. Fortune-telling is a sin when gypsies or conjurors do it, like the *nègres* making their nasty *gris-gris* to put curses on each other, but it can't be wrong if you use the Good Book. The Song of Solomon is the most puzzling bit of the Bible, but it's my favorite. Sometimes it seems to be a man speaking, and sometimes a woman; she says *I am black but comely,* but she can't be a *nègre,* surely? They adore each other, but at some points it sounds as if they are brother and sister.

My first question for the Book today is "did Cousine Eliza die a natural death?" I pull the bracelet down to my wrist and hold all the other little charms still, letting only the key dangle. I shake my hand as I recite the verse I've chosen, one that reminds me of Eliza: *Thy cheeks are comely with rows of jewels, thy neck with chains of gold.* When my hand stops moving, the key swings, most definitely anti-clockwise. I feel a thrill all the way down in my belly. So! Not a natural death; as I suspected.

What shall I ask next? I cross my legs to get more comfortable on the bare boards and study the Book. A verse gives me an idea. Was she—is it possible—was she murdered? Not a night goes by in a great city without a cry in the dark—I know that much. *The watchmen that went about the city found me,* I whisper. *They smote me, they wounded me.* I shake my wrist and the key dances, but every which way; I can't tell what the answer is. I search for another verse. Here's one: *Every man hath his sword upon his thigh because of fear in the night.* What if . . . I rack my imagination. What if two young Parisian gallants fought a duel over her after glimpsing her at the opera, and Eliza died of the shock? I chant the verse, my voice rising now, because no one will hear me up here. I wave my hand in the air, and when I stop moving the key continues to swing, anti-clockwise. No duel, then; that's clear.

But what if she had a lover, a favorite among all the gentlemen of France who were vying for the hand of the exquisite Creole maiden? What if he was mad with jealousy and strangled her, locking his hands around her long pale neck rather than let Tante Fanny and Oncle Louis take her back to Louisiana? *For love is strong as death; jealousy is cruel as the grave,* I croon, and my heart is thumping. I can feel the wet break out under my arms, in the secret curls there. I've forgotten to wave my hand. When I do it, the key swings straight back and forward, like the clapper of a bell. Like the thunderous bells in the high cathedral of Notre Dame de Paris. Is that an answer? Not jealousy, then, or not exactly; some other strange passion? Somebody killed Eliza, whether they meant to or not, I remind myself; somebody is to blame for the sad eyes in that portrait. For Tante Fanny walled up in her stifling room, and Oncle Louis who never comes home.

I can't think of any more questions about Eliza; my brain is fuzzy. Did she suffer terribly? I can't find a verse to ask that. How can I investigate a death that happened eight years ago, all the way across the ocean, when I'm only a freckled girl who's never left the plantation? Who'll listen to my questions? Who'll tell me anything?

I finish by asking the Book something for myself. Will I ever be pretty, like Eliza? Will these dull and round features ever bloom into perfect conjunction? Will I grow a face that will take me to France, that will win me the love of a French gentleman? Or will I be stuck here for the rest of my life, my mother's harried assistant and perhaps her successor, running the plantation and the wine business and the many complex enterprises that make up the wealth of the Famille Duparc-Locoul? That's too many questions. Concentrate, Aimée. Will I be pretty when I grow up? *Behold, thou art fair, my love,* I murmur, as if to make it so. *Behold, thou art fair.* But then something stops me from shaking my hand, making the key swing. Because what if the answer is no?

I stoop over the trunk and take out the death mask, as I now know it's called. I hold it very carefully in my arms, and I lie down beside the trunk. I look into the perfect white oval of my cousin's face and lay it beside mine. *Eliza, Eliza.* I whisper my apologies for disturbing her things, for borrowing her bracelet, with all its little gold trinkets. I tell her I only want to know the truth of how she died so her spirit can be at rest. My cheek is against her cool cheek, my nose aligns itself with hers. The plaster smells of nothing. I set my dry lips to her smooth ones.

"Millie," I ask, when she's buttoning up my dress this morning, "you remember my Cousine Eliza?"

The girl makes a little humming sound that could mean yes, no, or maybe. That's one of her irritating habits. "You must," I say. "My beautiful cousin who went away to Paris. They say she died of a fever."

This time the sound she makes is more like *hmph*.

I catch her eye, its milky roll. Excitement rises in my throat. "Millie," I say, too loud, "have you ever heard anything about that?"

"What would I hear, Mam'zelle Aimée?"

"Oh, go on! I know you house *nègres* are always gossiping. Did you ever hear tell of anything strange about my cousin's death?"

Millie's glance slides to the door. I step over and shut it. "Go on. You can speak freely."

She shakes her head, very slow.

"I know you know something," I say, and it comes out too fierce. Governing the *nègres* is an art, and I don't have it; I'm too familiar, and then too cross. Today, watching Millie's purple mouth purse, I resort to a bribe. "I tell you what—I might give you a present. What about one of these little charms?" Through my sleeve, I tug the gold bracelet down to my wrist. I make the little jewels shake and spin in front of Millie's eyes. "What about the tiger—would you like that one?" I point him out, because how would she know what a tiger looks like? "Or maybe these dance slippers. Or the golden cross, that Jesus died on?" I don't mention the key, because that's my own favorite.

Millie looks hungry with delight. She's come closer; her fingers are inches away from the dancing trinkets.

I tuck the bracelet back under my wrist ruffle. "Tell me!"

She crosses her arms and leans in close to my ear. She smells a little ripe, but not too bad. "Your cousine?"

"Yes."

"Your oncle and tante killed her."

I shove the girl away, the flat of my hand against her collarbone. "How dare you?"

She gives a luxurious shrug. "All I say is what I hear."

"Hear from whom?" I demand. "Your Pa Philippe, or your ma?" Millie's mother works the hoe gang. She's as strong as a man. "What would they know of my family's affairs?"

Millie is grinning as she shakes her head. "From your tante."

"Tante Marcelite? She'd never say such a thing."

"No, no. From your Tante Fanny."

I'm so staggered I have to sit down. "Millie, you know it's the blackest of sins to lie," I remind her. "I think you must have made up this story. You're saying that my Tante Fanny told you—you—that she and Oncle Louis murdered Eliza?"

Millie's looking sullen now. "I don't make up nothing. I go in and out of that dusty old room five times a day with trays, and sometimes your tante is praying or talking to herself, and I hear her."

"But this is ridiculous." My voice is shaking. "Why would—what reason could they possibly have had for killing their own daughter?" I run through the plots I invented up in the attic. Did Eliza have a French lover? Did she *give herself* to him and fall into ruin? Could my uncle and aunt have murdered her, to save the *famille* from shame? "I won't hear any more of such stuff."

The *nègre* has the gall to put her hand out, cupped for her reward.

"You may go now," I tell her, stepping into my shoes.

Next morning, I wake up in a foul temper. My head starts hammering as soon as I lift it off the pillow. Maman is expected back from New Orleans today. I reach for my bracelet on the little table beside my bed and it's gone.

"Millie?" But she's not there, on the pallet at the foot of my bed; she's up already. She's taken my bracelet. I never mentioned giving her more than one little trinket; she couldn't have misunderstood me. Damn her for a thieving little *nègre*.

I could track her down in the kitchen behind the house, or in the sewing room with Tante Marcelite working on the slave clothes, or wherever she may be, but no. For once, I'll see to it that the girl gets punished for her outrageous impudence.

I bide my time; I do my lessons with Tante Fanny all morning. My skin feels greasy. I've a *bouton* coming on my chin; I'm a martyr to pimples. This little drum keeps banging away in the back of my head. And a queasiness too; a faraway aching. What could I have eaten to put me in such a state?

When the boat arrives I don't rush down to the pier; my mother hates such displays. I sit in the shady gallery and wait. When Maman comes to find me, I kiss her on both cheeks. "Perfectly well," I reply. (She doesn't like to hear of symptoms, unless one is seriously ill.) "But that dreadful brat Millie has stolen a bracelet from my room." As I say it I feel a pang, but only a little one. Such a story for her to make up, calling my aunt and uncle murderers of their own flesh! The least the girl deserves is a whipping.

"Which bracelet?"

Of course, my mother knows every bit of jewelry I own; it's her memory for detail that's allowed her to improve the family fortunes so much. "A . . . a gold chain, with trinkets on it," I say, with only a small hesitation. If Eliza got it in Paris, as she must have done, my mother won't ever have seen it on her. "I found it."

"Found it?" she repeats, her eyebrows soaring.

I'm sweating. "It was stoppered up in a bottle," I improvise. "It washed up on the levee."

"How peculiar."

"But it's mine," I repeat. "And Millie took it off my table while I was sleeping!"

Maman nods judiciously and turns away. "Do tidy yourself up before dinner, Aimée, won't you?"

We often have a guest to dinner; Creoles never refuse our hospitality to anyone who needs a meal or a bed for the night, unless he's a beggar. Today it's a slave trader who comes up and down the River Road several times a year; he has a long beard that gets things caught in it. Millie and two other house *nègres* carry in the dishes, lukewarm as always, since the kitchen is so far behind the house. Millie's face shows nothing; she can't have been punished yet. I avoid her eyes. I pick at the edges of my food; I've no appetite today, though I usually like *poule d'eau*—a duck that eats nothing but fish, so the Church allows it on Fridays. I listen to the trader and Maman discuss the cost of living and sip my glass of claret. (Papa brings in ten thousand bottles a year from his estates at Château Bon-Air; our *famille* is the greatest wine distributor in Louisiana.) The trader offers us our pick of the three males he has with him, fresh from the auction block at New Orleans, but Maman says with considerable pride that we breed all we need, and more.

After dinner I'm practicing piano in the salon—stumbling repeatedly over a tricky phrase of Beethoven's—when my mother comes in. "If you can't manage this piece, Aimée, perhaps you could try one of your Schuberts?" Very dry.

"Certainly, Maman."

"Here's your bracelet. A charming thing, if eccentric. Don't make a habit of fishing things out of the river, will you?"

"No, Maman." Gleeful, I fiddle with the catch, fitting it around my wrist.

"The girl claimed you'd given it to her as a present."

Guilt, like a lump of gristle in my throat.

"They always claim that, strangely enough," remarks my mother, walking away. "One would think they might come up with something more plausible."

The next day I'm in Tante Fanny's room, at my lessons. There was no sign of Millie this morning, and I had to dress myself; the girl must be sulking. I'm supposed to be improving my spelling of verbs in the subjunctive mode, but my stomach is a rat's nest, my dress is too tight, my head's fit to split. I gaze out the window to the yard, where the trader's saddling his mules. He has four *nègres* with him, their hands lashed to their saddles.

"Do sit down, child."

"Just a minute, Tante—"

"Aimée, come back here!"

But I'm thudding along the gallery, down the stairs. I trip over my hem and catch the railing. I'm in the yard, and the sun is piercing my eyes. "Maman!"

She turns, frowning. "Where is your sun hat, Aimée?"

I ignore that. "But Millie—what's happening?"

"I suggest you use your powers of deduction."

I throw a desperate look at the girl, bundled up on the last mule, her mute face striped with tears. "Have you sold her? She didn't do anything so very bad. I have the bracelet back safe. Maybe she only meant to borrow it."

My mother sighs. "I won't stand for thieving or back-answers, and Millie has been guilty of both."

"But Pa Philippe, and her mother—you can't part her from them—"

Maman draws me aside, her arm like a cage around my back. "Aimée, I won't stoop to dispute my methods with an impudent and sentimental girl, especially in front of strangers. Go back to your lesson."

I open my mouth to tell her that Millie didn't steal the bracelet, exactly; that she thought I had promised it to her. But that would call for too much explanation, and what if Maman found out that I've been interrogating the *nègres* about private family business? I shut my mouth again. I don't look at Millie; I can't bear it. The trader whistles to his mules to start walking. I go back into the house. My head's bursting from the sun; I have to keep my eyes squeezed shut.

"What is it, child?" asks Tante Fanny when I open the door. Her anger has turned to concern; it must be my face.

"I feel . . . weak."

"Sit down on this sofa, then. Shall I ring for a glass of wine?"

Next thing I know I'm flat on my back, choking. I feel so sick. I push Tante Fanny's hand away. She stoppers her smelling salts. "My dear."

"What . . ."

"You fainted."

I feel oddly disappointed. I always thought it would be a luxuriant feeling—a surrendering of the spirit—but it turns out that fainting is just a sick sensation, and then you wake up.

"It's very natural," she says, with the ghost of a smile. "I believe you have become a woman today."

I stare down at myself, but my shape hasn't changed.

"Your petticoat's a little stained," she whispers, showing me the spots—some brown, some fresh scarlet—and suddenly I understand. "You should go to your room and ask Millie to show you what to do."

At the mention of Millie I put my hands over my face.

"Where did you get that?" asks Tante Fanny, in a changed voice. She reaches out to touch the bracelet that's slipped out from beneath my sleeve. I flinch. "Aimée, where did you get that?"

"It was in a trunk, in the attic," I confess. "I know it was Eliza's. Can I ask you, how did she die?" My words astonish me as they spill out.

My aunt's face contorts. I think perhaps she's going to strike me. After a long minute, she says, "We killed her. Your uncle and I."

My God. So Millie told the truth, and in return I've had her sold, banished from the sight of every face she knows in the world.

"Your cousin died for our pride, for our greed." Tante Fanny puts her fingers around her throat. "She was perfect, but we couldn't see it, because of the mote in our eyes."

What is she talking about?

"You see, Aimée, when my darling daughter was about your

age she developed some *boutons*."

Pimples? What can pimples have to do with anything?

My aunt's face is a mask of creases. "They weren't so very bad, but they were the only defect in such a lovely face, they stood out terribly. I was going to take her to the local root doctor for an ointment, but your papa happened to know a famous skin specialist in Paris. I think he was glad of the excuse for a trip to his native country. And we knew that nothing in Louisiana could compare to France. So your papa accompanied us—Eliza and myself and your oncle Louis—on the long voyage, and he introduced us to this doctor. For eight days"—Tante Fanny's tone has taken on a biblical timbre—"the doctor gave the girl injections, and she bore it bravely. We waited for her face to become perfectly clear again—but instead she took a fever. We knew the doctor must have made some terrible mistake with his medicines. When Eliza died—" Here the voice cracks, and Tante Fanny lets out a sort of barking sob. "Your oncle wanted to kill the doctor; he drew his sword to run him through. But your papa, the peacemaker, persuaded us that it must have been the cholera or some other contagion. We tried to believe that; we assured each other that we believed it. But when I looked at my lovely daughter in her coffin, at sixteen years old, I knew the truth as if God had spoken in my heart."

She's weeping so much now, her words are muffled. I wish I had a handkerchief for her.

"I knew that Eliza had died for a handful of pimples. Because in our vanity, our dreadful pride, we couldn't accept the least defect in our daughter. We were ungrateful, and she was taken from us, and all the years since, and all the years ahead allotted to me, will be expiation."

The bracelet seems to burn me. I've managed to undo the catch. I pull it off, the little gold charms tinkling.

Tante Fanny wipes her eyes with the back of her hand. "Throw that away. My curse on it, and on all glittering vanities," she says hoarsely. "Get rid of it, Aimée, and thank God you'll never be beautiful."

Her words are like a blow to the ribs. But a moment later I'm glad she said it. It's better to know these things. Who'd want to spend a whole life hankering?

I go out of the room without a word. I can feel the blood welling, sticky on my thighs. But first I must do this. I fetch an old bottle from the kitchen, and a candle stub. I seal up the bracelet in its green translucent tomb, and go to the top of the levee, and throw it as far as I can into the Mississippi.

CORNELIUS JUBB

Peter Robinson

Most of us around these parts had never seen a colored person until Cornelius Jubb walked into the Nag's Head one fine April evening in 1943, bold as brass and black as Whitby jet.

Ernie the landlord asked him if he had a glass. Glasses being in short supply, most of us brought our own and guarded them with our lives. He shook his head. Ernie's not a bad sort, though, so he dug out a dusty jam jar from under the bar, rinsed it off, and filled it with beer. The young man seemed happy enough with the result; he thanked Ernie and paid. After that, he lit a Lucky Strike and just stood there with that gentle, innocent look in his eyes, a look I came to know so well, and one that stayed with him throughout all that was to happen in the following weeks, for all the world as if he might have been waiting for a bus or something, daydreaming about some faraway sweetheart.

Now, most of us up here in Leeds are decent enough folk, and I like to think we measure a man by who he is and what he does. But there's always an exception, isn't there? In our case it was Obediah Clough, who happened to be drinking with his cronies in his usual corner, complaining about the meager cheese ration.

Obediah was too old to go to war again, and he drilled the local Home Guard and helped out with ARP, though air raids had been sporadic since 1941, to say the least.

Obediah swaggered up to the young colored gentleman with that way he has, chest puffed out, baggy trousers held up with a length of cord, and looked him up and down, an exaggerated expression of curiosity on his blotchy red face. His pals sat in the corner, sniggering at his performance. The young man ignored them all and carried on drinking and smoking.

Finally, not used to being ignored for so long, Obediah thrust his face mere inches away from the other man's, which must have been terrible for the poor fellow because Obediah's breath smells worse than a pub toilet at closing time. Give him his due, though: the lad didn't flinch.

"What have we got here, then?" Obediah said, playing it up for his cronies.

Whether because he recognized the question as rhetorical or because he simply didn't know the answer, the young man made no reply.

"What's your name, then?" Obediah asked.

The man put his glass down, smiled, and said, "My name's Jubb, sir. Lieutenant Cornelius Jubb. I'm very pleased to meet you." He held out his hand, but Obediah ignored it.

"Jubb?" Obediah's jaw dropped. "Jubb? But that's a Yorkshire name."

"It's the name I was given by my parents," said the man.

"Tha's not a Yorkshireman," Obediah said, eyes narrowing. "Tha's having me on."

"No word of a lie," said Cornelius Jubb. "But you're right, sir. I'm not a Yorkshireman. I'm from Louisiana."

"So what're you doing with a Yorkshire name, then?"

Cornelius shrugged. "Maybe my ancestors came from Yorkshire?"

Cornelius had a twinkle in his eye, and I could tell that he was joking, but it was a dangerous thing to do with Obediah Clough. He didn't take well at all to being the butt of anyone's joke, especially after a few drinks. He looked over to his friends and gestured them to approach. "Look what we've got here, lads, a black Yorkshireman. He must've come straight from his shift down t'pit, don't you think?"

They laughed nervously and came over.

"And what's that tha's got on thy wrist?" Obediah said, reaching toward some sort of bracelet on the G.I.'s right wrist. He obviously tried to keep it out of sight, hidden under his sleeve, but it had slipped out. "What is tha, lad?" Obediah went on. "A bloody Nancy boy? I've got a young lady might appreciate a present like that." The young man snatched his arm away before Obediah could grab the bracelet.

"That's mine, sir," he said, "and I'd thank you to keep your hands off it."

"Doesn't tha know there's a price for coming and drinking in here with the likes of us?" Obediah went on. "And the price is that there bracelet of thine. Give us it here, lad."

The boy moved a few inches along the bar. "No, sir," he said, adopting a defensive stance.

I could tell that things had gone far enough and that Obediah was about to get physical. With a sigh, I got to my feet and walked over to them, putting my hand gently on Obediah's shoulder. He didn't appreciate it, but I'm even bigger than he is, and the last time we tangled he came out with a broken rib and a bloody nose. "That's enough, Obediah," I said gently. "Let the lad enjoy his drink in peace."

Obediah glared at me, but he knew when he was beaten. "What's he think he's doing, walking into our pub, bold as you like?" he muttered, but his heart wasn't in it.

"It's a free country, Obediah," I said. "Or at least Mr. Hitler hadn't won the war last time I checked."

This drew a gentle titter from some of the drinkers, Obediah's cronies included. You could feel the tension ease. As I said, we're a tolerant lot on the whole. Muttering, Obediah went back to his corner and his pals went with him. I stayed at the bar with the newcomer.

"Sorry about that, lad," I said. "He's harmless, really."

The G.I. looked at me with those big brown eyes of his and nodded solemnly.

Now that I was closer, I could see that the object Obediah had referred to was some sort of gold chain with tiny trinkets suspended from it, a very unusual thing for a man to be wearing. "What exactly is that?" I asked, pointing. "Just out of curiosity."

He brought his arm up so I could see the chain. "It's called a charm bracelet," he said. "My lucky charm bracelet. I usually try to keep it out of sight."

Everything on the chain was a perfect miniature of its original: a gold locket, a cross, a monkey, an angel, a golden key, a tiny pair of ballet slippers, a lighthouse, a tiger, and a train engine. The craftsmanship was exquisite.

"Where did you get it?" I asked.

"Fishing," Cornelius said.

"Pardon?"

"Fishing. Caught it fishing in the Mississippi, down by the levee, when I was boy. I decided then and there it would be my lucky charm."

"It's a beautiful piece of work," I said. I held out my hand. "Richard Palmer. Dick to my friends."

He looked at my outstretched hand with suspicion for a moment, then slowly he smiled and reached out his own, the palm as pink as coral, and shook firmly. "Pleased to meet you, Mr. Palmer," he said. "I'm Cornelius Jubb."

I smiled. "Yes, I heard."

He glanced over at Obediah and his cronies, who had lost interest now and become absorbed in a game of dominoes. "And I don't know where the name came from," he added.

I guessed that perhaps some Yorkshire plantation owner had given it to one of Cornelius's ancestors, or perhaps it was a contraction of a French name such as Joubliet, but it didn't matter. Jubb he was, in a place where Jubbs belonged. "You don't sound southern," I said, having heard the sort of slow drawl usually associated with Louisiana on the radio once or twice.

"Grew up there," Cornelius said. "Then I went to college in Massachusetts."

"What are you doing here all by yourself?" I asked. "Most American soldiers seem to hang around with their mates, in groups."

Cornelius shrugged. "I don't know, really. That's not for me. They're all . . . y'know . . . fighting, cussing, drinking, and chasing girls."

"You don't want to chase girls?"

I could have sworn he blushed. "I was brought up to be a decent man," he said. "I'll know when the right girl comes along." He gestured to the charm bracelet again and smiled. "And this is for her," he added.

I could have laughed at the naivety of his statement, but I didn't. Instead, I offered to buy him another drink. He accepted and offered me a Lucky. That was the beginning of what I like to think of as an unlikely friendship, but I have found that war makes the unlikeliest of things possible.

You might be wondering by now why I wasn't at war with the rest of our fine lads. Shirker? Conchie? Not me. I saw enough carnage at Ypres to last me a lifetime, thank you very much, but the fact of the matter is that I'm too old to be a soldier again. After the first war I drifted into the police force and finally rose to the rank of Detective Inspector. Now that all the young men have gone off to fight, of course, they need us old codgers to carry the load back home. Just as I was getting ready to spend my twilight days reading all those books I never read when I was younger—Dickens, Jane Austen, the Brontës, Hardy, Trollope. Ah, well, such is life, and it's not a bad job, as jobs go. At least I thought so, until events conspired to prove me wrong.

Cornelius, as it turned out, was one of about three hundred colored persons—or Negroes, as the Yanks called them—in an engineering regiment transferred up from the West Country. During our conversations, mostly in the Nag's Head, but often later at my little terraced back-to-back over carefully measured tots of whiskey, no longer readily available, I learned about hot and humid Louisiana summers, the streets, sounds, and smells of New Orleans, and the nefarious ways of the color bar and segregation. I had already heard of problems between white and colored G.I.s in other parts of the country. Apparently, the American military command wanted to institute the same sort of color bar they had at home, but we British didn't want that. I had also heard rumors that in some towns and villages a sort of unwritten code had grown up, fostered by whispering campaigns, as regards which pubs were to be frequented by Negroes and which by whites.

I also learned very quickly that Cornelius was a shy young man, a bit of a loner, but no less interesting or intelligent for that. His father was a Baptist minister, and he had wanted his son to go to college and become a schoolteacher, where he might have some positive influence on young men of the future. Though Cornelius had instead followed a natural interest in and flair for the more practical and mechanical aspects of science, he was remarkably well traveled and well read, even if there were great gaps in his education. He had little geography, for example, and knew little beyond the rudiments of American history, yet he spoke French fluently—though not with any accent I'd heard before—and he was well versed in English literature. The latter was because of his mother, he told me. Sadly deceased now, she had read children's stories to him from a very early age and guided him toward the classics when she thought he was old enough.

Cornelius was homesick, of course, a stranger in a strange land, and he missed his daddy and the streets of his hometown. We both had a weakness for modern music, it turned out, and we often managed to find Duke Ellington or Benny Goodman broadcasts on the wireless, even Louis Armstrong if we were lucky, whenever the reception was clear enough. I like to think the music helped him feel a little closer to home.

All in all, I'd say that Cornelius and I became friends as that spring gave way to summer. Sometimes we discussed current events—the "bouncing bombs" raid on the Eder and Möhne dams in May, for example, which he tried to explain to me in layman's terms (without much success, I might add). We even went to the pictures to see Charlie Chaplin in *The Gold Rush* with a couple of broad-minded Land Girls I knew. That raised more than a few eyebrows, though everything was above board. As far as I could tell, Cornelius stayed true to his word about waiting for the right girl to come along. How he knew that he would be so sure when it happened, I don't know. But people say I'm married to my job, which is why my wife left me for a traveling salesman, so how would I know about such things?

One August night, just after the Allies had won the battle for Sicily, the local G.I.s all got a late pass in honor of Patton's role in the victory. After an evening in the Nag's Head, drinking watery beer, Cornelius and I stopped up late, and after he left I was trying to get to sleep, my head spinning a little from a drop too much celebratory whiskey, when there came a loud knocking at my door. It was a knocking I wish I had never answered.

Brimley Park was a thick wedge of green separating the terraces of back-to-backs on the east side and the more genteel semi-detached houses on the west. There was nothing else but a few wooden benches and some swings and a slide for the kiddies. Chestnut trees stood on three sides, shielding the heart of the park from view. There used to be metal railings, but the Ministry of Works appropriated them for the war effort a couple of years ago, so now you could make your way in between the trees almost anywhere.

Harry Joseph, who had been dispatched by the beat constable to fetch me, babbled most of the way there and led me through the trees to a patch of grass where PC Nash and a couple of other local men stood guard. It was a sultry night, and the whiskey only made me sweat more than usual. I hoped they couldn't smell it on me. It was late enough to be pitch-dark, despite double summer time, and, of course, the blackout was in force. As we approached, though, I did notice about eighteen inches of light showing through an upper window in one of the semis. They'd better be quick and get their curtains down, I thought, or Obediah Clough and his ARP men would be knocking at their door. The fines for blackout violations were quite steep.

Harry had babbled enough on the way to make me aware that we were approaching a crime scene, though I never did manage to find out exactly what had happened until I got there. PC Nash had his torch out, the light filtered by the regulation double thickness of white tissue paper, and in its diffused milky glow I could see the vague outline of a figure on the grass: a young woman with a Veronica Lake hairstyle. I crouched closer, careful not to touch anything, and saw that it was young Evelyn Fowler. She was lying so still that at first I thought she was dead, but then I noticed her head move slightly toward me and heard her make a little sound, like a sigh or a sob.

"Have you called an ambulance?" I asked PC Nash.

"Yes, sir," he said. "They said they'll be here straightaway."

"Good man."

I borrowed Nash's torch and turned back to Evelyn, whispering some words of comfort about the doctor being on his way. If she heard me, she didn't acknowledge it. Evelyn wasn't a bad sort, as I remembered. Around here, the girls were divided into those who didn't and those who did. Evelyn was one who did, but only the morally rigid and the holier-than-thou crowd held that against her. It was wartime. Nobody knew which way things were going to go, how we would all end up, so many lived life for the moment. Evelyn was one of them. I remembered her laugh, which I had heard once or twice in the Nag's Head, surprisingly soft and musical. Her eyes might have been spoiled for me by that cynical, challenging look that said, "Go on, convince me, persuade me," but underneath it all, she had been easily enough persuaded.

There was no mistaking what had happened. Evelyn's dirndl skirt had been lifted up to her waist and her drawers pulled down around her ankles, legs slightly spread apart at the knees. She was still wearing nylons, no doubt a gift from one of our American brothers, who seemed to have unlimited supplies. Her lace-trimmed blouse was torn at the front and stained with what looked like blood. From what I could see of her face, she had taken quite a beating. I could smell gin on her breath. I looked at her fingernails and thought I saw blood on one of them. It looked as if she had tried to fight off her attacker. I would have to make sure the doctor preserved any skin he might find under her nails.

I averted my gaze and sighed, wondering what sad story Evelyn would have to tell us when, or if, she regained consciousness. Men had been fighting a deadly campaign in Sicily, and even now, as we stood around Evelyn in Brimley Park, they were still fighting the Germans and the Japanese all over the world, yet someone, some man, had taken it into his mind to attack a defenseless young woman and steal from her that which, for whatever reason, she wouldn't give him in the first place. And Evelyn was supposed to be one of those girls who did. It didn't make sense.

My knees cracked as I moved. I could hear the ambulance approaching through the dark, deserted streets of the city. Just as I was about to stand up, the weak light from the torch glinted on something in the grass, half hidden by Evelyn's outstretched arm. I reached forward, placed it in my palm, and shone the torch on it. What I saw sent a chill down my spine. It was a tiny, perfectly crafted tiger. The very same one I had seen so many times on Cornelius Jubb's "lucky" charm bracelet.

It was with a heavy heart that I approached the U.S. army base in a light drizzle early the following morning, while Evelyn Fowler fought for consciousness in the infirmary. It was a typical enough military base, with Nissen huts for the men, storage compounds for munitions and supplies, and the obligatory squad of men marching around the parade ground. Along with all the Jeeps and lorries coming and going, it certainly gave the illusion of hectic activity.

My official police standing got me in to see the CO, a genial enough colonel from Wyoming called Frank Johnson, who agreed to let me talk to Lieutenant Jubb, making it clear that he was doing me a big favor. He specified that army personnel must be present and that, should things be taken any further, the matter was under American jurisdiction, not that of the British. I was well aware of the thorny legal problems that the American "occupation," as some called it, gave rise to and had discovered in the past that there was little or nothing I could do about it. The fact of the matter was that on the fourth of August, 1942, after a great deal of angry debate, the Cabinet had put a revolutionary special bill before Parliament that exempted U.S. soldiers over here from being prosecuted in our courts, under our laws.

The colonel was being both courteous and cautious in allowing me access to Cornelius. The special U.S.A. Visiting Forces Act was still a controversial topic, and nobody wanted an outcry in the press or on the streets. There was a good chance, Colonel Johnson no doubt reasoned, that early collaboration could head that sort of thing off at the pass. It certainly did no harm to placate the local constabulary. I will say, though, that they stopped short of stuffing my pockets with Lucky Strikes and Hershey bars.

I agreed to the colonel's terms and accompanied him to an empty office, bare except for wooden desk and four uncomfortable hard-backed chairs. After I had waited the length of a cigarette, the colonel came back with Cornelius and another man, whom he introduced as Lieutenant Clawson, a military lawyer. I must confess that I didn't much like the look of Clawson; he had an arrogant twist to his lips and a cold, merciless look in his eye.

Cornelius seemed surprised to see me, but he also seemed sheepish and did his best to avoid looking me directly in the eye. Maybe this was because of the scratch on his cheek, though I took his discomfort more as a reflection of his surroundings and hoped to hell it wasn't an indication of his guilt. After all, we were on his home turf now, where the colored men had separate barracks from the whites and ate in different canteens. Already I could sense the gulf and the unspoken resentment between Cornelius and the two white Americans. It felt very different from Obediah Clough's childish attempts at bullying; it ran much deeper and more dangerous.

"Tell me what you did last night, Cornelius?" I asked, the words out of my mouth before I realized what a mistake I had made calling him by his first name. The colonel frowned, and Lieutenant Clawson smiled in a particularly nasty way. "Lieutenant Jubb, that is," I corrected myself, too late.

"You know what I did," said Cornelius.

The others looked at me, curious. "Humor me," I said, feeling my mouth become dry.

"We were celebrating the victory in Sicily," Cornelius said. "We drank some beer in the Nag's Head and then we went back to your house and drank some whiskey."

The colonel looked surprised to hear Cornelius talk, and I guessed he hadn't heard him before. Where you were expecting some sort of barely comprehensible rural Louisiana patois, what you got in fact was the more articulate and refined speech of the New Englander, a result of the time Cornelius had spent in the north.

"Were you drunk?" I asked.

"Maybe. A little. But not so much that I couldn't find my way home."

"Which way did you go?"

"The usual way."

"Through Brimley Park?"

Cornelius hesitated and caught my eye. "Yes," he said. "It's a good shortcut."

"Did you notice anything there? Anyone?"

"No," he said.

I got that sinking feeling. If I could tell that Cornelius was lying, what would the others think? He certainly wasn't a natural liar. And why was he lying? I pressed on, and never had my duty felt so much of a burden to me before.

"Did you hear anything?"

"No," said Cornelius.

"Do you know a girl by the name of Evelyn Fowler?"

"Can't say as I do."

"About five foot three, good-looking girl. Wears nice clothes, makes a lot of them herself, has a Veronica Lake hairstyle."

"Who doesn't?" said Cornelius.

It was true; there were plenty of Veronica Lake look-alikes walking around in 1943. "She's been in the Nag's Head a couple of times," I added.

"I suppose I might have seen her, then," said Cornelius. "Why?"

"She was raped and beaten last night in Brimley Park."

Now, for the first time, Cornelius really looked me in the eye. "And you think I did it?" he asked.

I shook my head. "I'm only asking if you saw anything. It was around the time you left. And"—I dropped the tiger softly on the table—"I found this near the scene."

Cornelius looked at the charm, then turned up his sleeve and saw the missing spot on his bracelet. Clawson and the colonel both stared at him gravely, as if they knew they'd got him now and it was just a matter of time. I wasn't so sure. I thought I knew Cornelius, and the man I knew would no sooner rape and beat Evelyn Fowler than he would sully the memory of his own mother.

Finally, he shrugged. "Well," he said, "I did tell you I walked through the park. It must have dropped off."

"But you saw and heard nothing?"

"That's right."

"Bit of a coincidence, though, isn't it? The timing and all."

"Coincidences happen."

"Where did you get that scratch on your cheek?" I asked him.

He put his hand up to it. "Don't know," he said. "Maybe cut myself shaving."

"You didn't have it last night when you left my house."

He shrugged again. "Must have happened later, then."

"When you were attacking Evelyn Fowler?"

He looked at me with disappointment in his eyes and shook his head. "You don't believe that."

He was right; I didn't. "Well, what did happen?" I asked.

"I think that's about enough for now," said Lieutenant Clawson, getting to his feet and pacing the tiny room. "We'll take it from here."

That was what I had been afraid of. At least with me Cornelius would get a fair deal, but I wasn't sure how well his countrymen would treat him. I was the one who had brought the trouble, the one who couldn't overlook something like the little tiger charm found at the crime scene, even though I never suspected Cornelius of rape. But these men . . . how well would he fare with them?

"This girl who was attacked," Clawson went on, "is she still alive?"

"Evelyn Fowler? Yes," I said. "She's unconscious in hospital, but she's expected to pull through."

"Then maybe she'll be able to identify her attacker."

I looked at Cornelius and saw the despair in his face.

I thought I knew why. "Yes," I said. "Perhaps she will."

Within two days, Evelyn Fowler was sitting up and talking in her hospital bed. Before the Americans arrived, I managed to persuade Dr. Harris, an old friend, to give me a few minutes alone with her.

Not surprisingly, she looked dreadful. The Veronica Lake hair lay limp and greasy around her heart-shaped face. She was still partially bandaged, mostly around the nose, but the dark bruises stood out in stark contrast to skin as pale as the linen on which she lay. Her eyes had lost that light, cynical, playful look and were filled instead with a new darkness. When she tried to smile at me, I could see that two of her lower front teeth were missing. It must have been a terrible beating.

"Hello, Inspector Palmer," she said, her voice oddly lisping and whistling, no doubt because of the missing teeth. "I'm sorry, it's a right mess you see me in."

I patted her hand. "That's all right, Evelyn. How are you?"

"Not so bad, I suppose, apart from my face, that is. And a bit of soreness . . . you know."

I did know.

"He must have been disturbed or something," she went on. "I suppose I was lucky he didn't kill me." She tried another smile, and some of her natural sweetness and playfulness came through.

"Did you see your attacker at all?" I asked, a lump in my throat.

"Oh, yes," she said. "I mean, you can't help it, can you, when a great hulking brute's on top of you, thumping you in the face? I saw him, all right."

"Did you recognize him?"

Here she paused. "Well, it was dark, what with the blackout and all that. But I suppose in a way that's what made it easier."

"What do you mean?"

"The blackout. His face, it just blended right in, didn't it." She lowered her voice to a whisper and turned her head toward me. "He was a nigger."

"Evelyn, that's not a polite word to use."

"Well, it wasn't a polite thing he did to me, was it?" She pouted. "Anyway, Jim—that's my sweetheart G.I., Jim's a G.I., and he says them niggers are good for nothing and they have their way with white women at the drop of a hat. Said they're hanging them over there for it all the time. They're not the same as us. Not as intelligent as us. They're just like big children, really. They can't control themselves. I know what folks thought of me, that I'd go with anybody, but I wouldn't go with a nigger, not for a hundred pounds. No, sir."

"Was it someone you recognized?"

"I'd know him if I saw him again."

"But you'd never seen him before?"

"I didn't say that. My head still aches. I can't think clearly."

"Did you scratch him?"

"I certainly tried hard enough . . . Funny thing . . ."

"What is?"

"Well, it's just a feeling I got, I don't know, just about when I was passing out, but at one time I could have . . ."

"What?"

"Well, I could have sworn that there were two of them."

Apart from one or two brief consultations with Lieutenant Clawson and another U.S. military lawyer called William Grant, the case was taken out of my hands, and whatever investigation was done was carried out by the U.S. military. It's a sorry state of affairs indeed when a British policeman has no powers of investigation in his own country.

Naturally, the Americans were tight-lipped and I could discover nothing from them. Evelyn came out of hospital after a week and soon got back to her old self, and her old ways, though she seemed to be avoiding me. At least, she never came to the Nag's Head anymore, and I got the impression that whenever she saw me approaching in the street she crossed over to the other side. I guessed that perhaps the Americans had found out about our little chat and warned her off. Whatever the reason, they were keeping everything under wraps, and hardly a snippet of information even got out to the papers.

Of poor Cornelius, I had no news at all. I didn't see him again until the general court-martial at the base. As he sat there, flanked by a guard and his lawyer, he seemed lifeless and mechanical in his movements, and the sparkle had gone from his eyes, though the look of innocence remained. He seemed resigned to whatever fate had in store for him. When he looked at me, it seemed at first as if he didn't recognize me; then he flashed me a brief smile and turned back to examining his fingernails.

I had never been to an American GCM before, and I was surprised at how informal it all seemed. Despite the uniforms, there were no wigs in evidence, and the language seemed less weighty and less full of legal jargon than its British equivalent. There were twelve members of the court, all officers, and by law, because this was the trial of a Negro, one of them also had to be colored. This turned out to be a young first lieutenant, new to command, who seemed nervous and completely intimidated by the other eleven, all of whom had higher ranks and much greater seniority.

Cornelius pleaded not guilty and his defense was that he had interrupted the attack and chased off the attacker, whom he had not recognized because of the blackout. When he realized he was a colored American G.I. standing alone in a deserted park after nightfall with a raped and beaten white girl, he did what any colored man would do and hurried back to camp.

Naturally, I was called quite early in the proceedings to present my evidence, much as I would have been in an ordinary court. I described how I had been woken up and led to Brimley Park by

Harry Joseph, what I had seen there, and what I had found in the grass beside Evelyn Fowler. I was then asked about my relationship with the accused and about how previous to the attack we had spent the evening drinking. The problem was that whenever I tried to expand on Cornelius's good character and his virtues and to emphasize that, drunk or sober, he was not the sort of man who could have carried out such a brutal rape, they cut me off. Even Cornelius's lawyer never really let me get very far. As a policeman, of course, I was used to giving evidence for the prosecution, not for the defense, but this time the limitations galled me.

Evelyn Fowler was a revelation. In court, she looked a lot more demure than she ever had in the Nag's Head: no dirndl skirt, bolero dress, or Veronica Lake hairstyle for Evelyn today; only a plain utility dress and hair tied loosely behind her neck.

Lieutenant Clawson proceeded gently at first, as if afraid to stir up her feelings and memories of the events, but I guessed that his apparent sympathy was merely an act for the court. When he got to the point, he made it brutally and efficiently.

"What were you doing in the park that night, Miss Fowler?" he asked.

"I was walking home from a dance," she said. "My friends wanted to stay, but I had to get up early for work. It's a shortcut."

"And what happened?"

"Someone grabbed me and threw me to the ground. He . . . he punched me and tore my clothing off."

"And he raped you. Is that correct?"

Evelyn looked down at the handbag clasped on her knees. "Yes," she whispered. "He raped me."

"Miss Fowler, do you see the man who raped you and beat you here in this courtroom today?"

"I do," she said.

"Can you please point him out to the court?"

"That's him," she said, pointing at Cornelius without a moment's hesitation. "The accused. That's the man who raped me."

"You have no doubt?"

"Not a shred," said Evelyn, her lips set in a determined line. "That's him."

And did Cornelius's lawyer attack her evidence? Not a bit of it. Did he challenge her character and question how she had arrived at her identification? Not at all. I knew that Evelyn hated and feared colored people, and that she had been well versed in this by her beau, G.I. Jim, but did the lawyer ask her about her feelings toward Negroes? No, he didn't.

I was willing to bet, for a start, that Evelyn hadn't picked Cornelius out of a lineup of similar physical types, and that as far as she was concerned one Negro looked very much like another. And Cornelius did have a scratch on his face, after all. I wouldn't even have been surprised if she had been told in advance that a charm from his bracelet had been found right beside her arm after the attack. She had told me that at one point she had sensed two men. Couldn't one of them have been Cornelius fighting off her attacker? But neither lawyer asked about that.

All in all, it was a disappointing affair, one-sided and sloppy in the extreme. I spent the entire time on the edge of my seat, biting my tongue. On several occasions I almost spoke out, but I knew they would only expel me from the courtroom if I did so. I could only pray for Cornelius now, and I wasn't much of a believer in prayer.

After a short recess for lunch, which I spent smoking and trying, unsuccessfully, to gain access to Cornelius's lawyer, there was little else to be done. Dr. Harris gave evidence about Evelyn's condition after the attack, not forgetting to mention that the small piece of skin found under one of her fingernails was black.

In the end, it was an easy decision. Lieutenant Cornelius Jubb admitted to being in Brimley Park on the night in question, around the exact time the attack occurred. It was a particularly brutal attack, and Cornelius and Evelyn, while they might have recognized one another in passing, had no earlier acquaintance, which might have earned the court's leniency. A charm from a bracelet the accused was known to wear habitually was found at the scene. He had a scratch on his face and she had black skin under her fingernail. His defense—that he had seen a woman in trouble and come to her rescue—was too little, too late. They might as well have added that he was colored, but they didn't go that far.

But when the verdict finally came, it took the breath out of me: Lieutenant Cornelius Jubb was found guilty of rape and was sentenced to be hanged by the neck until dead.

That was the one little detail I had forgotten, and I cursed myself for it: under U.S. Article of War 92, rape is a crime punishable by life imprisonment or death, which is not the case under British law. They wanted to make an example of Cornelius, so they went for the death penalty, and there wasn't a damn thing I could do about it. In a way, I had gotten him into this, through my bloody devotion to my job, to duty. I could have hidden the tiger charm. I knew Cornelius wasn't a rapist, no matter what happened in Brimley Park that night. But no, I had to do the right thing. And the right thing was going to get Cornelius Jubb hanged.

They let me see Cornelius the night before his execution. He seemed comfortable enough in his tiny cell, and he assured me that he had been well treated. In the dim light of a grille-covered bulb, the small windows covered by blackout curtains, we smoked Luckies and talked for the last time.

"What really happened that night, Cornelius?" I asked him. "You didn't touch that girl, did you?"

He said nothing for a moment, just sucked in some smoke and blew it out in a long plume.

"I know you didn't," I went on. "Tell me."

Finally, he looked at me, the whites of his eyes big and round. "It was a good night," he said. "One of the best. I enjoyed our talk, the whiskey. I always enjoyed our talks. You treated me like a human being."

I said nothing, could think of nothing to say.

"It was a fine night outside. Hot and humid. It reminded me a bit of home, of Louisiana, and I was walking along thinking about all those years ago when I was a kid fishing off the levee, hooking the bracelet. When I got to the park I heard some sounds, stifled, as if someone was being gagged. It was dark, but I could make out two figures struggling, one on top of the other. I'm not a fool. I knew what was happening. When I got closer I could see that he was . . . you know, thrusting himself in her and beating her face. I grabbed him and tried to drag him off but it took all my strength. The girl was nearly unconscious by then, but she managed to lash out and give me that scratch. Finally I pulled him loose, and he ran off into the night." Cornelius shrugged. "Then I went back to the base."

"Did you recognize him?" I asked.

For a moment, he didn't answer, just carried on smoking, that faraway look in his eyes.

"Yes," he said finally. "I recognized him."

"Then why the hell didn't you say so?"

"What would have been the point?"

"The truth, Cornelius, the truth."

Cornelius smiled. "Richard, Richard, my friend." He always called me Richard though everyone else called me Dick. "You have the white man's trust in the truth. It's not quite the same for me."

"But surely they would have investigated your claim?"

"Perhaps. But the man who did it is a really bad man. People are scared of him. The morning after it happened, even before you came to see me, he made it clear that he wasn't going to take the blame, that if I tried to accuse him everyone in his hut would swear he was back on base when the attack took place."

"What about the guards on the gate?"

"They can't tell us apart. Besides, they don't even pay attention. They just sit in their gatehouse playing cards."

"So he's just going to let you die instead of him?"

Cornelius shrugged. "Well, I don't imagine he's too keen on dying himself. Would you be? It doesn't matter anyway. What happens to him. That's between him and God."

"Or the devil."

Cornelius looked at me, a hint of the old smile in the turn of his lips. "Or the devil. But even if he hadn't managed to get it all fixed, they wouldn't have believed me anyway. They'd have simply thought it was another trick, another desperate lie. They had all the evidence they needed, and then I came up with some crazy story about trying to save the girl. What would you think?"

"I know you wouldn't do what they accused you of."

"But they don't know me. To them I'm just another no-good nigger. It's the sort of thing we do. If I'd given his name, it would have been just one more nigger trying to lie his way out of his just deserts by pointing the finger at another." Cornelius shook his head. "No, my friend, there's no way out for me."

He lifted up his sleeve. "At least I got my bracelet fixed and they let me have it back," he said. "No longer evidence, I guess." Then he unfastened the clasp and handed it to me. "I want you to have it," he said. "I know I said it was going to be for my girl, but I never did find her. Now I'd like my friend to take it."

I looked at the bracelet resting in his palm. I didn't really want it, not after everything that had happened, but I couldn't refuse. I picked it up, feeling an odd sort of tingle in my fingers as I did so, and thanked him for it.

That was the last time I saw Cornelius Jubb. The morning they hanged him I walked and walked the length and breadth of the city, feeling as if I was the one living in a foreign country, and when I came to the biggest bomb site in the city center I took out Cornelius's charm bracelet and threw it as far as I could into the rubble.

DOWN AND DIRTY

Fidelis Morgan

My mummy always tells me to keep out of trouble, and when I go on a train I know I must be very careful. I should always go into a crowded compartment, she says, and if there aren't any then I must pick one with a lady in it, especially after dark. I must never go in a train carriage on my own with a man.

This is because men sometimes hurt people on trains, and stuff their bodies under the seats behind the heater, although I have looked down under the seats sometimes and do not think there is enough room there for a dead body. Ladies do not murder people, especially on trains. Ladies only poison their husbands sometimes, and that was usually in the old days when ladies wore long skirts. As strangers, ladies make safer traveling companions, my mummy says.

But not all ladies are nice. I will not tell her about the lady I met on the train yesterday, because she was not very nice at all, and said some horrible things about both Mummy and Daddy.

My daddy is a war hero. He flew planes during the war at a special airbase for the Airborne Forces Experimental Establishment at Sherburn-in-Elmet in Yorkshire. He is a test pilot now, a wing commander, at Boscombe Down. The planes he flies are not for passengers, but for battles. It is the most dangerous job a pilot can have, because no one knows whether the plane he flies will stay in the air, and sometimes they go very fast and explode in the sky. He has been testing a plane called the TSR2, which was in the newspapers, so I suppose he is quite famous compared to most people's fathers.

Mummy is a housewife. This means she organizes the staff (a cook, a cleaner, and Daddy's secretary) and has her hair done a lot. Sometimes she has migraines and has to go to bed in the daytime. On those days I have to be quiet and not play the gramophone. But I prefer playing with my trains to listening to pop music anyhow.

I like trains very much. At home in my bedroom I have a train set. It's a Hornby, an O gauge. Most boys have OO electric trains, but the O trains are bigger, and you have to wind them up with a key. I don't like electric trains. I like steam.

Every week I go on the train. Wednesday is my mummy's day for beauty treatment, so I use my pocket money on that day, buy a ticket, and go somewhere on my own.

I like to go to Eastleigh to see the engine shed. I sometimes go up to London. I know the London trip well because whenever my mummy goes shopping I go up to town with her. She goes first class and always eats breakfast in the restaurant car on the train, where she has coffee poured from a silver pot with a neck like a swan by a waiter called Ginger who wears a red short jacket, and in London she likes to go to Harrods and buy things. When I go with her we go in a black taxi where two of the seats face backward and pop down out of the wall. I like taxis. We do not have taxis like that in Salisbury.

Once I made Mummy laugh in the taxi. We came over a bridge across the river Thames and passed a big black building with a tower and a clock. Mummy says everything in London is black because of the Germans. They dropped a lot of bombs and the smoke from the bombs made everything in London black, just like the inside of the chimney. But that was almost twenty years ago now, so I wonder why the rain has not washed all the soot away.

I recognized the building with the clock because there is a picture of it on the HP sauce bottles, so I asked Mummy if it was the sauce factory.

She thought this was very funny. It is really a place called the Houses of Parliament, and some people call it Big Ben, though I think *that* is pretty funny. Whoever thought of calling a house by someone's name?

When I said that thing about the sauce factory Mummy ran her hand through my hair and smiled at me. Her smile sometimes looks quite sad when she looks at me, and sometimes she even has tears. But anyway, I think she shouldn't do that thing with my hair anymore, because I am not a child.

The lady on the train touched my hair too. But I don't like to think about it.

When I have been to London I have seen some very famous trains. I have seen the Golden Arrow which goes to France, and the Royal Scot. I wish I could see Mallard. Its number is 4468. It is blue and it broke the record for the fastest train at 126 miles per hour. In America the trains are huge, and I would like to see them. I am saving my pocket money because if I went to America I would go to Disneyland. Perhaps when I was there I would also see Superman or Batman. I like the Justice League of America very much. The Americans are lucky. I wish we had superheroes in England too. It's funny though, because they did not come and save President Kennedy, even though he saved the world from the atom bomb and the Communists. I think Dan Dare is probably better than Superman, even though he has to use a plane to fly.

In Swindon, which is very famous for railways, I saw Hereward the Wake and Shooting Star. These are sister trains. They are 7P6F 6-2 class with the numbers 70037 and 70029. I collect train numbers and write them down in a little black book. Mummy gave me the book. It has a leather cover with a gold line around it. When I get home I take my ABC books out and underline all the trains I have seen. I also write down the names of special trains, like the Winston Churchill, Tintagel, and Boadicea, and also Pullman carriages. Pullmans are special passenger cars for very rich and posh people. They have a brown and cream livery and little fancy lights on the tables. I would like to go on a Pullman but I think I will never have enough money for that. The Pullmans are divided into kitchen cars, brake cars, and parlor cars. I have seen Agatha, Evadne, Lucille, Philomel, Ursula, and Sheila. One day I would like to go on the Brighton Belle or the boat train to Southampton, but when I got to Southampton I would not go on the boat because I am frightened of the sea.

The lady on the train was called Rosemary, which is also the name of a Pullman parlor car. She was wearing a bracelet, and that was what started the trouble. I do not believe what she told me about that bracelet. Mummy says that because people think I am simple they sometimes make things up and I do not have to believe everything people say even if they are grown-ups, because grown-ups do not always tell the truth. And also she says that sometimes grown-ups do nasty things to people like me. Like that Rosemary in the train. But I don't want to think about her. She is a nasty piece of work.

As long as I remember my manners and am polite Mummy says I will always be all right, because I am quite handsome. I am tall and have dark hair. It is cut in the usual way for a man. I would like to have long hair like the Beatles, but I go to the barber with my daddy and the barber always uses the electric razor up the back of my neck. Daddy says the Beatles are like pansies.

I wish Daddy liked me a bit more, and I could play cricket with him or even football. Daddy does not like me to call him Daddy. I tried one day calling him Dad instead but he says there is no need to call him anything in front of people. Most people call him Bill, which is short for William. No one I have asked knows why Bill is short for William, but you would think Bill was short for Billiam, which would be a stupid name.

I don't know why Daddy doesn't like me very much. He is usually very friendly with men. He goes to the Red Lion with them and plays darts and drinks beer. But he never takes me with him. Even though I am over eighteen.

I can remember when I was still practically a child and he'd come to my bedroom in the night and read me stories by the nightlight, which was a red and white mushroom. When he thought I was asleep he would talk to me, saying horrid things in a hissing voice. One day he spat on my bed. But I didn't tell Mummy about that, even though I was frightened that she might think it was me who spat on the quilted bedspread. I am more scared of Daddy than Mummy. He has got very strong hands. Daddy whispered in my ear one night that I was not his son, and one day he told a lady in a shop that I was bitten by a monkey when I was a baby, but I cannot believe that this is true because whoever heard of monkeys living in Salisbury except when the circus comes? I am not saying that I think my daddy is a liar, though perhaps he was confused because he might have had a drink in the pub at lunchtime or something. I don't like being alone with him very much, and I told Mummy this, but she says I must always remember how brave Daddy is, and how he risks his life every day to put the food on our table, although I have never seen him do this. Cook usually puts the food on the table. Daddy's work sometimes means he has to go away for a few days, and sometimes he stays out till very late at night and comes in shouting because he is drunk. Sometimes this makes Mummy very sad, and while we are sitting watching the television I can see that she is crying, even though we might be watching something funny like *Steptoe and Son* or *Benny Hill*, or the comedy bits in *The Black and White Minstrel Show*.

Rosemary, the lady I met on the train, was like the girls in *The*

Black and White Minstrel Show. They all wear sparkly dresses and twinkling top hats and smile all the time. They are called the Television Toppers and I think they are all six feet tall, the same height as me. But this lady was much smaller than that, although she was very pretty, with that kind of yellow hair, all fluffed up, like Marilyn Monroe before she killed herself.

Her jumper was very tight for a lady. It was pink. She also wore a tight skirt and had a shiny patent-leather handbag. She was in a compartment without any men, which was why I went and sat with her, although I wish I had not. After the guard took our tickets I saw that we were both going to Salisbury. I had been up to Vauxhall, which is a good station for train-spotting, as all the trains coming out of Waterloo go through it. I saw quite a few Q1s. The Q1 locomotive weighs fifty-one tons and five hundredweights and its driving wheel is five feet, 1 inch in diameter. But mainly I saw diesels and electrics, which are not much fun. Electrics don't even look as though there is a locomotive, just a row of boring passenger cars. Soon I believe there will be no more steam trains, and that will be the beginning of the end for the railways. And a man called Dr. Beeching is planning to give many stations and branch lines the ax. In my opinion doctors should stick to looking after people and not waste their time fiddling about with our trains.

After Basingstoke (shed number 70D, Southern Region) nearly everyone got off the train. We were traveling on 80031, a standard 2-6-4, eighty-eight-ton, ten-hundredweight locomotive with a five foot, eight inch driving wheel. When I boarded the train at Waterloo I went to the buffet and treated myself to a sandwich and a cup of tea. I like the tea on trains, but most people do not.

When I was finished I moved along and sat in a crowded second-class slide-door compartment. But at Woking all the ladies in the compartment got out, and I was left on my own with two men in bowler hats, so I moved along and found a car near the back of the train with only two women in it.

Rosemary, in the pink pullover, was reading a magazine about pop music. Every time she turned the page her gold bracelet jangled. I couldn't take my eyes off the bracelet because it was all gold charms, and one of them was a wonderful train. It was a very early locomotive, maybe even a model of Stephenson's Rocket. There were other charms on the bracelet, but I wanted to look closely at Rocket. One day I will go to the Science Museum in London and see Rocket—maybe even touch it if there is not a fence in the way.

The woman Rosemary sighed when she saw me watching her, and she pulled at her jumper, so I looked down at my lap. I had bought myself a copy of the *Eagle* at Waterloo, and read that, trying to sneak glimpses at the charm over the top of the comic. Dan Dare, pilot of the future, was as usual in a good adventure, fighting the Mekon.

The lady who was sitting beside me on the window side started to make a noise like *tch-tch.* She was quite old, probably about thirty-five, and fat, and wore a tweed suit like Daddy's secretary wears, but Daddy's secretary is even older and fatter than this woman. The fat lady was staring at the *Eagle,* so I thought maybe she wanted to look at it. I held it out to her and said: "Perhaps, madam, you would like to read it when I am finished." But she made a noise like a steam locomotive when it comes to a station stop and turned her back to me. Rosemary giggled when the fat lady made this noise and gave me a wink, so I winked back and pulled a face to show I knew I was in trouble with the fat lady. Rosemary rolled her eyes in a conspiratorial kind of way, and then returned to reading her pop magazine.

I did not think that Rosemary would turn out in the end to be so horrible. If anyone was going to be unpleasant I would have thought it was the fat lady, but the fat lady got out at Basingstoke.

I think Rosemary is what Mummy would call a common little tart.

As the train pulled out of Basingstoke station it started to rain.

The windows were grimy, and the water came down in clean lines, cutting a diagonal pattern in the dirt.

I shuffled along into the fat woman's place near the window and started to look out. Sometimes at Basingstoke there are some good locomotives waiting the sidings, sometimes even rows of Pullman cars.

"Perhaps you'll let *me* read your comic," said Rosemary, out of the blue. I handed it to her.

"I like the train on your bracelet," I said. "Is it articulated?"

She pulled her sleeve down again, almost as though my mentioning the bracelet made her feel she had to hide it. Perhaps, I thought, she took me for a jewel thief or a robber who would overpower her, rip the bracelet from her petite wrist, and leap from the train with my ill-gained booty.

She turned the comic over and started to read the back page. It was a special cut-out article on the TSR2. She seemed to be very interested.

"Do you like planes?" I asked. "I live near Boscombe Down."

"My boyfriend is a pilot there," she said. "He's been working on this plane."

"So does my daddy." I clapped my hands together with excitement. "Do the wheels on the train move?"

"I should bloody hope so," said Rosemary, "or we'll never get home before *Late Night Line Up*."

I laughed and she smiled as she fiddled again with the bracelet. I think *Late Night Line Up* is a boring program, and after it the TV shuts down for the night so I am usually in bed anyway.

"It's pretty, isn't it?" She rolled her fingertips along the wheels and I could see them moving, but I could not see whether the wheels pushed the connecting rod in and out.

"Did you buy it?" I couldn't take my eyes off the wheels. I wanted to touch them too.

"My boyfriend gave it to me," she said. "He was stationed up north during the war. Leeds. He found it while they were clearing up after some Nazi bomb which almost blew up the flat he lived in. No one claimed it so he hung on to it." She pulled up her sleeve, held her arm out, and jangled the bracelet. "He used to keep it in the cockpits with him as a lucky mascot, but when these new planes came in, reaching such high speeds, he said it was a liability. He was frightened it would fly off the hook and knock his eye out, so then he kept it in the flight office. Until he gave to me, anyhow." She handed the *Eagle* back to me, then pulled her sleeve down, folded her arms, and edged nearer to the window. "How quickly it gets dark now. It'll be Christmas before we know it." She chewed the inside of her cheek.

The sky was dark gray with rain clouds and the sun had dipped below the horizon. You could see little cream-colored lights in people's houses, and parallel lines of yellow street lamps as we passed through Overton. We were on the fast train, so we didn't stop at the station.

"Perhaps your boyfriend knows my dad." I called him Dad because I didn't want her to turn all funny like Daddy does on me sometimes when I am with him and he meets people who work at the base and I call him Daddy. "He's a test pilot. He specializes in down in the dirt maneuvering. Low flight, you know. Down and dirty. He's very brave. He's got medals."

"Maybe." She didn't seem interested and went on staring out into the dark. "What's his name?"

So I told her, and I remembered to say Wing Commander. Mummy does this in shops, and then people are very nice to her and start bowing and scraping. I said Bill, too, rather than William. I wanted Rosemary to think I was very casual with Daddy, as though we go down to the Red Lion for drinks together every weekend.

"What's your name, then?" She had knotted her eyebrows together and was peering at my face.

"Tommy," I said. "Tommy Birkenshaw."

"Tommy?" She pursed her lips, her eyes went sort of slitty, and she crossed her legs, one over the other. "You're rather good-looking." She sounded surprised. "I thought . . ." Her voice drifted off, and she suddenly clicked open her handbag and pulled out a compact and lipstick. "What's your mummy like, then?" She was swiping the lipstick back and forth across her lips as she spoke. It was a pale coral pink, like a peeled shrimp.

"She's very nice," I said. "Very kind. Can I see the train on your bracelet?"

"Yes, yes. Of course." She wiggled her lips together and thrust the lipstick back into her bag, wiping each end of her mouth with her fingertip. "Is she pretty, your mummy? How old is she?"

"She's forty. I think she looks like Sophia Loren."

"Are you a mongol?" She was fidgeting with her hand inside her handbag, as though she was looking for something. "You don't look like one. You look normal."

"I'm just a bit slow, that's all. Mummy says . . ."

"Your mummy is a domineering cow," she said, almost as though she was spitting at me. I was frightened of her now, and I wanted her to stop talking and just show me the bracelet. "And your daddy is an ungrateful bastard, and you can tell him Rosemary said so."

I tried to get her talking about the bracelet again. "Does the rod go in and out of the piston cylinder?"

She opened her mouth and laughed in a loud way, like men laugh in the pub. I could see her uvula go up and down at the back of her throat. "In your father's case, deary, it does that rather too often for his own good."

I had barely noticed that the train had stopped. We were at Andover, and I prayed someone would get in, or that Rosemary would get out. But the platform was deserted, and I knew her ticket was for Salisbury, like mine.

The whistle blew and the train puffed out into the dark countryside.

"I might go to the buffet now," I said, getting up.

"No. Stay!" She grabbed my wrist and the train rattled and swayed as it crossed some points. She pulled me down beside her. "Tell me more about your daddy. Is he working late much at the moment?"

"Dad always works late." I could feel the spiky pieces on the charm bracelet pressing against my leg as she pushed her hand down, narrowly missing my flies.

"Well, he's not been working late with *me* these last few weeks, that's for sure. Does he smell of scent?"

"Of course not." I was trying to pull away from her, but she was stronger than you'd think and I didn't want her to think I was being rude. "Dad's a man. Men don't wear scent."

"Why don't you kiss me?" Her hand was rubbing now, up and down my thigh. It made my trousers feel uncomfortable. "Go on, Tommy. Give me a nice snog. And when you get home you can tell your dad all about it."

"It's all right, thanks," I said. "I'd better be off now. We'll be there soon."

She pushed me back and I fell along the seat. She sprawled on top of me, wriggling and slobbering. It made me feel quite dizzy and frightened.

"It's all right," I said again. "Perhaps you can show me your bracelet now, Rosemary. That would be nice, wouldn't it?"

She was tugging at my belt and unfastening my fly buttons. I grabbed at her hand to make her stop, but her bracelet got caught up in my watch strap and my hand was trapped beside hers as she slid her fingers into the front of my pants.

"Please . . ." I tried to sit up. "The guard will come . . ."

"The guard never comes after Andover, you silly bugger. Not unless people get on." She was pulling on my willy, making me feel all strange and hot.

"Please can I get up now, Rosemary?" I said, staring up at my mac in the nets for luggage. "I think I have to go to the toilet. Please can I go to the toilet?"

Her face loomed above me and she planted her lips on mine and started putting her tongue into my mouth. I think she was a bit mad, because whoever would do such a thing as that?

"Give it to me." She moaned, sliding her mouth over my lips. "Give it to me."

I didn't know what she was talking about, and kept wondering what Mummy would think if she saw me with all this pink lipstick Rosemary was smearing all over my face.

"Come on, come on, come on . . . Put it in. Put it inside me . . ." Her hand was right inside my pants now. I tried to pull it away, but my own wrist was bound to hers by that darned bracelet. So I yanked my hand away very hard and the bracelet sort of snapped and was hanging from my watch strap.

That stopped her, all right.

She glared down at my arm and started shouting at me. "What do you think you're playing at? You've gone and broken it."

She snatched at the bracelet, but I pulled my arm back and she lurched forward because the train was braking for the signals at Idmiston Halt.

She tumbled down onto the floor as I pushed her away from me. As she hit the ground her head caught on the edge of the seat and there was this cracking noise, like when you snap a twig or bite into a Ryvita.

Rosemary didn't move, she just lay curled up on the floor between the seats. Her head was twisted right around on her neck, like a doll's.

The train made a sound like a gasp and moved slowly forward.

I sat down and fiddled with the bracelet, which still hung from the catch on my watch strap. I could not remove it.

"Rosemary?"

She was still on the floor. She looked as though she was asleep.

The yellow rows of streetlights outside showed that we'd be arriving in Salisbury in a few minutes' time.

"Rosemary, I can't seem to get this bracelet off."

She didn't reply.

Her eyes were still shut and the train was slowing down. We'd be home in a few moments.

So I did something terrible.

I just yanked at the thing until it was free, snapping one of the links.

We were passing the Scats Seeds factory now. Any second, the train would pull in at the station.

"Rosemary?"

But she was still fast asleep.

I didn't know what to do.

Castle Street. The train was really slowing down, clouds of steam puffing past the window in the yellow light.

I couldn't take the bracelet with me. That would be stealing. But if I just left it on the seat—well, anything might happen to it. What if a passenger bound for Exeter got in and pinched it? Rosemary would lose the bracelet and it would be my fault.

I knelt down and tried to get to her handbag, which lay on the floor beneath her. But she was pressing the bag against the radiator grille and I didn't want to break that too. Imagine! To break both her bracelet and her bag in one day!

I could see that her skirt and jumper didn't have any pockets.

Her skirt was high up her legs. Because it was a miniskirt I could see her pants.

Maybe . . .

Well, it seemed as safe a place as any.

I pulled the opening of the pants toward one leg, and managed to slip the bracelet into her knickers, but my fingers were all slippy. I just couldn't make it stay still. The dratted thing just kept wriggling out of my hand onto the floor as if it was alive. "Put it in," she had said, when she was messing about with my flies. "Inside me." I gripped the bracelet and shoved it hard into the bit between her legs until it seemed safely tucked away.

It might be a bit uncomfortable when Rosemary woke up. But

that would teach her for calling Mummy and Daddy names, and for playing about with *my* pants.

I stood up, brushed myself down, and straightened my hair in the mirror on the wall under the luggage rack. There was a little bit of that pink lipstick on my cheek, so I made sure to rub it off with my finger. I wiped my fingers clean with a tissue and carefully put it into the waste bin.

I knew I ought to try to wake Rosemary up again. But if she went sailing on to Yeovil and Exeter St. David's, so what? It would serve her right. She could catch the next train back, even if that was the milk train.

I took my mac from the luggage rack and stepped over her, being careful not to tread on her hands, which lay in my path.

Before leaving the compartment I patted my pocket, making sure my train-spotting book was still there, before I slid the door closed after me.

After all, I'd seen quite a few Q1s today, and also noted down a string of Pullman cars on the boat train.

How awful if I'd had a wasted day.

THE GOBLIN

Lynda La Plante

Carol Mary Edge was sentenced to eight years for the manslaughter of her mother. In prison she had been closely monitored for the first two years and given sporadic sessions with a prison psychiatrist. A plump, lank-haired girl, she was well behaved but sullen and uncooperative. She changed radically when she was transferred to an open prison and, with other girls, put to work in the garden. Part of her duties was caring for the inmates' "pet corner"; they had a goat, three guinea pigs, and two rabbits. By the time Carol was released there were ten rabbits and the girls had bred over three hundred more and sold them on to the local pet shop.

On her release Carol had eighteen months of weekly visits with a parole officer; since she had no living relatives it was the parole board that arranged her accommodation and a job at an MFI store. Carol was still overweight, but she had muscle tone from working in the prison garden and she was very strong. Her dark hair was almost to her waist, worn in a braid down her back. She had made a few friends in prison, but none she intended to see again. Instead, she was determined to start a new life, listing as preferences for future employment anything to do with animals.

Sometimes the customers at MFI were like aggressive animals themselves, and she loathed her job. Carol constantly badgered her parole officer to find her alternative work.

After two years, Carol left the MFI store to work as a kennel maid at Battersea Dogs Home. She moved to a small one-bedroom flat on a large council estate near to her new job. Via the animals Carol saw firsthand the results of abuse on the creatures taken into care, but she also recognized that with careful training, love, and patience they could be healed and new homes found for them. She saw the tragic cases of the strays that were never taken and eventually ended up being put down. Equally heartbreaking were the dogs returned from their new homes; all her love and patience had not been enough and they had savaged their new owners or been too boisterous and so were rejected and brought back to eventually be destroyed.

Carol learned from these dumb creatures the need to be accepted as "normal." Being sweet-tempered and obedient secured them a safe existence. She watched her own behavior more at the kennels than at MFI. Eight years as a guest of Her Majesty had resulted in Carol's picking up from the other inmates their relish at using foul language, and so she made a great effort to not swear. The time spent working alongside the vets and qualified kennel maids made her determined to gain some qualifications, but, sadly, she failed the written examination to move up a notch from basically cleaning out the cages and walking the dogs. She took home the canine magazines and dog-show newsletters as bedtime reading. In one of the magazines she found an advertisement for an experienced receptionist at a veterinary practice in Highbury, North London.

Carol applied for the job and used her free afternoon for the interview, which was taken by the present receptionist, who was pregnant. It was a large practice run by two vets, Peter Frogton and Miles Richards, and two female veterinary assistants. They had a large open plan reception area with a high desk and clean tiled floors. There were three consulting rooms for the vets to examine the sick animals, behind which were the cages for overnight stays. The cages were close to a large, well-equipped operating room.

Carol was asked to fill in a "previous employment" form, and if she was suitable she would be asked to meet both the residing vets. Carol took the form home and spent hours poring over each question, writing down her replies on a notepad so she wouldn't make any mistakes when filling in the form itself. Previous employment and letters of recommendation worried her: prison, MFI, and eighteen months washing down dog shit was not exactly the best CV, even though it was only to act as a receptionist. The current pregnant one had implied that there was often a lot more to the job and it could even entail assisting the veterinary nurses.

Carol went to the head kennel maid at Battersea, mentioned the possible job, and asked if they could give her a letter of recommendation. They would be very sad to see her leave but knew that the wages were very low and, understanding that if there was a possibility of something more lucrative for her, they would of course give her the letter.

"To Whom It May Concern" was signed by the administration officer and stated that in the two years Carol had worked for Battersea she had been methodical, caring, and willing. She also had shown a very sympathetic and intuitive knowledge of the dogs, gaining their trust quickly and helping in their rehabilitation and training.

Carol went to a local print shop, carefully printed out the headed notepapers, and then copied the letter inserting nine years for two. As she was still only twenty-six years old, it would appear that she had gone to work for the kennels on leaving school. She was no longer required to visit her parole officer and from her mother's estate she now had ten thousand pounds in the bank.

Carol waited to hear from the veterinary clinic and eventually received a letter asking her to come into the surgery to meet the two partners. She spent a lot of time shopping for new clothes—neat skirts and blouses, a couple of jackets, and two pairs of court shoes. She was impressed by her own appearance, her long hair neatly braided, her new business suit; she even had a small brief-case. Yes, she thought, I look the fucking business!

It was love at first sight: Peter Frogton was charming and very good-looking, if older than she had expected. He was fifty-two, with dark hair graying at the temples, slim, about five foot ten, and dressed in tweeds, but the pale blue tunic was what really made him stand out. The high collar enhanced his blue, dark-lashed eyes, and he had a lovely gentle manner. The other partner was younger, blond, knew he was attractive. He was not all that interested in Carol. He seemed to be in a hurry and kept looking at his watch; he didn't even stay to show her around. Mr. Frogton did, and then sat and had a cup of coffee with her, asking her about herself, and did she feel she could cope with reception duties. Carol said there would be no problem as she had worked on a secretarial course before leaving school. It was a lie. But by the time she returned home she was elated; she had the job, starting the following Monday.

Carol had never been so happy, and the job was beyond her wildest dreams. Working at the desk taking appointments and phone calls was nerve-racking to begin with, but within a week she was relaxed and very competent. She also began assisting the training veterinary nurses and a number of times worked late with either one or other of the partners. It was a very busy practice, and the patients ranged from a mouse with a broken foot to birds and snakes, but mostly it was the cats and dogs that needed treatment. Carol kept her white uniform pristine, and she even bought a pair of white nurse's shoes to make herself look more efficient.

At night Carol studied the veterinary medical books, the journals and news circulars. Her whole life revolved around her work and her dreams of becoming closer to Mr. Frogton. She had never had a relationship with anyone, had never really had any sexual urges until now. Carol at no time showed her infatuation, but retained a very professional presence. However, she was becoming certain that Mr. Frogton was falling in love with her. She knew this by certain small things that he did: when he wore a flower-printed tie, it was a signal. On Valentine's Day he bought her a box of chocolates—that he also bought them for all the other women made no difference; he would have to do that so no one knew his intentions toward her.

Carol was careful when asking questions about his private life, but when she discovered that he was divorced, and quite recently, it was yet another signal: he had instigated the divorce because of his feelings toward her. She was loath to ask too many questions about his personal life, as she didn't want anyone becoming suspicious of their relationship.

Every day was a bonus. She became more and more indispensable, working late, arriving before she was required to be on duty. Frogton made her even more certain of their growing love affair when he asked if she would take the keys to the surgery home with her. This meant that she could open up for him, as she was always so early and it would be a relief for him to know she was there.

On a number of occasions when they were operating on the sick animals she offered to help out and proved so invaluable that Frogton started to ask for her specifically to assist him. It was yet another sign of his love. If he wrote a memo for her she treasured it as a love token. To her, a simple message that read "Call owner first thing in the morning" actually meant "I am desperate for the morning, to be near you!"

Carol would help Frogton into his smock and pass him his mask, and he was so patient and caring, always explaining what he was doing and why. She began to scrub up her hands the way he did, snapping on the rubber gloves in an identical manner, even wearing a mask. Bit by bit she began to know all the names of the different surgical instruments, always ready and waiting to pass them to him. One day he said to her that he felt she was more adept than his actual veterinary nurse. His compliments made her flush, not with embarrassment but with passion; she was by now adoring of his every move.

Carol made sure she was on good terms with the nurses, and she tried to be nice to Miles Richards, but she didn't like him. He used to get a little tetchy with her when she was supposed to be on reception and instead was with Mr. Frogton. The practice was a very busy one and they also sold customers dog food, cat litter, and certain over-the-counter nonprescription treatments for fleas and ticks. Part of her job too was to reorder and restock, plus take all the appointments and oversee the daily surgery requirements. The medical supplies were kept locked in a secure cabinet in the office, but Carol was often asked to check if they were running low and then to make a note for either vet to order more.

Hilda was the other receptionist, a middle-aged, friendly woman, and Carol made sure they remained on good terms. Come nine o'clock in the morning there were at least six or seven clients and their animals, and it would continue all day until evening. Sometimes they had late-night surgery and early starts in the morning for the operations, but Carol never once complained. Often she would take over Hilda's duties, as she was invariably late, so their friendship grew over the months.

Christmas 1972. The surgery had a little tree, decorated by Carol, who had brought in small wrapped gifts for everyone to place beneath the tinfoil-covered base. It was just the tree. Miles had felt that would be all that was necessary, but all the cards they were sent by their patients Carol threaded on a ribbon and pinned up around the reception desk. It was, she felt, going to be the happiest Christmas of her entire life.

The staff were to break for the Christmas holiday on December twenty-fourth and reconvene on the twenty-seventh, with another break for New Year's, and the roster of those required for emergencies was to be discussed. Miles had booked a holiday for all the Christmas period, leaving for St. Moritz on the twenty-fourth and not returning until January 6. This had caused a little friction between the partners, and then Frogton agreed to take his vacation later and not take a Christmas break; thus he could work over the holiday period for any emergencies. He asked if Carol had made any plans, and when she said that she hadn't and was prepared to work over the entire holiday, he kissed her, not on the lips but on the cheek. (He couldn't have kissed her lips, as there were other people there to witness his show of affection.) Frogton made her heart beat so hard it almost burst her uniform.

"You are so special, Carol, thank you. I really appreciate your loyalty; you have proved to be irreplaceable."

That night she couldn't sleep, going over and over every detail in her mind: his beautiful sweet kiss, every word he had said. She was irreplaceable! It was to her a sign of her lover's commitment to her, and the following day she received another as Mr. Frogton arrived with his gifts to place beneath the Christmas tree. One was prettily wrapped in gold paper with gold ribbon and had a small gift card that said "Happy Christmas, Carol, with love. Peter."

Christmas Eve surgery went on until eight-fifteen, and then the doors were locked and out came two bottles of champagne. All the staff were gathered, except Miles, who had already taken off for his Christmas break. They gathered around the tree as Mr. Frogton played Father Christmas, handing out their gifts; for Carol it was the best time she had ever had in her entire life. She sipped her champagne, her face glowing. Mr. Frogton had virtually drunk a bottle himself and was in high spirits as he produced a sprig of mistletoe and held it above his head, laughing. Carol stood on tiptoe to kiss him, and he swung her around in his arms before he planted a kiss on her forehead. She knew he couldn't kiss her lips as before, not in front of everyone, but she flushed with happiness and kept her arm around his waist as he insisted everyone open the presents.

The leather-bound desk diary with his initials in gold was, he said, the most perfect present. Carol's fingers shook as she carefully opened her gift from him. First she folded the gold paper neatly, then wrapped the gold ribbon around her fingers. She wanted to treasure every second. She sat down to open the small leather box. The eighteen-karat gold charm bracelet took her breath away. Mr. Frogton came and sat beside her, taking the bracelet from her and pointing out each of the charms. There was a tiger, a funny little train, a locket in the shape of a heart, a monkey, a tiny pair of ballet shoes, and a cross.

"Do you like it?" Frogton asked.

"Oh, yes, yes I do," she murmured, reading so many messages of his love into each charm.

Frogton patted his pockets and produced a small envelope. "They were all on the bracelet when I bought it, so I decided that I'd get one extra charm that is especially for you."

"Oh" was all she could utter.

"Open it," he said, smiling.

With trembling fingers Carol opened the envelope and tipped into the palm of her hand a small goblin sitting on a toadstool, with a gold loop on its back to attach it to the bracelet.

"Do you like it?" asked Frogton. "He's an antique charm."

"Oh, yes, it's perfect."

"Do you want me to put it on the bracelet for you?"

"Oh, yes, thank you."

Mr. Frogton went to the counter, found a small pair of scissors, and pried open the ring on the goblin's back, then hooked it onto one of the bracelet's links. Hilda stood by, watching. She found it touching the way Carol was so flushed, her cheeks bright pink.

"Isn't that lovely," she said, and Mr. Frogton, delighted by his own gift, passed it to Hilda.

"It has quite a history. It belonged to an elderly aunt."

Carol had to take a deep breath to control her emotions. An aunt—this meant the gift was very special, a family treasure, and he was giving it to her!

Hilda, much to Carol's annoyance, held up the bracelet for everyone to see, and they clustered around.

"It must have belonged to someone a long time ago. Some of the charms look very old," she said.

"The goblin's new," Carol blurted out.

"Isn't he cute?" Hilda said, draping the bracelet over her own wrist.

"And it's very heavy gold, isn't it?"

Frogton laughed and said he doubted it was of great value. He was still beaming, but by now was glancing at his watch, anxious to leave.

Hilda passed the bracelet back to Carol; she wanted to snatch it, never let it go, but she managed to keep control of her emotions. The bracelet, the little goblin, were to her a declaration of his love. No one else had been given such a special and thoughtful and expensive gift.

Mr. Frogton then bade everyone a Happy Christmas and said he would have to go, as he still had some last-minute shopping to do. Carol hurried to fetch his coat, holding it out for him.

"Are you spending Christmas here or going off somewhere special?" he asked.

"Yes," she said and added, "to my family. My mother is very elderly."

"Well, have a wonderful time."

He kissed her cheek and then bade everyone good night.

Carol was almost the last to leave. Hilda was putting on her coat, then picking up bulging grocery bags to take home, ready to prepare Christmas dinner.

"You're welcome to come and spend Christmas Day with us, Carol," she said.

"That's nice of you, Hilda, but I've got family commitments, and I'm on the emergency callouts and Mr. Frogton's bound to need me to help, as he's working over the holiday."

"All right, then, you have a wonderful time. He must certainly think a lot of you; that was a really lovely present."

Carol continued collecting all the Christmas wrapping paper and putting it into a black rubbish bag, but not her own paper from her present; that she would keep always. The cages were all empty and the surgery was silent as she turned off the lights, almost ready to go home.

"I'm off, then," Hilda said as she headed for the door; then, just as she was leaving, she chuckled. "I hope it doesn't come early; she must be close to having it. He said he thinks it's a boy."

"What?"

"The baby, Meryl's. You know, you took over her job. I suppose they'll get married, might even do it this summer."

Carol was not that interested, just eager for Hilda to leave; she liked being alone in the surgery, especially sitting in Mr. Frogton's section, looking over his things, tidying his desk.

"His divorce was through months ago, so he won't be able to get out of it." Hilda laughed.

Carol frowned. "Who are you talking about—Mr. Richards?"

"No, dear, Mr. Frogton. Didn't you know? It's his baby."

Whatever Hilda said after that, Carol didn't hear; she was hardly able to stand upright, her legs were shaking so badly.

"Happy Christmas," Hilda called out as the door closed, missing Carol sinking to her knees, tears streaming down her cheeks.

No matter how many times she tried to persuade herself that Hilda could be mistaken, she knew it was the truth. He had betrayed her, kept this bitch and the fucking baby a secret. He had lied to her—the bastard had egged her on, teased her with his kisses and smiles.

All over the Christmas break, Carol's fury built. She couldn't eat and hardly slept, thinking about how she had been betrayed and how she could make him pay for it. Then she began to feel better as the plan started to take shape. She never took off the bracelet; the jingle of the charms was a constant reminder. It was irritating because the goblin's pointed finger kept sticking into her wrist like a pinprick, but she even liked that, as it kept reminding her of his betrayal.

Christmas came and went, and she continued working and behaving normally, smiling and helpful. The arrival of Frogton's baby son created quite a party atmosphere in the surgery, everyone congratulating him and bringing gifts for the little boy. Carol bought a small teddy bear, removing the attached warning: "Not suitable for small babies," as the eyes were glass and attached by a lethal drawing pin. Secretly she had been fermenting in pain, and the arrival of the baby made it worse. At long last she was ready. She would make Peter Frogton pay for his betrayal with his life. She was sure he had bought the fucking bracelet for his whore. She'd probably disliked it; some of the charms were horrible and the gold heart didn't even open.

She left for work at exactly the same time as she usually did. It was only a twenty-minute walk to the clinic, and today was an early start. It was always early on Tuesdays and Thursdays, as that was when the more complex operations were done. When they were completed, the clinic would open for other business at nine. Mrs. Dart, the cleaner, wasn't given keys, so Carol had to let her in.

Carol had spent weeks preparing for this morning. It was imperative that she was above suspicion. By this time Carol had a rudimentary knowledge of the sedatives used for the animals, and she had decided to soak a rag in halothane, as well as lacing Frogton's morning coffee with the Halcyon tablets she had been prescribed for insomnia. In preparation, Carol had been stealing small amounts of halothane from the cabinet for weeks.

Carol had specifically chosen this morning, as there was a Dalmatian, a Rottweiler, and a Jack Russell to be put to sleep. The veterinary mortuary van would call for the collection of the animals' carcasses before surgery. The animals would be placed in heavy black plastic bags with their weight and a description attached and then carried on a small gurney to the rear entrance, ready to be driven to the incinerator. There were occasionally grieving owners who asked for their pet's ashes, but Carol knew the three that morning had no owner's requests. She was safe, and she had already made an excellent copy of the death certificate for a Great Dane called Felix who had been put to sleep a month earlier. There would be four bodies removed to the incinerator from the Miles and Frogton Veterinary Clinic: three canines and one human.

The careful planning of the murder had given Carol a strength of will she never realized she had. She was sure there was no hint of her turmoil, her fury, or her pain. She was certain that no one guessed her intentions, least of all Peter Frogton. She was just as certain that she was going to get away with it. It was all in the planning, and she had spent night after night making lists and destroying them, only to begin another the next night until she knew everything by heart.

Walk to work.
Open surgery, check operation room.
Prepare Peter Frogton's coffee.
Present morning operations.
Brew fresh coffee, wash out Frogton's mug.
Wait for the drugs to take effect.
Cover his mouth with the soaked rag.
Prepare animals for mortuary.
Kill Peter Frogton.
Place his body in mortuary bag.
Open rear door.
Place bags on gurney.
Relock the back door.
Open mail.
Let in Mrs. Dart.

Get ready for morning surgery.
Let out Mrs. Dart.
Open front door ready for morning surgery.

The lie she would tell Hilda had changed a few times. First Peter had taken ill, then he had been called away on an emergency. Then he had given her the perfect reason for him not being there. As he was now a proud father and had not taken time off at Christmas, he and his whore were going on holiday. The bitch had already left for their rented villa. Frogton had arranged to leave straight after surgery; it was perfect. The practice would be run in his absence by Miles Richards. The fact that Frogton was not returning, not ever, would therefore not become an issue for two weeks, and she had booked her own two-week vacation to begin during Frogton's absence. Even if the police were called, they would find no motive, no evidence. Peter Frogton had just disappeared off the face of the earth. Carol had even watched a television documentary detailing just how many people do disappear without a trace, and the amount was astonishing. She also watched all the television cop shows and knew it was imperative she leave no trace of what had happened, so cleaning up had to be done very methodically.

Carol was on hand for the disposal of the two large dogs, and Frogton helped her carry them to the rear door for collection. He was tired, complaining of being kept up all night by his new baby, and couldn't wait to get away. She watched as he sipped his coffee; he didn't even taste the Halcyon. The small Jack Russell was carried from his cage. He had been sedated during the night, but there was little hope that he would recover, so he was quickly injected and died peacefully on the table. Frogton was removing his rubber gloves, ready to scrub and wash his hands at the sink; as he bent forward he stumbled and then held on to the sink with his hands, leaning forward.

"Christ, I feel terrible," he muttered.

Carol moved behind him with the hammer. She hit him on the back of his skull, hard. He gasped and turned toward her, his face registering total shock, even more so when he saw her draw back her hand with the hammer, ready for another strike. He made a grab for her wrist, but she kicked him to his knees and hit him again on the side of his temple. She then dragged his body to lie face forward and covered his gasping mouth with the rag soaked in halothane; he gasped a few times, then lay still. She'd used the entire contents of two vials—one would have been enough, but she wanted to make sure, very sure, he was dead. She had to wait fifteen minutes, her hand pressed to his throat, a towel left over his face. Feeling for his pulse and satisfied he was dead, she stripped off his clothes; first his blue tunic, then his vest, his pants and socks, shoes and underpants. She placed everything carefully into a carrier bag, then bent over his naked body and tied his hands behind his back, looping the rope around his ankles and drawing his legs back almost to his arms. She then rolled his body over and began to ease the thick black bag around him, securing it at the top. For safety she wrapped a second bag around him. This she tied with strong, thick string, and then attached the label. *Great Dane. FELIX, aged ten years. Owner Mrs. Thompson,* and the address. She dragged the bag to the back door and propped it up beside the two other dead animals.

Carol was sweating as she returned to the table to lift the Jack Russell's corpse and stuff it into the black bag, ready for collection. She froze when the doorbell rang and rang; whoever it was kept a hand on the bell. Carol took deep breaths, wiped her face, and straightened out her uniform.

The woman was peering into the surgery, her hands cupped to see inside. Carol faced her.

"We're not open yet."

"I have to see Mr. Frogton. It's urgent."

"He's not here. You just missed him. He's gone . . ."

"You have to let me in. *Please* open the door. Please, I have to talk to you, talk to someone. *Open the door.*"

Carol had no option but to unlock the door. "What do you want?"

"It's about Jack. I have to see him."

"Who?"

"My dog, I have to see him. He's here."

"What dog?"

"Jack, the Jack Russell. My sister brought him in two days ago—he'd been run over. A Jack Russell. I have to see him—she said they were putting him to sleep. I have to see him."

"I'm sorry, you can't."

"But you don't understand. I've been away—my sister was looking after him. I have to see him. *It's important—I have got to see him.*"

"But you can't."

"Why not? He's here, isn't he?"

"Well, yes, he was, but I'm sorry . . ."

"Is he dead?"

"I'm afraid so. We couldn't save him. His injuries were too . . ."

"Can I see him?"

"Pardon?"

"Is he still here?"

Carol was in a state; she couldn't get rid of the hysterical woman, who was now sitting in one of the surgery chairs, crying, blubbering and sobbing loudly, saying over and over that she just had to see him.

"Did he have a brown right ear, or was it his left?"

"Pardon?" Carol snapped.

"My Jack Russell had a brown left ear; Battersea Dogs Home said they've got a Jack Russell stray, handed in two days ago. It could be Jack, do you see? Maybe my sister brought in the wrong dog. They don't open until ten, so if I could just see the one you've got here. It might not be my Jack. He's run off before. I think he was trying to get to my house, so maybe the dog that got hit by the bus isn't mine. He wasn't wearing a collar, was he? My sister said he didn't have a collar on. My Jack had a collar."

Carol checked her watch. Any minute now the mortuary van would be here.

"Wait here, please," she said, and hurried into the operating section. She had to stand for a moment to get her breath, then she opened the bag, lifted out the Jack Russell, snatched the towel from the floor, and carried him into the surgery.

"Oh, my God! Oh, my God. He's dead. Is he dead?"

"Yes, Mr. Frogton put him to sleep this morning."

"But you said he wasn't here."

"I said he'd just left. Now, is this your Jack Russell or not?"

The woman peeked at the dog curled in the bloody towel and then howled, "No, no, it's not mine. That's not Jack. Oh, thank God, thank God. You see, he's got a black ear, not brown. My Jack's ear is brown. Oh, thank you, thank you. I'm sorry to have bothered you."

Carol, with the dead dog in her arms, ushered the woman out and then locked the door. She kept repeating to herself that it was all right, everything was all right, she was just fifteen minutes behind schedule.

The mortuary van arrived two minutes later. Carol had to help him carry the three bags to his van. She had not had time to put the Jack Russell into his mortuary bag or fill in the form, but rather than delay getting rid of Frogton she decided she'd take the dead dog and Frogton's clothes to the local dump.

The mortuary van driver signed them out. The Rottweiler, the Dalmatian, and, lastly, heaving up the body of Frogton, he signed for the Great Dane.

"They don't have long lives, do they, these big dogs?"

"No, their hearts are quite small," she said with relief as the doors closed.

"I've got fifteen to collect all over London this morning. Do you want any ashes brought back?" he asked, heading for the driver's seat.

"No, no ashes required," she said, wishing he'd drive off and let her get down to cleaning up and getting rid of the clothes and the bloody Jack Russell.

Carol watched the van drive off, then returned to the final clearing up. She washed down the table, took off her soiled uniform, and stuffed it into the same bag with Frogton's clothes and the dead Jack Russell. She then went to the sink and cleaned up the blood from Frogton, where he'd bled from the hammer blows. She wiped it clean, replaced the hammer with the tools in the back room, returned, and gave the room a once-over with her eyes.

"Shit," she snapped.

The charm bracelet was just beneath the sink; somehow when Frogton grabbed her he must have broken the chain. On her hands and knees, she snatched it up and checked that all the charms were there. There was one missing—the fucking goblin.

"Fuck, fuck, where is the fucking thing?"

She sat back on her heels, her eyes roaming the room, but she couldn't see it. With the flat of her hand she felt under every surface, on top, down the sides; she began to pant with fear. The charm was not in the operating room—she even went back to reception, searched every inch of it, and went back to the operating room and re-searched, but there was no effing goblin. The reception phone rang, jangling her nerves. She snatched it up.

"Yes?"

She listened. It was Battersea Dogs Home; they had received a call from a very distraught woman who had lost her Jack Russell.

"Yes, she came here, then she left. It wasn't her Jack Russell; it was another Jack Russell."

"Did it have a collar on it?" asked the persistent kennel maid at the end of the line.

"No, it was hit by a bus. It had internal injuries, and Mr. Frogton put it to sleep."

"Could you describe it?"

"What?"

"We have a young man here who's lost his Jack Russell. He says it's got a black ear, on the left. Is that the one you have there? Only the stray we've got here has a brown ear, brown left ear."

"Yes, it's got a black ear and a sort of brown spot over its right eye," Carol snapped.

To Carol's fury she was left waiting as the kennel maid went to talk to the young man. When she came back, she asked if the dog was still at the surgery.

"Yes, it's still here."

"He's coming right over. Can you keep it there?"

"It's dead."

"Yes, you said, but he wants to make sure it's his dog, and if it didn't have a collar and it fits his description . . ."

Carol sighed. "No. No, I'm sorry, but he can't come here."

"Is that you, Carol?"

"What?"

"This is Barbara, remember? We worked together? I knew you'd got a job at the clinic. I didn't recognize your voice. Is it okay for the boy to come over? He's so upset, Carol. *Carol?*"

Carol closed her eyes and took a deep breath. "Yes, he can see it, but he had better come over right now."

Carol slammed down the phone. "Fucking dog, the fucking stupid fucking dog."

She checked her watch; her whole schedule was off now with this fucking Jack Russell, and she had to get rid of it before fucking Hilda or anyone else turned up for surgery.

At eight o'clock the doorbell went again. Carol steamed out and snatched it open. He was red-haired, with round owl glasses and wearing a dirty anorak.

"Can I see if you've got Rex?" he asked, gulping, almost in tears. Carol nodded and went and brought him the dead dog, still wrapped in the bloodstained towel.

"Yes, yes, that's Rex," he said, then burst into tears.

"Do you want to take him?" she asked brusquely.

He nodded, holding out his arms, and she passed over the dog wrapped in the towel.

"You can keep the towel," she said, opening the door to usher him out. In fact, it was quite useful that he wanted to take it. She wouldn't have to dump the dog along with the bloodstained clothes.

"I'll bury it at my grandma's. She's got a garden," he said, blinking, his eyes watering behind his owl glasses.

"Fine, thank you, good-bye." She shut the door, then had to open it again as the cleaner appeared.

"Morning, Carol, love. I'm ever so late today. My other job had left the place in a right state, so I had a lot of cleaning."

Carol didn't wait to listen as Mrs. Dart prattled on while she got out her cleaning equipment. By now she was way off schedule; she was supposed to have taken the clothes to the dump. All she could do was bundle them up and hide them under the counter until it was time for her to go home. She'd wasted time searching them for the charm, and now it was almost eight-thirty and the surgery would be open soon. Mrs. Dart washed down the floor in reception, dusted and watered the plants, all with a nonstop conversation to herself. She even washed the floor in the operating room, clanking her bucket and mop.

"Can you hurry it up, Mrs. Dart? It's almost time for surgery. Mrs. Dart?"

Mrs. Dart was still dusting when the first customers arrived. Carol couldn't believe it; they were fifteen minutes early. She almost felt as sick as their parrot! But at last Mrs. Dart left. Carol itched to ask her if she had found her goblin but decided against it.

Miles arrived to start his surgery and the day began. As Carol answered the calls, she could feel the bag close to her legs under the counter. It was a full morning, and come lunchtime she put the plan back on schedule.

"I'll get off at lunchtime. Going on my holiday, unless I'm needed. I wouldn't mind leaving at twelve-thirty."

"You do that, love," said Hilda as she proffered a coffee; she managed at least three mugs every morning. "You've done enough good turns, so you go on off."

Hilda stepped aside as Carol collected the bag and made to leave.

"Did the mortuary van come this morning?" Miles asked as he appeared at his surgery door.

"Yes."

"Frogton got off sharpish, didn't he?"

Hilda murmured that she had not actually seen him, as he'd gone before she arrived.

"Can you get him on the phone, Hilda? It's this German shepherd; I don't know what tests he's done, and I can't find the X-rays."

Carol was at the door, listening, as Hilda called and then replaced the phone.

"No answer, and his answerphone's not on. I'll try again, but I think they were all going straight to the airport."

"I thought she had already left," Carol said, feeling her color drain.

"No, she changed her mind. They were all going together—well, with the baby she didn't want to travel by herself. It's understandable."

Miles, irritated, snapped as he returned to his cubicle, "Just try and contact him, Hilda. I really need to speak to him."

"The X-rays are on his desk, second drawer are the details I think you'll need," Carol said, hovering, eager to leave.

"Thank you, Carol. We'll miss you, but have a good holiday." Miles stood at his doorway.

Hilda waved as Carol smiled and walked out.

"Bit inconvenient, isn't it?" said Miles. "Carol taking off the same time as old Froggy. Makes us very short staffed."

Hilda nodded, then said Carol had booked her break a good while ago, just after Christmas. She turned, smiling at the baby photographs pinned up on their noticeboard. Frogton's son, born January 4.

"Be nice for them both to get away with the new baby," Hilda said, checking down the appointments; they had a very busy day ahead.

Carol slammed her front door shut. She tipped out the clothes, felt in all the pockets, in the cuffs, everywhere, but found no charm. No fucking goblin. She then tipped everything into the sink and poured bleach over the clothes and shoes. She waited until they were almost shredded before she put on rubber gloves to wring the remains out and put them back into the bag. The shoes' rubber soles were sticky, the suede coming apart. She then went into the bathroom. The smell of bleach made her feel sick so she ran the shower, picked up a towel, and was about to put it on the heater rail when she stopped. "Shit. Fuck shit, the fucking towel."

She closed her eyes. The bloody Jack Russell! She'd wrapped it in a towel, the blood-covered towel, fucking shit. She was now certain the charm must have caught on the fluffy cotton towel. The fucking goblin had to be with the dead bloody Jack Russell dog.

Carol called the Dogs Home and got the boy's address. Shit, shit, he'd said he was going to bury it at his grandmother's house! Fuck shit, how the hell was she going to find that address?

At the surgery Hilda thanked a woman, Mrs. Palin, and as soon as she left looked down the entries. Miles appeared, ushering out a very elderly woman with an equally ancient cat in a cage.

"Just feed her once a day, small portions, and she should be fine."

He leaned in to Hilda as the elderly woman paid her. "Just a checkup, won't need to see Mitzie again."

He returned to his surgery, gesturing for a young boy to carry in his pet mouse. Hilda gave the receipt to the woman and put the money into the till before she went back to Mr. Frogton's lists. Something didn't quite make sense; Mrs. Palin had come in to thank them, as she had now got her Jack Russell back, and he was none the worse. But they had no record of it being released from the clinic. They did have a Jack Russell, but according to Frogton it was doubtful it would survive the night. It was scheduled to be collected for the mortuary.

Frogton's girlfriend had called three times, wondering where he was, as they were due to catch a flight and were going to miss it. Hilda said he had left in the early morning and she had no idea where he was, just as she had no idea why Carol had not made any mention of the Jack Russell's recovery and signed him out. There would be quite a bill to be paid. It was very unlike Carol, as she was usually so methodical. Hilda went into Miles's surgery.

"You know we had that Jack Russell in, been in an accident on the Seven Sisters Road, just by Holloway prison, bus ran over it; this woman came in with it, it wasn't hers, said it was her sister's."

"What?" Miles said, checking over X-rays.

"Well, a woman, the woman's sister, just came in to thank us. She said she's got him home and he's none the worse."

"What?"

"That's what she said. He's fine, none the worse."

"What?"

Miles went to the X-ray drawers, drew out a set, and pinned them up.

"None the worse?" he said, pulling a face. "He's got a fractured pelvis, two broken back legs, and damage to his kidneys and collarbone!"

"Well, that's what she said. Came in to thank Carol, but we were so busy I couldn't really talk much to her. He was going to be put down this morning."

"Well, miracles do happen, but that's beyond me, and I'm afraid this old boy's in very bad shape. I think he should be put out of his misery."

Miles was referring to the German shepherd—both back legs were dragging, and he had a congenital spinal deficiency that left his lower back weak.

"Better call his owners. And did you get hold of Froggy?"

"No, I didn't, and Mary's been calling; she's a bit frazzled as they're going to miss the flight."

Miles returned to the X-ray of the Jack Russell, frowning; there was no possible way this dog could be, as his owner had stated, "none the worse." He was in a wretched condition.

"Who was the bill made out to?" he asked.

Hilda had returned to reception.

"What?"

"I said, who was the bill made out to for this Jack Russell?"

Hilda looked confused.

"I don't know. There doesn't seem to be a record of it!"

Carol had gotten rid of the clothes, tied in a tight bundle of newspapers and tossed into a Dumpster. She had also made headway in discovering Owl Glasses's grandmother's address. When she had called the boy his friend had answered and given the address; it was actually not far from Carol's flat, in Highbury, so she went straight there.

Carol rang the doorbell and waited for what seemed an age before it was opened by a small, shriveled woman in thick-lensed glasses like her grandson's. Carol explained that she worked at the local veterinary clinic and had handed over the Jack Russell.

"Yes, he came here with it," the woman said, peering up at Carol, who was head and shoulders taller than her.

"Has he actually buried it?"

"Yes, in a shoe box in the garden."

"I'm very sorry, but I'm afraid I will have to dig it up."

"You must be joking. It's dead."

"Yes, I know, but we had a call from Battersea Dogs Home, and it seems there is some confusion regarding the ownership of the dog."

"But it's dead. It was Kevin's pet."

"Yes, I am sure it was, but I need to verify its markings, if it has a black or brown left ear, or if it is the other way round."

"Oh, I dunno. Kevin's not here. He's at college."

"I can do it, if I could just be shown where he is?"

Carol sighed with relief as the old lady let her in and led her down a dingy dark hallway, through an old-fashioned, equally dark kitchen, and into the small back garden. The garden was overgrown with weeds and rubbish, old bicycles, and an old pram minus its wheels. Bottles and Coke cans littered the base of the wall that backed to the street.

"Kids chuck things over the wall," the old lady said in disgust, "but he's buried by the tree. You can't miss it; we've only the one tree anyway."

"Do you have a shovel?"

"No, I got a trowel. That's what our Kevin used."

Carol smiled, waiting by the tree as the grandmother went to find it. The freshly dug mound had a small handmade wooden cross; printed on it in black felt-tipped pen was REX. The grandmother returned with her trowel.

"Do you know if Rex was still wrapped in the towel?"

"I don't know, love. You'd have to ask our Kevin, but he put him in a shoe box, I know that. He worshipped that little dog."

Carol got down on her knees. She told the old lady that she should go back inside, then started to dig.

Kevin had not dug a deep hole; it was only about six inches down and the earth came away easily. Carol eased up the shoe box; it was small and she was certain that the towel and the dog could not have fit in the box together. As she lifted the lid she saw she was right; there was no white bloodstained towel, just Rex.

Carol stamped on the earth to flatten it back into place, then she refixed the cross. Kevin's grandmother was standing at the kitchen door.

"I don't suppose you know what Kevin did with the white clinic towel, do you?"

"The trowel?"

"No, Rex was wrapped in a white *towel* when I gave him to your grandson."

"Oh, I don't know where that is; you'd have to ask our Kevin. Do you want it back?"

"No, I don't think so, but do you know if he found anything else?"

"What else?"

Carol tried to smile. "It's nothing, never mind. And thank you. I'm sorry to have bothered you."

Almost as an afterthought she asked if she could wash her hands, which were covered in dirt. She stood at the kitchen sink, the old grandmother hovering as she washed and soaped up her hands. She looked around for something to dry them on. There was a plastic washing basket in the corner. If Carol had just moved a shirt aside she would have seen the clinic towel, but instead she dried her hands on a tea towel with a large picture of Wonder Woman's face printed on it.

Carol sat in the darkness; she went over and over everything in her mind. She sighed; she was probably getting things out of proportion. Even if the charm was found, so what? It was true everyone knew it belonged to her; they'd all seen Mr. Frogton give it to her for Christmas. She was sure it wouldn't mean anything; she had simply mislaid it. If anyone asked for it or found it, all she had to say was she had lost it. It was only a charm. Nevertheless, it niggled at her, and she was unsure what to do. If she went and spoke to Kevin, it would be suspicious, never mind incriminating. Digging up his bloody dog had been bad enough, and now if Kevin went to visit his grandma she'd obviously say something about her wanting the stupid fucking towel.

"Fuck fuck fucking shit," she muttered as the phone rang; it had rung a few times since she'd been home, but she hadn't answered. No sooner had it stopped ringing than it started up again. She snatched it.

"Yes?"

"That you, Carol?"

"Yes."

"This is Miles Richards."

Pause.

"Are you there?"

"Yes."

"We're all a bit worried about Peter. He's not shown up and he's supposed to have gone on holiday. Did he mention anything to you?"

"No."

"Was he all right this morning?"

"Yes."

"What time did he leave the surgery?"

"Just after eight, maybe eight-fifteen."

"I see. Well, sorry to bother you. Good night."

Miles replaced the phone. He was alone in the surgery, waiting for the owner of the German shepherd. He checked his watch, impatient to leave but at the same time concerned about his partner. It was so out of character, and he hoped there hadn't been an accident. None of the hospitals they'd called had him registered. He turned to see the dark outline of a figure in the glass door. He opened it.

"Froggy?"

It was the owner of the German shepherd, who had asked to see him one more time before he was put to sleep. He was very calm, gently holding the big dog's head in his lap, stroking him. After a while he got up. The big dog struggled to rise to his feet but couldn't stand.

"Good boy, stay, stay, Hank—there's a good chap."

Miles waited patiently, shaking the man's hand. Still he maintained control of his emotions.

"Been a good pal to me. I'll miss him. It'll be painless?"

"Yes, and I feel that it is the best, or should I say the kindest, thing to put him out of his misery."

"Right, yes. Well, thank you for seeing me, and just send me the bill for Hank. Thank you."

Miles put in the call for the mortuary wagon to do a pickup the following morning. It was on answer machine, so he left the usual message and details, describing the dog. He then replaced the receiver and picked up the report book to enter the details, ready for the morning. The last entry was for a collection that morning: Dalmatian, Rottweiler, and Great Dane. He frowned; there was something wrong. There was a fourth dog listed, in Frogton's handwriting, a Jack Russell, but only three dogs had been taken!

Miles went into Frogton's office and sat behind his desk checking his diary; he read the report of the injured Jack Russell brought in after it had been found in the road. Also listed were the dog's injuries, its markings, that it had no collar and had been brought into the surgery by the owner's sister, who was taking care of the dog.

Miles shut the book. He recalled Hilda saying the woman had collected her dog and that it was fine. He remembered joking with her, saying it must have been some kind of miracle because the dog was so severely injured, that his partner had earmarked it for being put to sleep, even booking a place for it in the mortuary van. He picked up the phone and dialed.

Carol stared at the ringing phone. Her hand reached out, then withdrew; there was something ominous about the way it was ringing. She went to bed; tomorrow she would get the bus for the coach station, and then she would have two weeks in the Lake District.

The mortuary attendant collected Hank the following morning. Miles had every intention of speaking to him about the previous day's collection, but they had an emergency, so he was busy in surgery. By now the police had been contacted about the disappearance of Peter Frogton, and inquiries about him had begun. No one had seen him since the previous morning's surgery, so Carol became a vital witness to be questioned, but no one knew where she was, just that she had gone on two weeks' holiday. It was suggested that perhaps they might have gone together, but this was dismissed by all the staff.

One week later, there had been no sighting or contact by Peter Frogton, and no clue as to his whereabouts was forthcoming. It was a mystery because he had no money problems, no domestic problems; he was, everyone said, delighted with his new baby boy, and his distraught girlfriend could shed no light on why he would disappear. No bank card had been used, no checks had been cashed; he seemed to have no enemies. His car was left at his home; it was due for an MOT so he had caught the bus to work on the last morning he was sighted. For two weeks the inquiries continued with no results; no one came forward, even after the local papers had published a request for any information.

By the time Carol returned to work, the police still had no motive, nothing that gave them so much as a clue as to why the senior partner had disappeared. Carol appeared stunned when told. She said he had been perfectly normal the last time she had seen him. He had said he was looking forward to his holiday and he had left earlier than arranged as he was not driving. She even shed a few tears; it was dreadful to think something bad had happened to such a lovely man!

Carol was by now certain that she had committed the perfect murder. She went about her duties as diligently as always, the first to arrive, the last to leave. They were expecting a new partner to join the practice, as Miles could not deal with the clinic on his own. It appeared on the surface as if Peter Frogton had never worked there, but he had, and in six months the memory of him had not faded. Carol had intended moving on to somewhere else but decided against it; she felt that safe.

Then the idiot woman with the fucking Jack Russell returned, and now her bloody dog was sick and running a high temperature. She was almost as hyper as she had been when she'd called around to make sure the dead dog wasn't her fucking dog.

Miles was allocated the bitch, and he went into his surgery with the woman talking at screech level. Carol could hear her hysterical voice going on and on about how she had almost lost him once, had even presumed he was dead, but that nice girl at the desk had shown her the other dog, and it wasn't her dog because it had the wrong-colored ear. The pitch of her voice allowed everyone waiting in the surgery to hear how she had gone to Battersea Dogs Home and met this poor boy who had an almost identical Jack Russell, but his had a black ear and her Jack had a brown, and this poor boy was weeping because it wasn't his dog at Battersea but her naughty boy, and then this poor youngster had to identify his dead dog at the clinic.

Carol maintained her calm, staring fixedly at the appointments as the screaming bitch was led out, Miles assuring her that her dog was going to be fine but he just wanted to keep the little chap in for the night. The surgery continued until after six, and Carol couldn't wait to leave; seeing that woman again had really unnerved her.

"Could you stay for a moment, Carol?" It was the way he said it, like he had something important to discuss.

"Sorry, Mr. Richards, not tonight," she said, avoiding his eyes. She felt as though they were boring into her head as she went out the surgery door. She gave a furtive glance back through the glass door panel, but he wasn't even looking at her; he was on the phone.

Miles thumbed through the old appointment diary, back six months, as he held on for the caller. He then jotted down the address and stared into space. He went back to checking operations, interns, the dogs to be put down, and then he paused, flicked forward then backward over the dates. In the past eight months they'd had only one Great Dane, brought in for surgery with cancer of the bowel. Felix had not survived the intricate operation and died under anesthesia. He was already old for a Dane, at ten years. They had treated eight other Great Danes, but none had been in for an operation or had, according to the records, died within the time frame. So which was the Dane taken on the morning with the Dalmatian and the Rottweiler, and what had happened to the injured Jack Russell? Had it been claimed? There was no record, and no bills had been made out for the time it had been in the surgery. No X-rays had been taken. Mrs. Palin had said a boy had been at the Dogs Home, worried about his Jack Russell, so maybe they could shed some light on it all.

Miles contacted the Dogs Home, found out Kevin's address, and called him. Kevin agreed to see him at his grandmother's house.

Kevin answered the door. He had food stains around his mouth, and his owlish glasses looked crooked. His grandma stood behind him, saying this was ridiculous, they'd already sent one woman to dig it up, it'd be rotting by now.

"It was my dog. It was Rex," Kevin said, agitated.

Miles tried to make light of it, saying he was sure it was his dog but he needed to ask Kevin some questions about when he had collected the corpse from the veterinary clinic.

Miles stood in the old kitchen, the rotting carcass now in a large hatbox. He was very perplexed about the fact that someone from his clinic had been to the house, had dug up the dog! It didn't make any sense, unless there was some hidden agenda.

"I promise you will have Rex returned. I need him for just a few days, and I am not here about any vet fees. He wasn't given to you in this box, was he?"

"No, he was wrapped in a mucky towel. I think it's still in my toolbox. Gran was going to wash it, but I used it to wipe some chain tube off my bike."

Miles waited while Kevin fetched the towel, now streaked with oil stains as well as the dark red bloodstains that had turned rust brown.

"Thank you. I really appreciate your help."

"There was something else," Kevin said, flushing. "It was caught in the towel."

Miles nodded. Kevin looked even more embarrassed.

"I gave it to my girlfriend. It was like a charm, you know, off a bracelet. It was about so big." He indicated with his fingers how small the charm was.

"Does she still have it?" Miles asked.

"I dunno. We broke up. Is that what this is all about? I think it was quite old, like antique gold, but it was very small. A little man I think, like a pixie."

Miles hesitated; he didn't understand the importance of the charm because he had been the only one not present at the Christmas gift exchange.

At the police station, the detective in charge of Frogton's disappearance looked into the hatbox with distaste.

"What is it?"

"It's a dead Jack Russell dog, and its body was wrapped in this towel that belongs to the clinic. The kid also found a gold charm of a goblin—you know, a charm that hangs off a bracelet. I called Hilda, our other receptionist, and she recalls Peter Frogton giving it to Carol last Christmas. She said it was a little goblin, not a pixie. A gold goblin sitting on a mushroom."

"Does he still have it?"

"No, he gave it to his girlfriend, but they broke up and she threw it away; well, that's what she said. It was a goblin, but she couldn't remember if it was sitting on anything."

Miles remained at the station for two hours, going through all the details about how dogs were collected for the incinerator by the mortuary company. The dogs were burnt and the bones and fragments crushed, so there would be no remains left. It was possible that Peter Frogton was murdered, his body taken in the place of a Great Dane, and incinerated. The Jack Russell was supposed to have been incinerated that same morning, but Kevin had collected it for burial in his grandmother's garden.

There was a very long pause. Miles was flushed red in the face while the police officer grew paler by the minute.

"Jesus Christ. You think she put your partner in a doggy bag?"

Before they arrested Carol, they checked her background and discovered her previous prison record. This made for a lot of embarrassment, as they should have been more thorough.

"Apparently she lied to us on her letter from her previous employers. She had only worked there for two years," Miles said to a stunned, white-faced Hilda. "Before that, she was in prison."

"Prison?" Hilda stuttered, hardly able to take it all in.

"She murdered her mother," Miles said quietly.

"What, Carol did? But she couldn't have done. She was going to spend Christmas with her."

"Well, she lied, Hilda. Carol lied to all of us. She apparently hit her mother over the head with a hammer."

"No, surely not—her own mother?"

"Yes, that's what I was told."

"Why?" Hilda asked in a shocked gasp.

"No idea. They didn't tell me," Miles said flatly.

Carol was arrested at the surgery at nine-fifteen on July 3, 1973, and subsequently charged with the murder of Peter Frogton. She never gave an explanation, nor did she admit her guilt or deny it; she appeared totally uninterested in the whole proceedings. Without a body and with not one witness, it was doubtful that they would be able to make the charge stick. At the time DNA testing was not used, and although the white towel might have Peter Frogton's bloodstains on it, they could also have been the Jack Russell's.

The police had removed the gold charm bracelet as part of the evidence, noting that it was minus the goblin. They subsequently interviewed Kevin's girlfriend. She was evasive and tearful, but then admitted she had lied. She hadn't thrown the goblin away. She said she had thought Kevin might ask for it back, and she wasn't going to give it to him. The detective looked at the small gold charm in the palm of his hand; the little goblin sitting on a toadstool was identified as the charm given to Carol by Frogton. When shown to Hilda, she confirmed it was definitely the same one.

During Carol's final interrogation, she had become increasingly abusive, often laughing at some private joke she never shared with anyone. The detective held up the charm bracelet, letting it dangle.

"Does this belong to you, Carol?"

No reply.

"This was a gift to you from Peter Frogton, wasn't it?"

No reply.

"This charm was attached to this bracelet by Peter Frogton. It was a Christmas gift to you, wasn't it?"

No reply.

"Will you look at this little charm? It was on this bracelet when you killed Peter Frogton."

No reply.

"Carol, will you look at this charm and tell me what it is?"

At last there was a response; she looked up, her eyes like ice chips, and she let out a high-pitched screech.

"It's a fucking gold Jack Russell dog, you cunt."

Carol never admitted killing Peter Frogton. She was found mentally unfit to stand trial and sent to Broadmoor, a prison for the criminally insane. The bracelet was tagged, bagged, and listed as evidence, then stored in the police station's evidence lockup, with the goblin reattached in case it got lost.

THE SNAKE EATER BY THE NUMBERS

Lee Child

Numbers. Percentages, rates, averages, means, medians. Crime rate, clearance rate, clearance percentage, increase, decrease, throughput, input, output, productivity. At the end of the twentieth century, police work was about nothing but numbers.

Detective Sergeant Ken Cameron loved numbers.

I know this, because Cameron was my training officer the year he died. He told me that numbers were our salvation. They made being a copper as easy as being a financier or a salesman or a factory manager. We don't need to work the *cases*, he said. We need to work the *numbers*. If we make our numbers, we get good performance reviews. If we get good reviews, we get commendations. If we get commendations, we get promotions. And promotions mean pay and pensions. You could be comfortable your whole life, he said, because of numbers. Truly comfortable. *Doubly* comfortable, he said, because you're not tearing your hair out over vague bullshit subjective notions like safe streets and quality of life. You're dealing with numbers, and numbers never lie.

We worked in North London. Or at least he did—I was assigned there for my probationary period. I would be moving on, but he had been there three years and would be staying. And North London was a great place for numbers. It was a big manor with a lot of crime and a population that was permanently hypersensitive to being treated less well than populations in other parts of London. The local councillors were always in an uproar. They compared their schools to other schools, their transport spurs to other transport spurs. Everything was about perceived disadvantage. If an escalator was out at West Finchley Tube station for three days, then they'd better not hear that an escalator had been fixed in two days down at Tooting Bec. That kind of thing was the birth of the numbers, Cameron told me. Because stupid, dull administrators learned to counter the paranoid arguments with numbers. No, they would say, the Northern Line is actually sixty-three percent on time up here and only sixty-one percent on time down there.

So, they would say, shut up.

It wasn't long before police work fell in with the trend. It was inevitable. Everything started being measured. It was an obvious defensive tactic on the part of our bosses. Average response time following a 999 call? Eleven minutes in Tottenham, Madam Councillor, versus *twelve* minutes in Kentish Town. Said proudly, with a blank but smug expression on our bosses' meaty faces. Of course, they were lying. The Kentish Town bosses were lying too. It was a race toward absurdity. I once joked to Cameron that pretty soon we would start to see *negative* response times. As in, Yes, Madam Councillor, that 999 call was answered eleven minutes before it was made. But Cameron just stared at me. He thought I had lost it. He was far too serious on the subject to countenance such a blatant mistake, even in jest.

But certainly he admitted that numbers could be massaged.

He collected massage examples like a connoisseur. He observed some of them from afar. The 999 stuff, for instance. He knew how the books were cooked. Switchboard operators were required to be a little inexact with their timekeeping. When it was noon out there in the real world, it was four minutes past noon inside the emergency switchboard. When a sector car was dispatched to an address, it would radio its arrival when it was still three streets away. Thus, a slow twenty-minute response time went into the books as a decent twelve minutes. Everybody won.

His approach to his own numbers was more sophisticated.

His major intellectual preoccupation was parsing the inconvenient balance between his productivity and his clearance rate. For any copper, the obvious way to enhance a clearance rate was to accept no cases at all, except the solid gold slam dunks that had guaranteed collars at the end of them. He explained it like a Zen master: Suppose you have only one case a year. Suppose you solve it. What's your clearance rate? One hundred percent! I knew that, of course, because I was comfortable with simple arithmetic. But just for fun I said, Okay, but suppose you *don't* solve it? Then your clearance rate is zero! But he didn't get all wound up like I thought he would. Instead, he beamed at me, like I was making progress. Like I already knew the dance steps. *Exactly*, he said. You avoid the cases you know you *can't* solve, and you jump all over the cases you know you *can* solve.

I should have spotted it right then. *The cases you know you can solve*. But I didn't spot it. I was still inside the box. And he didn't give me much time to think, because he rushed straight on to the main problem, which was productivity. Certainly major points could be scored for a seventy-five percent clearance rate. That was obvious. But if you achieved that mark by clearing three cases out of four, you lost major points for a lack of productivity. That was obvious too. Four cases a year was absurdly low. *Forty* cases a year was low. In North London at that time, each detective was looking at hundreds of cases a year. That was Ken Cameron's big problem. The balance between productivity and clearance rate. Good productivity meant a bad clearance rate. A good clearance rate meant bad productivity. He said to me, *See?* Like the weight of the world was on his shoulders. Although that was a misinterpretation on my part. He was really saying: *So I'm not such a bad guy, doing what I'm doing*. I should have seen it. But I didn't.

Then, still in his Zen master mode, he told me a joke. Two guys are in the woods. They see a bear coming. "Run!" says the first guy. "That's ridiculous," the second guy says. "You can't run faster than a bear." "I don't need to run faster than the bear," the first guy answers. "I only need to run faster than you." I had heard the joke before, many times. I suppose I paused a moment to remember who had told it to me last. So I didn't react the way Cameron wanted me to. I saw him thinking *Fast-track training college wanker*. Then he regrouped and explained his point. He wasn't looking for extremely high numbers in and of themselves. He was just looking to beat the guy in second place. That's all. By a point or two, which was all that was necessary. Which he could do while maintaining an entirely plausible balance between his clearance rate and his productivity.

Which he could do. I should have asked, *How, exactly?* He was probably waiting for me to ask. But I didn't.

I found out how the day I met a prostitute called Kelly Key and a madman called Mason Mason. I met them separately. Kelly Key first. It was one of those perceived disadvantage things. Truth was, North London had a lot of prostitution, but not nearly as much as the West End, for instance. It tended to be of a different nature, though. It was definitely more in-your-face. You *saw* the hookers. Up west, they were all inside, waiting by the phone. So I was never really sure exactly what the locals were up in arms about. That their hookers were cheaper? That they wanted prettier girls? Or what? But whatever, there was always some street-clearing initiative going on, usually in the northern reaches of Islington and all over Haringey. Working girls would be dragged in. They would sit in police stations, looking completely at home and completely out of place all at the same time.

One morning we got back from the canteen and found Kelly Key waiting. Ken Cameron evidently took a snap decision and decided to use her to teach me all kinds of essential things. He took me aside and started to explain. First, we were *not* going to write anything down. Writing something down would put her in the system, which would aid our productivity but *would* damage our clearance rate, because solicitation cases were very hard to make. *But*, the longer we concealed our indifference, the more worried old Kelly would get, which *would* result in some excellent freebies after we finally let her go. A cop who pays for sex, Cameron told me, is a very bad cop indeed.

Bad cop. I suppose, in a relative way.

So I watched while Cameron harassed Kelly Key. It was late morning, but she was already dressed in her hooker outfit. I could see a lot of leg and a lot of cleavage. She wasn't dumb enough to offer anything off her own bat, but she was heavily into doing the Sharon Stone thing from *Basic Instinct*. She was crossing and uncrossing her legs so fast I could almost feel the disturbance in the air. Cameron was enjoying the interview. And the actual *view*, I suppose. I could see that. He was totally at his ease. He had the upper hand, so definitively it was just an absolute fact. He was a big man, fleshy and solid in that classic policeman way. He was probably forty-something, although it's hard to be precise with guys who have that sort of tight pink flesh on their faces. But he had his size, and his badge, and his years in, and together they made him invulnerable. Or together they *had*, so far.

Then Mason Mason was brought in. We still had an hour of fun to go with Kelly, but we heard a disturbance at the front desk. Mason Mason had been arrested for urinating in public. At that time we called the uniformed coppers woollies because of their wool uniforms, and on the face of it the woollies could handle public urination on their own, even if they wanted to push the charge upward toward gross indecency. But Mason Mason had been searched and found with a little more folding money in his pocket than street people usually carry. He had ninety pounds on him, in new tenners. So the woollies brought him to us, in case we might want to try a theft charge, or mugging, or even robbery with violence, because maybe he had pushed someone around to get the cash. It might be a slam dunk. The woollies weren't dumb. They knew how we balanced clearance rate with productivity, and they were self-interested too, because although individual detectives competed among themselves, there was also an overall station number, which helped everybody. There was a number for everything.

So at that point Cameron put Kelly Key on the back burner and Mason Mason on the front. He took me aside to explain a few things. First, Mason Mason was the guy's actual name. It was on his birth certificate. It was widely believed that his father had been drunk or confused or both at the registry office and had written *Mason* in both boxes, first name and surname. Second, Mason wasn't pissing in public because he was a helpless drunk or derelict. In fact, he rarely drank. In fact, he was pretty harmless. The thing was, although Mason had been born in Tottenham—in a house very near the Spurs ground—he believed he was American and believed he had served in the United States Marine Corps as part of Force Recon, who called themselves the Snake Eaters. This, Cameron said, was both a delusion and an unshakable conviction. North London was full of dedicated Elvis impersonators, and country-and-western singers, and Civil War reenactors, and Omaha Beach buffs, and vintage Cadillac drivers, so Mason's view of himself wasn't totally extraordinary. But it led to awkwardness. He believed that the North London streets were in fact part of the ruined cityscape of Beirut, and that to step into the rubble and take a leak against the shattered remains of a building was all part of a marine's hard life. And he was always collecting insignias and badges and tattoos. He had snake tattoos all over his body, including one on his chest, along with the words DON'T TREAD ON ME.

After absorbing all this information I glanced back at Mason and noticed that he was wearing a single snake earring in his left ear. It was a fat little thing, all in heavy gold, quite handsome, quite tightly curled. It had a tiny gold loop at the top, with a non-matching silver hook through it that went up and through his pierced lobe.

Cameron noticed it too.

"That's new," he said. "The Snake Eater's got himself another bauble."

Then his eyes went blank for a second, like a TV screen changing channels.

I should have seen it coming.

He sent Kelly Key away to sit by herself and started in on Mason. First he embarrassed him by asking routine questions, starting with a request that he should state his name.

"Sir, the marine's name is Mason, sir," the guy said, just like a marine.

"Is that your first or last name?"

"Sir, both, sir," the guy said.

"Date of birth?"

Mason reeled off day, month, year. It put him pretty close to what I guessed was Cameron's age. He was about Cameron's size too, which was unusual for a bum. Mostly they waste away. But Mason Mason was tall and heavily built. He had hands the size of Tesco chickens and a neck that was wider than his head. The earring looked out of place, all things considered, except maybe in some kind of a pirate context. But I could see why the woollies thought that robbery with violence might fly. Most people would hand over their wad to Mason Mason rather than stand and fight.

"Place of birth?" Cameron asked.

"Sir, Muncie, Indiana, sir," Mason said.

The way he spoke told me he was clearly from London, but his faux American accent was pretty impressive. Clearly he watched a lot of TV and spent a lot of time in the local multiplexes. He had worked hard to become a marine. His eyes were good too. Flat, wary, expressionless. Just like a real jarhead's. I guessed he had seen *Full Metal Jacket* more than once.

"Muncie, Indiana," Cameron repeated. "Not Tottenham? Not North London?"

"Sir, no, sir," Mason barked. Cameron laughed at him, but Mason kept his face blank, just like a guy who had survived boot camp.

"Military service?" Cameron asked.

"Sir, eleven years in God's own Marine Corps, sir."

"Semper fi?"

"Sir, roger that, sir."

"Where did you get the money, Mason?"

It struck me that when a guy has the same name first and last, it's impossible to come across too heavy. For instance, suppose I said, *Hey, Ken*, to Cameron? I would sound friendly. If I said *Hey, Cameron*, I would sound accusatory. But it was all the same to Mason Mason.

"I won the money," he said. Now he sounded like a sullen Londoner.

"On a horse?"

"On a dog. At Harringay."

"When?"

"Last night."

"How much?"

"Ninety quid."

"Marines go dog racing?"

"Sir, recon marines blend in with the local population." Now he was a jarhead again.

"What about the earring?" Cameron asked. "It's new."

Mason touched it as he spoke.

"Sir, it was a gift from a grateful civilian."

"What kind of civilian?"

"A woman in Kosovo, sir."

"What did she have to be grateful about?"

"Sir, she was about to be a victim of ethnic cleansing."

"At whose hands?"

"The Serbs, sir."

"Wasn't it the Bosnians?"

"Whoever, sir. I didn't ask questions."

"What happened?" Cameron asked.

"There was social discrimination involved," Mason said. "People considered rich were singled out for special torment. A family was considered rich if the wife owned jewelry. Typically the jewelry would be assembled and the husband would be forced to eat it. Then the wife would be asked if she wanted it back. Typically she would be confused and unsure of the expected answer. Some would say yes, whereupon the aggressors would slit the husband's stomach open and force the wife to retrieve the items herself."

"And you prevented this from happening?"

"Me and my men, sir. We mounted a standard fire-and-maneuver encirclement of a simple dwelling and took down the aggressors. It was a modest household, sir. The woman owned just a single pair of earrings."

"And she gave them to you."

"Just one, sir. She kept the other one."

"She gave you *an* earring?"

"In gratitude, sir. Her husband's life was saved."

"When was this?"

"Sir, our operational log records the engagement at oh-four-hundred last Thursday."

Cameron nodded. He left Mason Mason at the desk and pulled me away into the corner. We competed for a minute or two with all the one-sandwich-short-of-a-picnic metaphors we knew. One brick shy of a load, not the sharpest knife in the drawer, that kind of thing. I felt bad about it later. I should have seen what was coming.

But Cameron was already into another long and complicated calculation. It was almost metaphysical in its complexity. If we logged another case today, our productivity number would rise. Obviously. If we broke it, our clearance rate would rise. Obviously. Question was, would our clearance rate rise faster than our productivity number? Basically, was it worth it? The equation seemed to me to require some arcane calculus, which was beyond me, and I was a fast-track training college wanker. But Cameron seemed to have a handy rule of thumb. He seemed to suggest that it's *always* worth logging a case if you know you're going to break it. At the time I suspected that was a nonmathematical superstition, but I couldn't prove it. Still can't, actually, without going to night school. But back then I didn't argue the arithmetic. I argued the facts instead.

"Do we even have a case?" I asked.

"Let's find out," he said.

I imagined he would send me out for an *Evening Standard* so we could check the greyhound results from Harringay. Or he would send me to wade through incident reports, looking for a stolen snake earring from last Thursday night. But he did neither thing. He walked me back to Kelly Key instead.

"You work hard for your money, right?" he said to her.

I could see that Kelly didn't know where that question was going. Was she being sympathized with, or propositioned? She didn't know. She was in the dark. But like all good whores everywhere, she came up with a neutral answer.

"It can be fun," she said. "With some men."

She didn't add *Men like you.* That would have been too blatant. Cameron might have been setting a trap. But the way she smiled and touched his forearm with her fingertips left the words *It can be fun with men like you* hanging right there in the air. Certainly Cameron heard them, loud and clear. But he just shook his head impatiently.

"I'm not asking for a date," he said.

"Oh," she said.

"I'm just saying, you work hard for your money."

She nodded. The smile disappeared and I saw reality flood her face. She worked *very* hard for her money. That message was unmistakable.

"Doing all kinds of distasteful things," Cameron said.

"Sometimes," she said.

"How much do you charge?"

"Two hundred for the hour."

"Liar," Cameron said. "The twenty-two-year-olds up west charge two hundred for the hour."

Kelly nodded.

"Fifty for a quickie," she said.

"How about thirty?"

"I could do that."

"How would you feel if a punter ripped you off?"

"Like he didn't pay?"

"Like he stole ninety quid from you. That's like not paying *four times.* You end up doing him for nothing, and you end up doing the previous three guys for nothing too, because now *that* money's gone."

"I wouldn't like it," she said.

"Suppose he stole your earring as well?"

"My what?"

"Your earring."

"Who?"

Cameron looked across the room at Mason. Kelly Key followed his gaze.

"Him?" she said. "I wouldn't do *him.* He's mad."

"Suppose you did."

"I wouldn't."

"We're playing let's pretend here," Cameron said. "Suppose you did him, and he stole your money and your earring."

"That's not even a real earring."

"Isn't it?"

Kelly shook her head. "It's a charm from a charm bracelet. You guys are hopeless. Can't you see that? It's supposed to be fastened onto a bracelet. Through that little hoop at the top? You can see the wire doesn't match."

We all stared at Mason Mason's ear. Then I looked at Cameron. I saw his eyes do the blank thing again. The channel-changing thing.

"I could arrest you, Kelly Key," he said.

"But?"

"But I won't, if you play ball."

"Play ball how?"

"Swear out a statement that Mason Mason stole ninety quid and a charm bracelet from you."

"But he didn't."

"What part of let's pretend don't you understand?"

Kelly Key said nothing.

"You could leave out your professional background," Cameron said. "If you want to. Just say he broke into your house. While you were in bed asleep. The homeowner being in bed asleep always goes down well."

Kelly Key took her gaze off Mason. Turned back to Cameron.

"Would I get my stuff back afterward?" she asked.

"What stuff?"

"The ninety quid and the bracelet. If I'm saying he stole them from me, then they were mine to begin with, weren't they? So I should get them back."

"Jesus Christ," Cameron said.

"It's only fair."

"The bracelet is *imaginary*. How the hell can you get it back?"

"It can't be imaginary. There's got to be evidence."

Cameron's eyes went blank again. The channel changed. He told Kelly to stay where she was and pulled me back across the room, to the corner.

"We can't just *manufacture* a case," I said.

He looked at me, exasperated. Like the idiot child.

"We're not manufacturing a case," he said. "We're manufacturing a *number*. There's a big difference."

"How is there? Mason will still go to jail. That's not a number."

"Mason will be better off," he said. "I'm not totally heartless. Ninety quid and a bracelet from a whore—he'll get three months, tops. They'll give him psychiatric treatment. He doesn't get any on the outside. They'll put him back on his meds. He'll come out a new man. It's like putting him in a clinic. A rest home. At public expense. It's doing him a favor."

I said nothing.

"Everyone's a winner," he said.

I said nothing.

"Don't rock the boat, kid," he said.

I didn't rock the boat. I should have, but I didn't.

He led me back to where Mason Mason was sitting. He told Mason to hand over his new earring. Mason unhooked it from his earlobe without a word and gave it to Cameron. Cameron gave it to me. The little snake was surprisingly heavy in the palm of my hand, and warm.

Then Cameron led me downstairs to the evidence lockup. Public whining had created a lot of things, he said, as far as police work went. It had created the numbers, and the numbers had been used to get budgets, and the budgets were huge. No politician could resist padding police budgets. Not local, not national. So most of the time we were flush with money. The problem was, how to spend it? They could have put more woollies on the street, or they could have doubled the number of CID thief-takers, but bureaucrats like monuments, so mostly they spent it on building new police stations. North London was full of them. There were big concrete bunkers all over the place. Manors had been split and amalgamated and HQs had been shifted around. The result was that evidence lockups all over North London were full of old stuff that had been dragged in from elsewhere. Stuff that was historic. Stuff that nobody tracked anymore.

Cameron sent the desk sergeant out for lunch and started looking for the prefilm record books. He told me that extremely recent stuff was logged on the computers, and slightly older stuff was recorded on microfilm, and the stuff from twenty or thirty years ago was still in the original handwritten log books. That was the stuff to steal, he said, because you could just tear out the relevant page. No way to take a page off a microfilm without taking a hundred other pages with it. And he had heard that deleting stuff from computer files left telltale traces, even when it shouldn't.

So we split up the pile of dusty old log books and started trawling through them, looking for charm bracelets lost or recovered years ago in the past. Cameron told me we were certain to find one. He claimed there was at least one of everything in a big police evidence lockup like this one. Artificial limbs, oil paintings, guns, clocks, heroin, watches, umbrellas, shoes, wedding rings, anything you needed. And he was right. The books I looked at told me there was a Santa's grotto behind the door behind the desk.

It was me who found the bracelet. It was right there in the third book I went through. I should have kept quiet and just turned the page. But I was new and I was keen, and I suppose to some extent I was under Cameron's spell. And I didn't want to rock the boat. I had a career ahead of me, and I knew what would help it and what would hurt it. So I didn't turn the page. Instead, I called out.

"Got one," I said.

Cameron closed his own book and came over and took a look at mine. The listing read *Charm Bracelet, female, one, gold, some charms attached*. The details related to some ancient, long-forgotten case from the 1970s.

"Excellent," Cameron said.

The lockup itself was what I supposed the back room of an Argos looked like. There was all kinds of stuff in boxes, stacked all over shelves that were ten feet high. There was a comprehensive numbering system with everything stacked in order, but it all got a little haphazard with the really old stuff. It took us a minute or two to find the right section. Then Cameron slid a small cardboard box off a shelf and opened it.

"Bingo," he said.

It wasn't a jeweler's box. It was just something from an old office supplier. There was no cotton wool inside. Just the charm bracelet itself. It was a handsome thing, quite heavy, very gold. There were charms on it. I saw a key, and a cross, and a little tiger. Plus some other small items I couldn't identify.

"Put the snake on it," Cameron said. "It's got to look right."

There were closed loops on the circumference of the bracelet that matched the closed loop on the top of Mason's snake. I found an empty one. But having two closed loops didn't help me.

"I need gold wire," I said.

"Back to the books," Cameron said.

We put his "one of everything" claim to the test. And, sure enough, we came up with *Gold Wire, jeweler's, one coil.* Lost property, from 1969. Cameron cut a half-inch length with his pocketknife.

"I need pliers," I said.

"Use your fingernails," he said.

It was difficult work, but I got it secure enough. Then the whole thing disappeared into Cameron's pocket.

"Go tear out the page," he said.

I shouldn't have, but I did.

I got a major conscience attack four days later. Mason Mason had been arrested. He pleaded not guilty in front of the magistrates, and they remanded him for trial and set bail at five thousand pounds. I think Cameron had colluded with the prosecution service to set the figure high enough to keep Mason off the street, because he was a little worried about him. Mason was a big guy, and he had been very angry about the fit-up. *Very* angry. He said he knew the filth had to make their numbers. He was okay with that. But he said nobody should accuse a marine of dishonor. Not *ever.* So he stewed for a couple of days. And then he surprised everyone by making bail. He came up with the money and walked. Everyone speculated but nobody knew where the cash came from. Cameron was nervous for a day, but he got over it. Cameron was a big guy too, and a copper.

Then the next day I saw Cameron with the bracelet. It was late in the afternoon. He had it out on his desk. He slipped it into his pocket when he noticed me.

"That should be back in the lockup," I said. "With a new case number. Or it should be on Kelly Key's wrist."

"I gave her the ninety quid," he said. "I decided I'm keeping the bracelet."

"Why?"

"Because I like it."

"No, why?" I said.

"Because there's a pawnshop I know in Muswell Hill."

"You're going to sell it?"

He said nothing.

"I thought this was about the numbers," I said.

"There's more than one kind of numbers," he said. "There's pounds in my pocket. That's a number too."

"When are you going to sell it?"

"Now."

"Before the trial? Don't we need to produce it for evidence?"

"You're not thinking, kid. The bracelet's gone. He fenced it already. How do you think he came up with the bail money? Juries like nice little consistencies like that."

Then he left me alone at my desk. That's when the conscience attack kicked in. I started thinking about Mason Mason. I wanted to make sure he wasn't going to suffer for our numbers. If he was going to get medical treatment in jail, well, fine. I could live with that. It was wrong, but maybe it was right too. But how could we guarantee it? I supposed it would depend on his record. If there was previous psychiatric treatment, maybe it would be continued as a matter of routine. But what if there wasn't? What if there had been a previous determination that he was just a sane but bad guy? Right then and there, I decided I would go along to get along *only if* Mason was going to make out okay. If he wasn't, then I would torpedo the whole thing. Including my own career. That was my pact with the devil. That's the only thing I can offer in my defense.

I fired up my computer.

His name being the same first and last eliminated any confusion about who I was looking for. There was only one Mason Mason in London. I worked backward through his history. At first, it was very encouraging. He *had* had psychiatric treatment. He had been brought in many times for various offenses, all of them related to his conviction that he was a recon marine and London was a battlefield. He built bivouacs in parks. He went to the toilet in public. Occasionally he assaulted passersby because he thought they were Shiite guerrillas or Serbian militia. But generally the police had treated him well. They were usually kind and understanding. They got the mental health professionals involved as often as possible. He received treatment. Reading the transcripts in reverse date order made it seem like they were treating him better and better. Which meant, in reality, they were tiring of him somewhat. They were actually getting shorter and shorter with him. But they understood. He was nuts. He wasn't a criminal. So, okay.

Then I noticed something.

There was nothing recorded more than three years old. No, that was wrong. I scrolled way back and found there *was* in fact some very old stuff. Stuff from fourteen years ago. He had been in his late twenties then and in regular trouble for public disorder. Scuffles, fights, wild drunkenness, bodily harm. Some heavy-duty stuff, but normal stuff. Not mental stuff.

I heard Cameron's voice in my head: *He rarely drinks. He's pretty harmless.*

I thought, Two Mason Masons. The old one, and the new one. With an eleven-year gap between.

I heard Mason's voice in my head, with its impressive American twang: *Sir, eleven years in God's own Marine Corps, sir.*

I sat still for a minute.

Then I picked up the phone and called the American embassy, down in Grosvenor Square. I couldn't think of anything else to do. I identified myself as a police officer. They put me through to a military attaché.

"Is it possible for a foreign citizen to serve in your Marine Corps?" I asked.

"You thinking of volunteering?" the guy answered. "Bored with being a cop?" His voice was a little like Mason's. I wondered whether he had been born in Muncie, Indiana.

"Is it possible?" I asked again.

"Sure it is," he said. "At any one time we've got a pretty healthy percentage of foreign nationals in uniform. It's a job, after all, and it gets them citizenship in three years instead of five."

"Can you check records from there?"

"Is it urgent?"

I thought of Cameron on his way to Muswell Hill. Being shadowed by a recon marine with a grudge.

"It's very urgent," I said.

"Who are we looking for?"

"A guy called Mason."

"First name?"

"Mason."

"No, first name."

"Mason," I said. "Both his names are Mason."

"Hold the line," he said.

I spent the time working out Cameron's likely route. He would probably walk. Too short a journey to drive, too awkward on the Tube. So he would walk. *He would walk through Alexandra Park.*

"Hello?" the guy at the embassy said.

"Yes?"

"Mason Mason served eleven years in the Marines. Originally a U.K. citizen. Made the rank of first sergeant. He was selected for Force Recon and served all over. Beirut, Panama, the Gulf, Kosovo. Received multiple decorations and an honorable discharge just over three years ago. He was a damn fine jarhead. But there's a file note here saying he was just in some kind of trouble. One of the Overseas Veterans' associations just had to bail him out from something."

"Why did he leave the Marines?"

"He failed a psychiatric evaluation."

"You get an honorable discharge for that?"

"We kick them out," the guy said. "We don't kick them in the teeth."

I sat there for a moment, undecided. Should I dispatch sector cars? They would be no good in the park. Should I send the woollies on foot? Was I overreacting?

I went on my own, running all the way.

It was late in the year and late in the day, and it was already getting dark. I crossed the railway as a train rumbled under the bridge I was on. I watched the road ahead, and the hedges on each side. I didn't see Cameron. I didn't see Mason.

Alexandra Park's iron gates were already closed and locked. THIS FACILITY CLOSES AT DUSK, said the sign. I climbed over the gates and ran onward. The smell of night mist was already in the air. I could hear distant traffic all the way from the North Circular. I could hear starlings roosting somewhere to the south. In Hornsey, maybe. I followed the main path and found nothing. I saw the dark bulk of Alexandra Palace ahead and stood still. Go on or turn back? The streets of Muswell Hill, or the park? Surely the park was the danger zone. The park was where a recon marine would do his work. I turned back.

I found Cameron a yard off a side path.

He was half hidden under some low shrubbery. He was on his back. His coat was missing. His jacket was missing. His shirt had been torn off. He was naked from the waist up. He had been ripped open from the sternum to the navel with a sharp blade. Then someone had plunged his hands inside the wound and lifted his stomach out whole and rested it on his chest. Just pulled it out, the whole organ. It was *right there on his chest,* pale and purple and veined. Like a soft balloon. It had been squeezed and pressed and palpated and arranged until the faint gold gleam of the charm bracelet showed through the thin translucent lining. I saw it quite clearly in the fading evening light.

I think I was supposed to play the part of the Kosovo wife. I was Cameron's coconspirator, and I was supposed to recover the jewelry. Or Kelly Key was. But neither of us did. Mason's tableau came to nothing. I didn't try, and Kelly Key never even saw the body.

I didn't report it. I just got out of the park that night and left him there for someone else to find the next morning. And someone else did, of course. It was a big sensation. There was a big funeral. Everyone went. Then there was a big investigation, obviously. I contributed nothing, but even so Mason Mason became the prime suspect. But he disappeared and was never seen again. He's still out there somewhere, a mad recon marine blending in with the local population, wherever he is.

And me? I completed my probationary year and now I'm a detective constable down in Tower Hamlets. I've been there a couple of years. My numbers are pretty good. Not quite as good as Ken Cameron's were, but then, I try to live and learn.

STROKE OF LUCK

Mark Billingham

So many things could have been different.

An almost infinite number of them: the flight of the ball; the angle of the bat; the movement of his feet as he skipped down the pitch. The weather, the time, the day of the week, the whatever . . .

The smallest variance in any one of these things, or in the way that each connected to the other at the crucial moment, and nothing would have happened as it did. An inch another way, or a second, or a step and it would have been a very different story.

Of course, it's *always* a different story; but it isn't always a story with bodies . . .

He wasn't even a good batsman—a tail-ender, for heaven's sake—but this once he got everything right. The footwork and the swing were spot on. The ball flew from the meat of the bat, high above the heads of the fielders into the long grass at the edge of the woodland that fringed the pitch on two sides.

Alan and another player had been looking for a minute or so, using hands and feet to move aside the long grass at the base of an oak tree, when she stepped from behind it as if she'd been waiting for them.

"Don't you have any spare ones?"

Alan looked at her for a few long seconds before answering. She was tall, five-seven or -eight, with short dark hair. Her legs were bare beneath a cream-colored skirt, and her breasts looked a good size under a sleeveless top. She looked Mediterranean, Alan thought. Sophisticated.

"I suppose we must have, somewhere," he said.

"So why waste time looking? Are they expensive?"

Alan laughed. "We're only a bunch of medics. It costs a small fortune just to hire the pitch."

"You're a doctor?"

"A neurologist. A consultant neurologist."

She didn't look as impressed as he'd hoped.

"Got it."

Alan turned to see his teammate brandishing the ball, heard the cheers from those on the pitch as it was thrown across.

He turned back. The woman's arms were folded, and she held a hand up to shield her eyes from the sun.

"Will you be here long?" Alan said. She looked hesitant. He pointed back toward the pitch. "We've only got a couple of wickets left to take."

She dropped her hand, smiled without looking at him. "You'd better get on with it then . . ."

"Listen, we usually go and have a couple of drinks afterward, in the Woodman up by the Tube. D'you fancy coming along? Just for one maybe?"

She looked at her watch. Too quickly, Alan thought, to have even seen what time it read.

"I don't have a lot of time."

He nodded, stepping backward toward the pitch. "Well, you know where we are . . ."

The Woodman was only a small place, and the dozen or so players—some from either team—took up most of the back room.

"I'm Rachel, by the way," she said.

"Alan."

"Did you win, Alan?"

"Yes, but no thanks to me. The other team weren't very good."

"You're all doctors, right?"

He nodded. "Doctors, student doctors, friends of doctors. Anybody who's available if we're short. It's as much a social thing as anything else."

"Plus the sandwiches you get at halftime . . ."

Alan put on a posh voice. "We call it the tea interval," he said.

Rachel eked out a dry white wine and was introduced. She met Phil Hendricks, a pathologist who did a lot of work with the police and told her a succession of grisly stories. She met a dull cardiologist whose name she instantly forgot, a male nurse called Sandy who was at great pains to point out that not all male nurses were gay, and a slimy anesthetist whose breath would surely have done the trick were he ever to run short of gas.

While Rachel was in the ladies', a bumptious pediatrician Alan didn't like a whole lot dropped a fat hand on his shoulder.

"Sodding typical. You do fuck all with the bat and then score *after* the game . . ."

The others enjoyed the joke. Alan glanced around and saw that Rachel was just coming out of the toilet. He hoped that she hadn't seen them all laughing.

"Do you want another one of those?" Alan pointed at her half-empty glass before downing what was left of his lager.

She didn't but followed him to the bar anyway. Alan leaned in close to her, and they talked while he repeatedly failed to attract the attention of the surly Irish barmaid.

"I don't really know a lot of them, to tell you the truth. There's only a couple I ever see outside of the games."

"There's always tossers in any group," she said. "It's the price you pay for company."

"What do you do, Rachel?"

She barked out a dry laugh. "Not a great deal. I studied."

It sounded like the end of a conversation, and for a while they said nothing. Alan guessed that they were about the same age. She was definitely in her early thirties, which meant that she had to have graduated at least ten years before. She had to have done something, had to *do* something. Unless of course she'd been a mature student. It seemed a little too early to pry.

"What do you do to relax? Do you see mates or . . . ?"

She nodded toward the bar, and he followed her gaze to the barmaid, who stood, finally ready to take the order. Alan reeled off a long list of drinks, and they watched while the tray placed on the bar began to fill up with glasses. Alan turned and opened his mouth to speak, but she beat him to it.

"I'd better be getting off."

"Right. I don't suppose I could have your phone number?"

She gave a noncommittal hum as she swallowed what was left of her wine. Alan handed a twenty-pound note across the bar, grinned at her.

"Mobile?"

"I never have it switched on."

"I could leave messages."

She took out a pen and scribbled the number on the back of a dog-eared beer mat.

Alan picked up the tray of drinks just as the barmaid proffered him his fifty pence change. Unable to take it, Alan nodded to Rachel. She leaned forward and grabbed the coin.

"Stick it in the machine on your way out," he said.

Alan had just put the tray down on the table when he heard the repetitive chug and clink of the fruit machine paying out its jackpot. He strode across to where Rachel was scooping out a handful of ten-pence pieces.

"You jammy sod," he said. "I've been putting money into that thing for weeks."

Then she turned, and Alan saw that her face had reddened. "You have it," she said. She thrust the handful of coins at him, then, as several dropped to the floor, she spun around, flustered, and tipped the whole lot back into the payout tray. "I can't . . . I haven't got anywhere to put them all . . ."

She'd gone by the time Alan had finished picking coins off the carpet.

It didn't take too long for Rachel to calm down. She marched down the hill toward the Tube station, her control returning with every step.

She'd been angry with herself for behaving as she had in the pub, but what else could she do? There was no way she could take all that loose change home with her, was there?

As she walked on she realized that actually there *had* been things she could have done, and she chided herself for being so stupid. She could have asked the woman behind the bar to change the coins into notes. Those were more easily hidden. She could have grabbed the coins, left with a smile, and made some beggar's day.

She needed to remember. It was important to be careful, but she always had options.

She reached into her handbag for the mints. Popped one into her mouth to mask the smell of the wine. The taste of it . . .

As she walked down the steps into Highgate station she dropped a hand into her pocket, groping around until she could feel her wedding ring hot against the palm of her hand. There was always that delicious, terrifying second or two, as her fingers moved against the lining of her pocket, when she thought she might have lost it, but it was always there, waiting for her.

She stood on the platform, the ring tight in her fist until the train came in. Then, just as she always did, she slipped the ring, inch by inch, back onto her finger.

Lee pushed his chicken Madras around the plate until it was cold. He'd lost his appetite, anyway. He'd ordered the food before the row, and now he didn't feel like it, so that was another thing that was Rachel's fault.

She'd be in the bedroom by now, crying.

She never cried when it was actually happening. He knew it was because she didn't want to give him the satisfaction, or some such crap. That only proved what a stupid cow she was, because he couldn't stand to see her cry, to see *any* woman cry, and maybe if she *did* cry once in a while he might ease off a bit.

No, she saved it up for afterward, and he could hear it now, coming through the ceiling and putting him off his dinner.

The row had been about the same thing they were all about. Her, taking the piss.

He'd backed down on this afternoon walking business, on her going out to the woods for an afternoon on her own. He'd given in to her, and today she'd been gone nearly six hours. Half the fucking day and no word of an apology when she'd eventually come strolling through the front door.

So, it had kicked off . . .

Lee was bright, always had been. He knew damn well that it wasn't *just* about her staying out of the house too long. He knew it all came down to the pills.

There'd been a lot more rowing, a lot more crying in the bedroom, since he'd found that little packet tucked behind her panties at the back of a drawer. He was clever enough to see the irony in *that* as well. Contraceptive pills, hidden among the sexy knickers he'd bought for her.

He'd gone mental when he'd found them, obviously. Hadn't they agreed that they were going to start trying for a kid? That everything would be better once they were a family? He was furious at the deceit, at the fool she'd made of him, at the time and effort he'd wasted in shafting her all those weeks beforehand.

There'd been a lot more rowing since . . .

Christ, he loved her though. She wouldn't get to him so much if it wasn't for that, wouldn't wind him up like she did. He could feel it surging through him as he lost his temper, and it caused his whole body to shake when it was finished and she crawled away to cry where he couldn't see her.

He hoped she knew it—now, with her face buried in a sopping pillow—he hoped she knew how much he loved her.

Lee dropped his fork and slid his hand beneath the plate, wiggling his fingers until it sat balanced on his palm. He jerked his forearm and sent the plate fast across the kitchen.

Watched his dinner run down the wall.

He watched them.

He lay on the grass, just another sun worshipper, and with his arm folded across his head he spied on them through a fringed curtain of underarm hair. He watched them from his favorite bench. His face hidden behind a newspaper, his back straight against the small, metal plaque.

FOR ERIC AND MURIEL, WHO LOVED THESE WOODS . . .

He watched them, and he waited.

He watched *her,* of course, at other times too. He'd followed her home that very first day and now he would spend hours outside the house in Barnet, imagining her inside in the dark.

He couldn't say why he'd chosen her; couldn't really say why he'd chosen any of them. Something just clicked. It was all pretty random at the end of the day, just luck—good or bad, depending on which way you looked at it.

When he was caught, and odds on he would be, he would tell them that and nothing else.

It all came down to chance.

They'd begun to spend their afternoons together. They walked every inch of Highgate Woods, ate picnics by the tree where they'd first met, and one day they held hands across a weathered wooden table outside the cafeteria.

"Why can't I see you in the evenings?" Alan said.

She winced. "This is nice, isn't it? Don't rush things."

"I changed my shifts around so we could see each other during the day. So that we could spend time together."

"I never asked you to."

"There's things I want, Rachel . . ."

She leered. "I bet there are."

"Yes, *that*. Obviously that, but other things. I want to take you places and meet your friends. I want to come to where you live. I want you to come where *I* live . . ."

"It's complicated. I told you."

"You never tell me anything."

"I'm married, Alan."

He drew his hand away from hers. He tried, and failed, to make light of it. "Well, that explains a lot."

"I suppose it changes everything, doesn't it?"

He looked at her as if she were mad. "Just a *bit*."

"I don't see why."

"For fuck's sake, Rachel . . ."

"Tell me."

"I don't . . . I wouldn't like it if I was the one married to you, put it that way."

She looked at the table.

"Don't cry."

"I'm not crying."

Alan put a laugh into his voice. "Besides, he might decide to beat me up."

Then there *were* tears, and she told him the rest. The babies she didn't want and the bruises you couldn't see, and when it was over Alan reached for her hand and squeezed, and looked at her hard.

"If he touches you again, I'll fucking kill him."

She appreciated the gesture but knew it was really no more than that, and she was sad at the hurt she saw in Alan's eyes when she laughed.

Afterward, Rachel leaned down to pull the sheet back over them. A little shyness had returned, but it was not uncomfortable or awkward.

"I *would* tell you how great that was," she said. "But I don't want you to get complacent." She turned on her side to face him and grinned.

"I was lucky to meet you," he said. "That day, looking for the ball."

"Or *un*lucky . . ."

He shook his head, ran the back of his hand along her rib cage.

"Did you know that a smile can change the world?" she said. "Do you know about that idea?"

"Sounds like one of those awful self-help things."

"No, it's just a philosophy, really, based around the randomness of everything. How every action has consequences, you know? How it's *connected*." She closed her eyes. "You smile at someone at the bus stop and maybe that person's mood changes. They're reminded of a friend they haven't spoken to in a long time and they decide to ring them. This third person, on the other side of the world, answers his mobile phone doing ninety miles an hour on the motorway. He's so thrilled to hear from his old friend that he loses concentration and plows into the car in front, killing a man who was on his way to plant a bomb that would have killed a thousand people . . ."

Alan puffed out his cheeks, let the air out slowly. "What would have happened if I'd scowled at the bloke at the bus stop?"

Rachel opened her eyes. "Something else would have happened."

"Right, like I'd've got punched."

She laughed, but Alan looked away, his mind quickly elsewhere. "I want to talk to you later," he said. "I want to talk to you tonight."

She sighed. "I've told you, it's not possible."

"After what you told me earlier, I want to call you. I want to know you're okay. There must be a way. I'll call at seven o'clock. Rachel? At exactly seven."

She closed her eyes again. Then, fifteen seconds later, she nodded slowly.

It was a minute before Alan spoke again. "Only trouble is, you smile at *anyone* at a bus stop in London, they think you're a nutter."

This time they both laughed, then rolled together. Then fucked again.

When they'd gotten their breath back they talked about all manner of stuff. Films and football and music.

Nothing that mattered.

Alan lay in bed after Rachel had left and thought about all the things that had been said and done that day. He wanted so much to do something to help her, to make her feel better, but for all his bravado, for all his heroic notions, the best that he could come up with was a present.

He knew straightaway what he could give her, and where to find it.

It was in a shoe box at the back of a cupboard stuffed with bundles of letters, a bag of old tools, and other odds and sods that he'd collected from his father's place after the old man had died.

Alan hadn't looked at the bracelet in a couple of years, had forgotten the weight of it. It was gold, or so he presumed, and heavy with charms. He remembered the feel of Rachel's body against his fingers—her shoulder blades and hips—as he ran them around the smooth body of the tiger, the edges of the key, the rims of the tiny train wheels that turned . . .

After his father's death, Alan had spoken to his mother about the bracelet. He asked her if she knew where it had come from. The skin around her jaw had tightened as she'd said she hardly remembered it, then in the next breath that she wanted nothing to do with the bloody thing. Not considering where it had damn well come from.

Alan put two and two together and realized how stupid he'd been. He knew about his father's affairs and guessed that, years before, the bracelet had been a failed peace offering of some sort. It might even have been something that he'd originally bought for one of his mistresses. His father had been a forensic pathologist and Alan was amazed at how a man who exercised such professional skill could be so clumsy when it came to the rest of his life.

It wasn't surprising that his mother had reacted as she had, that she'd wanted no part of the charm bracelet. It had become tainted.

Alan was not superstitious. He sensed that Rachel would like it. He wouldn't give it to her as it was, though. He would make it truly hers before he gave it.

He knew exactly what charm he wanted to add.

From Muswell Hill it was a five-minute bus ride to Highgate Tube. Rachel leaned back against the side of the shelter. Her hair was still wet from the shower she'd taken at Alan's flat.

She'd thought so often about how she might feel afterward. It had been a vital part of the fantasy, not just with Alan but with other men she'd seen but never spoken to. The sex had been easy to imagine, of course. It had been gentler than she was used to and had lasted longer, but the mechanics were more or less the same. Where she'd been wrong was in imagining the feelings that would come when she'd actually done it. She'd been certain that she'd feel frightened, but she didn't. Fear was familiar to her, and its absence was unmistakable. Heady.

She waited a couple of minutes before giving up on the bus

and making for the station on foot. Had there been anybody else at the bus stop, she might well have smiled at them.

Lee didn't think that he asked too much. Not after a long day talking mortgages to morons and assuring mousy newlyweds that damp was easily sorted. At the end of it, all he wanted was his dinner and some comfort.

He couldn't stand her so fucking cheerful.

Taking off his jacket and tie, opening a beer, and asking just what she was so bloody chirpy about.

Had she been up to those fucking woods again?

Yes.

Who with?

Don't be silly, Lee.

Sucking off tramps in the bushes, I'll bet.

Then she'd laughed at him. No outrage like there should have been. No anger at his filthy suggestions, at the stupid suspicions that he'd only half tarted up as a joke.

A jab to the belly and another to the tits had shut her up and put her down on the floor. Now he straddled her chest, knees pressed down on her arms, his hands pulling at his own hair in frustration.

"We were going to do the business later on. I was well up for it, and tonight could have been the night we did something special. Made a new life."

"Lee, please . . ."

"You. Fucking. Spoiled. It."

"We can still do it, Lee. Let's go upstairs now. I'm really horny, Lee . . ."

He shook his head, disgusted, gathering the spit into his mouth. She knew what was coming. He could see it in her eyes, and he waited for her to try to turn her head away as he leaned down and pushed the saliva between his teeth. Instead, she just closed her eyes, and he thought he saw something like a smile as he let a thick string of beery spit drop slowly down onto her face.

As soon as the seven o'clock news had begun, Alan reached for the phone and dialed the number.

It was answered almost immediately, but nobody spoke.

Alan whispered, realized as soon as he had that he was being stupid. He wasn't the one who needed to be secretive.

"Rachel, it's me . . ."

Suddenly, there was a noise, above the hiss and crackle on the line. It was a guttural sound that echoed. That it took him a few moments to identify. An animal sound: a gulp and a grind, a splutter and a swallow. It was the sound of someone sobbing uncontrollably but trying with every ounce of strength to assert control. Trying desperately not to be heard.

Alan sat up straight, pressed the phone hard to his ear.

"Rachel, I'm here, okay? I'm not going anywhere."

He watched the comings and goings with something like amusement.

For a fortnight he watched her leave the house in Barnet mid-morning, then come home again by late afternoon. He stayed with her most of the day when he could, saw her meet him in the woods or sometimes go straight to his flat when they couldn't be arsed with preliminaries.

When they wanted to get straight down to it.

He watched her leave the flat, eyes bright and hair wet. The smell of one man scrubbed away before she went home to another.

He wondered if the man he saw climbing into the silver sports car every morning knew that he was a cuckold. On a couple of occasions he thought about popping a note under his windscreen to let him know. Just to stir things up a bit.

He hadn't done because he didn't want to do anything that might disturb the routine. Not now that he was ready to take her. Besides, mischief for its own sake was not his thing at all.

Still, he couldn't help but marvel at the things people got up to.

On the day Alan had hoped to give Rachel the bracelet, his mother tripped on the stairs.

So many things that could have been different . . .

Two weeks before, the jeweler had shown him a catalog. There *had* been charms that would have carried more or less the same meaning, but Alan knew what he wanted. He'd ordered one specially made. He'd decided against the diamond spots and gone for the enamel, but still, it wasn't cheap. He'd thought of it as a dozen decent sessions with one of his private patients. He always thought in those terms whenever he wanted to splash out on something.

A fortnight later, half an hour before he was due to meet Rachel in the woods, he walked out onto Bond Street with the bracelet. Then, his mother called.

"Don't worry, Alan. It's just my ankle, it's nothing . . ."

A message that said, *Come and see me now, if you give a shit.*

He phoned Rachel and left a message of his own. She was probably on her way already, was almost certainly somewhere on the Northern line. He made for the Underground himself, steeling himself for the trip to his mother's warden-controlled flat in Swiss Cottage.

As he walked, he realized that his mother would see the bag. It was purple with white cord handles and the name of the jeweler in gold lettering. He couldn't show her the bracelet for obvious reasons . . .

He decided that if she asked he'd tell her he'd bought himself a new watch . . .

Lee wasn't stupid—God, it would all have been a lot easier if he were—but it couldn't be very much longer before he noticed how often she was going to the toilet or taking a shower just before seven o'clock . . .

She collected her bag on the way upstairs, and then, once she'd locked the bathroom door, she switched the phone on, set it to vibrate only, and waited.

Tonight she was desperate, had been since Alan had failed to meet her at lunchtime. She'd waited in the woods for twenty minutes before she'd got a signal, before the alert had come through. She'd listened to his message once then erased it as always. Walked back toward the Tube, unraveling.

Sitting with her back against the side of the bath, she thought there was every chance that he might not ring at all. His excuse for not turning up had sounded very much *like* an excuse. Not that she could blame him for wanting to call a halt to things; she knew how hard it was for him in so many ways . . .

She almost dropped the phone when it jumped in her hand.

"Where were you?"

"Didn't you get the message? I was at my bloody mother's."

"I thought you might have made it up."

"Jesus, Rachel."

"Sorry . . ."

A sigh. Half a minute of sniffs and swallows.

"God, I wish I could see you," he said. "Now, I mean. I've got something for you. I wanted to give it to you this afternoon . . ."

"I'd like to see you too."

"Can you?"

The hope in his voice clutched at her. "There might be a way . . ."

"By the tree in half an hour. The woods don't shut until eight."

"I'll try."

When she'd hung up she dialed another number. She spoke urgently for a minute, then hung up again. When she heard the landline ringing a few moments later, she flushed the toilet and stepped out of the bathroom.

Lee was holding the phone out for her when she walked into the lounge. She took it and spoke, hoped he could hear the shock and concern in her voice despite the fact that he hadn't bothered to turn the television down.

"That was Sue," she said afterward. "Her brother's been in a car accident. Some idiot talking on his mobile phone plowed into the back of him on the motorway. I said I'd go round . . ."

Lee's team had been awarded a penalty. Without turning around to her, he waved his consent.

He was astonished to see her leave the house alone at night. The husband did, of course, jumped in his sports car every so often to collect a takeaway or shoot down to the off-license, but never *her* . . .

He'd been planning to do it during the day; he knew the quiet places now, the dead spots en route where he could take her with very little risk, but he wasn't a man to look a gift horse in the mouth.

This was perfect, and he was as ready as he'd ever be.

He presumed she'd be heading for the Tube at High Barnet. He got out of his car and followed her.

It took Alan ten minutes to get to the woods. By half past seven he'd gotten everything arranged.

He hadn't wanted to just give her the bracelet. He'd wanted her to come across it, to find it as if by some piece of good fortune. Luck had played such a big part in their coming together, after all, which is why he'd chosen the charm that he had. There was only really one place that he could leave it . . .

The light was fading fast. The few people he saw were all moving toward one or another of the various exits. He dialed her number.

"It's me. You're probably still on the Tube. Listen, come to the tree, but don't worry if you can't see me. I'll be nearby, but there's something I want you to find first. Stand where the ball was found, then look up. Okay? I'll see you soon."

He moved away from the tree so that he could watch from a distance when she discovered the bracelet. It worried him that it would soon be too dark to see the expression on her face when she found it. He sat down, leaned back against a stump to wait.

It was the away leg of a big European tie, and one up at halftime was a very decent result.

Lee was at the fridge, digging out snacks for the rest of the game, when the car alarm went off. That fucking Saab across the road again—he'd told the tosser to get it looked at once. The wailing stopped after a couple of minutes but started up again almost immediately, and Lee knew that uninterrupted enjoyment of the second half had gone out the window.

He picked up his keys and stormed out of the front door. The prat was out by the looks of it, but Lee fancied giving his motor a kick or two anyway. He might come back afterward, grab some paper, and stick a none-too-subtle note through the wanker's letterbox. Maybe a piece of dog shit for good measure . . .

Rachel's phone was lying on the tarmac halfway down the drive.

Lee picked it up and switched it on. The leather case had protected it, and the screen lit up immediately.

He entered the security code and waited.

There was a message.

Rachel had realized her phone was missing as soon as she came out of the station. She knew Alan would be worried that she'd taken so long and had reached for the phone to see if he'd left a message. A balloon of sickness had risen up rapidly from her gut, and she'd begun running, silently cursing the selfish idiot who'd thrown himself on to the line at East Finchley, then feeling bad about it.

A few minutes into the woods and still a few more from where Alan would be waiting. It was almost dark, and she hadn't seen anyone since she left the road. She looked at her watch—the exits would close in ten minutes. She knew that people climbed over fences to get in—morons who lit bonfires and played chase me with the keepers—so it wouldn't be impossible to get out, but she still didn't fancy being inside after the woods were locked up.

She thought about shouting Alan's name out; it was so quiet that the sound would probably carry. She was being stupid . . .

Still out of breath, she picked up her pace again, looking up at the noise of feet falling heavily on the path ahead and seeing the jogger coming toward her.

Alan rang again, hung up as soon as he heard her voice on the answering machine.

He looked at his watch, leaned his head back against the bark. He could hear the distant drone of the traffic and, closer, the shrill peep of the bats that had begun to emerge from their boxes to feed. Moving above him like scraps of burned paper on the breeze.

He slowed as he passed her, jogged on a stride or two, then backed quickly up to draw level with her again. She froze, and he could see the fear in her face.

"Rachel?" he said.

She stared at him, still wary but with curiosity getting the better of her.

"I met you a few weeks ago in the pub," he said. "With Alan." Her eyes didn't move from his. "Graham. The cardiologist?"

"Oh, God. Graham . . . right, of course . . ."

She laughed, and her shoulders sagged as the tension vanished.

He laughed too, and reached around to the belt he wore beneath the jogging bottoms. Felt for the knife.

"Sorry," she said. "I think my brain's going. I'm a bit bloody jumpy, to tell you the truth."

He nodded, but he wasn't really listening. He spun slowly around, hand on hip, catching his breath. Checking that there was no one else around.

"Well . . ." she said.

He'd have her in the bushes in seconds, the knife pressed to her throat before she had a chance to open her mouth.

He saw her check her watch.

It's time, he thought.

"Rachel!"

He looked up and saw the shape of a big man moving fast toward them. She looked at the shape, then back to him, her mouth open and something unreadable in her eyes.

He dug out a smile. "Nice to see you again . . ." he said.

With the blade of the knife flat against his wrist, he turned and jogged away along the path that ran at right angles to the one they'd been on.

"Was that him? Was that him?"

"He was a jogger. He just . . ." Lee's hand squeezed her neck, choked off the end of the sentence. He raised his other hand slowly, held the phone aloft in triumph. "I know all about it," he said. "So don't try and fucking lie to me."

There were distant voices coming from somewhere. People leaving. Laughter. Words that were impossible to make out and quickly faded to silence.

Lee tossed the phone to the ground, and the free hand reached up to claw at her chest. Thick fingers pushed aside material, found a nipple, and squeezed.

She couldn't make a sound. The tears ran down her face and neck and onto the back of his hand as she beat at it, as she snatched in breaths through her nose. Just as she felt her legs go, he released her neck and breast and raised both hands up to the side of her neck.

"Lee, nothing happened. Lee . . ."

He pressed the heels of his hands against her ears and leaned in close, as though he might kiss or bite her.

"What's his name?"

She tried to shake her head, but he held it hard.

"Or so help me I'll dig a hole for you with my bare hands. I'll leave your cunt's carcass here for the foxes . . ."

So she told him, and he let her go, and he shouted over his shoulder to her as he walked farther into the woods.

"Now, run home."

Alan had given it one more minute ten minutes ago, but it was clear to him now that she wasn't coming. She'd sounded like she was really going to try, so he decided that she hadn't been able to get away.

He hoped it was only fear that had restrained her.

He stood up, pressed the redial button on his phone one last time. Got her message again.

There were no more than a couple of minutes before the exits were sealed. He just had time to retrieve the bracelet, to reach up and unhook it from the branch on which it hung.

He'd give it to her another day.

Standing alone in the dark, wondering how she was, he decided that he might not draw her attention to the newest charm on the bracelet. A pair of dice had seemed so right, so appropriate in light of what had happened, of everything they'd talked about. Suddenly he felt every bit as clumsy as his father. It seemed tasteless.

Luck was something they were pushing.

He stepped out onto the path, turned when he heard a man's voice say his name.

The footwork and the swing were spot on.

The first blow smashed Alan's phone into a dozen or more pieces, the second did much the same to his skull, and those that came after were about nothing so much as exercise.

It took half a minute for the growl to die in Lee's throat.

The blood on the branch, on the grass to either side of the path, on his training shoes looked black in the near total darkness.

Lee bent down and picked up the dead man's arm. He wondered if his team had managed to hold on to their one-goal lead as he began dragging the body into the undergrowth.

Graham had run until he felt his lungs about to give up the ghost. He was no fitter than many of those he treated. Those whose hearts were marbled with creamy lines of fat, like cheap off-cuts.

He dropped down on to a bench to recover, to reflect on what had happened in the woods. To consider his rotten luck. If that man hadn't come along when he had . . . A young woman with Mediterranean features was waiting to cross the road a few feet from where he was sitting. She was taking keys from her bag, probably heading toward the flats opposite.

She glanced in his direction, and he dropped his elbows to his knees almost immediately. Looked at the pavement. Made sure she didn't get a good look at his face.

The next High Barnet train was still eight minutes away.

Rachel stood on the platform, her legs still shaking, the burning in her breast a little less fierce with every minute that passed. The pain had been good. It had stopped her thinking too much; stopped her wondering. She sought a little more of it, thrusting her hand into her pocket until she found her wedding ring, then driving the edge of it hard against the fingernail until she felt it split.

Alan had thought it odd that she still took the ring off even after she'd told him the truth, but it made perfect sense to her. Its removal had always been more about freedom than deceit.

An old woman standing next to her nudged her arm and nodded toward the electronic display.

CORRECTION. HIGH BARNET. 1 MIN.

"There's a stroke of luck," the woman said.

Rachel looked at the floor. She didn't raise her head again until she heard the train coming.

TWO DEATHS AND A MOUTHFUL OF WORMS

Denise Mina

The insistent mobile phone was tucked down in front of the gear stick. Keeping his eyes on the road, Phil leaned forward, straining slightly against the seat belt as he reached for it. The caller display said "Pete2," so he knew it was Anya, ringing him to sort it out. He turned the phone off and threw it into the passenger seat, as if carelessly. He'd call her tomorrow. In the evening. He glanced at the dead phone. Let her wait. He shouldn't contact her until she'd had time to cool off and think about him and everything he had to offer.

The sleek car slid effortlessly along the Westway, and his heart slowed to the rhythm of the wiper. He licked his upper lip and found it salted. Dried sweat. From the exertion. He smiled softly to himself and glanced in the rearview mirror, looking back down the dark empty road behind, half expecting to see Anya standing in the middle lane, naked as he had left her, black blood tumbling down her pretty chin, dripping off her finger to the floor. He tried to imagine an expression on her face but couldn't. He didn't know what she would be feeling now. It was their first time together, and he wanted it to be all right. He wanted that very much.

He couldn't stop seeing her face as she went down beneath

him; her skirt riding up to her thighs as she slid onto the sofa bed, glaring up at him, eyes brilliant with alarm. She was beautiful. Even in submission, she was beautiful. She wasn't like Helena, who gradually lost all mystery and beauty for him after their first time. He licked his lip again and smiled, happy at the reminder in the salty tang. He wasn't even afraid of her calling the police, because she didn't have a visa. Russian women weren't like French women. He would give her the bracelet tomorrow, when the swelling had gone down a little.

As he pulled up the steep drive the car dipped on the high-tech suspension, jolting his stomach, making him feel sick and proud at the same time as he always did when he pulled up at the white town house. The rooms at the front were dark.

Phil couldn't resist. He leaned over and turned the phone on, typing in the pin number, being careful not to touch any extraneous buttons in case she was phoning him right now and he would be answering. The phone came to life, the pale blue panel lighting up to tell him the time and date. One new message.

He called the answerphone service and selected Listen. Anya was sobbing, calling his name: "Pheeleep, Pheeleep." She gasped for breath. "Please to come. My Pheel, please to come." Spluttering as she spoke, perhaps spluttering blood. He smiled as she hung up and selected Listen to Messages again. "Please to come. My Pheel." That charged wetness about her mouth was gorgeous. He'd phone her tomorrow, in the evening or afternoon at the earliest.

He lifted the green velvet box from his lap, bundled it into the glove compartment with the dead phone, and opened the car door, trying, even alone in the dark, not to grunt as he pulled himself out of the bucket seat. He locked the car carefully, his eyes lingering on the glove compartment, testing it with fresh eyes to see if Helena could have spotted anything through the glass and metal and leather. She'd know the whole story if she found the gaudy present, she'd know about the cheap woman and the why. He couldn't face a showdown. She'd divorce him and take everything. He didn't want her anymore, couldn't take her anywhere. She had too many scars. The best that could happen would be if she just ran back to France and left him alone.

He put his key in the large front door and opened it to a thick, fetid silence. The hall was dark. Following his nightly ritual, Phil put his house keys on the silver calling card plate in the center of the hall, emptying his pockets of small change and a couple of tenners, giving the impression of openness.

The edge of the large bowl of lilies reflected what was behind him: a brightly lit kitchen door with a shadow moving through it, holding on to the wall to steady herself.

"Well, well, well," she said, "if it isn't Jesus H. Christ himself."

She talked in stupid clichés when she was drunk, her French accent coarser and thickening. Phil ignored her and walked across the hall to the bottom of the stairs.

"Where the hell are you going?" He turned. Helena was silhouetted against the light, wearing a long black silk nightgown with lace on the arms and chest. The sort of nightgown an older woman might wear, imagining it to be alluring. Naked and young was alluring, sweet and vulnerable was alluring. Drunk Helena swaying in the doorway, her mouth a bitter button, her eyes blinking slowly, was not.

"I made you dinner," she said. "You said you'd be in from work at fucking nine o'clock, and I made you a beautiful soufflé."

Phil stopped on the stairs, holding on to the banister, letting the weight of his body swing him back to face her.

"Supper," he corrected quietly.

Helena rolled her eyes up in her head, shutting them tightly, and tried to start the argument again.

"I made you fucking dinner—"

"A meal served at that time is commonly called supper. Not dinner." He swung back to face the stairs, suppressing a smile. "Supper."

She was too drunk to think of a comeback. By the time she opened her mouth to start again he was out of sight on the upstairs landing. He heard her drawn breath, enough to shout with, and felt along the wall, flicking the hall light off. He left her flummoxed in the darkness. Silly cow.

He was halfway across the bedroom to their en suite when he heard the first crash from downstairs. She was trashing the kitchen again, smashing up the new set of crockery he had bought her to replace the previous set she had smashed up.

He locked the door to the bathroom, something he hadn't done in weeks. Helena had been up here already, pouring talcum powder on the head of his electric toothbrush, in his aftershave bottles, and in his basin. Hers was pristine. The talc was all over the floor, trapped between the biscuit-colored tiles. She'd have to clean it up in the morning, or at least arrange for someone else to come in and do it. She never seemed to realize that she was only making work for herself.

Phil went to the cupboard and pulled down a spare head for his toothbrush and a packet of floss. He'd broken Anya's tooth tonight, knocked part of a premolar right out of her mouth and across the room with a single punch. Anya was beautiful. She had large brown eyes, thick black hair. When he first saw her at the champagne bar, it was her legs he noticed. She had a scrawny thinness that made her look like a suspect, a high-strung woman too nervous to eat properly.

Slammo saw him eyeing her up and leaned across the table, dipping his silk tie in a puddle of cheap champagne and cigar ash. "Is she a drug courier?" he said, and Phil laughed.

That was exactly what she looked like. She wore too much makeup, teased her hair in ways it didn't want to go.

The champagne bar was a cheap con serving viscose Cava for twenty quid a glass. The real reason anyone went there was for the striptease and the nearly naked women serving. They were good-looking women, though, there was no denying it, but their purpose was to get you to drink more. They got a cut of the tab from their tables. Anya made him buy four bottles, each costing eighty-five quid, before she would sit on his knee. He bought another four for the privilege of kissing her hand.

He had money to spare, and he wouldn't be like the other contenders for her affections: he wasn't old or fat. He was a successful broker, not hypersuccessful and not obsessed with the work. He was never placed on the top table at functions, but in her eyes he was a god. He owned a large house outright, he drove a Ferrari, he was generous and handsome and young. Most of the men who went in there were forty or fifty, she said, most of them were fat or sweaty. He was a good catch for her.

They had been together for four months now, long enough to swap sexual histories. He told her about Helena and how they met at a barbecue in Henley, he told her about Helena's drinking but left the rest of it out. Anya had loved a boy at home but he'd died, sadly, when she was out of town on business for the shop (she worked in an aunt's clothes shop at home—top class, designer things like Dior and Chanel and Versace). She had only had one boyfriend since she came to London, Johnny, who wasn't nice to her. Phil wanted to ask her outright, Did he hit you? But he didn't want to sound outraged or disapproving. Part of the grooming was never to talk about it in other than positive terms: there are worse things you can do, at least he loved you enough to do that, he didn't mean it. Set up excuses for himself in the future. Johnny was very rich, but she didn't see him anymore. She didn't miss him at all.

Helena was rattling the bathroom door, cursing him for locking it. Phil ignored her, running the warm water into his basin to wash his face. She kicked it; he could hear her grunting as she did.

He could imagine Anya working in a designer shop at home, the most beautiful girl in her small, mud-encrusted town. It was a shame he couldn't tell the boys in the office about her, but a few of their wives knew Helena from Christmas parties. It was a shame. If he groomed her properly, if it worked out right, Anya could turn out to be sustainable, the woman he could come home to every night, want every night and have. It could work. Russian women had different expectations.

He didn't know where she was from or why she had come here. She told him the name of the place several times, and he would playact, shrugging, watching her lips, making her say it again. She finished by smirking and saying, "It near Siberia, Pheel. You don't know Russia's towns." He didn't have to engage with her personal history. She was twenty-three and living in a flat in Soho and working for her cousin Fat Eugene in a champagne bar. Fat Eugene had the flat in payment for some debt and let her use it exclusively because she was family.

Helena kicked the door. "Let me in, you fucker."

Every night they went through this charade now, Helena trying to get attention from him by behaving badly and then he'd come bursting out of the bathroom and leather her, slap and punch. "Is this what you want?" He'd fall on his knees by her side and take out the pocket knife, nick her skin with the business end of the bottle opener. He sharpened it for her, to make the cuts uniform. Helena lay on the floor and took it, groaning like a whore in ecstasy, climbing slowly into bed after him, sorry for all the mess she'd caused.

She kicked the door again. "Let me in, you fucker. Let me in and I'll fucking kill you. I'll mark you, and then we'll see what your friends at work think about it."

She stood back, waiting for him to open the door and go for her. Her complicity was pathetic to him now. Role play, even hard-core role play, wasn't what he wanted, not after Anya's horror and fright. Poor Anya, so shocked by the change of mood in him. He snapped the lock off the door and let it swing open. Helena stood outside, staggered back a little step, bracing herself for the first blow.

"Do what you like," said Phil. "I don't give a shit."

He brushed past her on the way to bed, and as he passed she saw something and caught her breath, gave a little inadvertent cry.

"For fuck's sake, I didn't touch you." He turned and saw that her eyes were fixed on the back of his hand. Helena's knees buckled. She slid to the floor, seeming to whither as she did so, still staring. He had fresh cuts on his knuckles. She crumpled to the floor, real tears in her eyes. He had cut the back of his hand on someone else. Phil was embarrassed.

He tutted hard and covered the cut hand with the other, muttering "for fuck's sake" and "just a cut" as he busied himself taking off his rings and his watch. He stripped down to his boxers and hung his clothes up, ignoring Helena. He saw her in the reflection of the window, sitting in the shaft of harsh light from the hall. Her hands were clasped to her chest and, even in a reflection, Phil could see a hundred tiny white scars, each a centimeter long, crisscrossing her face and hands, intersecting her eyebrows and lids, crawling over her lips like a hundred tiny worms.

When he met Helena she was young and pert and game for anything. She said something cheeky to him in front of all the men gathered around the barbecue, something about her needing a good slap. They became inseparable. They traveled when they could take holidays, went to visit her cold parents in Paris, and bought the house after the wedding. It began in this house, drunken arm-twisting and small hits, getting bigger and closer to her face until she couldn't go to work for more than a day a week and they sacked her. But now it was no more than a hollow ritual, a reminder of when she'd really had something worth taking away.

"Good night, Helena." He climbed into bed and turned off the light.

She stayed on the floor in the shaft of light, sobbing while her energy lasted, ending up sniffing and lonely on the big white floor.

Phil lay in the bed facing the windows with his eyes shut. He pulled the sheets up to his mouth and felt, for the first time in years, a little guilty. He listening as she cried quietly. He listened as she tried to get up, her feet scrabbling on satin nightie against the woolen carpet, looking for purchase, trying hard to get up but failing, like a spider caught in the bath.

He didn't want to ring too early in the evening. He wanted her to wait and get desperate, to reach the stage where she expected him not to phone but dearly wanted him to. Helena had told him how she'd waited by the phone the day after the first real beating, praying for his call, wishing, wishing. He ordered a steak sandwich at the bar and another pint of Stella. The pub was at Charing Cross, an anonymous theme bar less than half a mile from Anya's flat. He didn't know anyone in there and mingled happily with the other commuters relaxing with the paper on their way home. He flicked through the *Evening Standard*, skimming the articles, thinking about the bracelet in his pocket.

They had been seeing each other for four months, all of it very nice, out to dinners or staying in, having a good time while he waited. When he saw the charm bracelet dangling from the tree he knew that now was the time. She was attached enough. He would give the bracelet to her afterward, pretend he had bought it in a flurry of remorse.

It looked like something a Russian girl would like, gold and rich, vulgar and an obvious antique. It had individual charms hanging off it: a tiger, two dice, a little steam train with wheels that moved, all heavy and expensive. Not designer, not pretty; she wouldn't necessarily like the thing but she'd feel the weight of it and know how much it was worth, and that alone would endear him to her. And then, when she had calculated how much it was worth and what he would have spent retail (she knew he didn't know anyone in wholesale; they'd had that conversation when he bought her the watch), when she was already pliable and forgiving, then he'd give her the smaller box in matching green velvet with the pink egg inside.

The bracelet had been dun and stuck with leaves and mold when he found it. It had been left hanging in a branch like a child's glove lost on the ground and left sitting on a gatepost, advertising itself to passersby. The sun passed overhead, and he caught a glimpse of it. He was sitting on the bench in the overgrown path, phoning her. He told her he was thinking about her and touching himself (he wasn't) and wanted to kiss her all over and look after her (he didn't). On the other end of the phone Anya was saying that she'd gotten a hundred-quid tip from a handsome man the night before.

It was all she talked about, money, all she wanted, poor immigrant. Perhaps the man would come back, perhaps he would give her more money and try to become her lover. Would that make him jealous? Would that make him angry? He could hear her boss Fat Eugene laughing at her.

"You know, Anya," he said, picking the bracelet off the branch like a fruit, "all that glistens is not gold."

She didn't understand, of course. She asked him "What?" twice and then brushed over it.

He stopped himself from telling her he had a gift for her.

He had paid to have the bracelet cleaned and polished and bought the best box the jewelers had to present it in. The green box had a yellow coat of arms stamped on it, some spurious connection to an obscure European family of aristos prepared to exploit their family history to make and sell trinkets for tourists. It had a gold satin interior. And then he saw the egg in pink enamel with gold weave around it, a poor man's Fabergé. The elderly jeweler showed him how to open it. "A special message can be placed inside, you see, for a loved one." He glanced at Phil's wedding ring. "For an anniversary. It's a brand-new piece, valuable, from a very reputable maker, intricate." It was yellow gold meshed over menstrual pink enamel. Phil could see it was crap. That's why he bought it.

He finished his sandwich and stepped outside the sticky hub to make the phone call. He found an alley away from the pedestrians and faced the back, hanging his head low, getting the voice right.

"Please don't hang up" was his anxious opener. He loved her. He needed her. He was sorry. He finished by telling her that she deserved so much more.

She was delighted to hear from him, he could tell by the high tone of her voice. "Please to come," she said. "We can talk please."

"I'm so sorry."

"Come to me, Pheel." She sounded quite turned on, a little breathy, even.

He hung up and went back into the pub for another quick half.

It was a cheap room in a pricey area. Soho might have been the center of the red light district, but it was still expensive. Small rooms in overpriced, narrow houses. The buzzer system was ramshackle, with Biroed names taped to the buzzers. Some of them weren't even names, just descriptions: *Young Model, Swedish Girl, Lonely Guy.* Anya had only a number on hers. She must have been waiting by the entry phone, because the moment his finger came off it she buzzed him up.

The stairs were wooden and narrow and worn in the center where eager feet had rattled up them and sloped down for a hundred years. Anya was waiting for him on the second landing, dressed in a sheer black silk shirt and jeans, standing in the doorway, watching for his face to appear on the bend. She looked tentative and nervous. He brought his eyebrows together in the middle, whispering her name as he ran up the three final steps.

"Forgive me." He brought her hand to his lips, looking at her face and noticing a small black crescent on her cheek where the tooth had gone into it. He kissed the mark lightly. She kept his big hand in her small one and pulled him into the flat.

The house had been chopped up from a grand whole, and there was no hallway. She maneuvered him to the sofa and sat him down. He stayed on the edge of the seat, acting anxious still.

"I have something for you," she said, and skirted behind him to a sideboard. "I bought for you."

She bent down, presenting him with her tight little arse in denim, and pulled from the cupboard a bottle of Remy Martin XO Special. It was very good cognac, and she had the presentation bottle: a flat oval with ornamental ridges all along the side. They had it in the drinks cabinet at work. It was a delicious, cool fit on the well of the palm and cost extra to buy. In the four months they had been together, he had never known her to spend any money on anything, and he knew that this bottle cost closer to a hundred quid than fifty.

"You like?"

He nodded dumbly. There was less work for him to do here than he could possibly have supposed. She was already forgiving him, already smiling at him as she unwrapped the lid and poured the glittering caramel liquid into two waiting glasses.

"I bought you a gift too," he said quietly, looking back at her.

Anya looked him in the eye as she ran her sharp little tongue around the neck of the bottle. "That's lovely, honey. Put on the table for me to see."

"It's nothing much." He took out both of the green boxes and placed them on the cluttered coffee table next to each other, the big one and the matching little one, and for a moment he considered them and thought they looked like him and Anya, a big one and a little one by its side, perfectly matching.

Behind him Anya raised both hands high, using all her slight weight to bring the heavy ornamental glass bottle down on the left side of Phil's head.

Stunned at the blow, he slumped to the side, and she hit him again, holding the bottle by the neck, smashing the deep heavy ridges across the right of his head this time, hearing a dull crack. Frowning, she looked at the bottle, but the glass was intact. The noise hadn't come from the bottle. Phil was lying on the sofa, staring intently at the legs of the coffee table, a bubble of red at his ear. She hit him once again, on the temple this time, and his head caved in like a smashed egg. He rolled forward, tumbling paralyzed onto the floor, unable to bring his hands up to break his fall. His blood began to spill free, and the thirsty carpet sucked it up.

As he lay on the ground listening to his own hot blood glug into the nylon shag, the last thing he heard was Anya, tiny, hitherto compliant Anya, spit words at him. "Fuck you," she said. "You can fucking hit me? Fuck you."

He couldn't hear her anymore, but his vision was suddenly as sharp as it had ever been. The last image ever to register on his retina was Anya, drinking straight from the bottle, clutching the blood-smeared glass with both her tiny hands.

She sat alone and still for a long time, drinking brandy, whispering to Phil's cooling body, telling him what a cunt he was. She opened the boxes and saw the bracelet and put it on. It looked ridiculous on her slim wrist.

"Fucking rubbish."

And then the egg. She opened it in the middle and found a note in Phil's handwriting: *I love you*. She screwed it up and threw it into the wet blood. It sucked the blood up from the ground, smothering itself in gore until it was as bloated with blood like a happy tick. Anya clipped the egg to the bracelet and sat back, poking the body with her toe.

"Go fucks yourself."

The fury ebbed away as the drink warmed her. She would have cried, but she wasn't sorry or afraid. Phil had stopped bleeding, and the edges of the blood had started to dry by the time she picked up the phone and called the club.

It was nine o'clock, and the punters were few and far between. The music blared insistently on the other end, and she could hear the girls talking to each other. Eugene? Please to put Eugene. Thanks you, Sally.

She shook a cigarette out of the packet and lit up, inhaling deeply, tipping her head back, closing her eyes, and stroking her slim throat with her fingertips. Eugene picked up the phone and grunted hello, and Anya lapsed into her own language. "Eugene," she whispered, "I've done it again."

Suddenly he was attentive. "By 'it' do you mean what happened at home, the Johnny situation?"

He sounded annoyed. She jackknifed slowly forward over her knees, contracting every muscle in her face until she looked like a small, grieving child.

"He hit me, Euge," she keened. "I can't . . . Euge, I can't take that. My face, it's my face."

Eugene turned from the bar, cupping his hand over the receiver. "What's wrong with you? Why do you keep doing that?"

"I got angry. He hit me. Please help."

He sighed, a breathy, exasperated fluster in her ear. "Anya, I can't help you."

"Please, Euge, please help me."

Eugene was a gangster born of gangsters, and he had seen some hair-raising sights in his life, but those were accidents of birth and cast. Deep in his heart he was a gentleman. He used violence as a tool, for a reason, but disposing of needless bodies depressed him. It made him question the purpose and point of life.

"No," he said. "You'll have to run."

Contemplating difficulties for herself made Anya howl with grief.

"But, Eugene, I'm your family. How can you leave me unprotected? How can you abandon me?"

Eugene waited until she had calmed down and said, "After Johnny, never again."

She heard the finality in his voice, remembered wearing the blood-soaked kimono as she sat curled up on the sofa, watching Eugene and his two friends, who knew about those things, coming out of the kitchen for smoking breaks, covered in blood and bits, avoiding her eyes. She had liked that kimono. It was yellow and she suited yellow. It looked good with her black hair.

"Anya, wherever you go, remember to call your mother. Good-bye."

"But, Eugene—"

But Eugene was gone.

The international departures lounge was chic and modern, but one small escalator ride up took Anya into Waterloo train station itself, a gray, cavernous building filled with a yellow light filtering slowly down through the dirty glass above. Disease-riddled pigeons and pedestrians intermingled, all feeding and waiting. It was nine-thirty A.M. and the commuter traffic was slowing down.

Anya perched on the coffee bar stool for a long time, watching the women come and go from the toilets across the concourse, looking for someone of her build with luggage. She had seen a couple of hopefuls, but one woman only had a briefcase with her and the other was too fat. The train was leaving in thirty minutes when she finally saw her, a perfect match; the woman was petite, had a suitcase, a red coat, and a matching wide-brimmed hat. She was well dressed, which pricked at Anya's vanity. The hat would be the perfect way to hide her face.

She slipped off the stool and walked across the busy concourse to the entrance, walking past a bucket of filthy mop water waiting to be emptied into a toilet. She dropped a twenty-pence piece into the turnstile and followed her into the ladies' toilets. The tail of the woman's red coat switched the bottom of a cubicle door. She was hanging it up. Anya waited silently, watching for an attendant, although there didn't seem to be one, listening for other customers. The place was empty. Everyone was gathering down by the platform, waiting to get through customs before the train embarked. The toilet flushed behind the door and the end of the red coat was lifted up.

Anya slipped into a cubicle opposite the sinks, pulling the door to. The woman walked across to the basin and turned on the water, rolling first one hand and then the other under the tap, watching her hands as she did so. Anya had her hands around her neck before she even realized that she was not alone.

The woman struggled, but not for long and not too hard. She couldn't have had a lot of breath in her to begin with, because she was unconscious in thirty seconds and dead in two minutes. As she slumped into Anya's arms, her hat fell to the side. The woman's face was covered in small healed cuts, like paper cuts. They were all over her neck, rioting up her chin and cheeks, swarming into her mouth. Anya dragged her backward to the cubicle and sat her on the toilet, peeling the coat off her, taking her money and papers. She stood in front of the mirror and fixed the hat on her head. It was a little big, but it would do. She tipped it to the side at a jaunty angle and noticed the heavy charm bracelet that she still wore. It was all wrong, too vulgar for the cashmere coat and matching luggage. As she left the toilets, she let the bracelet slide out of her hand and into the mop bucket, the splash barely audible, a flash of gold swallowed by black water.

She was waiting at passport control when it occurred to her: she did not have scars all over her face. They would know it wasn't her. Suddenly alive, she looked left and right for an escape. They were in a corridor.

Surgery. Could she say she had had surgery and gotten rid of them, a skin graft, a peel? They might send her back and tell her to get another passport then. The fat man in front shuffled off, and she was motioned forward. The woman found the photo and looked at her. She looked closer and handed the book back.

"Merci, madame."

She waited until she was in the departure lounge to look through her papers. She was called Helena, and when she had applied for her passport five years ago, her skin was as soft and perfect as Anya's.

FAVOR

John Harvey

Kiley hadn't heard from Adrian Costain in some little time, not since one of Costain's A-list clients had ended up in an all-too-public brawl, the pictures syndicated around the world at the touch of a computer key, and Kiley, who had been hired to prevent exactly that kind of thing from happening, had been lucky to get half his fee.

"If we were paying by results," Costain had said, "you'd be paying me."

Kiley had had new cards printed. *Investigations. Private and Confidential. All kinds of security work undertaken. Ex-Metropolitan Police.* Telephone and fax numbers underneath. Cheaper by the hundred, the young woman in Easy Print had said, Kiley trying not to stare at the tattoo that snaked up from beneath the belt of her jeans to encircle her navel, the line of tiny silver rings that tinkled like a miniature carillon whenever she moved her head.

Now the cards were pinned, some of them, outside news agents' shops all up and down the Holloway Road and around; others he'd left discreetly in pubs and cafés in the vicinity; once, hopefully, beside the cash desk at the Holloway Odeon after an afternoon showing of *Insomnia,* Kiley not immune to Maura Tierney's charms.

Most days, the phone didn't ring, the fax failed to ratchet into life.

"E-mail, that's what you need, Jack," the Greek in the corner café where he sometimes had breakfast assured him. "E-mail, the net, the World Wide Web."

What Kiley needed was a new pair of shoes, a way to pay next month's rent, a little luck. Getting laid wouldn't be too bad either: it had been a while.

He was on his way back into the flat, juggling the paper, a pint of milk, a loaf of bread, fidgeting for the keys, when the phone started to ring.

Too late, he pressed Recall and held his breath.

"Hello?" The voice at the other end was as suave as cheap margarine.

"Adrian?"

"You couldn't meet me in town, I suppose? Later this morning. Coffee."

Kiley thought that he could.

When he turned the corner of Old Compton Street onto Frith Street, Costain was already sitting outside Bar Italia, expensively suited legs lazily crossed, *Times* folded open, cappuccino as yet untouched before him.

Kiley squeezed past a pair of media types earnestly discussing first-draft scripts and European funding and took a seat at Costain's side.

"Jack," Costain said. "It's been too long." However diligently he practiced his urbane, upper-class drawl, there was always that telltale tinge of Ilford, like a hair ball at the back of his throat.

Kiley signaled to the waitress and leaned back against the painted metal framework of the chair. Across the street, Ronnie Scott's was advertising Dianne Adams, foremost among its coming attractions.

"I didn't know she was still around," Kiley said.

"You know her?"

"Not really."

What Kiley knew were old rumors of walkouts and no-shows, a version of "Stormy Weather" that had been used a few years back in a television commercial, an album of Gershwin songs he'd once owned but not seen in, oh, a decade or more. Not since Dianne Adams had played London last.

"She's spent a lot of time in Europe since she left the States," Costain was saying. "Denmark. Holland. Still plays all the big festivals. Antibes, North Sea."

Kiley was beginning to think Costain's choice of venue for their meeting was down to more than a love of good coffee. "You're representing her," he said.

"In the U.K., yes."

Kiley glanced back across the street. "How long's she at Ronnie's?"

"Two weeks."

When Kiley was a kid and little more, those early cappuccino days, a girl he'd been seeing had questioned the etiquette of eating the chocolate off the top with a spoon. He did it now, two spoonfuls before stirring in the rest, wondering as he did so where she might be now, if she still wore her hair in a ponytail, the hazy green in her eyes.

"You could clear a couple of weeks, Jack, I imagine. Nights, of course, afternoons." Costain smiled and showed some teeth, not his but sparkling just the same. "You know the life."

"Not really."

"Didn't you have a pal? Played trumpet, I believe?"

"Saxophone."

"Ah, yes." As if they were interchangeable, a matter of fashion, an easy either-or.

Derek Becker had played Ronnie's once or twice, in his pomp—not headlining but taking the support slot with his quartet, Derek on tenor and soprano, occasionally baritone, along with the usual piano, bass, and drums. That was before the booze really hit him bad.

"Adams," Costain said, "it would just be a matter of babysitting, making sure she gets to the club on time, the occasional interview. You know the drill."

"Hardly seems necessary."

"She's not been in London in a good while. She'll feel more comfortable with a hand to hold, a shoulder to lean on." Costain smiled his professional smile. "That's metaphorically, of course."

They both knew he needed the money; there was little more, really, to discuss.

"She'll be staying at Le Meridien," Costain said. "On Piccadilly. From Friday. You can hook up with her there."

The meeting was over. Costain was already glancing at his watch, checking for messages on his mobile phone.

"All those years in Europe," Kiley said, getting to his feet, "no special reason she's not been back till now?"

Costain shook his head. "Representation, probably. Timing's not quite right." He flapped a hand vaguely at the air. "Sometimes it's just the way these things are."

"A little start-up fund would be good," Kiley said.

Costain reached into his suit jacket for his wallet and slid out two hundred and fifty in freshly minted twenties and tens. "Are you still seeing Kate these days?" he asked.

Kiley wasn't sure.

Kate Keenan was a freelance journalist with a free-ranging and often fierce column in the *Independent*. Kiley had met her by chance a little over a year ago, and they'd been sparring with each other ever since. She'd been sparring with him. Sometimes, Kiley thought, she took him the way some women took paracetamol.

"Only I was thinking," Costain said, "she and Dianne ought to get together. Dianne's a survivor, after all. Beat cancer. Saw off a couple of abusive husbands. Brought up a kid alone. She'd be perfect for one of those pieces Kate does. Profiles. You know the kind of thing."

"Ask her," Kiley said.

"I've tried," Costain said. "She doesn't seem to be answering my calls."

There had been an episode, Kiley knew, before he and Kate had met, when she had briefly fallen for Costain's slippery charm. It had been, as she liked to say, like slipping into cow shit on a rainy day.

"Is this part of what you're paying me for?" Kiley asked.

"Merely a favor," Costain said, smiling. "A small favor between friends."

Kiley thought he wouldn't mind an excuse to call Kate himself. "Okay," he said, "I'll do what I can. But I've got a favor to ask you in return."

The night before Dianne Adams opened on Frith Street, Costain organized a reception downstairs at the Pizza on the Park. Jazzers, journalists, publicists, and hangers-on, musicians like Guy Barker and Courtney Pine, for fifteen minutes Nicole Farhi and David Hare. Canapés and champagne.

Derek Becker was there with a quartet, playing music for schmoozing. Only it was better than that.

Becker was a hard-faced romantic who loved the fifties recordings of Stan Getz, especially the live sessions from the Shrine with Bob Brookmeyer on valve trombone; he still sent cards, birthday, Christmas, and Valentine, to the woman who'd had the good sense not to marry him some twenty years before. And he liked to drink.

A Bass man from way back, he could tolerate most beer, though he preferred it hand-pumped from the wood; in the right mood, he could appreciate a good wine; whiskey, he preferred Islay single malts, Lagavulin, say, or Laphroaig. In a pinch, anything would do.

Kiley had come across him once, sprawled along a bench on the southbound platform of the Northern Line at Leicester Square.

Vomit still drying on his shirt front, his face bruised, a cut splintering the bridge of his nose. Kiley had pulled him straight and used a tissue to wipe what he could from around his mouth and eyes, pushed a tenner down into his top pocket, and left him there to sleep it off. Thinking about it still gave him the occasional twinge of guilt.

That had been a good few years back, around the time Kiley had been forced to accept that his brief foray into professional soccer was over: the writing on the wall, the stud marks on his shins; the ache in his muscles that never quite went away, one game to the next.

Becker was still playing jazz whenever he could, but instead of Ronnie's, nowadays it was more likely to be the King's Head in Bexley, the Coach and Horses at Isleworth, depping on second tenor at some big band nostalgia weekend at Pontins.

And tonight Becker was looking sharp, sharper than Kiley had seen him in years, and sounding good. Adams clearly thought so. Calling for silence, she sang a couple of tunes with the band. "Stormy Weather," of course, and an up-tempo "Just One of Those Things." Stepping aside to let Becker solo, she smiled at him broadly. Made a point of praising his playing. After that his eyes followed her everywhere she went.

"She's still got it, hasn't she?" Kate said, appearing at Kiley's shoulder.

Kiley nodded. Kate was wearing an oatmeal-colored suit that would have made most other people look like something out of storage. Her hair shone.

"You didn't mind my calling you?" Kiley said.

Kate shook her head. "As long as it was only business." Accidentally brushing his arm as she moved away.

Later that night—that morning—Kiley, having delivered Dianne Adams safely to her hotel, was sitting with Derek Becker in a club on the edge of Soho. Both men were drinking scotch, Becker sipping his slowly, plenty of water in between.

Before the reception had wound down, Adams had spoken to Costain, Costain had spoken to the management at Ronnie's, and Becker had been added to the trio Adams had brought over from Copenhagen to accompany her.

"I suppose," Becker said, "I've got you to thank for that."

Kiley shook his head. "Thank whoever straightened you out."

Becker had another little taste of his scotch. "Let me tell you," he said. "A year ago, it was as bad as it gets. I was living in Walthamstow, a one-room flat. Hadn't worked in months. The last gig I'd had, a pub over in Chigwell, I hadn't even made the three steps up onto the stage. I was starting the day with a six-pack and by lunchtime it'd be cheap wine and ruby port. Except there wasn't any lunch. I hardly ate anything for weeks at a time, and when I did I threw it back up. And I stank. People turned away from me on the street. My clothes stank and my skin stank. The only thing I had left, the only thing I hadn't sold or hocked was my horn, and then I hocked that. Bought enough pills, a bottle of cheap scotch, and a packet of old-fashioned razor blades. Enough was more than enough."

He looked at Kiley and sipped his drink.

"And then I found this."

Snapping open his saxophone case, Becker flipped up the lid of the small compartment in which he kept his spare reeds. Lifting out something wrapped in dark velvet, he laid it in Kiley's hand.

"Open it."

Inside the folds was a bracelet, solid gold or merely plated Kiley couldn't be certain, though from the weight of it he guessed the former. Charms swayed and jingled lightly as he raised it up. A pair of dice. A key. What looked to be—an imitation, this, surely?—a Fabergé egg.

"I was shitting myself," Becker said. "Literally. Shit-scared of what I was going to do." He wiped his hand across his mouth before continuing. "I'd gone down into the toilets at Waterloo station, locked myself in one of the stalls. I suppose I fell, passed out maybe. Next thing I know I'm on my hands and knees, facedown in God knows what, and there it was. Waiting for me to find it."

An old Presley song played for a moment at the back of Kiley's head. "Your good-luck charm," he said.

"If you like, yes. The first piece of luck I'd had in months, that's for sure. Years. I mean, I couldn't believe it. I just sat there, staring at it. I don't know, waiting for it to disappear, I suppose."

"And when it didn't?"

Becker smiled. "I tipped the pills into the toilet bowl, took a belt at the scotch, and then poured away the rest. The most I've had, that day to this, is a small glass of an evening, maybe two. I know you'll hear people say you can't kick it that way, all or nothing, has to be, but all I can say is it works for me." He held out his hand, arm extended, no tremor, the fingers perfectly still. "Well, you've heard me play."

Kiley nodded. "And this?" he said.

"The bracelet?"

"Yes."

Forefinger and thumb, Becker took it from the palm of Kiley's hand.

"Used it to get my horn out of hock, buy a half-decent suit of clothes. When I was sober enough, I started phoning round, chasing work. Bar mitzvahs, weddings, anything, I didn't care. When I had enough I went back and redeemed it." He rewrapped the bracelet and stowed it carefully away. "Been with me ever since." He winked. "Like you say, my good-luck charm, eh?"

Kiley drained what little remained in his glass. "Time I wasn't here."

Standing, Becker shook his hand. "I owe you one, Jack."

"Just keep playing like tonight. Okay?"

The first few days went down without noticing, the way good days sometimes do. Adams's first set, opening night, was maybe just a little shaky, but after that everything gelled. The reviews were good, better than good, and by midweek word of mouth had kicked in and the place was packed. Becker, Kiley thought, was playing out his skull, seizing his chance with both hands. Adams worked up a routine with him on "Ghost of a Chance," just the two of them, voice and horn, winding around each other tighter and tighter as the song progressed. And, when they were through, Becker gazed at Dianne Adams with a mixture of gratitude and barely disguised desire.

Costain didn't have to call in many favors to have Adams interviewed at length on *Woman's Hour* and more succinctly on *Front Row;* after less than three hours' sleep, she was smiling from behind her makeup on *GMTV;* Claire Martin prerecorded a piece for her Friday jazz show and had Adams and Becker do their thing in the studio. Kate's profile in the *Indy* truthfully presented a woman with a genuine talent, a generous ego, and a carapaced heart.

All of this Kiley watched from a close distance, grateful for Costain's money without ever being sure why the agent had thought him necessary. Then, just shy of noon on the Thursday morning, he knew.

Adams paged him and had him come up to her room.

Pacing the floor in a hotel robe, sans paint and powder, she looked all of her age and then some. The photographs were spread out across the unmade bed. Dianne Adams onstage at Ronnie Scott's, opening night; walking through a mostly deserted Soho after the show, Kiley at her side; Adams passing through the hotel lobby, walking along the corridor from the lift, unlocking the door to her room. And then several slightly blurred and taken, Kiley guessed, from across the street with a telephoto lens: Adams undressing; sitting on her bed in her underwear talking on the telephone; crossing from the shower, nude save a towel wrapped around her head.

"When did you get these?" Kiley asked.

"Sometime this morning. An hour ago, maybe. Less. Someone pushed them under the door."

"No note? No message?"

Adams shook her head.

Kiley looked again at the pictures on the bed. "This is not just an obsessive fan."

Adams lit a cigarette and drew the smoke deep into her lungs. "No."

He looked at her then. "You know who these are from."

Adams sighed and for a moment closed her eyes. "When I was last in London, 'eighty-nine, I had this . . . this thing." She shrugged. "You're on tour, some strange city. It happens." From the already decimated minibar she took the last miniature of vodka and tipped it into a glass. "Whatever helps you through the night."

"He didn't see it that way."

"He?"

"Whoever this was. The affair. The fling. It meant more to him."

"To her."

Kiley caught his breath. "I see."

Adams sat on the edge of the bed and lit a cigarette. "Victoria Pride? I guess you know who she is?"

Kiley nodded. "I didn't know she was gay."

"She's not." Tilting back her head, Adams blew smoke toward the ceiling. "But then, neither am I. No more than most women, given the right situation."

"And that's what this was?"

"So it seemed."

Kiley's mind was working overtime. Victoria Pride had made her name starring in a television soap in the eighties, brittle and sexy and no better than she should be. After that she did a West End play, posed nearly nude for a national daily and had a few well-publicized skirmishes with the law, public order offenses, nothing serious. Her wedding to Keith Payne made the front page of both *OK* and *Hello!*, and their subsequent history of breaking up to make up was choreographed lovingly by the tabloid press. If Kiley remembered correctly, Victoria was set to play Maggie in a provincial tour of *Cat on a Hot Tin Roof*.

But he didn't think Victoria was the problem.

"Payne knew about this?" Kiley said.

Adams released smoke to the ceiling. "Let's say he found out."

One image of Keith Payne stuck in Kiley's memory. A newspaper photograph. A tall man, six-four or -five, Payne was being escorted across the tarmac from a plane, handcuffed to one of the two police officers walking alongside. Tanned, hair cut short, he was wearing a dark polo shirt outside dark chinos, what was obviously a Rolex on his wrist. Relaxed, confident, a smile on his handsome face.

Kiley couldn't recall the exact details, save that Payne had been extradited from Portugal to face charges arising from a bullion robbery at Heathrow. The resulting court case had all but collapsed amid crumbling evidence and accusations of police entrapment, and Payne had finally been sentenced to eight years for conspiracy to commit robbery. He would have been released, Kiley guessed, after serving no more than five. Whereas his former colleague, who had appeared as a witness for the prosecution and was handed down a lenient eighteen months, was the unfortunate victim of a hit-and-run incident less than two weeks after being released from prison. The vehicle was found abandoned half a mile away, and the driver never traced.

Payne, Kiley guessed, didn't take kindly to being crossed.

"When he found out," Kiley said, "about you and Victoria, what did he do?"

"Bought her flowers, a new dress, took her to the Caprice, knocked out two of her teeth. He came to the hotel where I was staying and trashed the room, smashed the mirror opposite the bed, and held a piece of glass to my face. Told me that if he ever as much as saw me near Victoria again he'd carve me up."

"You believed him."

"I took the first flight out next morning."

"And you've not been back since."

"Till now."

"Costain knew this?"

"I suppose."

Yes, Kiley thought, I bet he did.

Adams drained her glass and swiveled toward the telephone. "I'm calling room service for a drink."

"Go ahead."

"You want anything?"

Kiley shook his head. "So have you seen her?" he asked when she was through.

"No. But she sent me this." The card had a black-and-white photograph, artfully posed, of lilies in a slim white vase; the message inside read *Knock 'em dead* and was signed *Victoria* with a large red kiss. "That and a bottle of champagne on opening night."

"And that's all?"

"That's all."

Kiley thought it might be enough.

Adams ran her fingers across the photographs beside her on the bed. "It's him, isn't it?"

"I imagine so."

"Why? Why these?"

Some men, Kiley knew, got off on the idea of their wives or girlfriends having affairs with other women, positively encouraged it, but it didn't seem Payne was one of those.

"He's letting you know he knows where you are, knows your every move. If you see Victoria, he'll know."

Adams's eyes flicked toward the mirror on the hotel wall. "And if I do, he'll carry out his threat."

"He'll try."

"You could stop him."

Kiley wasn't sure. "Are you going to see her?" he asked.

Adams shook her head. "What if she tries to see me?"

Kiley smiled; close to a smile, at least. "We'll try and head her off at the pass."

That night, after the show, she asked Becker back to her hotel for a drink and, as he sat with his single scotch and water, invited him to share her bed.

"She's using you," Kiley said the next morning, Becker bleary-eyed over his coffee in Old Compton Street.

Becker found the energy to wink. "And how," he said.

Kiley told him about Payne, and all Becker did was shrug.

"He's dangerous, Derek."

"He's just a two-bit gangster, right?"

"You mean like Coltrane was a two-bit sax player?"

"Jack," Becker said, grasping Kiley by the arm, "you worry too much, you know that?"

The following afternoon Adams and the band were rehearsing at Ronnie's, Dianne wanting to work up some new numbers for the weekend. Kiley thought it was unlikely Payne would show his hand in such a public place, but rang Costain and asked him to be around in case.

"I thought that was what I was paying you for," Costain said.

"If he breaks your arm," Kiley said, "take it out of my salary."

Kiley had been checking out the *Stage. Cat on a Hot Tin Roof* was already on the road, this week Leicester, next week Richmond. Close enough to make a trip into the center of London for its star a distinct possibility. He sat in the Haymarket bar and waited for the matinee performance to finish. Thirty minutes after the curtain came down, Victoria Pride was sitting in her robe in her dressing room, most of the makeup removed from her face, a cigarette between her lips. Close up, she didn't look young anymore, but she still looked good.

"You're from the *Mail*," she said, crossing her legs.

Kiley leaned back against the door as it closed behind him. "I lied."

She studied him then, taking him in. "Should I call the management? Have you thrown out?" Her voice was still smeared with the southern accent she'd used in the play.

"Probably not."

"You're not some crazy fan?"

Kiley shook his head.

"No, I suppose you're not." She took one last drag at her cigarette. "Just as long as you're here, there's a bottle of wine in that excuse for a fridge. Why don't you grab a couple of those glasses, pour us both a drink? Then you can tell me what you really want."

The wine was a little sweet for Kiley's taste and not quite cold enough.

"Are you planning to see Dianne Adams while she's in town?" Kiley said.

"Oh, shit!" A little of the wine spilled on Victoria's robe. "Did Keith send you?"

"I think I'm batting for the other side."

"You think?"

"He threatened her before."

"That's just his way."

"His way sometimes extends to hit-and-run."

"That's bullshit!"

"Is it?"

Victoria swung her legs around and faced the mirror; dabbed cream onto some cotton wool and wiped the residue of makeup from around her eyes.

"Keith," Kiley said. "You let him know about the card and the champagne."

"Maybe."

"Just like you let him know about you and Dianne."

Victoria laughed, low and loud. "It keeps him on his toes."

"Then shall we say it's served its purpose this time? You'll keep away? Unless you want her to get hurt, that is?"

She looked at him in the mirror. "No," she said. "I don't want that."

His phone rang almost as soon as he stepped through the door. Costain.

"Why don't you get yourself a mobile, for fuck's sake? I've been trying to get hold of you the best part of an hour."

"What happened?"

"Keith Payne came to the club, walked right in off the street in the middle of rehearsals. Couple of his minders with him. One of the staff tried to stop them and got thumped for his trouble. Wanted to talk to Dianne, that's what he said. Talk to her on her own."

Kiley waited, fearing the worst.

"Your pal, Becker, all of a sudden he's got the balls of a brass monkey. Told Payne to come back that evening, pay his money along with all the other punters. Miss Adams was an artiste and right now she was working." Costain couldn't quite disguise his admiration. "I doubt anyone's spoken to Keith Payne like that in twenty years. Not and lived to tell the tale."

"He didn't do anything?"

"Someone from the club had called the police. Payne obviously didn't think it was worth the hassle. Turned around and left. But you should have seen the expression on his face."

Kiley thought he could hazard a guess.

Later that evening he phoned Victoria Pride at the theater. "Your husband, I need to see him."

The house was forty minutes north of London, nestled in the Hertfordshire countryside, the day warm enough for Payne to be on a lounge near the pool. A gofer brought them both a cold beer.

"Hear that?" Payne said. "Fuckin' birdsong. Amazing."

Kiley could hear birds sometimes, above the noise of traffic from the Holloway Road. He kept it to himself.

"Vicki says you went to see her."

"Dianne Adams, I wanted to make sure there wouldn't be any trouble."

"If that dyke comes sniffin' round."

"She won't."

"That business with her and Vicki, a soddin' aberration. All it was. Over and done. And then Vicki, all of a sudden she's sending fuckin' champagne and fuck knows what."

"You want to know what I think?" Kiley said.

A flicker of Payne's pale blue eyes gave permission.

"I think she does it to put a hair up your arse."

Payne gave it a moment's thought and laughed. "You could be right."

"And Becker, he was just sounding off. Trying to look big."

"People don't talk to me like that. Nobody talks to me like that. Especially a tosser like him."

"Sticks and stones. Besides, like you say, who is he? Becker? He's nothing."

Swift to his feet for a big man, Payne held out his hand. "You're right."

"You won't hold a grudge?"

Payne's grip was firm. "You've got my word."

The remainder of Dianne Adams's engagement passed without incident. Victoria Pride stayed away. By the final weekend it was standing room only and, spurred on by the crowd and the band, Adams's voice seemed to find new dynamics, new depth.

Of course, Becker told her about the bracelet during one of those languorous times when they lay in her hotel bed, feeling the lust slowly ebb away. He even offered it to her as a present, half hoping she would refuse, which she did. "It's beautiful," she said. "And it's a beautiful thought. But it's your good-luck charm. You don't want to lose it now."

On the last night at Ronnie's, she thanked him profusely onstage for his playing and presented him with a charm in the shape of a saxophone. "A little something to remember me by."

"You know," she said, outside on the pavement later, "next month we've got this tour, Italy, Switzerland. You should come with us."

"I'd like that," Becker said.

"I'll call you," she said, and kissed him on the mouth.

She never did.

Costain thanked Kiley for a job well done and with part of his fee Kiley acquired an expensive mobile phone and waited for that also to ring.

Three weeks later, as Derek Becker was walking through Soho after a gig on Dean Street, gone one A.M. A car pulled up alongside him and three men got out. Quiet and quick. They grabbed Becker and dragged him into an alley and beat him with gloved hands and booted feet. Then they threw him back against the wall and two of them held out his arms at the wrist, fingers spread, while the third drew a pair of pliers from the pocket of his combat pants. One of them stuffed a strip of toweling into his mouth to stifle the screams.

Becker's instrument case had already fallen open to the ground, and as they left one of the men trod almost nonchalantly on the bell of the saxophone before booting it hard away. A second man picked up the case and hurled it into the darkness at the alley's end, the bracelet, complete with its newly attached charm, sailing unseen into the deepest corner, carrying with it all of Becker's newfound luck.

It was several days before Kiley heard what had happened and went to see Becker in his flat in Walthamstow, bringing a couple of paperbacks and a bottle of single malt.

"Gonna have to turn the pages for me, Jack. Read them as well."

His hands were still bandaged and his left eye still swollen closed.

"I'm sorry," Kiley said and opened the scotch.

"You know what, Jack?" Becker said after the first sip. "Next time, don't do me no favors, right?"

PLAN B

Kelley Armstrong

Monday, August 10

Deanna lifted the charm bracelet and shifted closer to the bedside lamp for a better look.

"Oh, God," she said. "Reminds me of the bracelet my dad bought me when I turned thirteen. I asked for the new Guns N' Roses tape, and he gave me one of these. Bastard."

Gregory double-checked his tie in the mirror. "Think Abby will like it?"

"Shit, yeah. If any grown woman was made for charm bracelets, it's Abby." Deanna rolled onto her back and draped the bracelet around her breast. "Looks better on me, though, don't you think?"

Gregory chuckled but continued adjusting his tie. Deanna slid the bracelet down her stomach, spread her legs, and dangled it there.

"Wanna play hide and seek?" she asked.

She wrapped the bracelet around her index finger and waggled it closer to her crotch. Gregory stopped fussing with his tie and watched. Before the bracelet disappeared, he grabbed her hand.

"Uh-uh," he said. "Tempting, but no. I've heard of giving your wife a gift smelling of another woman's perfume, but that would go a bit far."

"Like she'd notice." Deanna flipped onto her stomach. "Probably doesn't even know what it smells like. The only time Abby lets her hand drift south of her belly button is when she's wiping her twat, and she'd probably avoid that if she could."

"That, my dear, sounds remarkably like jealousy."

"No, *my dear*, it sounds remarkably like impatience."

He shrugged on his jacket. "These things take time. Every detail must be planned to perfection."

"Don't pull that shit on me, babe. You aren't dragging your heels plotting how to get away with it. You have that figured out. Now you're just trying to decide how you want to do it. You're in no rush to get to the reality, 'cause you're too busy enjoying the fantasy."

He grinned. "This is true. Shooting versus stabbing versus strangulation. It's a big decision. I only get to do it once, sadly."

"At this rate, you'll never get around to doing it at all."

"How about Friday?"

Deanna popped up her head, then narrowed her eyes. "Ha-ha."

"I'm quite serious." Gregory patted his pockets and pulled out his car keys. "Does Friday work for you?"

She nodded, eyes still wary.

"It's a date, then," he said. "I'll see you tomorrow and we'll talk. I'm thinking stabbing. Messier, but more painful. Abby deserves the best."

He smiled, blew her a kiss, and disappeared out the door.

Deanna sat up and looked out the window. The cottage Gregory had rented for her was perched on a cliff overlooking the ocean. When she cast her gaze out across the water, it looked mirror smooth, with brightly colored yachts and sailboats bobbing about like children's toys. Cotton-candy clouds drifted across the aquamarine sky. Farther down the shore, a freshly painted red and white lighthouse gleamed like a peppermint stick. It was a picture so perfect that if you painted it, no one would believe it was taken from life. Yet if she looked down, straight down, she found herself staring into a maelstrom of mud and garbage. All the trash those distant boats tossed overboard wound up here, at the bottom of the cliff, where beer cans and empty sunscreen bottles swirled in whirlpools crested with dirty foam.

Be not deceived, for as ye sow, so shall ye reap. The Bible quote came so fast it brought a chill, and she shivered, yanking down the window shade.

For as ye sow, so shall ye reap. How deeply the lessons of youth burrow into the brain. She could still see her father in the pulpit, his lips forming those words. The lessons of youth, driven in with the help of a liberally wielded belt.

At fifteen, Deanna had run from those lessons, run all the way to Toronto, and found the hell her father prophesied for her. At seventeen, she mistook Satan for savior, becoming a wealthy businessman's toy in return for promises of gold rings and happily ever after. After two years, he discarded her like a used condom.

Before he could pass her apartment to his next toy, she'd broken in, intent on taking everything she could carry. Then she'd found the photos he'd taken of them together. And they'd given her an idea. For as ye sow, so shall ye reap. There had to be consequences. A price to be paid . . . but not by her.

It had been laughably easy. Of course, she hadn't asked for much. She'd been naive, having no idea how much those photos were worth to someone who valued his family-man reputation above all. But, with practice, she'd learned. For ten years now, she'd made her living having affairs with wealthy married men, then demanding money to keep her mouth shut.

Now, finally, that had all come to an end. One last mortal sin, and she'd be free.

Deanna opened the drawer of her bedside table and reached inside. Beneath the pile of lingerie was a postcard of the French Riviera. She didn't pull it out, just ran her fingers over its glossy surface. She closed her eyes and remembered when they'd bought it. She'd seen it in the display rack and pulled it out, waving it like a flag.

"Here! This is where I want to go."

An indulgent smile. "Then that's where we'll go."

He'd said Friday. Did he mean it? Could she book the tickets now? She stroked the postcard. No, not yet. Give it another couple of days. Make sure he meant it this time.

"How retro," Abby said, waving her wrist above the plate of mussels.

She snaked her hand over her head and wriggled in her seat like a belly dancer, her laughter tinkling chime for chime with the bracelet. The tiny dock-turned-patio held only a half-dozen tables, but every male eye at every one of those tables slid an appreciative look Abby's way, and an envious one at Gregory. He snorted under his breath. Fools.

He stabbed through his chowder, looking for something edible.

"It's so cute," Abby said. "Did you pick it up in London?"

"You could say that. So, you like it?"

"Love it." She fingered the charms. "Which one's for me?"

"All of them."

"No, silly, I mean: which charm did you buy for me? That's the tradition, you know. If you give someone a charm bracelet, you have to buy them the first charm, something meaningful."

Like hell. He wasn't about to waste money on another trinket. Not when it'd be lying on the ocean floor by the weekend. He peered at the charms. A key, a train, a saxophone . . .

"The lighthouse," he said. "I bought you the lighthouse."

"Oh?" she said, nose wrinkling as she examined the charm. "That's . . . interesting. Why'd you pick that?"

He waved his hand at the ocean. "Because it made me think of here. Your favorite restaurant."

"But the lighthouse isn't—" She leaned as far back in her chair as she could. "Well, I guess maybe you could see it from here. On a clear day. If you squint hard enough. Well, it's the thought that counts, and I *do* love it here. The lights over the water. The smell of the ocean. Heaven."

Heaven. Right. They lived in a town with two four-star restaurants, and Abby's idea of heaven was a wharfside dive where the specialties were beer, beer, and mussels soaked in beer. At least in town he could hope to see someone, make a contact that would lead to a sale. But none of the summer people came here. Only locals, and no local bought a thousand-dollar painting of the Atlantic Ocean when they could see it through their kitchen window.

The screen door leading to the patio creaked open. Out of habit, he looked, half hoping it might be one of the American celebrities who summered in town. He caught a flash of sun-streaked blond hair and a male face hidden by the shadows of the overhang.

The man scanned the patio, then stepped back fast. The door squeaked shut. Gregory's eyes shot to Abby as her gaze swiveled back to the harbor.

"Was that Zack?" he asked.

"Hmm?" Her bright blue eyes turned to meet his, as studiously vacant as ever.

Gregory's jaw tightened. "Zack. Your summer intern. Was that him?"

"Where, hon?"

Gregory bit off a reply. This wasn't the time to start sounding like a jealous husband, not now, when all it would take was one such comment passed from Abby to a friend to give him motive for murder. If Abby wanted to cheat on him, she'd had plenty of opportunity to do so before now. As lousy as their marriage was, Abby was satisfied with it. She was satisfied with him. And why not? She had not only a wealthy handsome husband but a husband who owned a successful art gallery, where every pathetic seascape she daubed onto canvas found a prominent place on the walls. The perfect catch for a pretty young art student of mediocre talent.

The moment he'd laid eyes on Abigail Landry at a Montreal art show, he thought *he* had found his perfect catch. A beautiful, lauded young painter, the ideal showpiece artist for his new Nova Scotia seaside gallery, and the ideal showpiece wife for him. The trouble had started three months after the wedding, when she'd refused to paint a custom-ordered portrait of a schnauzer wearing sunglasses. He'd lost his temper and smacked her. She'd said nothing, just gone into her studio and started the dog's portrait. Then the next day she'd waltzed in on a private meeting with two of his best clients, her black eye on full display, smiling sweetly and asking if anyone wanted iced tea, leaving him stammering to explain.

Before long, divorce was out of the question. Her silly seascapes accounted for seventy percent of the gallery's income. Then, two years ago, when the stock market plunge had wiped out his finances, she'd glided to his rescue with her own well-invested nest egg, offered as sweetly and as easily as the iced tea. So he was trapped.

"But not for long," he murmured.

Another vacant-eyed "Hmm?"

He smiled and patted her hand. "Nothing, my dear. I'm glad you like the bracelet."

Wednesday, August 12

Abby lifted the crimson-coated brush, in her mind seeing the paint move from the bristles to the canvas. No, not quite right. She lowered the brush and studied the picture. The red would be too harsh. Too *expected*. She needed something more surprising there. She laid the brush aside. Tomorrow she'd be better able to concentrate on finding the right shade. Tonight . . . She smiled. Well, tonight she had other things on her mind.

She moved the painting to the locked room in the back, then picked up the canvas propped against the wall and placed it on the now-vacant easel. She looked at the half-finished seascape. No room for surprises there. Blue sea, blue sky, white and gray rocks. Assembly-line art. This was what her talent was reduced to, putting her name on schlock while her true work was shipped out of the country and sold under a false name so Gregory didn't find out. Seascapes made money. Money made Gregory happy. So Abby painted seascapes, seascapes, and more seascapes, with the occasional crumbling barn thrown in for variety.

She glanced at the clock. Soon, very soon.

She lifted the brush to clean it, then stopped and stared at the painting. As if of its own accord, her hand moved to the canvas and the bristles streaked red across the surf. Too much red. She daubed the tip in the white and brushed it lightly through the red, thinning and spreading it until it became a pink clot on the wave. The surf tinted with blood. A small smile played on Abby's lips. Then she took a fresh brush and blotted out the red with indigo.

As she painted, a blob of blue fell on her arm. She swiped at it absently, then stopped, seeing the blue swirl against her pale skin. It looked like a Maori tattoo. She dabbed her finger in the paint and accentuated the resemblance. There. Cheaper than henna, less permanent than ink. As she laughed, she caught a glimpse of herself in the mirror across the room and grinned.

Any minute now she'd hear the key turn in the back lock. And then . . . A rush of heat started in her belly and plunged down. She looked at her reflection again, gaze dropping to the twin dots pressing hard against the front of her sundress. She rolled her shoulders and sighed as the fabric brushed her nipples. Still looking in the mirror, she unzipped her dress and let it fall. She grinned at her reflection. Not bad. Not bad at all.

Her eyes went to the blue tattoo on her forearm. An unexpected burst of color. She turned to the easel, lifted the paintbrush, and grazed it lightly over one hardened nipple. She sighed, then tickled the brush hairs around the aureole of her other nipple.

Another dip of paint, ocher this time. She stroked lines down her torso, shivering at the cool touch of the paint against her skin. Next the red, on her stomach, drawing lazy circles and zigzags. She parted her legs, lowered the brush, and swirled it across her inner thigh. As she painted lower, she let the end of the brush dart between her legs, prodding like an uncertain lover's finger, hesitant yet eager. Each time it made contact, she caught her breath and glanced at her expression in the mirror. She forced herself to finish her work, painting the other thigh to match the first, letting the brush tip probe her only when it came in contact naturally. Then, when she finished, she took the brush and turned it around, so her hand wielded the plastic tip instead of the paint-soaked bristle. She spread her legs and used the tip to tickle the hard nub within.

The back door clicked open. Abby grinned and lifted the brush, painting one last stroke of red from her crotch to her breasts. A bustle of motion in the doorway, silence, then a sharp intake of breath.

Abby looked up and flourished a hand at her painted body.

"What do you think?" she said. "A work of art?"

"A masterpiece."

Friday, August 14

Gregory switched the cell phone to his other ear and took his keys from the ignition.

"Yes, that's right, a room on the west side. Not the east side.

There was construction on the east side last time and it kept me up all night." He paused. "Good. Hold on, there's more. I want extra towels. Your housecleaning staff never leave enough towels."

The hotel clerk assured him everything would meet his satisfaction. It wouldn't, though. Gregory would make sure of that. He'd find something to pester them about at the front desk, raise a little fuss, just enough so that when the police asked the clerk whether she remembered Gregory, she'd roll her eyes and say "Oh, yes, I remember him."

Once he'd finished here, he'd stop by Deanna's cottage and make sure everything was ready. He chuckled. Deanna was ready, that was certain. Ready, willing, and chomping at the bit. She wanted to be free of Abby almost as much as he did. Last night when he'd gone by to finalize the plans, he'd barely made it through the door before she'd pounced and given him a taste of what life would be like post-Abby. He felt himself harden at the memory. A remarkable woman, Deanna was. He only hoped everything went well tonight. It would be a shame to lose her.

Last night she'd suggested—not for the first time—that she join him at the hotel, so she could corroborate his alibi. He'd gently reminded her that this wasn't a wise idea. When the police dug into his personal life, he knew they'd find he had a history of infidelity, but there was no sense doing their homework for them. Or so he'd told Deanna. The truth was that Gregory didn't want anyone seeing them together tonight. Better to leave her behind . . . in close proximity to his about-to-be-murdered wife.

Not that he had any intention of offering up Deanna as a scapegoat. But, well, if things went bad, it always helped to have a plan B. Deanna had bought the weapons and the tools, so it would be easy enough to steer the police in her direction. If the need arose, he had a speech all prepared, the heartrending confession of an unfaithful husband who had realized he still loved his wife and told his mistress it was over, then made the tragic mistake of leaving on a business trip to Halifax that same day, never dreaming his scorned lover might wreak her revenge while he was gone. He'd practiced his lines in front of the mirror until he could choke up on cue.

He pushed open the door to the gallery. A muted laugh tinkled out, followed by a deep chuckle that grated down Gregory's spine. He paused, holding the door half shut so the greeting bell wouldn't alert Abby and Zack. The murmur of their voices floated out from the back room. Zack laughed again. Gregory eased the door open, trying to slide in before it opened wide enough to set off the bell. He was halfway through when it chimed.

The voices in the back room stopped suddenly. Zack peeked around the corner, saw who it was, then said something to Abby, too low for Gregory to hear. The intern backed out of the studio.

"Ab? I'll grab coffee on my way back, okay?"

Abby appeared from the back room, carrying a wrapped canvas, and beamed a smile at Zack. "Perfect. Thanks."

As Zack strode out the front door, he slid a half-smirk Gregory's way, as if being allowed to play errand boy for Abby was some great honor Gregory could only dream of. Art student, my ass. The kid looked as if he should be riding the waves, not painting them. Not that Gregory cared. If Abby wanted to play teacher with California Picasso, she was welcome to him. He only hoped the kid wouldn't cause trouble later.

"I sold the new Martin's Point oil," Abby said, laying the canvas on the counter. "Got the asking price too. A couple from Chicago. Once they heard the exchange rate, they didn't care to dicker."

"Good, good. I just stopped by to make sure everything was okay before I left for my meeting."

"You'll be staying for the weekend, I assume."

Being little more than an hour from Halifax, there was no need for him to stay the weekend and they both knew it, just as they knew that he usually stayed and why he usually stayed. Yet Abby asked as casually as if she'd asked whether he'd take Highway 3 or 103, a matter of no interest to her either way. The thread of anger that rippled through him surprised him, as it always did, and in surprising him only angered him more.

"Yes, I'll be staying the weekend. With a friend."

He hated himself for tacking that on the end, hated himself for studying her reaction, and hated her even more for not giving one.

"Don't forget we're having dinner at the Greenways' on Sunday," she said. "Eight o'clock."

"I'll be there."

She nodded, then disappeared into the back room. He stifled the urge to call out a good-bye, turned on his heel, and left.

"You've reached the voice mail of Gregory Keith—"

Abby sighed and hung up.

"Still no answer?" Zack asked as he flipped the gallery OPEN sign to CLOSED.

"He must have turned off his cell. Maybe he's still in a meeting."

Zack cast a pointed look into the darkening night. "Uh-huh."

"Sometimes his meetings run late," she offered lamely. "I'll try once more from home, then call Mr. Strom back and tell him we're still considering his offer."

She turned off the main lights as Zack locked the front door. He followed her into the studio and trailed out the back door after her.

"Go," Gregory hissed.

Deanna lurched from behind the bushes as Abby parked at the top of the long drive. Gregory had to squint to see her. For a half mile in either direction, the only lights were the security floods beaming on the renovated farmhouse.

Abby climbed from her car. She started to lock it, then stopped, seeing Deanna stumbling up the driveway, her clothes torn and bloodstained. From this distance Gregory couldn't see his wife's expression, but he could imagine it. Eyes wide, mouth dropping open, a whispered "oh."

Abby jogged down the driveway toward Deanna. Smatterings of their conversation drifted to him.

"—accident—help—"

Abby gestured at the house. "—nine one one—?" She didn't have a cell phone, hated them.

Deanna grabbed Abby's arm, her voice shrill with panic. "—son—trapped—please—"

Then Abby did what Gregory knew she'd do. She followed Deanna. When Deanna stumbled, Abby grabbed her arm and draped it around her shoulders, supporting the injured woman. Very heroic. Also very stupid, because when she reached the shadows of the cedar hedge, all Deanna had to do was trip Abby, then throw her weight on top of her, and Abby went down. Deanna shoved a chloroform-soaked cloth over Abby's mouth and nose, and she stayed down.

Deanna turned toward Gregory's hiding spot, but he didn't step out. Not yet. First, he was making damn sure Abby was out cold. If anything went wrong, Deanna's face would be the only one she remembered seeing. He motioned for Deanna to slap Abby. She did. When Abby didn't move, Deanna slapped her again, the sound cracking through the silence.

"I think that's enough, my dear," Gregory said, stepping from the bushes.

He tossed Deanna the rope and watched her tie Abby up. Then he took over.

Deanna slapped Abby again, the sound echoing the rhythmic smack of the waves against the boat hull. Gregory shifted, fighting the growing worm of pique in his gut. She wasn't waking up.

What if she didn't? He'd have to go through with it, of course, killing her, but he'd really hoped she'd be awake. He wanted her to see who wielded the knife, to regain the power she'd sucked from him over the years.

Gregory grabbed the knife.

"I'll wake her—"

Deanna snatched it from his hand. "No, let me."

Deanna lowered the knife tip to Abby's cheek and pressed it against her pale skin. A single drop of blood welled up. Abby's eyes flew open. Gregory reached for the knife, but Abby bucked suddenly, startling them both, and the knife clattered to the deck. Abby jerked against her bonds, wriggling wildly. Deanna dove to hold her down. In the struggle, Deanna's foot knocked the knife across the deck.

"Don't!" Gregory said. "She's tied. She's not going anywhere."

Deanna nodded and pulled back from Abby. She looked around, gaze going to the knife by the cabin door.

"I'll get that," Deanna said.

As she pushed to her feet, Gregory took her place, and loomed over his terrified wife.

"Ah, now she's afraid," he said, smiling down at her. "Smart girl. Don't worry. This won't hurt a bit." He grinned. "It'll hurt a lot."

"Gregory?" Deanna said behind him.

His lips tightened at the interruption. He turned to her. "What?"

"Yesterday you asked if I was looking forward to this. I said I wasn't." She bit her lip, looking sheepish. "Well, I just wanted to let you know, I lied. We are looking forward to this."

"Good. Now—" He stopped. "We—?"

Deanna smiled. Her gaze moved over his shoulder.

"Yes," she said. "We."

He turned, following her gaze. Behind him, Abby sat up, tugging the rope from her wrists.

"Wha—?" he began.

Something cracked against the side of his head. He stumbled and managed to turn just enough to see Deanna raise the fire extinguisher again. She swung it.

Abby and Deanna stood at the side of the boat, watching Gregory's body sink into the inky water. A late-night fog was rolling in, a dense gray blanket barely pierced by the distant lighthouse beam.

"You're sure he won't wash up on shore?" Deanna asked, nibbling her thumbnail.

"Which way is the tide going, hon?" Abby asked gently.

"Out. Right. You said that. I forgot. Sorry."

"That's okay. You did a good job."

Good, but not perfect, Abby thought as she bent to wipe a smear of blood from the deck. She'd have to treat that later. If the first blow had succeeded, there wouldn't be any blood. It took a second hit to the head to induce bleeding. But Deanna hadn't known that, and Abby hadn't thought to mention it, and, really, it wasn't as if Abby would have changed her mind when the first blow failed.

She stood to see Deanna frowning as she squinted overboard, trying to see Gregory's body through the fog.

"It's okay, hon," Abby said. "He's definitely heading out to sea and will be for a few hours yet. Even if he does eventually wash up on shore, it won't be near here."

"But they'll identify him, won't they?"

"Yes. But then what? He wasn't shot. He wasn't stabbed. He hit his head and drowned. Happens all the time. Even if they suspect something, it can't be linked to us. We were careful."

"You're right," Deanna said, forcing a small smile. "You're always right."

Abby walked to Deanna, smiling. "Not always. I married that bastard, didn't I?"

She put her arms around Deanna's neck and leaned in. Their lips met. Deanna's parted, hesitant at first, as always, as if unsure, maybe still a little shocked at herself. A minister's daughter in spite of everything, Abby thought. She kept the kiss gentle and tentative, their lips barely touching. After a moment, Deanna tried to pull Abby closer, but she held back, teasing Deanna with modest kisses.

Abby reached down to the bottom of Deanna's blouse and began to unbutton it, her hands moving as slow as her lips. Deanna gave a soft growl of impatience, but Abby only chuckled. Only when the blouse was fully unbuttoned did Abby let her hands touch Deanna's skin. She pressed her fingertips against Deanna's stomach, then traced twin lines up her rib cage. She cupped Deanna's bare breasts and slid her thumbs over her hard nipples. Deanna groaned, grabbed the back of Abby's head and kissed her, all shyness gone. As Abby returned the kiss, heat throbbed through her. Perhaps just once more . . . But no. She couldn't.

She wrapped her hands in Deanna's hair and eased her back a step. Deanna's balance faltered. She tore her lips from Abby's to shout a warning that she was too close to the edge of the boat. But Abby already knew that.

She put her hands around Deanna's wrist and thrust her away. Deanna started to fall. She grabbed blindly and caught Abby's charm bracelet, but the clasp came apart. Deanna's arms windmilled as she fell over the edge.

Abby walked to the back of the boat and pulled up the anchor. In the water below Deanna thrashed and screamed. As Abby headed to the cabin, she looked down to see Deanna frantically trying to get a hold on the smooth side of the boat.

"I can't swim!" Deanna shouted.

"Yes," Abby said. "I know."

She walked into the cabin and started the engine. She moved the boat out of Deanna's reach, then waited and watched as Deanna's blond head bobbed like a beacon through the fog.

When Deanna finally sank and didn't resurface, Abby pushed the throttle forward and headed for shore.

Thursday, August 20

Abby parked at the top of the driveway and she rubbed her hands over her face. God, she was so sick of playing the distraught wife. How much longer did she have to do this? The last week had seemed endless. Pretending to look up expectantly each time the bells chimed over the gallery door. Murmuring "I'm sure he will" whenever someone reassured her that her missing husband would come home soon. Enduring Zack's constant, mooning "I'm here for you" glances.

It hadn't taken long for the police to discover that her missing husband had been renting a cottage outside town for his mistress, who was, conveniently, also missing. A quick check of their shared bank accounts showed that Gregory had slowly drained out nearly ten thousand dollars over the last month. That had been Abby's idea, passed through Deanna to Gregory's ear. As Deanna had warned Gregory, he couldn't be seen dipping into the money right after his wife's murder. Better to siphon some out early so they'd have celebration cash during the mourning period. Now, with a missing husband, a missing mistress, and missing money, it didn't take a genius to realize Gregory had cut his losses and left. Too bad all their assets were jointly held, meaning his abandoned wife could now use them as she wished. She even had the ten grand in cash Deanna had squirreled away for them.

Abby grabbed the pile of mail from the passenger seat and climbed out. As she circled around the front of the car, she leafed through the bills, flyers, and notes of sympathy. An unfamiliar postage stamp caught her attention. France? Who did she know in France? When she looked at the handwriting on the front, she froze. It wasn't possible. It *wasn't.*

Hands trembling, Abby tore open the envelope. In her haste, she ripped it too fast and the contents flew out. A postcard sailed to the ground.

"No," Abby said. "No!"

Deanna stood by the water's edge, her arms wrapped around her, shivering as a cool night breeze blew off the Mediterranean. Behind her the lights of the French Riviera flickered in the darkness, a scene that nearly matched the one on her postcard . . . the postcard Abby now had.

Deanna felt the sharp edges of the charms biting into her palm. She looked down at the bracelet in her hand. When she'd dove into the ocean, leaving Abby to think she'd drowned, Deanna had still clutched the bracelet. She'd kept it, thinking maybe she'd send it back to Abby as proof that she was alive. But then she'd decided the postcard would be enough . . . the postcard they'd picked out together when they'd first hatched their plan, when Deanna had still thought—hoped—that Abby and her promises had been real.

Deanna fingered the charms on the bracelet, stopping at the lighthouse. She remembered her last evening with Abby, sitting behind the cover of the lighthouse, dipping their feet in the surf, their clothing strewn over the rocks and bushes. Abby had asked, oh so casually, how well Deanna could swim. And, as accustomed as she was to lies and deceit from her lovers, Deanna still almost fell for it. The truth had been on her lips, ready to tell Abby that she'd been captain of the swim team before she'd dropped out of school. Instead, when she opened her mouth, she heard herself say, "Me? Can't swim a stroke. Never learned how."

Deanna had tried to look past it, told herself she was too suspicious. And yet . . . Well, it never hurts to have a plan B.

She let the lighthouse charm fall from her fingers. That had been *her* lucky charm that night, when the unexpected fog rolled in. She'd followed its beam back to shore. Then, before she'd left town, she'd returned to the lighthouse one last time, to leave something for Abby. On the postcard, she'd written only one line, instructing Abby to look for further "correspondence" at the "charmed" place. There, in the very spot where she'd deceived her lover, Abby would find detailed instructions on how to make her penance, on the exact penalty she must pay. The demand was fair. Not enough to send Abby into bankruptcy, just enough to hurt. For every action, there is a price to be paid. Deanna knew that, and now so would Abby.

Deanna drew back her arm and pitched the bracelet into the water. Then she turned and headed back to the hotel.

THE SUMMER OF '66

Tomas Ross

There is a theory that claims writing has a salutary effect on the writer. This is why therapists and psychiatrists sometimes advise their clients not to talk but to write; to write down everything that is bugging, frustrating, or traumatizing them. It is the time-honored function of the young girl's "Dear Diary," of the desperate jottings of spurned lovers, psychopaths, would-be suicides, and prisoners. It sometimes produces wonderful poetry, prose, or drama, but first and foremost it has always been intended as a mirror for the writer.

I'm a writer, so you'd think it would be no problem for me, but I couldn't manage it. I did my best, I started with myself, with my life, with what made me tick (to the extent that anyone knows that about himself), but somehow, without wanting to, I kept digressing, inventing people and circumstances that had nothing to do with me or with Lilly. A psychiatrist would call it repression. Perhaps that was what it was, though I put it down to routine: I'm just a writer who feeds on his imagination. No unresolved personal past as my inspiration, like all those authors who milk their own lives for book after book. Perhaps I should have stayed at home, in my own study, in the house where until recently Lilly also lived, so that I would be forced to think of her just by looking around me, but I'd left precisely because I didn't want that. Couldn't handle it.

I'd taken the "writer's block" line, which was of course partly true. But I hadn't told Ruth anything about Lilly. Why would I? Ruth is my new publisher: Three months ago, to our mutual satisfaction, she bought me from my old publisher. Her publishing house is the best an author could wish for: a prestigious list, pleasant editors, lots of attention, and a fantastic sales and publicity machine. Of course she knew Lilly: The three of us had celebrated the signing of the contract in style. The working title of my first thriller for Ruth was *The Club* and it was to be set on the Antillean island of Sint Maarten, where I planned to have a certain Freddy realize fifteen years down the line that his apparently successful life out there was totally futile. The first chapter, thirty-three pages long, was written in less than a week—I knew the island, I knew lots of types like Freedy. I had just decided that in the next chapter he would be sent a mourning card that would take him back home to Holland (where a criminal relative would turn his complacent neocolonial existence completely upside down)—when my girlfriend Lilly left me. Just like that, after five years, without warning. Classic, clichéd scene: Man comes home and finds a note. Not that there was anyone else, she just wanted to be alone for a few months and think things over. In the meantime she did not want to see or talk to me. She hoped I would understand.

A hack author would write: like a bolt from the blue. Try and find something better. I told my circle of friends that she'd gone to the U.S. for a bit—plausible, since she's American and her mother still lives there; so I added that my mother-in-law was gravely ill. (Crazy, of course, for a grown-up man with friends. Why didn't I just say that we were having a marital crisis? False modesty? A good theme to write about. If you can.)

No one asked me why I hadn't gone with her; they know me,

they know I like to be alone when I'm working on a novel. But of course not under these circumstances. Now I was being driven out of my mind with loneliness, by the house with her things all over the place and her clothes hanging up. I couldn't sit alone at the table where we had eaten and drunk together, let alone sleep in our bed. Let alone write in that house; when I sat down at my computer, my much-vaunted imagination deserted me and I thought of Lilly—why she had left, what I had done wrong, where she might be, and with whom. I tried to model Freddy's childhood sweetheart on her, marrying her to a writer whom she left in order to think things over. Sentimental, melodramatic prose that I knew was full of fury.

With Ruth, as I said, I blamed it on the traditional writer's block. She smiled understandingly. "Now do you see how helpless men are when their wives are gone?" If only she knew!

"Why don't you get away for a bit yourself? It sometimes helps, believe me. Do you know Cap d'Ail?"

Another perk. The publishing house had once been a successful Jewish family business but the war had put an end to that, as it had to so much else besides. The Polak family had died in Auschwitz, except for the youngest son Joseph, who had returned as the sole survivor in June 1945 but had immediately sold the publishing business. He no longer wanted to live in the country that had betrayed his parents and sisters. He had settled in Cap d'Ail in the South of France, in a house that the publishing house had made available even before then to authors in need of a retreat to get over their writer's block. Later Polak and his wife had moved to England and had rented out the house in Cap d'Ail to the publishing house, so that it had resumed its original function.

"You've everything you need. It has a small swimming pool, an Internet connection, and even a private beach that once belonged to Greta Garbo."

I've never been that crazy about the Côte d'Azur with its built-up coastline and rich, flashy inhabitants, but I accepted her offer, if for no other reason than that it had been raining for weeks in Amsterdam and there they had bright sunshine. And of course I was going to get Lilly out of my system. And to write. Before I forget.

The beach was accessible down thirty-one steps cut into the cliff. The house, a small stone 1930s villa, sat on a kind of plateau that had been transformed into a marvelous subtropical garden with huge agaves and tall cypresses. From the study I could reach the terrace by the swimming pool, from where I had a wonderful view of the Mediterranean and Monte Carlo. To the left and a little higher up was a neglected house with closed shutters that really had once belonged to Garbo but had been empty for years. Cap d'Ail itself was about two hundred meters higher, a tough scramble through pine trees and opulent villas.

The first day I packed the rental car full of groceries and stowed them away in the roomy freezer and well-appointed bar so that I did not have to bother about provisions for the time being. The little house had been excellently maintained—a living room, two bedrooms, a bathroom, a study—and a cleaning lady came once a week. In the event of problems I could contact an estate agent in Cap d'Ail. But why should I have any problems? It really was brilliant weather for April, already nearly twenty degrees Celsius on the beach, and I gloated when I saw on the weather report that Les Pays Bas was being ravaged by fierce northeast winds, though I must admit that I had a dreadful flash of a happy Lilly hand in hand with her someone else, braving the wind on a completely different beach. *What the hell!* I thought, pouring myself a second glass and trying to concentrate on Freddy, who in Chapter III arrived at a rainy Schiphol. The writing was going better than I could have expected. Two hours every morning after an early breakfast, after which I basked like a king on the beach until noon. Though there were hundreds of books in the house—what else did I expect?—when I'm writing I never read, frightened of being distracted or unconsciously plagiarizing. To my surprise the collection included lots of reference books about the Second World War belonging to old Polak; I had always thought that former victims of the Nazi regime were keen not to be reminded, but there was even an old book with the most gruesome pictures of Auschwitz, where his family had been gassed. I leafed through it but found it too nauseating and took my mind off it by studying a cookery book of regional recipes that I had found in the kitchen. Cooking has always been a hobby of mine, of necessity, since Lilly was a stereotypical American in that respect, regarding a stuffed pepper in the microwave as haute cuisine. My French is reasonable, but for a recipe with octopus, my favorite when it comes to *fruits de mer*, I needed the dictionary. "Small octopus, as fresh as possible," it said, "preferably cut up into small pieces immediately after catching and marinated as indicated above." That was the problem of the tourist plague: Cap d'Ail might be saturated with souvenir shops, but I hadn't seen a fishmonger's, and the days when fishing boats moored instead of luxury yachts were gone for good. Gloomily I ate my deep-frozen steak and peered at the darkening sea lapping against the rocks below me. Somewhere there underwater it must be teeming with those juicy little octopuses! Then I remembered that it was precisely the small kind that liked shallow waters, lying in wait in clefts in the rock till their unsuspecting prey swam past. . . .

The next morning I was in the water early. I hadn't the faintest idea how you were supposed to catch this kind of eight-tentacled mollusk, and there was no scoop net or suchlike to be found in the house, but I knew that some kinds secrete poison—it said so in the cookery book, and you had to wash and clean them really carefully—so I had put on household gloves. So there I stood, glad it was a private beach, with no sign of anyone on the slopes or near the house where Garbo had spent her last years in nunlike seclusion. I glanced up at the cloudless sky and wondered if she were laughing at me from up there, a grown-up guy with those gloves on, a diving mask, a rubbish bag in one hand for keeping the catch in, and a short stick in the other.

I took a deep breath, dived under, and swam past the capriciously shaped rocks. As the water was still no more than two meters deep, filtered sunlight penetrated and produced a kaleidoscopic effect. Hundreds of purple fishes flashed ahead of me like photons, punctuated by the occasional silvery gleam of a larger specimen. Clinging to the dark brown rocks were bright pink and purple sea anemones, their tentacles waving in the current, ready at any moment to grab a prawn or a hermit crab. But I was looking for different tentacles, surfaced for a moment for a gulp of fresh air, dived again, and gingerly poked the stick into the inky black crevices and holes. You never knew what might be hiding in there and a pair of latex gloves didn't strike me as much protection against the claws of a crab or the bite of a moray eel.

After nearly half an hour I was just coming to the gloomy conclusion that old Polak's stretch of sea was somehow octopus-free when I pulled one out of a hole in the rock on the seabed with the stick, slightly bigger than my fist and crimson in color. I drew it carefully toward me and had just put the bag over it when I saw something gleaming in the hole. At first I thought it was one of those mother-of-pearl shells, but once I had carefully extricated it from the hole, I saw to my astonishment that it was a bracelet, one of those charm bracelets that girls used to wear. How had the thing found its way there? Had that little octopus found it and made off with it like a magpie carries shiny objects to its nest? Nonsense of course—most probably someone had lost it and the current had swept it into the hole.

I surfaced, took off the mask, and held up the bracelet. In the sunlight it shone with a golden glow. Was it gold? There were about ten charms on it: a cross, a key, a kind of angel, and an animal that looked like a tiger. One charm seemed out of place; it was clearly a different shape, a bird with a small head, spread wings, and a long fan-shaped tail. The same color as the two links that had obviously been inserted at a later point to make the bracelet bigger. Had the bracelet first belonged to a girl who later wanted to wear it as a woman? How long had the thing been underwater? It had not been corroded by the seawater, but did that happen with gold? Who did the bracelet belong to? Ruth? The thought crossed my mind that Garbo had worn it, seeing that the beach had once belonged with her villa! It would have been nice to be able to say to Lilly on my return: "There you are, babe, for you. It was worn by the woman who never laughed."

Despondently I climbed the steps up to the house. Lilly. Lilly, who on the contrary was always laughing, and was now perhaps ecstatically happy, in love with another guy!

I washed the octopus, cut it into little pieces, let them marinate in wine, garlic, and herbs, and started on Chapter IV, in which Freddy bumps into a childhood sweetheart he hasn't seen for years and, like Lilly, is living happily with someone else. Somehow the description went very smoothly, but then I knew that I was eventually going to bring Freddy and her back together again. As I writer I've always been one for happy endings, and doubtless a psychiatrist would have had an explanation. Anyway, sitting out on the terrace in the evening eating the octopus with a full-bodied Burgundy, the lights of Monaco twinkling like a garland over the sea, the smell of sea and resin in my nostrils, I felt better than I had in weeks and went to bed pleased and satisfied.

Had I not cleaned the octopus properly, or had the Burgundy been too heavy? The funny thing was that I knew I was dreaming, but however awful the dream became I did not want to wake up, mesmerized as I was like a rabbit by a snake. At first I did not know where I was. I stared blinking into the sun at rows of wooden huts on either side of a wide, sandy roadway that ran parallel to a railway line. Scores of people shuffled out of several huts; men on one side, women and children on the other. They carried bundles of clothing, some of them old-fashioned wicker cases. I saw policemen and armed soldiers, and then with a start I recognized their helmets. No mistaking them. German soldiers!

Against the light sky I could make out the contours of barbed-wire fences and the stockades of watchtowers, farther away a white villa ringed with trees and beyond it, rolling cornfields. Perplexed, I followed with my eyes what were by now hundreds of people standing motionless along the road in front of the huts, with a girl with short cropped hair at the front. She was a bit like Lilly, as she used to look in childhood photos.

Suddenly a policeman shouted a name: "Aalbers, Mirjam!"

An old woman shuffled forward at the moment I heard the noise of a thundering train.

The next name rang out: "Polak, Joseph!"

On the other side a pale man with a case stepped onto the road. Beyond the villa the sun glinted on the moss green of a train that braked with a screech.

"Cohen, Naomi!"

As the girl stepped forward, I saw the man who was shouting the names. A young blond man, dressed in a kind of boiler suit with a white armband, holding a blue-black pistol with which he beckoned the girl, and actually smiled, for God's sake. She went over to the pale man called Polak and took his hand for a moment, in such a way that I was sure they were lovers. As she withdrew her hand, I saw she was wearing a bracelet on her wrist, a glittering charm bracelet. That book of photos, the name Polak, the charms—in my sleep my brain worked overtime, out of control like a computer gone haywire. I knew I was dreaming and I knew where I was in my dream. I knew where those poor devils would soon be headed in that damned train. I was dreaming about the transit camp at Westerbork in Drenthe, from where there were daily transports to Auschwitz. As the train wheezed to a stop, the young man with the pistol ran right past me with a policemen and I heard the policeman snap, "Christ, Wim, I've just heard the Allies have taken Breda. We've got to get out of here, man, before it's too late!"

Then I woke up bathed in sweat, although the window was open. Head spinning, I got out of bed, switched on a lamp, and still half asleep went to the kitchen for a drink of water. I had once heard that you can't dream of something that you haven't experienced consciously. So how could I dream of Westerbork? I had never been there. And those names? Polak was obvious, but Naomi Cohen? Who was she? And that blond camp guard Wim?

Christ! I thought grimly, *Stop it! Save that rubbish for your books. And in the future don't drink a liter of wine and half a bottle of brandy before bedtime!*

Worn out by the long journey I took a taxi home from the station; in my street I found myself looking against my better judgment for Lilly's dark-green Morgan, a very rare and valuable sports car that was a souvenir of her last film role. Had I already mentioned that she was a popular actress? If anyone could act, it was Lilly, you're telling me! But the only car outside the door was my own Alfa, too old and too unreliable to drive to the South of France.

I took a shower, poured a stiff drink, and listened to my voice mail as I went through the post. Nothing special in either, no word from Lilly. Gloomily I put a pizza in the oven and started unpacking my things, stuffed my dirty clothes into the laundry basket, too tired even to go through a newspaper. I decided on an evening in front of the telly, something I never usually do, since before you know it Lilly will flash past in some soap or other.

Then something happened that no author with the slightest self-respect would describe, but that when I think back to it now, still sends shivers down my spine. Let me first say that it was May 4, the National Commemoration Day for the Dead of the Second World War, something that because of my trip had completely passed me by. Nor had I seen any flags at half mast from the taxi, but that means nothing, since over sixty years on people don't make that much fuss about it.

So I switched the TV on, took my pizza out of the oven, poured myself a red wine, and went back to the living room, where I stood as if rooted to the spot. On the screen, less than two meters away from me, a young woman, still a girl, with dark cropped hair was looking into the camera with a rather sad smile. In my bewilderment I first thought I was looking at a childhood photo of Lilly. It is rule number one in prose, my genre: Coincidence is out, but that doesn't mean it doesn't exist. How else could you explain what did not add up? In retrospect of course it was not that much of a coincidence, a documentary that evening about Jewish children who had survived the Nazi camps. Beneath the sweet, typically Jewish girl's face was her name: Naomi Cohen. Behind it—but I didn't take that in until, as if in a daze, I saw a charm bracelet sparkling on her narrow wrist—were her date of birth and death: 1929–1966. She vanished from the screen and in her place there appeared another Jewish woman, but I did not really see her because the image of the last girl was etched so indelibly in my mind. This was insane! The same girl as in my dream, the same name that I had heard. Naomi Cohen! Or was it a mistake? It had to be! It must have been someone else, someone who looked like her, someone whom, tired as I was, I had confused with that dream image! But then, why 1966 as the year of her death? I was certain I had seen that on the screen. Surely it should have been a year in the war! And that bracelet? At that moment it dawned on me what I was looking at. Over an old black-and-white shot of huts, a sandy road with a railway line alongside, a watchtower, a white villa with cornfields beyond—an image that again made me shiver—appeared the caption "The Survivors of Westerbork."

Apart from writing novels, I occasionally do work for television, not out of ambition—the jobs are usually commissions for knocking other people's stories and scripts into shape—but simply because it pays well. The following morning I rang a producer I knew who referred me to the maker of the documentary of the night before. I found myself talking to a charming woman whose name I did not know, but who knew mine, which made a difference. I complimented her, which also makes a difference, and reeled off my fictitious story—who was it who said all writers are born liars? I pretended I was researching a new novel in which a survivor of Westerbork plays a major role, which is why the night before I had been so struck by a girl with cropped black hair who had been in her documentary. "I think her name was Cohen. . . ."

"Naomi Cohen," she said. "That's really sad. We couldn't talk to her because she died a long while ago, in 1966 I think. Still young, in her thirties. . . ."

I said nothing, completely thrown. Naomi Cohen. So it was true! Why had I dreamed of her? I had an explanation, an explanation that had haunted me all through the last sleepless night, but that I did not dare admit to myself. I might be famed for my imagination, but I absolutely did not believe in paranormal phenomena.

"Are you still there?"

"Yes, yes!"

"As I said, very sad. Think about it, first she's in Westerbork, then she survives the hell of Auschwitz, she tries to build a new life after the war, and then she goes and drowns!"

"She drowns?" I repeated stupidly.

"Yes. Somewhere in France. She was on holiday I think. I'm looking through my papers as I'm talking to you. . . . Yes, here it is, in the summer of 1966 on the Riviera . . . at least that's where they found her in the sea."

I could hear how hoarse my voice was. "Do you know where on the Riviera it was?"

"Um . . . yes. Somewhere near Monaco, it says here."

"It's lovely," said Ruth, studying the bracelet admiringly. "Actually it looks as if that bird charm has been added later, as have those links." She put down the bracelet and pulled a face. "It's really weird."

I nodded and took a sip of the white Sancerre she had treated me to. If only she knew just how weird it all was, but naturally I hadn't told her about that bizarre dream and the documentary. I had simply said I had found the bracelet in the water.

"It might very well be Mary's," she said cheerfully. "Joseph Polak's wife. Don't you think? She might have lost it while she was swimming? Gosh, that would be nice, they've invited me next weekend for his eighty-fifth birthday. Can you picture it if I give them this as an extra present?"

I smiled and shook my head. "It's not hers."

"Oh. Oh no?"

"No. I think it belonged to a Jewish girl, a certain Naomi Cohen."

She looked at me in astonishment. "How do you know that?"

"Because . . ." I covered my hesitation by taking another sip. Should I tell her about the dream after all? "Because I took it to the gendarmerie. Didn't I tell you that? I mean, it's gold after all, valuable." I smiled and looked at the bracelet. "I actually thought it might have been Garbo's! But the police told me that long ago a young woman drowned thereabouts."

"How awful."

"Yes."

"When was it, do you know?"

"Yes. The summer of 1966."

She frowned. "And her name was Cohen?"

I nodded.

"But then she may have been a friend of Joseph and Mary!"

"What?" Now it was my turn to be astonished. "But I thought they moved to England in the 1950s."

"Yes, they did, but they still often spent their summers there. They've only recently stopped going because of their age. What was the woman's name did you say?"

"Naomi. Naomi Cohen."

She grabbed her mobile excitedly. "Do you know what? I'll call right away. I had to anyway to confirm arrangements!" She smirked and was already keying in the number. "Why don't you come with me tomorrow? Joseph knows your books and it's your treasure trove, isn't it?" She nodded to the printouts of the first six chapters that I had brought. "You can afford a weekend in Devon, now you've made such good progress!"

She frowned as she listened to her mobile and turned it off. "Voice mail. I'll call them this evening, okay?"

I said nothing, in fact I scarcely heard her, but my brain was in overdrive as I recalled the images of that dream. The blond man who shouted out the names of those who were put on a transport to Auschwitz that day—he had also called the name Joseph Polak!

"What is it?" asked Ruth.

"Was Joseph in Westerbork first back then?"

"What? Yes. Why?"

"No reason. I saw books about it in the house."

"Aha."

Her mobile rang. Obviously one of her many business conversations. I drank and gazed at the rain-lashed window. That morning I had even asked my old friend Wim about a camp guard at Westerbork called wim! Just because of a dream and a charm bracelet! For Christ's sake. Was the Joseph Polak from that strange dream really the son of the publisher? It was obvious that Naomi had loved the pale young man, from the way she had grabbed him for a moment before they began their journey to hell. Joseph and she, both returning to postwar chaos. Probably she had looked for him, heard that he had gone to France and was married, and had visited him only much later, in 1966. Perhaps she had stayed there for a few days and then lost the bracelet. Then she had probably gone for a swim near Monaco and drowned.

"I had no idea you did nonfiction as well, old man!" said Bert on the telephone.

"What?" I said in surprise.

"Come on now. A young, blond camp guard called Wim. Why else would you ask about it? By the way, I'd like to know how you got your hands on a photo with him in it, as Van der Valk was smart enough not to let himself be photographed. . . ."

I was at a loss for words, saw him sitting there in the State Archive for War Documentation, Bert van der Laar, a childhood friend whom I frequently asked for information for my novels. A photo, I had said, a photo from Westerbork at that time. What else was I supposed to say? Bert, I had this really odd dream?

"Breda," said Bert in my ear, "was taken by the Allies on September 10, 1944. I don't know what you're getting at with your question, but the guy you mean was called Wim van der Valk and really was a camp guard at Westerbork. A real bastard. Stole everything those poor sods had with them before they were sent to the gas chambers. Well, German records show—you know how thorough the Huns were—that four days later he was given leave and went to Arnhem with a friend who was a policeman to visit his fiancée." He sniggered. "If you ask me you know all this already but want it confirmed. Okay, that's fine by me. On September 17, Arnhem, my dear Timo, was heavily bombed by the British. And according to a later statement by his fiancée Wim van der Valk and his colleague were killed in the raid. Bodies were certainly found, but they were unidentifiable. Not that strange, since it was a bit like a crematorium that morning. But of course you are hatching a plot in which on the strength of that alibi he is even now celebrating his birthday together with other Nazis somewhere in Paraguay!" He laughed and spluttered, "If you find him, I want to be the first to know, old man! Ha, ha!"

Van der Valk! I gazed vacantly into space and remembered that there was an Indian tribe that believed that dreams were reality and reality a dream.

"Hello?" asked Bert. "Are you still there?"

"What? Yes, yes." My temples were pounding but I had my wits about me again. "Bert, listen! One more thing, if you can. Joseph Polak, born 1919, in Westerbork and transported to Auschwitz. Whole family exterminated. Can you check at your end whether he survived and came back after the liberation?"

"Polak? The publisher?" He laughed in amazement. "Of course he did. Surely you must know that if you're with that publisher? I don't need to look that up, my friend. Polak was made an honorary French citizen immediately after the war when he moved there after his marriage. Anything else? I'm just about to go home—you know what women are like, old fellow."

I managed to laugh back. I hadn't yet told him a thing about Lilly. "And that fiancée of Van der Valk's, what became of her?"

"She was in the Nazi party, but like so many other traitors she escaped to South Africa in the chaos. Listen, Timo, you old conspiracy theorist, I really am hanging up now. If you need any more information, you'll just have to ring tomorrow. And if you write that novel, I want an acknowledgment at the front!"

He laughed again and hung up. With the receiver still in one ear I looked sheepishly at the bracelet before me on the desk. Was that charm really a falcon? Christ, Bert was right, just as I had thought myself after my conversation with Ruth that afternoon: Professional involvement with all those books was warping my sense of reality, a charge Lilly often leveled at me. "My sweet, you're gradually getting lost in your own imaginary world!" It's true that it flashed through my mind that Van der Valk might have assumed the identity of Joseph Polak after the war. In that case Polak died in the gas chambers, like the rest of his family. Concentration camp changed people, physically as well. Perhaps he had dyed his hair or something. Who would suspect or trouble a war victim? He had sold the publishing business and left for the South of France almost immediately. . . .Van der Valk alias Polak, an ex-camp guard who stole everything, even from his victims. Including poor Naomi's bracelet. Had he given it to his wife, the fiancée who had supposedly fled to South Africa? And as an extra had a charm made, a falcon, as a tangible reminder of his old identity, which he had had to exchange for, of all things, that of a Jew? But he had reckoned without Polak's old girlfriend Naomi. . . .

Timo Dekker, old conspiracy theorist! Bert was right. Turn it into nice book. All this because of a charm that was a bit like a falcon! And what was I supposed to say tomorrow to that nice old Joseph Polak on his birthday?

God almighty! What I should do, instead of going to England, was stay here at my desk and get on with *The Club*! I would give the bracelet to Ruth to take. If it were really true that Naomi Cohen knew Joseph Polak from the camp, it was bound to delight the old man.

I started when I heard a sound behind me, footsteps. "Timo?"

I turned round as if in a trance. Lilly was standing in the doorway, more beautiful than ever. There was a faint smile on her lips, guilty but also so sweet and disarming that I almost burst into tears when she came up to me and put her arms around me.

"Do you hate me?"

My tongue seemed to be blocking my throat so that all I could do was shake my head.

"I've been so stupid, so stupid!" She sniffed and kissed me. "Will you please forgive me?"

My mobile rang for so long that finally, cursing softly, I got out of the bed where Lilly was still sound asleep. No wonder, after what can safely be called a second honeymoon. Not a weekend as a jilted loser visiting an old couple in Devon with my publisher, but with the regained Love of my Life in a secluded hotel in the woods.

Sunday morning. Who the hell was stupid enough to call me here and now? Still drowsy, I answered.

"Hello?"

"Is that the writer Timo Dekker?"

A rather hoarse, unfamiliar voice, clearly that of an older man. How had the guy got hold of my mobile number?

"This is Joseph Polak, Mr. Dekker. You know my name, I assume. . . ."

I was instantly wide awake.

"I'm afraid I'm calling with very sad news. Mrs. Ruth Kroeze, your publisher, who was here for my birthday, drowned yesterday."

"What?" I wanted to scream, but could scarcely hear my own voice.

"It's terrible. She went for a walk along the local cliffs yesterday and according to the police probably lost her footing. . . . She was found this morning, hundreds of meters away, dragged along by the current."

He stopped talking for a moment and in the silence I could hear the blood pounding in my temples.

"I'm calling you personally because I understood you were staying in our old summer house. Ruth told us that you happened to find something in the sea. She was a bit secretive about it and promised it today as a present. . . ." He gave a short laugh and in a flash I saw the face of the camp guard before me, laughing as he called out the names of his victims. "But we couldn't find it. I was wondering if you . . ."

My mind a blank, I rang off, while my thoughts churned like a maelstrom.

According to the police here and in Devon everything Polak had told me was true. But of course everything about him was a lie, even his name. Ruth, poor Ruth, who for Christ's sake knew nothing. Who had probably shown him and his wife the bracelet unsuspectingly and told them my fibs about the gendarmerie in Cap d'Ail! Would things have been different if I hadn't said that? I was certain they would not. Naomi had known and they drowned her. Van der Valk must have done it with his wife, who had been wearing Naomi's bracelet, with two extra links and a falcon added. Had Naomi fought for her life and in the struggle pulled off the bracelet? How long, I wonder, had the couple hunted for it in vain?

Had they also pushed Ruth off the cliffs? Nothing easier, the three of them taking an evening walk along the deserted coast, Ruth with no inkling. No witnesses, no proof, just as before with Naomi.

And the bracelet?

Back in the sea, where it had lain for so long?

I sat there in a daze and stared at my distorted reflection in the window.

Was I really right? Why would he have killed her? Just because of the bracelet? Panic? Was it that bloody imagination after all? Nothing more than coincidence, two women who through a strange quirk of fate both had accidents and drowned?

But what about the charm then? Damn, damn!

"What is it, darling? Isn't it working?"

I turned around in alarm and smiled stupidly at Lilly who had brought me a cup of coffee and kissed me on the cheek. I hadn't told her anything either; undoubtedly she would have shaken her beautiful head pityingly. She glanced at my computer screen and frowned. "A nice opening," she said, and with her mellifluous actress's voice she read the first line out loud: "In the summer of 1966 Naomi Cohen knew that what she had suspected all those years was true. . . ."

"What's it about?" she asked inquisitively. "Who is this Naomi?"

I returned her kiss.

"To tell the truth," I lied, "I haven't a clue yet."

THE INKPOT MONKEY

John Connolly

Mr. Edgerton was suffering from writer's block; it was, he quickly grew to realize, a most distressing complaint. A touch of influenza might lay a man up for a day or two, yet still his mind could continue its divinations. Gout might leave him racked with pain, yet still his fingers could grasp a pen and turn pain to pennies. But this blockage, this barrier to all progress, had left Mr. Edgerton a virtual cripple. His mind would not function, his hands would not write, and his bills would not be paid. In a career spanning the best part of two decades he had never before encountered such an obstacle to his vocation. He had, in that time, produced five moderately successful, if rather indifferent, novels; a book of memoirs that, in truth, owed more to invention than experience; and a collection of poetry that could most charitably be described as having stretched the capacities of free verse to the limits of their acceptability.

Mr. Edgerton made his modest living from writing by the yard, based on the unstated belief that if he produced a sufficient quantity of material then something of quality was bound to creep in, if only in accordance with the law of averages. Journalism, ghostwriting, versifying, editorializing; nothing was beneath his limited capabilities.

Yet for the past three months the closest he had come to a writing project was the construction of his weekly grocery list. A veritable tundra of empty white pages stretched before him, the gleaming nib of his pen poised above them like a reluctant explorer. His mind was a blank, the creative juices sapped from it and leaving behind only a dried husk of frustration and bewilderment. He began to fear his writing desk, once his beloved companion but now reduced to the status of a faithless lover, and it pained him to look upon it. Paper, ink, desk, imagination: all had betrayed him, leaving him lost and alone.

To further complicate matters, Mr. Edgerton's wallet had begun to feel decidedly lightweight of late, and nothing will dampen a man's ardor for life more than an empty pocket. Like a rodent gripped in the coils of a great constricting snake, he found that the more he struggled against his situation, the tighter the pressure upon him grew. Necessity, wrote Ovid, is the mother of invention. For Mr. Edgerton, desperation was proving to be the father of despair.

And so, once again, Mr. Edgerton found himself wandering the streets of the city, vainly hunting for inspiration like a hungry leech seeking blood. In time, he came to Charing Cross Road, but the miles of shelved books only depressed him further, especially since he could find none of his own among their number. Head down, he cut through Cecil Court and made his way into Covent Garden in the faint hope that the vibrancy of the markets might spur his sluggish subconscious into action. He was almost at the Magistrates Court when something caught his eye in the window of a small antique shop. There, partially hidden behind a framed portrait of General Gordon and a stuffed magpie, was a most remarkable inkpot.

It was silver, and about four inches tall, with a lacquered base adorned by Chinese characters. But what was most striking about it was the small, mummified monkey that perched on its lid, its clawed toes clasped upon the rim and its dark eyes gleaming in the summer sunlight. It was obviously an infant of its species, perhaps even a fetus of some kind, for it was no more than three inches in height, and predominantly gray in color, except for its face, which was blackened around the mouth as if the monkey had been sipping from its own inkpot. It really was a most ghastly creature, but Mr. Edgerton had acquired the civilized man's taste for the grotesque, and he quickly made his way into the darkened shop to inquire about the nature of the item in question.

The owner of the business proved to be almost as distasteful in appearance as the creature that had attracted Mr. Edgerton's attention, as though the man were somehow father to the monkey. His teeth were too numerous for his mouth, his mouth too large for his face, and his head too great for his body. Combined with a pronounced stoop to his back, his aspect was that of one constantly on the verge of toppling over. He also smelled decidedly odd, and Mr. Edgerton quickly concluded that he was probably in the habit of sleeping in his clothes, a summation that briefly led the afflicted writer to an unwelcome speculation on the nature of the body that lay concealed beneath the layers of unwashed clothing.

Nevertheless, the proprietor proved to be a veritable font of knowledge about the items in his possession, including the article that had brought Mr. Edgerton into his presence. The mummified primate was, he informed the writer, an inkpot monkey, a creature of Chinese mythology. According to the myth, the monkey provided artistic inspiration in return for the residues of ink left in the bottom of the inkwell.

Mr. Edgerton was a somewhat superstitious (and, it must be said, sentimental) man: he still wore, much to the amusement of his peers, his mother's charm bracelet, a ragtag bauble of dubious taste that she found one day while walking upon the seashore and had subsequently bequeathed to him upon her death, along with a set of antique combs, now pawned, and a small sum of money, now spent. Among the items dangling from its links was a small gold monkey. It had always fascinated him as a child, and the discovery of a similar relic in the window of the antique store seemed to him nothing less than a sign from the divine. As a man who was profoundly in need of inspiration from any source, and who had recently been considering opium or cheap gin as possible catalysts, he required no further convincing. He paid over money he could ill afford for the faint hope of redemption offered by the curiosity and made his way back to his small apartment with the inkpot and its monkey tucked beneath his arm in a cloak of brown paper.

Mr. Edgerton occupied a set of rooms above a tobacconist's store on Marylebone High Street, a recent development forced on him by his straitened circumstances. Although Mr. Edgerton did not himself partake of the noble weed, his walls were yellowed by the fumes that regularly wended their way between the cracks in the floorboards, and his clothing and furnishings reeked of assorted cigars, cigarettes, pipe tobaccos, and even the more eye-watering forms of snuff. His dwelling was, therefore, more than a little depressing, and would almost certainly have provided Mr. Edgerton with the impetus necessary to improve his finances were he not so troubled by the absence of his muse. Indeed, he had few distractions, for most of his writer friends had deserted him. They had silently, if reluctantly, tolerated his modest success. Now, with the taint of failure upon him, they relished his discomfiture from a suitably discreet distance.

That evening, Mr. Edgerton sat at his desk once again and stared at the paper before him. And stared. And stared. Before him, the inkpot monkey squatted impassively, its eyes reflecting the lamplight and lending its mummified form an intimation of life that was both distracting and unsettling. Mr. Edgerton poked at it tentatively with his pen, leaving a small black mark on its chest. Like most writers, he had a shallow knowledge of a great many largely useless matters. Among these was anthropology, a consequence of one of his earlier works, an evolutionary fantasy entitled *The Monkey's Uncle*. (The *Times* had described it as "largely adequate, if inconsequential." Mr. Edgerton, grateful to be reviewed at all, was rather pleased.) Yet, despite searching through three reference volumes, Mr. Edgerton had been unable to identify the origins of the inkpot monkey and had begun to take this as a bad omen.

After another unproductive hour had gone by, its tedium broken only by the spread of an occasional ink blot on the paper, Mr. Edgerton rose and determined to amuse himself by emptying, and then refilling, his pen. Still devoid of inspiration, he wondered if there was some part of the arcane ritual of fueling one's pen from the inkpot that he had somehow neglected to perform. He reached down and gently grasped the monkey in order to raise the lid, when something pricked his skin painfully. He drew back his hand immediately and examined the wounded digit. A small, deep cut ran across the pad of his index finger, and blood from the abrasion was running down the length of his pen and congregating at the nib, from which it dripped into the inkpot with soft, regular splashes. Mr. Edgerton began to suck the offended member, meanwhile turning his attention to the monkey in an effort to ascertain the cause of his injury. The lamplight revealed a small raised ridge behind the creature's neck, where a section of curved spine had burst through its tattered fur. A little of Mr. Edgerton's blood could be perceived on the yellowed pallor of the bone. The unfortunate writer retrieved a small bandage from his medicine cabinet, then cleaned and bound his finger before resuming his seat at his desk. He regarded the monkey warily as he filled his pen, then put it to paper and began to write. At first, the familiarity of the act overcame any feelings of surprise at its sudden return, so that Mr. Edgerton had dispensed with two pages of close script and was about to embark on a third before he paused and looked in puzzlement first at his pen, then at the paper. He reread what he had written, the beginning of a tale of a man who sacrifices love at the altar of emptiness, and found it more than satisfactory; it was, in fact, as fine as anything he had ever written, although he was baffled as to the source of his inspiration. Nevertheless, he shrugged and continued writing, grateful that his old talent had apparently woken from its torpor. He wrote long into the night, refilling his pen as required, and so bound up was he in his exertions that he failed entirely to notice that his wound had reopened and was dripping blood onto pen and page and, at those moments when he replenished his instrument, into the depths of the small Chinese inkpot.

Mr. Edgerton slept late the following morning and awoke to find himself weakened by his efforts of the night before. It was, he supposed, the consequence of months of inactivity, and after coffee and some hot buttered toast he felt much refreshed. He returned to his desk to find that the inkpot monkey had fallen from its perch and now lay on its back amid his pencils and pens. Gingerly, Mr. Edgerton lifted it from the desk and found that it weighed considerably more than the inkpot itself and that physics, rather than any flaw in the inkpot's construction, had played its part in dislodging the monkey from its seat. He also noted that the creature's fur was far more lustrous than it had appeared in the window of the antique shop, and now shimmered healthily in the morning sunlight. And then, quite suddenly, Mr. Edgerton felt the monkey move. Its arms and legs stretched wearily, as if it were waking from some long slumber, and its mouth opened in a wide yawn, displaying small, blunt teeth. Alarmed, Mr. Edgerton dropped the monkey and heard it emit a startled squeak as it landed on the desk. It lay there for a moment or two, then slowly raised itself on its haunches and regarded Mr. Edgerton with a slightly hurt expression before ambling over to the inkpot and squatting down gently beside it. With its left hand, it raised the lid of the inkpot and waited patiently for Mr. Edgerton to fill his pen. For a time, the bewildered writer was unable to move, so taken aback was he at this turn of events. Then, when it became clear that he had no other option but to begin writing or go mad, he reached for his pen and filled it from the well.

The monkey watched him impassively until the reservoir was filled and Mr. Edgerton had begun to write, then promptly fell fast asleep.

Despite his unnerving encounter with the newly animated monkey, Mr. Edgerton put in a most productive day and quickly found himself with the bulk of five chapters written, none of them requiring more than a cursory rewrite. It was only when the light had begun to fade and Mr. Edgerton's arm had started to ache that the monkey awoke and padded softly across a virgin page to where Mr. Edgerton's pen lay in his hand. The monkey grasped his index finger with its tiny hands, then placed its mouth against the cut and began to suck. It took Mr. Edgerton a moment to realize what was occurring, at which point he rose with a shout and shook the monkey from his finger. It bounced against the inkpot, striking its head soundly against its base, and lay unmoving on a sheet of paper.

At once Mr. Edgerton reached for it and raised it in the palm of his left hand. The monkey was obviously stunned, for its eyes were now half closed and it moved its head slowly from side to side as it tried to focus. Instantly, Mr. Edgerton was seized with regret at his hasty action. He had endangered the monkey, which he now acknowledged to be the source of his newfound inspiration. Without it, he would be lost. Torn between fear and disgust, Mr. Edgerton reluctantly made his decision: he squeezed together his thumb and forefinger, causing a droplet of blood to emerge from the cut and then, his gorge rising, allowed it to drip into the monkey's mouth.

The effect was instantaneous. The little mammal's eyes opened fully; it rose onto its haunches and then reached for and grasped the wounded finger. There it suckled happily, undisturbed by the revolted Mr. Edgerton, until it had taken its fill, whereupon it burped contentedly and resumed its slumbers. Mr. Edgerton gently laid it beside the inkpot and then, taking up his pen, wrote another two chapters before retiring early to his bed.

Thus it continued. Each day Mr. Edgerton rose, fed the monkey a little blood, wrote, fed the monkey once again in the evening, wrote some more, then went to bed and slept like a dead man. The monkey appeared to require little in the way of affection or attention beyond its regular feeds, although it would often touch fascinatedly the miniature of itself that dangled from Mr. Edgerton's wrist. Mr. Edgerton, in turn, decided to ignore the fact that the monkey was growing at quite an alarming rate, so that it was now obliged to sit beside him on a small chair while he worked and had taken to dozing on the sofa after its meals. In fact, Mr. Edgerton wondered if it might not be possible to train the monkey to do some light household duties, thereby allowing him more time to write, although when he suggested this to the monkey through the use of primitive sign language it grew quite irate and locked itself in the bathroom for an entire afternoon.

In fact, it was not until Mr. Edgerton returned home one afternoon from a visit to his publisher to find the inkpot monkey trying on one of his suits that he began to experience serious doubts about their relationship. He had noticed some new and especially disturbing changes in his companion. It had begun to molt, leaving clumps of unsightly gray hair on the carpet and exposing sections of pink-white skin. It had also lost some weight from its face; that, or its bone structure had begun to alter, for it now presented a more angular aspect than it had previously done. In addition, the monkey was now over four feet tall, and Mr. Edgerton had been forced to open veins in his wrists and legs in order to keep it sated. The more Mr. Edgerton considered the matter, the more convinced he became that the creature was undergoing some significant transformation. Yet there were still chapters of the book to be completed, and the writer was reluctant to alienate his mascot. So he suffered in silence, sleeping now for much of the day and emerging only to write for increasingly short periods of time before returning to his bed and collapsing into a dreamless slumber.

On the twenty-ninth day of August, he delivered his completed manuscript to his publisher. On the fourth of September, which was Mr. Edgerton's birthday, he was gratified to receive a most delightful communication from his editor, praising him as a genius and promising that this novel, long anticipated and at last delivered, would place Mr. Edgerton in the pantheon of literary greats and assure him of a most comfortable and well-regarded old age.

That night, as Mr. Edgerton prepared to drift off into contented sleep, he felt a tug at his wrist and looked down to see the inkpot monkey fastened on it, its cheeks pulsing as it sucked away at the cut. Tomorrow, thought Mr. Edgerton, tomorrow I will deal with it. Tomorrow I will have it taken to the zoo and our bargain will be concluded forever. But as he grew weaker and his eyes closed, the inkpot monkey raised its head and Mr. Edgerton realized at last that no zoo would ever take the inkpot monkey, for the inkpot monkey had become something very different indeed . . .

Mr. Edgerton's book was published later that year, to universal acclaim. A reception was given in his honor by his grateful publishers, to which the brightest lights of London's literary community flocked to pay tribute. It would be Mr. Edgerton's final public appearance. From that day forth, he was never again seen in London and retired to the small country estate that he purchased with the royalties from his great, valedictory work. Even his previous sentimentality appeared to be in the past, for his beloved charm bracelet could now be found in the window of a small antique shop in Covent Garden where, due to some imaginative pricing, it seemed destined to remain.

That night, speeches were made, and an indifferent poem recited by one of Mr. Edgerton's new admirers, but the great man himself remained silent throughout. When called on to give his speech, he replied simply with a small but polite bow to his guests, accepting their applause with a gracious smile, then returned to toying with the small gold monkey that hung from a chain around his neck.

And while all those around him drank the finest champagne and feasted on stuffed quail and smoked salmon, Mr. Edgerton could be found sitting quietly in a corner, stroking some unruly hairs on his chest and munching contentedly on a single ripe banana.

ACTS OF CORPORAL CHARITY

Jane Haddam

Later, John Robert Mortimer would remember that it had all happened by accident, and because it had happened by accident, it couldn't possibly be his fault. God only knows that he hadn't intended to be in England, ever. When he was growing up, sitting by himself at a long table in the cafeteria at lunch, sitting in the back of one classroom or another so that no teacher would even think of calling on him, the only traveling he had ever imagined himself doing was to Florida or Los Angeles. He was a child of northern New England. Cold was his heritage. Sometimes he thought the only thing he could count on in life was snow.

This morning, standing on an unfamiliar street still mostly empty at the start of workday traffic, he was not only cold but tired. Last night had been worse than hideous. Whatever had given him the idea that he could make a life teaching English to adolescents? Whatever had given him the idea that he could function on less than three hours' sleep? But no, he'd never had that idea. He'd known as soon as he'd seen the time on his bedside clock that he was going to have a horrible day. It wouldn't even matter that this was his one day "off." There was no "off," not really. To be "off," he'd have to be home in New Hampshire, barricaded into his faculty apartment by books and a wall of noise, the Emperor's Concerto pumping through his headset, the ringers on all the phones made mute. Today he was not so much off as in hiding. He hated the idea of going back to the hotel.

"You'll have some time to yourself while you're there," Mr. Cadwallader had told him when he'd been assigned as a chaperon for the senior trip. "You'll have a day to yourself in the city. The only concern we have is that our students should be protected at all times."

Protected, my ass, John Robert had thought at the time, and he hadn't changed his mind. He was more in need of being protected from his students than his students were in need of being protected from London. That's what happened when you had to deal with kids who had no concept of the value of money—or of the fact that it was limited, for most people. That was a problem he hadn't considered when he'd signed on to teach at Meredith Academy. He'd thought that between his college, which had been both famous and infamously expensive, and his childhood, which had taken place in one of the most excruciatingly "normal" towns in all of the Northeast, he'd perfected the song and dance a poor boy had to do to survive among people much richer than himself. He'd been wrong about that too.

"Look," Lisa Hardwick had said the night before, hanging on to the door to his room as if she intended to swing on it, "we found this. We thought you'd like it."

"Found it where?" he'd asked, taking the slip of paper from her hand without looking at it. He was trying not to look at Lisa herself, or at her friend Marianne, who followed her around like gum stuck to a shoe. They were dressed in this year's version of cool, as far as cool was permitted within the dress code. They both had stockings on, and skirts that fell modestly to their knees. The problem was that the skirts had slits in them, cut high on their legs to the very edges of their underwear, and they wore necklines that plunged toward their navels and hugged everything too tightly to be ignored. They weren't wearing bras, either. They never did. With all that skin on display, it didn't matter that Lisa was pug-nosed and thick-waisted, or that Marianne had a line of pimples along her jaw that were rough and red from handling. Hormones were hormones. He wanted to reach out and pinch Lisa's nipples until they bled.

"We found it in a phone booth," Lisa said. Then she looked at Marianne, and they both burst out laughing.

A moment later they were gone, trailing beer fumes he should have recognized as soon as they'd appeared in the hall. He could hear them in the stairwell, stumbling and giggling. He looked down at the scrap of paper. It had a fringe of phone numbers at the bottom. They'd taken down somebody's posted advertisement. Whoever it was would get no answer now. He turned the paper over and over in his hands. *Are you a naughty boy?* it said, in bright red letters. The rest of it was not so bright, and for a moment he didn't understand what he was seeing. *Mistress Pamela knows what you are. You need discipline. Come up to my office and take your punishment—now.*

He let the paper fall to the floor. Could they really have found that in a phone booth? He bent down and picked it up. The last thing he needed was for somebody to find it directly outside his door. He went back into his room and locked himself in. He sat down on the edge of the bed and wondered what Mistress Pamela looked like. To make it really work, she'd have to be a middle-aged woman who wore the kind of button-to-the-neck dress they sold at home in JC Penney's, and those shoes that nobody wore anymore, the thick ones with the ties. Better yet, she'd have to be really fat, the way his foster mother had been fat, enormous, so that she could only fit into shifts and knee-high stockings that were always rolling down. It was very close in this room, very hot. The hotel must have turned up the heat after they'd all complained. He had sweat on his forehead and on the palms of his hands. He was finding it very hard to breathe.

He went into the bathroom and turned on the shower as hard as he could make it. That wasn't very hard. There didn't seem to be any decent water pressure in the entire city of London. He put his head under the water and left it there until the wet seeped down his neck and chest and soaked through his white button-down shirt and ratty thin tie. He'd bought the tie in a knockoff place in Boston. He'd bought the shirt at Sears. His foster mother had ended up in a pool of blood at the bottom of the long driveway that led to her house, stabbed forty-six times by a man she thought she was going to sell cordwood to. He could still hear the sound of the knife going in and coming out, the thud and the suck, thud and suck, thud and suck, over and over again, like the metronome on the piano in the music room at school.

He went back into the bedroom and sat down on the bed again. It was cold instead of hot. His head hurt. He took Mistress Pamela's advertisement and set fire to it with his green Bic lighter. He let it curl into his hand until the last moment. Then he dropped it into the empty tin of Myntz he'd brought all the way from the airport in New York. Thud and suck was a sound lots of things made. It was the sound sex made. It was probably the sound Mistress Pamela made when she did whatever she did to the men who called her number. He found he couldn't imagine what she did without imagining other things, and the other things he was imagining were all wrong. He wondered if she let men reverse the roles if they paid her enough to do it.

"You'll have a day to yourself in the city," Mr. Cadwallader had said, and it was true. He had this day, the day before they were due to go home. He could walk around as much as he wanted. He had no obligations but to be back at the hotel first thing tomorrow morning, to help supervise the packing up and getting to the airport. Lisa and Marianne would sit together at the back of the plane and giggle all the way to New York. The other teachers would huddle together toward the front and try to pretend they didn't know what the students were getting up to. All in all, both

England and American Airlines would be left with the impression that the students of Meredith Academy were spoiled brats with no consideration for anybody but themselves. It was true.

Mistress Pamela could do a job on you, John Robert thought, meaning Lisa, or Marianne, or even himself, or nobody at all. Thud and suck. Thud and suck. It was the sound of the waves going in and out on the New Hampshire shore.

There were crowds on the street now. John Robert was being pushed against the buildings and their windows, odd windows, not what he was used to. He looked at the people going by and thought they were no different from the people he saw in Boston, or Nashua. He inched along the pavement, looking at things that didn't interest him: newspapers, candy, small grocery items called garlic pickle and Marmite and mushy peas. He wished he knew where he was, in what part of the city. That way, he would know what to think of the women who were passing him. They didn't attract him. Most of them were too old. All of them were too hard. He could feel their hardness when they brushed against him, and they always did.

The bracelet was in the window of an antique shop when he saw it, and it stopped him dead. It had been years since he'd seen a charm bracelet. They were so out of style in the States, he never came across them anymore. This one was gold, not silver like the ones his foster sisters had owned before their mother died and he had been moved back to the children's shelter. Theirs had probably not really been silver, either—silver plate, maybe, if they were lucky—and they had worn them on their ankles instead of their wrists. His foster mother had worn no jewelry at all, but like his sisters she had always had her hair "done," blonded to the point of surreality, teased high over the top of her head, as if she had to anchor a Vegas headdress and wanted to make sure there was enough to keep it from falling off. Mistress Pamela hadn't worn any jewelry that he'd recognized when he'd gone to see her the night before. She'd barely worn any clothes. It wasn't any good, the way these women went about it. It was much too obvious that they were playing a game. He'd had a picture of her stuck in his mind, stuck so firmly that he had been unable to erase the number from his memory even by burning it, but when he'd gone up to the flat at the top of that long narrow flight of stairs, she'd been nothing at all like he had pictured her.

"If you want to make sure to get what you want," one of the other teachers at Meredith had said, "go to New York. They have them every which way in New York. You can get them made to order."

John Robert didn't want to get one made to order. He wasn't in the habit of visiting prostitutes. He wasn't in the habit of indulging himself in any way. If he wanted to indulge himself, he could always take up the offer Lisa Hardwick was making him. Maybe she'd be willing to make a party of it and invite in Marianne.

The bracelet had a lot of charms on it: a monkey, a tiger, a tiny key. There was even a miniature Fabergé egg. His foster sisters always chose charms for good luck, as if having a heart-shaped charm with their boyfriend's initials on it would call forth a proposal of marriage. There was a heart-shaped charm here, but he couldn't see initials on it. There was a pair of dice. They would have liked that one. He wondered what had happened to them after their mother died. Thud and suck. Thud and suck. He went into the shop and looked around.

Mistress Pamela had turned out to be a small woman trying to make up for her lack of stature by wearing very high heels. Her hair had been dyed red but very thin. Her voice had been high and stressed. The only truly impressive thing about her had been her fingernails, and he had told her how much he appreciated them: grown long and filed sharp, painted red with flecks of gold glitter in them, so that they winked in the light. It was about money, that was the problem. It was always about money, and he needed it to be about something else. She had had her instruments laid out on a table: a hairbrush, a tawse, a paddle, a cane. She'd had a cigarette going in a blue plastic ashtray on top of a heating grate. He could feel the whack and grate against the bare skin of his ass as the paddle came down, over and over again, the air whistling through its holes, the edges of her nails scratching him every time her hand made contact with his skin. He could feel the sting, still, under his clothes. All his muscles hurt. There were no women like his foster mother here in England, not that he had seen. Englishwomen did not seem to put on that kind of weight.

The woman at the counter in the back of the antique shop was not fat at all. She was compact and middle-aged, her gray hair pulled back tightly at the nape of her neck.

"Is there something I can do for you?" she said. "Is there something you've come to sell?"

John Robert wondered who this woman was. Did she own the shop or just work here? Did antique shops in England always have saleswomen who could speak so precisely, as if delivering lines from a textbook exercise on educated speech? He looked back at the window.

"There's a charm bracelet," he said.

"That's right." She came around her counter and to the front. The back of the window was open, covered only with a cloth, which was supposed to provide a background for the things that were offered for sale. She reached through the slit in the cloth and came back with the bracelet.

"It really is gold, this one," she said. "You don't get that very often in a place like this. Antique, too, some of it."

"Some of what?"

"Some of the charms," she said. She held the bracelet out on the palm of her hand. "That steam engine is old, I think. And the bear. Nineteenth century. You have to wonder who would have brought it here."

"You don't remember who did?"

"I wasn't the one who took it in," she said. "It's well past its date for sale. People bring things here and leave them. I don't know why. I've always wondered if this one belonged to somebody's mother."

"It could take a lot more charms," John Robert said.

"I even have charms," the woman said. "Those we get, all the time. Little bits of gold. People think it's valuable, gold."

"Isn't it?"

"Sometimes. But little bits are little bits. You're not going to get rich with a charm the size of a thumbnail. Do you mean to give that to your sweetheart? I have those other charms, if you want to put some on. I've got them right behind the counter."

"I was thinking of a souvenir," John Robert said. "Something special to bring home from England. We're only here for a week."

"From America," the woman said.

"From America."

"I've got an American charm too," the woman said. "A dollar sign, in gold. But that wouldn't do as a souvenir from England, would it?"

They were at the counter now. John Robert couldn't remember how they had gotten there. He shouldn't try to operate on too little sleep. The woman reached under the counter and came up with a tray. It was full of gold, not only charms, but bangle bracelets, earrings, rings, studs that might have gone through someone's nose, or someone's penis. In Mistress Pamela's room the wallpaper had begun to peel in strips off the walls, and the single window hadn't shut properly. Every time the cane came down on him, he had cried out. He knew when he began to bleed because he could feel the slickness dripping onto the tops of his thighs. He thought somebody would hear them. He imagined the street below them filled with undercover police, all of them holding tape recorders. His body began to buck and rise against the table she had forced him to bend over. His arms pulled against the wrist restraints. His legs strained against the ropes that secured him to the table legs, pulling him wide. The cane came down again and again, again and again, and he was shrieking long before he began to find release. He thought about Lisa and Marianne and his foster mother and his foster sisters and the long line of women down the years, old and young, young and old, it didn't matter. He was spurting out on to the carpet and the wall. Mistress Pamela was getting back to business.

The woman here flicked through the bits of gold in the tray and came up with the dollar sign. "See?" she said. "A dollar sign. An American must have brought it. Or somebody who thought they could buy a charm and it would make them rich."

"I knew people who did that," John Robert said.

"We all know people who do that," the woman said. Her hands were soft and lined. The nails were short and clean and without paint. She put the dollar sign down on the counter by itself. "I can put it on for you, if you like," she said. "It's not hard to do. You only need a soldering iron. I have one."

"Could you do that?"

"Of course I could. I offered. It's not people like you we get in here most of the time. I didn't realize it, when I bought the business."

"Realize what?"

"How sad the people are," the woman said. "It's just that, you know, that was the shock, taking this on. You see them every day, in the street, and you don't notice it. You don't think of it. But you have to think of it in here."

"Acts of corporal charity," John Robert said.

"I'm sorry?" the woman said.

"I was thinking of it," John Robert said. "That word, *corporal.* You only hear it used one of two ways. Corporal punishment. Acts of corporal charity. I've always thought they were much the same thing."

"Do you want me to put the dollar sign on the bracelet?" the woman said. "Maybe your sweetheart will think you're trying to bring her good luck."

Mistress Pamela's nails were fake. She broke one during their session, and as he stood in the middle of her room putting his clothes back on she fixed it with a kit she kept in the table drawer.

"That's a souvenir to take home from a holiday in England," she'd told him.

That was true. He was going to have the marks on his ass for a long time. He was going to have the embarrassment, too, the way he felt standing naked in the middle of her room with blood running down the back of his legs.

"I'll just go and put this on then," the woman in the shop said. "I don't care what kind of charity it is. There isn't much in the way of charity anymore. Not around here. People are sad. There's sadness everywhere."

The woman in the shop did not look sad. She walked away into the back and the lights glinted on the gold in her hand.

He was late getting to the plane in the morning. He was supposed to go on the bus with the rest of them, but he wasn't back in time to get the bus, and the only way they knew to leave without him was because he had remembered the number of one of the other teachers' cell phones.

"I'll be at Heathrow," he'd said, giving as little as possible in explanation. It wasn't their business, anyway, and he wasn't holding anybody up. His free day had been the last. The rest of them expected to be on duty now, right up to the end. He wouldn't have gone back to the hotel at all except that he had to get his clothes, and he needed his flight bag to pack away the charm bracelet.

"You have to be at the airport at least an hour before we're supposed to leave," Carla Massey had said—it was her cell phone, the least sympathetic of the teachers on the trip—and then she'd hung up on him, as if she thought he didn't know what was necessary for traveling these days. He was standing in a phone booth on a windy street he didn't recognize. He still had no idea where he was. He shifted the parcel in his hands and looked at the advertisements taped to the sides of the cubicle. He'd been looking forward to the tall red boxes he'd seen on *Doctor Who*, but this phone booth was nothing like that. It might as well have been a booth in Boston or New York.

He had the charm bracelet in the pocket of his shirt. It was bulky and awkward there. Bits and pieces of the charms stabbed at him. He moved it around for comfort and went out on the street to find a cab. The parcel felt warm to the touch, as if body heat did not dissipate after death.

"A sticker" his foster mother had called him when the social workers asked. The social workers came once a month to sit in the plastic chairs at his foster mother's metal kitchen table. They looked at the cheerful yellow curtains and the samplers she bought at crafts fairs: *If home is where the heart is, I live at Nieman Marcus; My dust bunnies bring Easter eggs; I fight poverty, I work.* They took notes on yellow legal pads with plastic pens printed with the words "Department of Children and Families." They tried not to look at his foster mother's size, or at the dogs coming in and out of the pet door with the mud of the yard all over them, or at the smoke curling up from the tip of her cigarette. "He sticks to things," his foster mother would say, putting the cigarette out in an ashtray overflowing with butts and pale pink wads of chewing gum.

Back at the hotel room, he sat down on the edge of his bed one more time and put the parcel on the bedside table. He went into the shower and washed for the first time in nearly two days. He put his dirty clothes in his suitcase among the clean ones, not really caring one way or the other if the clean ones would be ruined or stained. There was no blood on his clothes. There had been blood on him the night his foster mother was murdered, because he'd gone slipping and sliding in it (thud and suck) when he knelt down to turn her over on the drive. She had been chewing gum when she died. When he nudged her, the gum fell out of her mouth. When he looked up to find the moon, the sky was covered with clouds. Once, in the student center, Lisa Hardwick had grabbed his crotch and squeezed, and he had never been able to tell anybody about it. You couldn't tell people that kind of thing. You could get brought up on charges of sexual harassment.

"It's not so common to find men who like it real," Mistress Pamela had said as he was reaching for his clothes when the session was over. "They want to play at it, that's what. They don't want pain. You do."

"I do what?"

"Like pain," she'd said.

He got clean underwear and a clean shirt and a pair of jeans out of the same suitcase he'd put his dirty clothes in. He put his loafers on without bothering to look for socks. He found the charm bracelet where he'd left it on the bed. The gold dollar sign was shinier than the other charms. He'd noticed it before. That made sense, somehow. Money was always more fascinating than any of the things it could buy. He wondered who would want to buy a zoo full of miniature animals, especially a snake. He wondered what the dice were for. His foster sisters had bought charms for special occasions as well as for luck. They'd had their nails done at a salon in a strip mall just outside of Keene, carved up like topiaries, studded with glass crystals and multifaceted beads.

"He never lets you know what he's thinking," his foster mother had said—but she'd had that one wrong. The truth was, he wasn't thinking anything most of the time. His head was like an enormous seashell broadcasting the sound of the ocean. Thud and suck. Thud and suck. Everything drifted. Everything was the same.

"It would look better with more charms," the woman in the antique shop had said, fastening the bracelet around her wrist to model it for him. "I've never worn charm bracelets myself. I've never understood them."

He reached forward and raised her arm into the light.

"Charms are supposed to mean something," the woman said.

He took the parcel off the table and unwrapped it. He'd been careful to cut the hands off up over the wrists. It was easier that way. Wrist bones were impossible to saw through. He had tried. Fingers lacked what he needed: definition, maybe, or just a place to put the bracelet. He always left them with bracelets. He always bought them something before he let them go.

"It's beautiful," his foster mother had said, that night in the kitchen, before she'd walked down to the end of the drive to talk to the man who wanted cordwood. "Turquoise plastic. I don't think I've ever seen a bracelet made of turquoise plastic."

"I've got a bracelet in turquoise plastic," one of his foster sisters had said. "I bet he stole it from my room."

Down at the end of the drive there was a wooden gate and a big mailbox, big enough to put packages in. His foster mother hated to go down to the post office with those little yellow call slips to pick up whatever she'd had mailed to her from catalogs. She liked to order special-edition plates with pictures of angel children painted on them that she could prop up on little stands in a display case in the living room. She liked people to admire her collections.

"It's beautiful," she'd told him again, ignoring her daughter, which she usually did. Then she got up and started down the drive to the gate and her appointment. If he'd waited another month or two before he killed her, it would have been maple season and she would have been boiling syrup on the stove.

"I never saw anybody come before just from the pain," Mistress Pamela had said, straightening the instruments on her table. "I never saw anybody as young as you before, either. It's old guys I get, most of the time. Sour old men all shriveled up and waiting to die. You have to wonder what they've done they think they need to be punished for."

"It won't look right until it has a few more charms," the woman in the shop said. "Not to me." Then she took the bracelet off and laid it on the counter.

He had meant to buy the charm bracelet for Miss Pamela, but when he had seen it on the arm of the woman in the shop he hadn't been able to imagine it anywhere else. He'd bought another bracelet later, a tin and copper one in a souvenir shop in Leicester Square, with the outline of Tower Bridge engraved on it. He found that one in the pocket of his soiled pants and put it down on the bed next to the charm bracelet. Then he picked them both up and put them away in his flight bag. This was not the first time he had brought a hand back from Europe. He'd done it only last year, after the German trip. The trick was to know what they were looking for, and to keep all things made of metal in their own separate place.

The hands lay in plastic sandwich bags he'd brought from the States. He'd had no idea if they sold plastic sandwich bags in London, and he still didn't know. Miss Pamela's hand was curled in on itself, the nails long and glittery, bare of the rings she'd been wearing the night before. He had had to take off the rings because they could have tripped a metal alarm. The old woman's hand had never had any rings on it, and its fingernails were as plain as ever. She wouldn't waste her money getting bits of plastic and glass drilled into them. His jeans were loose and fluid—"relaxed fit," they were called, meaning they were made to be worn by men who were growing fat. He was not, but he liked the looseness in the legs. He put the bag with Miss Pamela's hand in it down the inside leg on the right and pinned it there. He put the bag with the old woman's hand in it down the inside leg on the left and did the same. He was careful to keep the fingers pointing upward so that the tips under the plastic brushed against his balls. He liked the feel of the plastic-covered palms pressing against his inner thighs. He would take Miss Pamela's hand out of its bag in the bathroom on the plane and put the bangle with Tower Bridge around the wrist. He would leave it under the tissues in the wall dispenser so that nobody would find it until the plane was being readied for takeoff down the line. By then, he would be in a cab in Manhattan, leaving the other one.

"Listen," Lisa Hardwick had said to him that day she'd grabbed his crotch in the student center. "Don't kid me. You always think with your dick."

Maybe he would sit next to Lisa Hardwick on the plane, in one of those three-across arrangements, with Marianne parked between them. He would take the old woman's hand off his thigh in the bathroom at JFK and put the bracelet on it. He would put the hand and the bracelet in the pocket of his jacket, so that he'd be ready with it when it came time to leave it in the cab. The bracelets always came off. They fell into sewer grates and onto tables. They fell down the cracks in couches. He had left the one from Germany in a drawer in a hotel room on I-95 in New Jersey, next to a Gideon Bible, and although the story had made the papers the very next day, there had been nothing said about a sterling-silver bangle bracelet with clusters of daisies around the edges.

He zipped up his pants and reached for the one clean shirt he had left. He put a plain blue crewneck sweater over the shirt. He put his hands between his legs and felt their hands there. If he pressed against them hard enough, they felt alive.

Thud and suck, he thought, piling his suitcases up in front of the door to the hotel room. When he'd started, he'd meant to take their hearts, but he always went on too long. Thud and suck, thud and suck, thud and suck. The knife went in and out and up and down and back again, with its own rhythm, like a dance he'd learned to do and could only do again by rote.

"You think with your dick," Lisa Hardwick had said, and John Robert Mortimer thought that was true.

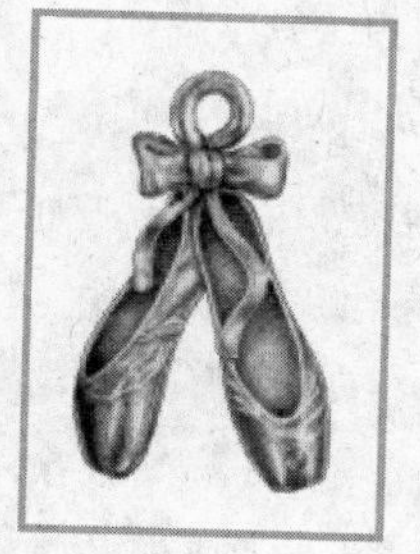

NOT QUITE U.

Laura Lippman

The newspaper had a story the other day about sisters who discovered each other at Princeton, or maybe it was Rutgers. It was definitely a school in New Jersey, I remember that much. Literally separated at birth in Mexico or someplace like that, they had been placed for adoption with two different families—one Jewish and obviously rich, the other Catholic and without so much money, so I guess their daughter was on scholarship, like me. Like I? As I am, yes, that's it. She was on scholarship, *as I am.* Or, as I was, at the time of the story I'm telling.

I was a sophomore at what I'll call Not Quite U., a place that was no one's first choice, except for the premeds. Not Quite wasn't a safety school exactly. In fact, some of the students who didn't want to be there had failed to get into places with lesser reputations. Sure, we had the usual mix of would-be Ivy types, but also people who hadn't made the cut at, say, Washington University or Bucknell. Not Quite U. was a consolation prize, a future line on your résumé, a drag in the present tense. Whenever some magazine did a roundup of the top ten party schools, Not Quite could be found in the correlating list of places where no one had any fun.

That was fine with me. I wasn't in college to have fun. I was pretty pleased with myself, getting into Not Quite with a good financial aid package, although it did feel like crashing a party where no one wanted to be. Even with the scholarship, I had to work two jobs to make ends meet. But I didn't mind either. It meant I spent less time in my dorm, listening to everyone whine about how miserable they were.

My first job was a work-study gig, decorous and dull. I worked at one of the information desks in the Great Glass Library, which afforded me plenty of time to study, but it paid only a dollar above minimum wage. So I fudged my age and my ID, took a second job in a working-class bar not far from campus. Most girls would have gone the glamour route at one of the downtown bars, figuring it would pay better. But a woman who sips a single twelve-dollar cocktail tends to be a lot stingier than a guy drinking six one-dollar drafts. Most people don't get that, but growing up where I did, I know there's no one more generous than a poor man on payday. I made a hundred dollars in tips on Friday night shifts, and while the men were flirty, they were more respectful than the ones you meet in nicer places, the guys who seem to think a handful of ass goes with the drink, another little bowl of snacks.

But I'm getting ahead of myself. This was two years ago, and I had been working at Long John's for six months and liking it almost too much. The whole point of going to Not Quite U., after all, was to do better than my parents had done. When I was in junior high, my father had run a small bar near the racetrack. *Run it right into the ground,* my mother would chime in here. My mother always said that if you wanted to know where to put your money, watch what my father did and run in the other direction. To which my dad said, "True enough, given that I've sunk most of my money into you, and it's the worst bargain I ever made."

This was drunk talk, late at night. My parents weren't generally mean, just disappointed. In life, in each other, in themselves.

And they weren't alcoholics—they just needed a vice they could afford, and a six-pack of Carling Black Label cost $3.69. Me, I don't much care for alcohol. I'll nurse a drink to keep a guy company, but I can't understand why anyone wants to dull the edges that way. I like to keep my mind sharp. Mind sharp, body hard. Did I mention I was on the track team in college? Which wasn't a prestige thing at NQU, which had love in its heart only for lacrosse, but still helped to get me in. I ran the mile, which I think requires the most discipline. Anyone can turn it on for a sprint—you're finished before your brain and body have had the chance to register the effort—while the marathon is a dull, plodding affair. The mile requires speed *and* strategy. And discipline. Even on the days I worked until two A.M., I was up at six for my morning run, back out in the afternoon to practice with the team. All the while, I maintained a B+ average, and I would have made straight A's if it weren't for all the general requirements outside my major, econ.

Everything began in late February of my sophomore year. Long John's was slow because a freak snowstorm had blown in, keeping most of the regulars at home. It was almost nine P.M. and there were only a few hard-core regulars along the bar when the door opened and four students fell in, giggling and stamping their feet. I disliked them on sight. They were so taken with themselves, so self-adoring that it had never occurred to them that anyone could find them less than fascinating. They kept collapsing in hilarity at their own jokes, and I knew that taking their orders would be pure torture. I let them arrange themselves in a booth—more hysterical laughter as they shrugged out of their coats and scarves and hats—before I approached.

"I don't suppose I could get a gin rickey here," one girl said, and the others laughed as if this was the funniest thing they had ever heard. Pretty and haughty, she was the apparent leader, the one they deferred to. Excuse me—*the one to whom they all deferred.* That's it. The one to whom they all deferred.

"The bartender here can do pretty much anything, but I should tell you we don't have a lot of premium brands in stock."

"I like Boodles," she said, prompting another round of laughter. "It's a British gin," she added helpfully, in case I couldn't put it together for myself.

"We have Beefeaters and Gordon's."

"Not even Bombay?"

"Beefeaters and Gordon's," I repeated.

She ran her fingers through her hair and I heard the bracelet before I saw it, and the sound it made was like another laugh at my expense. As an econ major, I didn't have to take too many English classes, but I knew about Daisy Buchanan and the silvery tinkle in her voice. That's what the bracelet sounded like to me, a woman's voice, full of money. The girl who wore it had long dark hair, falling loose to her shoulders, and a heart-shaped face. Staring at her was like looking into a mirror, only my hair has a lighter cast, and my cheekbones aren't as pronounced.

They eventually settled for beers and asked if the kitchen was open. They had apparently been lurching from place to place in the neighborhood, trying to find someone who was open, which is how they ended up at Long John's. They all asked for cheeseburgers, except for bracelet girl, who wanted a chef salad. I brought them their drafts and prayed that they would drink slowly so I could ignore them as much as possible.

"Hey, you and Maya look alike," said one of the boys, the better-looking of the two. He was a short guy, thin yet muscular, with dirty-blond hair curling under the rim of his ski cap.

The girl who wasn't Maya stifled a laugh, as if he had said something forbidden, but the other boy nodded. "Yeah, the resemblance is uncanny."

"What is this, another remake of *The Parent Trap*?" asked Maya. She began fiddling with her bracelet, unhooking the clasp, sliding it from her arm, sliding it back on. "Am I the proper one from Boston or the tomboy from California?"

"They walk alike, they talk alike," the ugly boy sang.

"That was Patty Duke," the other girl corrected him. "What's your name? Where are you from? Maybe you're distant relations and you don't even know it."

"I'm Kate," I said, using the shorter version of my real name. My parents had named me Caitlin. It was the year everyone was naming their daughters Caitlin. Only my mother, being my mother, had spelled it Katelyn. I had shortened it to Kate when I was in high school and the crisp, sharp sound fit me much better. Hard and sharp, like me. "And I'm from around here, more or less."

"Well, I'm from New York," Maya said. "And I have to say, I really don't see it. I mean, we have dark hair and green eyes. So what? Do *you* see it?"

Her look at pretty boy said: You'd better not.

"No," I said. "Our bone structure is completely different."

And I almost ran to the kitchen, heart pounding. It's not easy to give bad service to your only table of the night, but I managed it that evening, hiding in the kitchen as much as possible. They stiffed me on the tip, but they probably would have anyway. Besides, the last thing I wanted was for them to come back, bring other students interested in slumming for a night. If Maya wanted to disavow me, then I was just as anxious to deny her. Although, by all accounts—judging from her clothes, her averred preference for Boodles, and especially that bracelet dangling from her wrist—she had done just fine, better than me. Better than I.

The next week I checked the freshmen face book from her year in an idle moment at the library. She had gone to a private school in New York City. The last name didn't mean anything to me, but maybe she used her mother's name. She was majoring in art history with a minor in dance, a sure tip-off to how wealthy her family must be. No one who was worried about getting a job ever majored in art history.

I should have left it there, and I think I would have, but one of the boys from the bar came into the library one afternoon while I was working. "Hey, it's you," he said. "Maya's twin. Kay."

"Kate. I think I remember you too." He was the sort of cute one.

"I'm Clay, by the way. Why are you working at that bar if you've got a gig here?"

I shrugged, hoping it seemed devil-may-care, I do it for the *experience*, my good man. Not everyone at Not Quite is rich, but even the average kids seem kind of sheltered. I had heard a few stories that made me realize that not everyone's life was glossy perfection—the loss of a parent, a sibling's drug problem. But I hadn't heard anyone yet confess to being on intimate terms with the 911 dispatcher, or knowing the code for a domestic. Hey, nothing's ever a complete loss. The Fraternal Order of Police gave me five hundred dollars toward my tuition.

"I still think you and Maya look alike," he said. "If I didn't know better, I'd say you were long-lost sisters."

"Maybe we are," I said, trying to keep my tone light. "Was her father the mailman?"

"See, that's the funny thing. Maya doesn't know her *real* dad. I think it was some scandal. Luckily, her mom met this great guy and remarried while Maya was still really young. But no one ever talks about it. I've known her since junior high."

"Are you her boyfriend?"

"More of a friend," he said swiftly, as if sensing an opportunity. But I'm not sure the opportunity was there, not when I asked.

Two hours later, I was letting him screw me in his dorm room. His roommate came in not long after we finished, while I was putting on my socks, and said, "Hey, Maya."

"Hey," I said, my voice sweet and tinkly, not at all my own, and Clay didn't bother to correct his roommate's notion of what happened. And if I had been trying to make trouble, wouldn't I have made sure the roommate, ugly boy, knew I wasn't Maya?

It wasn't a big deal, by the way. My generation, whatever our problems, we're level-headed about sex. It feels good, and dorm life provides a lot of opportunities. I've been with guys and I've been with girls, and it's more about warmth than anything else, like puppies in a pet shop window, piled together in a heap. Plus, NQU is in this boring Rust Belt city where there isn't a lot to do. (Are you getting it yet? First choice of premeds, the Great Glass Library, big on lacrosse, Rust Belt city, a college with a two-word name? Look, I'd name it outright, but they have some scary lawyers, men who are very keen that the school's name not be connected with me in any form.) Anyway, it wasn't a big deal, sleeping with Maya's maybe, maybe-not boyfriend. It wasn't some Bette Davis movie where she plays twins, or even that stupid flick where the girl puts the spike heel through the guy's eye after a little mistaken identity action. Sex at NQU was about as meaningful as going out for a latte with somebody, only it didn't cost three dollars. Condoms were free, thanks to the student health clinic.

But sex with Clay was one degree of separation from Maya, and it made me feel as if I had, I don't know, *permission* to remove that one degree, to talk to Maya one-on-one, figure out if I was right about what I suspected. We didn't have any classes together, her being a year ahead and a dilettante art history major, but it was a small enough campus to cross someone's path, if you really put your mind to it.

I put my mind to it.

"Hey," I said, coming across her as she left a rehearsal one night. It was early spring now, just a month after we first met, warmer but by no means balmy. Still, all Maya wore was a pair of sweats over her skimpy leotard. I've got a nice body too, a body very much like Maya's—long-legged, small-boned—but I don't walk around in my track shorts, showing everyone my ass.

"Yeah?" she asked, not looking up. She was bent over her wrist, fastening the charm bracelet. I guess she couldn't wear it when she danced, loud as it was.

"We met at Long John's that one time? Remember? Those crazy guys thought we looked alike."

"Oh, sure." Sizing me up now, still trying to decide if the comparison was an insult.

"I like your bracelet," I said, then hated myself for sounding as if I was sucking up. "I mean, they're very fashionable right now, aren't they? Charm bracelets."

"Are they? This was a gift from my father, so I wear it all the time. It's an odd story—he found it in a cab."

"Was he the driver?"

"No." She laughed as if the idea of a cab-driving father was something quaint. But my dad had driven a cab once upon a time, although I had never heard of him doing it in New York. Then again, my dad's life had a lot of gaps; even the parts I knew about were filled with gaps. "He just found it in the backseat. Normally, he would have handed it over to the driver, but the guy looked kind of shady. So my dad called the cab company and told him what he had found, and they said they would turn it over to him if no one claimed it. No one ever did, so he kept it and gave it to me on my sixteenth birthday."

It sounded like the sort of story my dad would tell, except it had a happy ending. *I put a deposit down on the most beautiful bike, baby, but the guy sold it from under my nose. I went to the toy store, baby, but they didn't have the doll you wanted. I meant to have something for your birthday, honey, but I got held up at work and all the stores were closed.* Until I was ten, I believed it all. That was when I found out about the two things that kept us so broke—Daddy's poker habit and Daddy's other family.

"I'm going for coffee. You want to come?" Again, I could have kicked myself for sounding so needy. But Maya said yes. I don't know why. Maybe she wanted a cup of coffee. Maybe she liked me, in spite of herself. Maybe she wanted to know more about this strange girl with her face. We went to a place just off campus, Grounds for Life. That was the year when all the coffee places around Not Quite U. had *grounds* in the name. Grounds for Life, Urban Grounds, Common Grounds. Only the last one made sense to me.

"Hey, maybe someday someone will open up a Grounds Zero," I said as we fixed our coffees, just to be saying something. I noticed we took our coffees the same, with skim and two Equals.

Maya wrinkled her nose. All my life, I had been seeing that phrase in books, but I didn't really get it until that moment. She looked like a cat, a cat that had smelled something bad. I wondered if I would look like that if I made the same face.

"I'm sorry, my dad is a stockbroker. We knew like a dozen people who were killed that day."

"Your stepdad, right?"

She didn't like that word. She played with the clasp on her bracelet, easing it on and off her wrist, just as she had that first night in Long John's. "Who told you that?"

I shrugged, determined not to mention Clay. See, I didn't have any intention of hurting her. If I wanted to blow up her life, I could have done it right there, introduced Clay into the mix and let her draw her own conclusions. "I don't know. I probably just confused you with someone else. You know how it is on this campus, you hear bits and pieces of people's lives, all out of context. It gets jumbled up."

"Well, he is my stepdad, technically. But I think of him as my father. I never knew my *biological* father." She hit that word hard, as if it was something distasteful. "He ran out on the family when I was less than a year old."

"You never knew him?"

"I don't want to know him. Creep."

"Still, he paid child support, right?"

"I'm sure I don't know. It couldn't have been much—he was a real loser. It was my mother's lucky day when he left. She met my dad, Frank, six months later and they were married before I was three years old. I grew up on Park Avenue."

The last detail bugged me. Why would she tell me that she grew up on Park Avenue if she didn't know it would get under my skin? We had moved nine or ten times, but not one of our former addresses was Park Avenue. I had lived on streets with names like Meushaw and Hinton, places as ugly as they sounded, in stripped-down apartments that were still more than we could afford. We usually left owing a month or two of rent, although once my dad played the hand too far and they put our stuff on the street. Whatever happened, the excuse for everything we didn't have was that my father had another family before he met my mom and his ex-wife took him for every penny he had, even though she didn't need it. My mom tried to make it sound more proper than it was, but I did the math and I figured out that the last child of his first marriage and the first child of his second marriage—me, me, me—had been born within a few months of each other. Four to be exact. My birthday was October, which meant I was always the youngest in my class.

"I took a sociology and statistics class last semester, and they say the average household sees its income drop after divorce. Guess your family bucked that trend."

"Thanks to my father, yes. If my mother hadn't met him, life would have been pretty hand-to-mouth for us."

"Your *stepfather,*" I said because precision in language is important to me.

"Right," Maya said.

"I have both parents, and life is really hand-to-mouth for me."

I was trying to make a joke, or at least be a little self-deprecating, but Maya didn't laugh. She suddenly glanced at the big neon clock over the counter and said she had to go. She left in such a hurry that she didn't notice her charm bracelet was still on the table. Maybe that was because it had sort of scooted under a napkin, so she didn't see it as she gathered up her stuff. Or maybe she thought it was in her tote. At any rate, she left it behind and she was long gone before I realized it was there. So I did what anyone would do. I picked it up, planning to give it to her later.

Of course, I examined it first. It was surprisingly heavy and some of the charms were almost lethally sharp. A person would have lots of little nicks and cuts on her wrist, wearing a bracelet like that day in and day out. You couldn't dance in it, or work on a computer, or—if Maya had a life more like mine—wait tables with it on. You wouldn't want to wear it with a fine dress, because it would end up catching a thread here or there, creating runs. And you couldn't make love with it. You'd put someone's eye out, as my mom might say, although not about sex.

I fingered the charms. There was a heart-shaped locket with a catch and I tried to pry it open, certain my father's photo was inside. I know, I know, Maya said it was her stepfather who had found it in the cab, but I didn't believe that. She was so keen to write our father out of her life that she had revised the story in her head.

The charm I couldn't help noticing were the ballet slippers, two tiny gold cylinders with ribbons so fine you couldn't imagine one not getting broken over the years, with a jewel sparkling at one toe. It could have been cubic zirconium, but how would I be able to tell? The most precious stone I ever saw was the green glass in my high school ring. But I was sure it was a diamond glistening on those toe shoes.

I had wanted to take dancing lessons, wanted it more than anything. I was graceful, I had the right build for it, long and lean. But even the half-assed amateurs who teach ballet and tap and jazz at ten bucks a pop still expect to be paid, up front and in full. Twice I got into a class, only to have to drop out when my dad stopped paying. I can still see myself at eight, bare-legged because the leotard and the shoes were a big enough stretch—no money left over for the pink tights—being told that I can't come to class again until my mommy or daddy calls Madame Elena. After the second time I was barred from class—barred from the barre—I just didn't go back. I began running. To run, all you need is a pair of shoes and an open road.

I tucked the bracelet in my jacket pocket, thinking I would

give it to Maya the next time I saw her. It was the natural thing to do, right? She was gone, I couldn't run after her, and I didn't know exactly where she lived. I couldn't see giving it to the manager at Grounds for Life—he looked pretty skeevy. But what with one thing and another, I didn't see her for a while. Midterms came, and then spring hit the area hard, with a wave of almost summer-like days. Even the mopey types at Not Quite U. knew what to do with good weather. The grassy hill in front of the Great Glass Library was filled with sunbathing girls and Frisbee-tossing boys. They told us not to tan—Not Quite put on a big information push about skin cancer, just like with STDs and eating disorders—but we know, okay? We knew and we made our choices.

Anyway, I was sitting on the lawn with my sociology text when Clay approached me. He seemed kind of nervous, but guys often act weird after they've had sex with you. Why is that? I haven't been with that many guys, but I haven't found one yet who wasn't nervous after screwing you. Maybe it's because I don't get hooked on them, don't follow them around. The only thing guys dislike more than a clingy girl is a nonclingy girl.

"Hey," he said. "Kate." He looked around, as if he was proud of knowing my name and wanted to see if anyone appreciated the great effort he had made, dredging it up.

"Hey," I said, refusing to give him a name at all.

"Um, you know Maya? My girlfriend?" So she was his girlfriend now. I hope she appreciated her promotion. "She said you two had coffee a while back."

I figured he was feeling me out, trying to find out if I had told her anything.

"Yeah, for all of ten minutes. We didn't really get in too deep." See, I was being nice, letting him off the hook. I didn't sleep with him to make trouble for anyone, especially myself.

"Well, she thinks maybe she left her bracelet there, and she wonders if you took it."

Took it. Not *picked it up*, or *remember if she was wearing it that night*, or anything like that. He went straight to *took it*.

"Bracelet? I don't know anything about a bracelet."

"Oh." He was standing over me, his shadow blocking the sun, so I was beginning to catch a chill. It was that time of the year when there is a huge difference between sun and shadow, when you can lie in a bikini if you are out in the open, but would freeze in a lane of trees if you aren't carrying a sweater. "She was pretty sure she wore it that night."

"I just don't remember it. I guess I didn't notice it."

"She said you talked about it, that you asked her about it."

Shit, I had. But so what? "Maybe I did. I just don't remember."

"The thing is, she's always taking it on and off. It's like a nervous habit with her."

"Sorry."

It wasn't just that Maya had all but accused me of being a thief. It was the fact that she did it secondhand, sent her boyfriend to claim it for her, as if she were some lady fair and he was a knight trying to win her devotion.

"Well, if you see it around—" Clay said, looking more nervous than ever. He was scared to go back to Maya empty-handed. He was that whipped.

"What does it look like?" I asked. I wish I hadn't. The lie was too perfect in its nonchalance, and Clay caught it. He ambled away with a careless backward glance at my body, as if congratulating himself for knowing what it looked like without a bathing suit.

A week passed, then another, and no one came to talk to me about the bracelet again. I can't say I completely forgot about it—I kept the bracelet in my top drawer, next to my underwear, so I saw it every morning—but it wasn't uppermost in my mind. If I thought about the bracelet at all, it was to wonder how I could get it back to Maya anonymously. No plan seemed right.

And then I came back to my room one night and found Maya standing there with the resident adviser, demanding to be let in. The RA thought it was bogus, I could tell. He took me aside and asked me to let her look through my room as a favor, so she would back off. Apparently her stepfather had been making calls to various people and he was a big giver and an alum, so they had to indulge him. Yet the RA was so sympathetic and kind that I began to think the bracelet *wasn't* in my room, that it was all a horrible misunderstanding. But once the door was unlocked, Maya went straight for it, as if the bracelet had a homing device.

"How did that get there?" I asked. And the thing is, I meant it. I really couldn't remember.

"Because you *stole* it. And you're just lucky that all I care about is getting it back, because my father said this bracelet is so valuable that I could bring felony theft charges against whoever had it."

My father. Two simple words, people say them all the time. But it was a lie, in Maya's mouth, and the lie made me furious.

"Your *stepfather*. Because I know who your father was, and he happens to be my father too. And while you were living on Park Avenue and going to private school, he was either broke from paying your child support or moving us around so they couldn't find him to pay the child support. Five hundred dollars a month was nothing to you, but it was a lot to us, as much as we paid for rent in some places."

"Don't be ridiculous," Maya said. "We're practically the same age and my father didn't leave until I was two. How could we have the same father?"

"Pretty much in the same way we ended up having the same boyfriend." I turned to the RA, the lie now fully formed. "She planted this here because she's jealous of me for having sex with her boyfriend, Clay. She's setting me up."

I looked to the RA, then Maya. She was clearly shocked, and she sagged into him, whimpering a little. The RA, so recently my ally, looked at me as if I were pure evil. So I did the only thing that made sense to me at that moment: I grabbed the bracelet back from Maya and began to run, just run, with no plan or thought. I was too busy doing the math in my head. The child support checks my father made out every month had been for $500. But $500 a month was $6,000 a year and almost $100,000 over sixteen years. The money my father spent on Maya, who didn't need a dime, could have covered my tuition at Not Quite U. And she was going to begrudge me a bracelet, found by our father, in his cab? The way I see it, she had gotten to have the bracelet and now it was my turn. I ran, the bracelet in my hand, and, remember, I was fast, a miler.

But Maya chased me, and she had stamina from dancing, if not speed. She chased me down the steps of our dorm and onto the street. She chased me up the main drag, the one that separated the housing units from the campus, and into a neighborhood of grand old houses. The fruit trees had lost their blooms and the tulips were beginning to lose their petals, but the azaleas were coming in and the trees were past the budding stage. Funny, the things you notice at such a moment, but I was breathing hard and those green spring smells went deep into my lungs. It occurred to me that Maya's family could afford a house as nice as the ones we ran past, possibly nicer, given how much more stuff cost in New York. I wondered if she had a car and a horse, if all the charms on the bracelet digging into my palm represented the abundance that Maya took for granted.

She was not close to catching me, and I knew the gap between us would only increase the longer we ran. But I also knew I'd have to go back eventually, face the RA and whatever consequences Not Quite U. had in store for me. They probably wouldn't let me have student housing next year, which was fine with me. I already planned to move off campus. But I didn't want to let go of the bracelet, not yet, so I ran and Maya continued to run after me. I wonder now why she didn't scream for someone to stop me, but I was still in my practice clothes and people were used to seeing young women jog down these streets around the university. I reached a busy intersection and crossed the street just as the light changed. I gather that Maya tried to put on a burst of speed, thought she could cross on the diagonal and pick up some ground. At any rate, I heard the screechy sound of failing brakes and then a scream, just one.

Maya was hit by a car, an ordinary car. Campus rumor blew it into a bus, but it wasn't that dramatic. I'm tempted to say it was a cab because that would give the story a nice shape, and maybe over the years I'll allow myself that one little tweak. But it was just a car, and a fairly small one. Luckily for Maya, the woman saw her and braked, so she wasn't going that fast when she hit her. Unluckily for Maya, her left knee absorbed most of the impact.

Plenty of people gathered around her, so there was no reason for me to go back, nothing I could do. I slowed to a walk, turned the first corner I came to, and sank onto a bench, as if waiting for a bus. The bench said THE GREATEST CITY IN AMERICA, a claim so pathetically untrue that I wanted to laugh. This was the kind of place, the kind of people, I came from: all brag, no do. I had tried everything I could to set myself apart. I wasn't going to be like my father, too busy dreaming to ever get it right. I certainly wasn't going to be like my mother, who had settled for being the dreamer's wife. But for all I had done, I would never be my sister, fate's favorite up until five minutes ago, one of life's natural-born winners. True, she's never going to dance again, but that will probably be for the best too. She'll marry some rich guy, sit on the board of the New York City Ballet, and spend the rest of her life alluding to the dance career she might have had if she hadn't been hit by a car.

The bracelet had left dozens of tiny red marks, like a cat's tooth prints, inside my right palm. I let it dangle from my index finger, watching the play of light on the diamond on the ballet shoes. I wondered if Maya's stepfather had really found it in a cab, or if that was simply a story he had invented, a cover for something more disreputable—a card game, a payoff for a bad debt. No, that's what my father would do. What was the logic of a world in which someone like Maya got a bracelet and a new father, while I had to make do with the cheap, pathetic bastard I'd known since birth? My dad was capable of a lot, but the bottom line was that he wasn't organized enough to run back and forth between two families, not even for a few months. Maya was not my sister, which meant that I couldn't show up at Park Avenue or wherever she lived and demand that her stepfather save me as he had saved her. I couldn't even justify keeping the bracelet he had given her, but I didn't see why she should have it back. I tossed it under the bench in the greatest city in the world a few blocks from the greatest university where no one wanted to be and went back to the dorm.

When I told them I had lost the bracelet, they asked me to leave school. My folks said a twenty-year-old who wasn't in school had to support herself, and I didn't bother to point out that I had been supporting myself even while in school. So here I am two years later in the airport bar, wearing a black polyester skirt that gives me permanent visible panty line and dusting peanut skins from the seat. I am taking classes at the community college, but I still have a few years to go before my degree, and then I'm going to look at MBA programs. What do you think, Wharton or Kellogg?

I hope business picks up again soon. It's not just that fewer people are flying, but that people aren't as anxious to get blotto before a flight anymore. Everyone thinks they're going to be wrestling a terrorist to the ground somewhere over Pittsburgh. They almost seem to wish for it. But my mother said this is a good place to meet men, and I guess she should know. She met my father this way, back in the day when they called this airport Friendship.

So—are you married? Do you have a family? I don't mind. I know how to keep things casual.

THE THINGS WE DID TO LAMAR

Peter Moore Smith

We gave him noogies, Indian burns, charley horses, wet willies. We tickled him till he peed in his pants. We dangled him by his underwear from the dogwood tree in front of his house and left him hanging there. We held him down and let daddy-longlegs crawl all over his face. Once we gave him a potato chip and after he ate it we told him it had been dipped in formaldehyde; later, he hugged his stomach, rocked back and forth against the chain-link fence between our houses, and puked. The two of us, me and Benjamin, we'd trap Lamar in the concrete playground tube by the school, one of us on each side, and not let him out until he held his ears and squealed. Lamar had this sideways smile that flashed, all crooked and weird, even when we were beating the crap out of him. Christ. The things we did to that poor fucker. We shaved stripes into his head with Benjamin's dad's barbershop clippers. Sometimes we'd ask him if he wanted to go to the movies, and after he got the money from his mom we'd just take it to the 7-Eleven and buy SlimJims.

Lamar. Oh, Jesus.

One afternoon we took his latchkey and threw it up on the roof. Next thing we knew old Lamar was up there, hanging by one hand from the rain gutter, smiling and giggling.

"Jump!" we said. "We'll catch you!"

Yeah, right.

Lamar's fat friend Anthony, who followed Lamar everywhere, had to call the fire department to get him down.

We took his comic books; we took his baseball cards; we took his clothes and made him run home in his underpants; we took his money, his food, his toys. Anything he had, we took it. One time we noticed he was wearing a girl's bracelet. He said he found it under a park bench when he went to Baltimore to visit his grandma. Benjamin took it and threw it to me. I pretended to drop it down a sewer drain but really I stuck it in my pocket. We played keep-away with his hat, his books, his Scooby-Doo lunch box; we took his homework so many days in a row that Lamar started making multiple copies, hiding little squares of folded paper all over his clothes.

And fat Anthony, who was always just sort of standing around while we tortured poor Lamar, even *he* would laugh, his stomach jiggling like one of Mom's church picnic Jell-O molds.

This is a good one:

One time we told Lamar that if he put on girls' underwear we'd let him come over to Benjamin's house and listen to Benjamin's dad's quadrophonic hi-fi system. Then, in the vacant lot behind the Safeway, after he'd slipped on my sister's training bra and underpants, we took a Polaroid and dropped it into the mail slot of Lamar's house.

There was also the time Benjamin said Lamar was retarded but that no one was telling him.

"I am not retarded," Lamar said. "I get straight A's."

"Sure," Benjamin said. "In retard class. You're a straight-A *retard*."

"It's not a *retard* class."

"How do you know?"

"Because it's the *advanced* class."

"How do you know they're not just saying that to make you feel smart, and that you're really all a bunch of retards?"

Lamar's eyes grew wide.

"Retard," Benjamin said.

Lamar put his hands over his ears.

" 'Tard."

We'd punch Lamar in the same place on his arm until the bruise turned black, with concentric rings of purple and yellow. When we punched Lamar he would close his eyes but keep smiling. Then, after a few days of getting punched in the same spot, Lamar would do anything to guard it, offering up almost every other part of his body, giggling and at the same time twisting away in this grotesque, prissy dance.

The more he danced, the more we laughed.

Even Anthony.

It wasn't any fun to beat up Anthony, incidentally. He would just fall down, never saying anything, never begging or squealing or giggling like Lamar. Funny thing was, I remember seeing Lamar really give it to Anthony, so I guess *he* got a kick out of it. Lamar would punch his poor fat friend in the same place in the arm that we punched him, but Anthony would just rub it with his hand, a look of stupefaction on his stupid, fat face. Lamar called Anthony Fat-Boy, Fatty-Boomba-Latty, Fatty-McFat-Fat, the President of the Fat States of Fat-merica.

This made Benjamin crazy.

I can say this now—if I had said *then* he would have beaten the crap out of me—but Benjamin was kind of fat himself.

"You wanna pick on someone just because they're fat?" Benjamin would say to Lamar, defending Anthony. "You wanna make fun of somebody just because they're a little bit overweight?" He punctuated each word with a hard punch to Lamar's arm.

"You do it," Lamar would say.

"I"—*punch*—"do"—*punch*—"not"—*punch.*

"Stop it." Lamar twisted his body and fell to the ground.

"It's all right," Anthony said softly. "He was just joking."

We were on the school playground, on the swings.

"Shut up, faggot," Benjamin said. "Just because I'm beating up

Lamar because he called you fat doesn't mean I won't beat the crap out of you because you're a faggot, you faggot."

So Anthony and I waited until Benjamin got tired of beating the crap out of Lamar.

Then, as they walked away, Lamar rubbing his arm, Anthony a few steps behind, Lamar turned around to Anthony and sang, "Fatty fatty fat-butt! So fat you ate the cat's butt!"

From where I was on the swings I could see Anthony's face. I could almost feel the hot tears exploding down his cheeks.

Infuriated, Benjamin took off after Lamar, chasing him across the soccer field, over the pedestrian overpass, and into the vacant lot behind the Safeway. I ran behind Benjamin, Anthony huffing and puffing behind me. I thought the whole thing was hilarious, to tell the truth. Benjamin *was* fat, and Lamar had found this weird, indirect way of saying it. Lamar jumped up on a rock and held his tight little fist in the air, smiling hugely, like he was about to say something magnificent. But Benjamin just crashed into him, grabbing him around the waist and pushing him into a huge pile of trash. "It's not nice"—*punch*—"to call someone"—*punch*—"fat"—*punch*.

"I didn't call *you* fat," Lamar said.

"I didn't say I *was* fat," Benjamin said, punching him again. "Are you saying *I'm* fat?"

Lamar squirmed and tried to twist away.

Benjamin reached for the nearest thing, which happened to be a rusted tin top to an old can of something, and held it to Lamar's throat.

Me and Anthony were standing on the rock, looking down.

"You better go ahead and do it," Lamar said. "Because one day I'm going to—"

"What?" Benjamin said. "You're going to do what, fag fucker?"

Anthony's eyes were huge, and he was out of breath. "One day," he gasped, "he's going to kill you."

Benjamin and I just laughed.

"He will." Anthony looked around, even more surprised. "He's crazy."

Benjamin laughed so hard he actually rolled off Lamar into the heap of trash. "Crazy?" He went into hysterics. *"Lamar?"*

Lamar got up and brushed the filth from his clothes. "I'd kill you now," he said, giggling hysterically, "but these are my good pants."

There was a party at Clarista Siedbetter's once. Her family had an aboveground backyard pool. Everyone was there. Even Lamar and Anthony showed up, Lamar in a pair of tight red swimming trunks and a Scooby-Doo towel wrapped around his skinny shoulders, Anthony in his dad's plaid boxer shorts and a minuscule green and white towel that had been stolen from a Holiday Inn. Lamar and Anthony climbed up on the platform and were about to get in when Clarista said, "Oh, I'm so sorry, Lamar, but the law only allows eleven kids in the pool at a time."

"The law?" Lamar lifted an eyebrow.

"You know"—Clarista had it all worked out—"safety regulations."

I gave the pool a quick count.

There was me, Benjamin, Clarista, Billy Elliman, Tiffany Engleton, Todd Skrillitz, Sheri Bristol, Jonathon and Bobby Bintliff, Kelly Fritz, and Parker Townsend.

Eleven.

Sheri Bristol, who was already one of the prettiest girls in our neighborhood, offered to get out so Lamar could swim. "I don't mind," Sheri said.

But Clarista gave her this look. It was like in *Star Wars* when Darth Vader strangled that guy without even touching him.

Sheri just shut the fuck up.

The sunlight that day was a narcotic; morphine light mixed with the heavy chlorine in my eyes and I saw a film over everything—blue, green, yellow, like I was looking through sheets of plastic. Everything seemed slo-mo, far away, disconnected. "It's all right." Lamar, smiling as always, wrapped his Scooby-Doo towel around his shoulders and climbed down from the platform. Anthony remained a few steps behind. "We have a hose in our backyard, and my dad just bought me a Slip 'n Slide."

Benjamin laughed. "Yeah. Go play with your Slip 'n Slide!"

It seemed like time folded in half. It seemed like I saw myself from above.

The sun heated the blue water and glanced off the tanned faces of the neighborhood kids.

Clarista swam directly over and kissed me. I was twelve, two weeks from thirteen. She tasted like cigarettes.

At home that night I considered giving Clarista the charm bracelet I had stolen from Lamar. I took it out of the drawer and examined it. It was pretty old, I guess, with a tiger, a little train that had actual moving wheels, a saxophone, little ballet slippers, and even a monkey.

But for some reason I decided to keep it.

Fuck Clarista, I thought. And then I actually thought about fucking Clarista.

And that was weird.

Two weeks later it was just me and my sister. No other kids. No party. My mom had made a chocolate cake, and we were sitting around after a dinner of Kentucky Fried Chicken, my favorite, picking at the bones, when we heard the doorbell. "Answer the door," Jean said.

"It's my birthday. You answer it."

By that time my mom was already opening the door, revealing Lamar and a brightly wrapped package. "Happy birthday!" He wore that usual sideways smile.

I got up.

The package was tied with curly red ribbons and silver bows.

"Come in, Lamar." Mom was speaking to Lamar but looking at me. "Isn't that nice?" she said. "A birthday present." Whenever there was a stranger in the house, my mother started using her June Cleaver voice.

"Hi, Lamar." I walked over to the living room, and Lamar stepped inside.

"Would you like a piece of birthday cake?" my mother asked. "I'll bet you'd like a nice big piece of chocolate birthday cake."

Lamar gave me that look, all sideways and smiley.

"Yeah, Lamar," I said weakly, "have some cake."

"Open it," he said, holding the package forward.

"What is it?"

My sister rolled her eyes. "Open it, *moron*."

I took the package, sat down on the living room floor, and carefully slid the ribbon off, and then I tore some of the wrapping away.

"It's an ant farm." Lamar was standing above me.

"An ant farm?"

"You better keep that thing out of my room," Jean said. "I don't want ants crawling all over my stuff."

The paper torn back, I could see the box cover. In big, yellow words it said ANT FARM! THE FUN, SCIENTIFIC WAY TO LEARN ABOUT THE INSECT KINGDOM!

My mother looked at me. "What do you say?"

I looked at Lamar. "Thanks, Lamar."

My mother was standing behind Lamar, and she was about to touch his shoulder, but for some reason she stopped herself halfway through and disappeared into the kitchen.

I remember seeing Lamar through the picture window of his house. He would stand on a chair and look out at us when we were playing. He had a way of pushing his chest forward and holding his hands up in front of him, his fingers moving slowly, like he was strumming a harp.

What a fucking freak.

The subdivision of our neighborhood was organized around a series of alternating blocks and cul-de-sacs. There was a block, and going into the middle of each block was a street, at the end of which was a circular drive. Organized around the circle was a series of houses, each of them pretty much the same. Some had gray roofs; some had black. Some of the houses were made of red brick; some had colored siding. Our circle, which was called Galaxy Court, was the last part of the development and butted right up against the turnpike. On the other side of the pike was the Andromeda Shopping Plaza, which included the Safeway, Dart Hardware, Hallmark, 31 Flavors, H&R Block, and 7-Eleven. Behind the Safeway was a vacant lot. There were a bunch of large, flat rocks, big enough to stand on, a couple of rusted-out Dumpsters, and a fascinating glacier of trash.

I can't tell you how many times we beat the crap out of Lamar back there. Or threw him into one of the Dumpsters. Or covered him with garbage.

Anyway, for the past couple of weeks I hadn't seen Benjamin around much. I had seen him with Clarista Siedbetter's brother Eddie once, who was fifteen. They were getting into some other teenager's car. I had thought to call after them, to see if they were going to the mall, but I was pretty sure Benjamin had seen me. I had even seen him smoking inside the concrete tube with Clarista, and I didn't think it was just a cigarette, and he had his arm around her. So, since I had nothing to do I went over to the Safeway lot and just sort of poked through the trash.

Anyway, I was jabbing a stick at a super-gross dead rat when I heard a voice say, "You're going to catch a disease."

I turned around. "Hey, Lamar." It was a Sunday morning, I remember, and I was surprised to see him because Lamar's family was usually in church on Sunday mornings.

He came up beside me and sniffed. "My father said you shouldn't play with dead animals, that you can get diphtheria."

I pushed the stick under the rat and flicked it toward him. "He's right." It grazed his bare leg.

"Stop it." He rubbed his hands over the piece of skin the dead rat had touched. Then he said, "You want to play something?"

"Like what?"

"I don't know. Make-believe?"

Make-believe was a game I was trying to leave behind. I had just turned thirteen. "You mean like *Star Trek?*" I said. "Or war?"

"That would be cool." Lamar nodded. "Or what about religion?"

"What do you mean, religion?"

"We could have our own religion," he said, "and we could be gods." He jumped up on a rock and pointed down at me. "We could pretend this rock is a mountain, and that there's an entire civilization down there in the trash. You know, countries and cities. And sometimes we can be nice gods and give them good weather, and other times, for no reason whatsoever, we can smash everything in sight." Lamar was smiling his maniac smile.

"And they have to worship us?" I said. "They have to get down on their knees and pray to us, like, three times a day?" I climbed up on the rock next to him. "Because if they don't—"

"Yeah," Lamar said, "if every single person doesn't worship the heck out of us three times a day"—he jumped down from the rock and started smashing imaginary cities—"we'll kill everyone." I was feeling like a regular Mahatma Gandhi for not punching Lamar, and was also a little surprised by the vividness of his imagination. "Except for this little family," he went on. He picked up an empty box of kitchen matches and placed it gently on top of the rock. "A devout family of four, who always worships us every day. They get to live and to be the founders of a new, futuristic civilization."

"Nah." I stepped on the matchbox, grinding it beneath the ball of my foot. "Fuck *them*."

I looked at Lamar's face. He was biting his lip and for once his smile had disappeared.

Over the course of my childhood Benjamin and I had broken, mangled, or destroyed pretty much every toy this kid ever had. We took away his baseballs, snapped the arms off his GI Joes, slipped his Tonka Toys into our pockets and told him we didn't know where they went. I had never felt bad about it. Not once. But now, for some reason, after stepping on an empty matchbox . . . "I'm sorry about that, Lamar." I reached down and reconstructed it.

Lamar released his lower lip and smiled. "So this family that worships us can be the beginning of an entirely new civilization." He placed the now-smashed-but-pathetically-reconstructed matchbox on a flat part of the rock, then went to the trash glacier to find other items. "The first thing they build," he said, "is a temple in our honor." He found an empty orange juice carton and placed it next to the matchbox.

"Oh, man," I said, suddenly excited. "Check out *this* temple." I selected an empty bottle of Sprite and placed it on the rock.

"Okay," Lamar said, smiling full out, "okay. So maybe that temple can be in your honor, and this one"—he grabbed another soda bottle, placing it at the end of our imaginary civilization—"can be for me."

"And they become rivals," I said, "and one part of the world starts to worship me and the other half starts to worship you, and they start to have wars and crap."

"An excellent idea, Mr. Watson."

We played silently for a while, going back and forth from the trash glacier to the large flat rock and placing imaginary houses, schools, and temples in a grid pattern. The cities grew, side by side, and I couldn't help but notice that Lamar's civilization was somehow more clever than mine, that the way he placed his bits and pieces of trash actually resembled a metropolis as though seen from an airplane. We completely covered the rock, and then I felt it was time. I flicked a white plastic bottle cap toward Lamar's city. It struck and toppled a milk carton.

"What are you doing?"

"My people have been secretly amassing weapons," I said, "and now they're ready for battle."

"All right." I saw Lamar's smile, wide and white. He grabbed an old pen and flung it toward my biggest temple. I laughed and picked up a flattened Coke can, skimming it off Lamar's city. We went back and forth a few times this way until Lamar said, "And now the gods themselves are called on to fight." We started walking over our cities, smashing everything with our feet, kicking down the schools and auditoriums, the city halls and restaurants. We shattered and scattered all our work until the entire civilization was reduced to rubble. "And now," he said, fully absorbed in the game, "it is time for me to send my only son to live among the people." Lamar knelt down on the rock and placed a red twist tie that he had fashioned into the shape of a cross in the middle of all the rubble.

For some reason I felt my face turn hot. I said, "That is ridiculous bullcrap."

"What do you mean?"

"You're just repeating some crap they told you in church." I was repeating my father, actually, who hated everything about religion and went into a tirade whenever it came up.

"Okay," he said, "forget it."

"I've already forgotten," I informed Lamar, walking away.

"We could play *Star Trek*." Lamar got up and came after me. "Or war. You could be Spock."

I turned around. "I don't feel like playing *Star Trek*."

"Do you want to watch TV?" he said. "You could come to my house."

I punched him. He rubbed the patch of skin I had punched

and kept walking beside me. "We could build up the civilization and smash it down again."

"I don't think so."

"We could—"

"You never know when to shut up, Lamar," I said, "do you?"

We walked back across the pedestrian overpass, crossed the turnpike, me angry for no real reason and Lamar with his head down, and continued that way until we came to our houses.

Then, right before I walked into my yard, I punched him in the arm so hard he fell on the ground.

I was in the driveway, listening to music on an old transistor radio I had found in my dad's closet, when two police cars drove up next door, one black and white, the other a plain sedan. The policemen got out, went to Lamar's house, and knocked. Lamar's mom answered. She wore a beige pantsuit. I turned the radio off and went to stand by the fence to hear what was happening. I remember her saying, "What?" I remember Lamar's sister, Estelle, coming to the door. She'd had her hair done. I turned around from the fence and saw my mother standing at the door of our house. She had a package of Kraft macaroni and cheese in her hands. I heard one of the policemen ask for Lamar. Then the two policemen in suits went inside and the other two waited for a while on the front lawn.

One of them turned his face toward the sun.

A couple of minutes later I saw Lamar come out. His mother was right behind him. They went to the police car, and one of the officers opened the door to the backseat. They got in, and the plainclothes policemen got in the front. They started the car up again and drove away, leaving me standing in the yard holding the transistor radio, Estelle in the door of Lamar's house, and my mother behind me. When I turned to look at my mother's face I saw something in it, some delicate movement along the jaw.

"I want you to tell me what happened." She sat me down at the kitchen table.

"What happened to what?"

"What did Lamar do?"

"Lamar didn't do anything."

"Why did the police come for him?"

I remember this: I was crying. I didn't know why. I felt like an idiot. Thirteen years old, and I was crying.

"If you know something," my mother said. "If you know anything, you have to tell me . . ." Her voice was shaking. She was thin and tall, with short curly hair. It occurred to me for the first time just then that she was a person.

A local girl—it was Tiffany Engleton, I found out later—had discovered the body of a boy in the vacant lot behind the Safeway supermarket on the turnpike. The police suspected that a fight between two neighborhood boys had gone too far, and for the time being they were calling it an accident.

It was Benjamin, I realized. Benjamin was dead.

Lamar had actually killed Benjamin, just like he said he would. I went to my room and sat on the edge of the bed with my hands in front of me. I wondered what I should do. What are you supposed to do when someone kills someone? I felt like I should pray or visit his grave or do something solemn.

Then, right around seven-thirty, there was a knock at the door. "Mom," I heard Jean say, "it's the police."

My mother went into the living room, and I walked in behind her.

They were the same two plainclothes detectives I had seen earlier.

"Good evening, ma'am," the older one said. "I'm Detective Alta, and this is Assistant Detective Claridge. We were wondering if we could have a few words with your son."

The older detective had short gray hair and a polyester blue blazer. The younger one, I'll never forget, had hair that was completely white.

"Of course," she said. "Please. Come in."

My father reclined in his vinyl easy chair in front of the television. He turned the volume down with the remote control.

The police detectives nodded to him and sat down on the couch.

"Can I get you some coffee?" my mother asked in her idiotic June Cleaver voice. "A soda, perhaps?"

"Thank you for offering," the older detective said. "But we're just fine."

I stood in front of the coffee table.

"And how are you?" the detective asked.

"Me?"

"Yes."

I looked at my Adidas. "Fine."

"The boy who lives next door," he said. "Are you friends with him?"

"Lamar?"

"Yes, Lamar Duncan."

I had breathed out, I think, but for some reason I couldn't breathe in.

The detective said, "Is he a friend of yours?"

I looked at my mother.

"They're friends," she said. "Lamar gave him an ant farm."

"An ant farm?"

"For his birthday."

"Is Lamar a nice boy?" the detective asked me.

"He's nice," I managed to say.

"Does he . . . does he pick on other kids sometimes?" The detective came forward off the couch, almost crouching on the floor.

I couldn't think of a response. My face was on fire. I kept

thinking of Benjamin. I kept imagining him naked on a stretcher in a hospital somewhere. The freckled skin, the long black hair.

"Tell the truth," my mother said.

"We pick on him."

"What's that?" the detective asked quietly.

"We pick on Lamar. Benjamin does, mostly."

"I see." The detective put a hand over his mouth and his eyes closed for a moment. He cleared his throat, then slapped his legs. "All right then." He smiled a thin smile.

"One day Lamar said he would kill Benjamin," I blurted.

"Lamar said that?"

"Yes, sir." I never said *sir*. I don't even know where I got it. There was snot coming out of my nose. I wiped it away.

"What is Benjamin's last name?"

"Herman," I said.

"Why don't you go to your room now?" my father said. It was the first thing my father had said to me in weeks.

I turned to look at him. I knew from one look that I was going to get it later.

I hadn't bothered to open the ant farm yet, and in my room I ran my hands over the box, tracing the words with my fingers. ANT FARM! THE FUN, SCIENTIFIC WAY TO LEARN ABOUT THE INSECT KINGDOM! I kept picturing Benjamin without his Judas Priest T-shirt on for once, lying naked on a steel examining table like the victims in an episode of *Columbo*. I opened the ant farm box and started flipping through the booklet that came with it. There were line drawings that showed all the different types of ants in the colony. There was the queen, the worker ants, or drones, the nursing ants that took care of the larvae.

My parents restricted me to my room that whole next day, only allowing me to come downstairs for a baloney sandwich at lunch and, later, a TV dinner. The entire neighborhood was talking about Lamar, I could feel it. On the one hand I was dying to get out there, to find out exactly what had happened. On the other, I was absorbed by Lamar's ant farm booklet. There was an ad on the back for other kits from the same company; there was a chemistry set, a microscope, a junior electrician's set . . . THE FUN, SCIENTIFIC LEARNING SERIES. I kept staring at it, thinking of all the things there were to know, and of how I didn't know a fucking thing.

The following morning I saw Lamar through my bedroom window. He had his legs folded under him and was sitting near the chain-link fence that separated our yards and was tearing blades of grass into smaller and smaller pieces and then throwing them up in the air while making soft, slo-mo exploding noises. I sneaked downstairs and slipped through the kitchen door.

"Hey," I whispered.

He didn't turn around.

"Lamar," I said a little louder.

He barely looked up.

"What happened?"

He shrugged.

"Are you in trouble?"

He started moving funny, his whole body kind of shaking. I took that as a yes.

"What did you do?"

"They didn't tell you?"

"Who?"

"The police."

"They just asked if we were friends."

He nodded.

"Did you kill Benjamin?"

He threw a few blades of grass into the air. "I killed Anthony."

I had leaned my arms over the fence and had been rocking the whole thing back and forth. Now I stopped. "Anthony?"

"Yup."

"Why?"

He tore a handful of grass into tiny pieces, then scattered them, his arms beating like wings. "I don't know."

"What do you mean, you don't know?"

"I mean, I don't know."

"Was it an accident?"

"No."

"Did he fall down and hit his head—"

"No."

"—on a rock or something?"

"I pushed a piece of wire into his neck."

I imagined it, the sharp end of an old broken wire hanger going into the soft part of Anthony's neck. "And then what happened?" Involuntarily, I touched my own neck.

"He started to bleed." Lamar turned to look at me. "Really fast. It was like all the blood in his body came out at once."

"Oh, man."

"Where was it?" I said. "I mean, exactly."

"By the dumpsters," he answered. "Right between them."

It was late afternoon, and there was an almost imperceptible coolness in the air. Autumn was weeks away, but I could feel its approach, like an airplane about to land.

"Are you going to go to jail?"

He thought for a minute. "First I'm going to go stay with my grandmother, and then there's going to be court." Lamar threw some grass into the air. "And then they'll send me to jail, I guess." Then he looked up at me. "Where's Benjamin?"

I shrugged. "I haven't been hanging out with Benjamin."

"Why not?"

"Why *Anthony*?" I pictured that kid, his fat stomach, the way his eyebrows looked like two caterpillars crawling across his face. "Why didn't you kill Benjamin?" I said, and then more softly, "Or me?"

Lamar started shaking his head back and forth, not like he was saying no, more like he was getting ready for something, like he was about to break into a run. "I wouldn't kill you guys," he said. "You and Benjamin . . . you guys are my best friends."

Then autumn came just like I knew it would, and then the winter, and the next spring, and so on. There was a trial. At first there was a subpoena for me to go and tell them about what Anthony had said that day on the god-rock, about Lamar threatening to kill Benjamin, but then they said I didn't have to, after all. I never really hung out with Benjamin much after that. We kind of went in different directions. Lamar's family stayed just as they were, only Lamar wasn't there anymore. He went to live with his grandmother and then was put into a state facility for young people who've committed dangerous crimes. I finished junior high, and then high school, and then, if you can believe it, I was accepted to college on a partial swimming scholarship. After the whole thing with Lamar, my parents tried to get me into sports, thinking it would keep me out of trouble, and swimming was the only physical activity I could stand. I spent my whole first semester of college swimming and reading. I had a talent for the butterfly, it turned out. I was no superstar, believe me, but I placed third in the five-hundred meter a couple of times. And sometimes when I was swimming I would start to think of Lamar and how he thought we were his friends and I would stop, and I would have to get out of the pool and tell the coach I had a cramp.

Anyway, when I came back for that first winter break my parents picked me up at the airport and drove me home. I saw him there, standing in the window. Lamar. Jesus. He was a lot older now, and taller. But he was still skinny. He was still the same old Lamar. He had his chest out and his fingers were kind of moving around in front of him, the way he had stood there when he was a kid and we were all playing in the yard, and he was watching. He had that faraway look. I couldn't tell if he saw me, because his eyes didn't move.

I went upstairs, and when I was unpacking I came across that charm bracelet, the one I had stolen from him when we were just kids. It was just sitting there in the back of a drawer. I hadn't looked at it in so long, and I noticed the little charms it had: the little train engine, the tiger, the sax, ballet slippers, monkey. One of the charms was an angel, one of those angels down on its knees with its hands pressed together in prayer. For some reason I thought of Lamar sitting that way that day in the backyard, tossing handfuls of grass in the air and telling me so matter-of-fact how he had killed Anthony.

I threw the charm bracelet out the window.

I remembered the feeling of my fist hitting Lamar's arm, knuckles in his flesh, and I remembered one particular Saturday morning—we must have been around nine or ten—when Lamar just lay down.

"Go ahead," he said. "I don't care anymore. I don't care what you do to me."

Benjamin stood over him with his angry black hair and his mean freckles and his hands on his hips. "What do you mean?" he said. "Aren't you going to dance around like a scared little John Travolta?"

"Why should I?" Lamar said, smiling. "You'll just catch me."

Fat Anthony chuckled, his stomach jiggling.

Benjamin was confused, grabbing a handful of his own hair. "Where do you want me to hit you?"

"It doesn't matter." Lamar was defiant. He presented his bruised arm to Benjamin like a prize.

"I've been punching his arm," I told Benjamin helpfully.

"Yeah," Anthony said, "hit his arm."

"I don't know." Benjamin tossed it off like he was turning down a dessert. "I don't think I want to punch Lamar right now."

Still on the ground, Lamar rolled his eyes. "Just get it over with."

"Yeah," I said. "Punch him."

Benjamin started to walk away, and Lamar rose to his feet, lifting himself up with that sideways smile on his face, the same smile he would wear a couple of years later when he gave me that ant farm.

"Benjamin," I said, "what are you—"

Suddenly Benjamin turned around. "I'll tell you," he said, hitting Lamar to the rhythm of his words, "when"—*punch*—"I will beat"—*punch*—"the crap"—*punch*—"out of you"—*punch, punch*. And he wailed on Lamar, fists like pistons, his face full of hate, punching his message home, and my own hate was in there with each and every punch—worse, because I was standing beside Benjamin, me and fat Anthony, standing there smiling idiotically, laughing and grinning and enjoying every second of it.

And goddamn it if Lamar—it still kills me to think of this—if Lamar wasn't smiling too.

Man, the things we did to that kid.

THE EASTLAKE SCHOOL

Jerrilyn Farmer

"Fix Mommy a drink, Megan."

My mom. She works so hard. She gets stressed. I looked at the kitchen clock. Four P.M. "Do you want to wait a little?"

"I'm dying here, pumpkin. Be a good girl." My mom put her key ring down on the counter, the keys sounding all jangly upset.

Our house has just been redone, by a quality architect, my mom says, but I'm still getting used to it. I tugged hard on the vacuum seal of the built-in refrigerator to open the door. Arctic Circle–type air rushed out as I grabbed a bottle of Diet Coke.

"That's good," she said. "Why is your hair in your face?"

I got out a crystal glass, tall and delicate, the kind mom likes, and filled it with cubes. The Diet Coke splashed in, stopping at about three-quarters full.

I looked up and noticed my mother's lipstick was smudged almost completely off.

She must have read my mind or something. Maybe seen where I was looking. Her hand flew to her face. "My lipstick?"

My mother looks like a movie star. She's blond and gorgeous. She has perfect skin, the perfect tan. She has a great figure. Incredible, actually. She's skinnier than any of my friends. She's really amazing, my mom.

I went to the cabinet and found the bottle of Barbados rum. I poured a lot in. Mom likes it that way.

By then my mom had opened her little purse and found her little compact. She got very still, looking in that little mirror. "I don't have on one single trace of lipstick." Her voice had that stunned sound you hear when a guy in a movie suddenly notices the sky is filled with alien spaceships.

I handed her the drink, setting it down on the counter in front of her on a fabric cocktail napkin that matched the lemon yellow of the tiles. Neat. Not one drop spilled. Mom needed a pick-me-up every afternoon. It was my job to fix it. She'd start drinking rum and Diet Cokes about four-thirty every school day and keep on drinking until just before Daddy came home from the firm.

"Aren't you interested in where I've been?" my mom asked. I have learned to decipher what my mom says as she twists her mouth in the application of lipstick. She quickly capped the tube and looked at me.

"Sure."

"I know you've been depressed, darling. I know what it must feel like to be rejected by Eastlake."

My neck hurt. My wrist itched.

"Honey?" My mom was so worried about me it made me feel awful.

The Eastlake School. It was the most prestigious school in the universe. It ran from grades seven through twelve. Not everyone can get in, though. They are famous for rejecting everybody. My application had been rejected and I have been working hard, hard, hard. At least three hours each and every night since kindergarten. And I get straight A's. It doesn't matter to them. They get dozens of girls applying who get straight A's. They get hundreds. All the parents around here want their daughters to be Eastlake girls and Eastlake gets to choose. That's the way it is with the Eastlake School.

"You've been very depressed, Megan, isn't that right?"

My mom really didn't deserve all the trouble I brought. The arch in my left foot began aching pretty badly.

"Well, your problems are solved. I just saw the director of admissions, Mrs. Williams. She's agreed to move you up to the waiting list. See? And after Daddy talks to the head of the school, I'm sure they'll find a spot for you in their seventh-grade class, after all." My mother smiled a fresh-Chanel-lipstick smile and then raised her glass.

I watched her drink. In a few seconds the glass wore the perfect outline of my mom's beautiful smile on its rim.

The truth about my mother is she doesn't look old enough to have a twelve-year-old daughter. I'd heard people tell her that all my life, adding a year every time I'd had another birthday.

"Did you hear what I said, Megan?"

I guess I must be the most ungrateful teenager in America. Here my mother and father have been doing everything in their power to move me across the chessboard of my life toward their wonderful goals, and I'm like some sort of imbecile pawn who doesn't even say thank you.

"Thank you, Mom."

"You're more than welcome, honey." She looked radiantly beautiful at that moment.

"Do you think maybe the teachers there are kind of hard, Mom? Maybe . . ."

"They'll love you at Eastlake. All the best girls go there. You'll have a wonderful time. You'll see. And look what I've brought you."

My mom opened her little purse and pulled out a jewelry store box. She opened the hinge and set the box before me.

"Is this for me?"

"Isn't it adorable? Try it on! We're celebrating you getting into Eastlake, silly. I found it at that cute antique store at the Plaza where they have all that funky old stuff and it just called out to me. It's got charms, see?"

My mom is always super sweet like that. Always giving me gifts when I get down at heart. I don't have her cheery temperament. I don't have her naturally upbeat personality, so she gets me little gifts, she loves me so much.

"Don't you adore it? Now why are you pulling so hard on your hair? That's got to hurt, Megan. Stop it, please."

I picked up the bracelet and let it dangle, clinking the charms together. One, a small gold puffy heart, glinted in the downbeam of the fancy recessed lights Mom had chosen with her decorator. I examined the heart more closely, noticing it had a tiny jewel, as Mom kept on talking about Eastlake and refilled her own glass.

Along the edge of the heart I detected a fine seam. This was too cool. The puffy heart was a locket! I tried to pry my fingernail into the creased edge, but it just slipped off. It was no use. The locket was maybe welded shut. Totally stuck. And my fingernails are pathetic, really. My fault. I bite them—isn't that gross? Ugly nails. Ugly hands.

Mom's voice: "Honey, are you zoning out on me? I was talking about how you're going to have to do your part. Give Eastlake your best effort. You can do it."

"Mom . . ." I fiddled with the little heart, unable to open it, unwilling to let it alone.

"Yes, dollface?"

"Eastlake . . ."

"Yes?"

"It's a very tough school."

My mother held her drink between her two beautifully manicured hands and smiled. "So you'll work harder."

You know how you can be fine one minute and then suddenly the next minute you find some dumb thing is happening, like tears are pouring out of your eyes? That's the sort of thing that happens to me all the time, lately. For no reason. And it began happening right then. Somehow, my face was just all wet. Luckily my hair was hanging down or my mom would have been really worried, wondering what was wrong with me now. I turned to get her more ice from the freezer and wiped my face with a dishtowel when she wasn't looking.

Mom was happy about the fresh ice. "So what have you been up to while I was out?"

"Me? Just drawing."

I pulled my sketch pad from the corner of the breakfast nook table and opened it to the page.

Mom slowly took the pad. "Is that *me?*"

It was a sketch using oil pastels. I'd made my mother's skin a little too peachy, I realized, having colored it without her there to look at while I drew. And I hadn't remembered just how light were the golden highlights in her hair. But other than that, I thought it was maybe not too bad. I had gotten her chin just right.

Mom took a while to tell me what she thought of it. And while I was waiting, standing in the cool kitchen, I realized that I got her nose wrong. Completely. And her eyes. My neck started hurting again. And I couldn't wait any longer. I wanted to snatch the sketchbook out of her hands. Grab it. And rip out the page, punch it into a ball, and throw it away. Fast.

"Do you like it, Mommy?"

"It's just fine."

Fine? No. It was awful. The eyes were horrible. I'd gotten the nose all wrong. What was I thinking? My mother's eyes were a million times prettier than I had drawn them. I could just kill myself for showing her that picture.

"It's just . . . honey, I don't think this artsy stuff is for you. I know you met the art teacher at the public high school."

"Miss Sanchez. She said . . ."

Mom put her hand up gently. "She tells *all* the kids they have talent, honey. That's her job. I will not have you attending the public high school simply because one teacher appealed to your vanity. So just get that idea right out of your head. Next thing you'll be telling me you want to drop out of the honors program and hang around with a lot of troubled kids, is that right?"

How could I keep on letting my mom down like this? I was way too selfish. My mom once said I had my father's selfish gene, and I guess that's so. I made a secret promise right then to stop thinking like this. To stop disappointing my mother.

Mom looked at me closely. I wondered if she could see I was going to try harder, because I really, really was. "You need to be more positive, sweetie. You'll do fine at Eastlake. I've gotten you this far, haven't I?"

My mom's smile faded immediately when she saw my face.

I stopped looking at her, stopped breathing, even, for a few seconds. It was the thing we never talked about.

I pulled my hair down over my face, which I know I shouldn't do since she doesn't like it, but sometimes I can't help it. My grades are a subject that's tricky. It's like something we can't talk about, because we both know it's been my mom who has been earning all my A's at Pasadena Country Day, practically doing all my homework and projects and papers since kindergarten. Everyone in my sixth-grade class suspects it. My teachers know it. And so do I. That's why when the rejection letter from Eastlake came in the mail, I wasn't surprised. I was kind of expecting it.

"Are you worrying again? About the letter?"

"No. Honestly." I gave her the kind of smile she deserved, real nonchalant and carefree.

Last Saturday was like a funeral around my house. My father glared at my mother. My mother was so trembly she asked me to fix her a drink at noon! Even with Daddy at home.

"Are you worrying, Megan? Please don't. I'll help you, sweetie. You'll love Eastlake."

She held out her glass and I got up to refill it, making it mostly Diet Coke this time, hiding behind my hair.

When the letter came and Mom was so disappointed, I realized something. She regrets having me. I know she does. I could tell by the look on her face. And you know something else? I can't blame her one bit. She's right. I'm just a screwed-up kid and she deserves so much better. As much as I always try to be just perfect for her, I always find some supremely stupid way to muck it all up. Typical me. Instead of making her happy, like I always, always try, I just end up embarrassing her. How screwed up is that?

And parents aren't very tolerant, you know? They hate being embarrassed. They just hate it. It's like when I feel embarrassed, only a thousand times worse because she's a grown-up and has worked terribly hard and all. I wish I could be good enough to make her proud, I really do. Then she could be happy. Or maybe it would be better to wish for something else. I looked at the bracelet on the counter. Maybe if I were just *gone,* my mom wouldn't be so sad.

The first thing she said, after reading the rejection letter from the Eastlake School, was what was she going to tell her friend Carrie? Carrie's daughter Zoë is in sixth grade at Country Day too. When I showed up to school on Monday, I wasn't surprised to learn that Zoë got accepted to all the schools she applied to. She was going to go to Eastlake, of course.

"Carrie?" My mother was already on the phone as I handed her the fresh rum and Diet Coke. "Guess what? I just spoke to Mrs. Williams at Eastlake."

I guess my mom couldn't wait to call Carrie. I heard her laugh for the first time in a week. She said, "So if they give the girls four hours of homework every night and make them work on projects all weekend, the girls will do it. I know the school is academic, Carrie, but so are our girls."

I stood in the kitchen, feeling pretty much like throwing up.

Mom, what if I just can't keep up at Eastlake? What if I fail all my classes? What if I can't breathe there? What if I let you down, again and again and again?

My mom didn't hear me, though. I wasn't really talking out loud.

My mom put her hand over the telephone and whispered, "Put on the bracelet, doll. It's so you."

I jumped up to put the bracelet on, just like she asked. But I could tell she was disappointed I hadn't thought to put it on myself.

One year later . . .

Right before the start of Mrs. Gold's Latin class was the first time I heard it. Clarissa Blake stopped talking as soon as she saw I was standing behind her. Katie Hardy's face still looked shocked, and she couldn't cover it up fast enough once she realized I was standing right there.

I bet in all the history of the Eastlake School, no other seventh-grade girl had ever before gotten a D in Latin. And right before I entered the classroom, I bet someone must have been asking how I got into Eastlake, then, if I was so stupid. And that's when Clarissa shared her family's theory. Her mother said that my mother had sex with the admissions director. Right on the office floor. With Mrs. Williams, who all the girls know is a lesbian.

My cheeks burned. Burned hot as fire. It was such a sudden, unexpected pain I almost tripped. I couldn't go on living one more second with that burning. And at the same time, there was such dizziness. I was falling down a deep, deep pit. Standing there like a dork. Blushing hotter and hotter.

"What's going on in the back of the room?" Mrs. Gold called too loudly, looking at us all tied up in a knot of girls near the door. "Settle down. Take your seats. We're going to have our Latin final in a few days and we have a lot to review, young ladies."

I don't know how I got to my seat. I don't know how I found the right book and opened it to the right page. I could do nothing more than tell myself to breathe. I was numb, mostly, with not even one thought in my head for a full ten minutes. I think the only thing that brought me back to earth was the burning pain. I looked down at my left wrist. I had been twisting my gold bracelet, mindlessly twisting it harder and harder, around and around. The little gold charms had scratched my skin raw. I stopped, surprised at what I was doing.

As Mrs. Gold talked about the genitive case, I played with each little charm, daydreaming about the tiny tiger devouring my enemies, the tight clique of smart girls, including Katie and Clarissa, who sat together in the front row with their hands in the air for every question.

I fiddled, as I always did, with the heart-shaped gold locket, the one with the tiny jewel. It was stuck shut, like always. I had been frustrated I couldn't see if anything was locked inside, but I'd feared pushing on it too hard, afraid it was too delicate and I might damage the charm, and then what would my mother say? But as Mrs. Gold didn't see me very well in my seat in the back, I got a little bolder and began to look for things in my backpack with which to pry open the seal of the locket. A ball point pen wasn't doing it. I tried another, but nothing. A paper clip—carefully straightened out—was too thick. But the sharp tip of my math compass! That was perfect.

As Mrs. Gold praised Lucy McCook's brilliant freaking declensions, I stabbed at the locket. I don't know my own strength, I guess. The point of the compass skittered off the shiny gold heart and punctured my wrist. I held my breath, willing myself not to gasp, and heard the girl next to me giggle. Blood was coming from the small puncture wound, and I was startled when she nonchalantly passed me a tissue.

I picked up the compass once again and fit its dangerous silver tip right against the groove that ran all around the locket. I tried to use a prying pressure, but again the compass point slipped off the charm, scraping my wrist, not drawing blood this time, but close.

The girl next to me smirked. Her name is Hannah Miller. She

pantomimed that I should hold the charm steady and she would wield the compass. We girls are pretty good at giving Mrs. Gold a face that looks interested while we're busy doing what we like. Hannah picked up the compass, gripping it like a dagger, and drew it back a good nine inches. I thought about what it might feel like to get stabbed with such force. And I wondered how the pain could be any worse than hearing secondhand that your mother slept with the lady who works in the admissions office, moaning and writhing on the floor, lipstick smeared all the way off, to get her stupid daughter into a decent school.

Hannah brought the sharp point of the compass down hard, striking directly on the seam of the locket with all the force of Eastlake's star middle school volleyball spiker. The gold heart charm cracked open.

From inside, a slip of yellowed paper, folded very slim, popped out onto my Latin book. I grabbed at it greedily, using my fingernail to unroll the note. On the slip, in green fountain pen ink, were the words: *Mors stupebit, et natura*. Bloody Latin.

I thought about opening my Latin dictionary.

Hannah pulled the note closer and read the faint handwritten scrawl. She pointed to the first word and whispered," 'Death.' Cool."

There wasn't a flash of light or a clap of thunder, but I wasn't such a big idiot that I couldn't tell when God was sending me a message. Death. And something more. I read the note again. Maybe "Death, stupid, is natural." Something like that. And, of course, it all made sense! I almost laughed, it seemed so right. *Death is natural.* Why should anyone go on and on and suffer? And wasn't I suffering?

And with this new thought, my pain seemed to disappear. I think I might have even smiled. I pushed my long hair behind my ears and kept smiling.

Maybe, I thought, I could go home right after school. And maybe, I thought further, while my mother was out shopping and

I should be starting on my homework, I could get out the rum and the Diet Coke and see if I could stand the taste. And then maybe I could go find those Xanax tablets of my mom's. And it could be over that fast! I could be free! I could do it before my mom came home from the store.

I smiled up at Hannah, who looked startled to see me so happy.

I could do it. I knew I could. End the misery. End the pretending. And if I timed it just right and didn't lose my nerve, I wouldn't even have to do tonight's homework in Latin.

The pills were in my mother's bathroom cabinet. I shook them all into my hand and counted. Fifteen pills. I guessed that would be enough to do it.

In the kitchen I was a pro at mixing a rum and Diet Coke. I crushed the pills using this cute old marble mortar and pestle my mom's decorator found in England. It made like a teaspoonful of chunky white powder, all crushed. I stirred it into the drink. There was no reason for me to be sad. I wouldn't ever have to go back to Eastlake. I wouldn't have to sit and be judged by girls who could say such cruel things about another girl's mother.

I set the drink onto a yellow fabric napkin, nice and neat, and then ran out to the main hall, up the steps, my feet suddenly not clumsy. I dashed into my bathroom, the pink tiles giving me the rosy glow my mom thought was the best for us girls. I found my hairbrush and brushed my hair until it was shining, and then, pulling my hair back off my forehead, put on a fresh headband. In the mirror, I saw the face that my mother would approve of. A neat face. With neat hair.

I was feeling lighter than ever, almost giddy with lightness. Time stretched out, but I really didn't care. No homework was pulling at me. No Latin and math and ethics hiding around each corner, waiting to bite me each night. No hours and hours of trying to get into my head all the stuff I just didn't get. Not anymore.

In my room I pulled off my dark blue Eastlake School sweater and put it neatly in the laundry basket. I stepped out of the navy and white plaid uniform skirt, inspected it to see if it was clean enough for another day, and then caught myself and smiled a nice, free smile. I put it neatly on top of the sweater. I did the same with my white polo shirt. The last time, I thought.

In my closet, a straight row of school uniforms hung in silent judgment, but I just shut the door. I had to make a careful choice. From my drawer I chose my favorite pair of bright yellow shorts and a silky blue tank top that had thin straps. I ran back into the bathroom and checked myself out in the full-length mirror. And I didn't look so bad at all.

I took off the charm bracelet and threw it into the pink trash can. I'd memorized its message. I didn't need it anymore.

I was so calm. That was the oddest thing. Calm and happy. I was ready. I was. Sometimes you just know what to do.

I walked down the stairs, and the house looked different somehow. Down in the hall, I felt blessed. Then I walked back into the kitchen. There, on the counter, was my mother's key ring. She must have come home a little early.

There on the floor lay my dead, dead, dead mother. She looked really beautiful, lying there like that, but her hair was a real mess.

The kitchen clock read 3:55. My mom needed her pick-me-up earlier every day. I had noticed that. I wasn't so dumb. I wasn't.

I picked up my sketch pad and walked over to the mirror in the hall. I didn't look different at all. Not at all. Same lumpy body. Same geeky braces. And I started to draw my self-portrait.

THE BLESSING OF BROKENNESS

Karin Slaughter

Mary Lou Dixon sat in the front pew of the church, her eyes raised as she watched the cross over the pulpit being slowly lowered to the floor. She fiddled with the bracelet on her wrist as the cross, which had seemed so small hanging a few inches from the ceiling, began to grow larger as it descended in front of her like a broken bird.

"Hold up," the foreman said, and the three men working the pulleys stopped. The cross shook in the air, its broken right arm dangling by a few slivers of wood as it tapped ominously against the side. The noise reminded Mary Lou of a clock, ticking away time.

"Easy, now," the foreman instructed, using his hands to illustrate. He was the only English-speaking person in the four-man crew, and the Mexicans were slow to understand his orders. They finally seemed to comprehend, though, because the cross began its journey to the floor once again, finally coming to a gentle resting point on the carpet.

The Mexicans genuflected, and Mary Lou wondered if that was entirely appropriate in the Christ Holiness Baptist Church of Elawa, Georgia. The cross was a simple wooden affair, lacking a Jesus, but with a fine polish that shone in the morning sun. It was hardly the ornamental icon most Catholics were used to exalting, if that was what Catholics did—Mary Lou had no idea. She had been Christ Holiness for the last twenty years and before that Lord and Savior, which was two steps below Primitive and one above snake handling.

Although plenty of contractors attended the church, none had volunteered their time to help repair the ailing cross. Bob Harper, who had been a deacon for the last ten years, owned his own construction company, but he was still more than five hundred dollars more expensive than the black man and his crew. The job was too small to make it worth his time, he had said. Mary Lou had commented that she was glad Jesus had not felt the same way about dying for Bob's sins, but the deacon had not been swayed by her remark.

So here Mary Lou was with a black foreman and his Catholic Mexicans, trying to get the cross repaired before Easter Sunday—at considerable expense—with no help whatsoever from the more capable men of the congregation. This sort of thing was typical of the church lately. Long gone were the times when people happily volunteered to do routine maintenance or send out mailers to collect donations for foreign missionaries. No one visited the sick in the hospital anymore. No one wanted to go on Bible retreats unless they were assured there would be a pool and twenty-four-hour room service. The last two antiabortion rallies down to Atlanta had been canceled because the weather report had predicted rain, and Lord knew no one wanted to stand out in the rain.

"Mrs. Dixon?" the black man asked. His name was Jasper Goode, she knew. He was a dark-skinned older man with a bald head that showed a significant amount of perspiration despite the air-conditioning in the church. Mary Lou did not trust this show of overperspiration, as if it somehow made him shifty. He had done nothing but stand and direct the crew all morning, yet he was sweating as if he had been running a marathon.

"Ma'am?" he prompted.

"Yes?" Mary Lou answered, shifting in the hard pew. She put her hand to her stomach to calm it.

Jasper walked toward her, down the stairs that lined the stage. He kept walking until he was about three feet away, looming over her.

Mary Lou squared her shoulders, willing herself not to fidget. He was a tall man and knew it. She could not help but glance down at the floor before bracing herself to look back up at him.

"Sorry," he said, smiling as he kneeled down on one knee in front of her.

"What is it?" she snapped, aware she had no reason to. The truth was she did not like him standing so close to her. The sight of him was almost too much to bear.

The man had been badly burned, and up close his face was a synthetic-looking mess, his skin stretched unnaturally tight in places, the pigment a patchwork quilt of varying skin tones around his cheeks so that from afar he looked as if someone had stitched his face together from borrowed flesh. He had no eyebrows or eyelashes, giving his eyes a perpetually startled look. His hands, too, were scarred, and the skin that bunched around his wrists resembled a slouching sock. Even in this heat, he wore his sleeves long, tightly buttoned at the wrists, hiding what Mary Lou imagined was an even more horrific sight.

He said something to his crew, and she tried not to watch him speak. The most startling thing about the man's appearance was his lips—an unnatural shade of pink, like the bright pinkness of a mouse's nose, and delicate-looking, more suited for a maiden than an old black man with no facial hair to speak of. The lips had a constant sheen, as if they had been made for him only recently. Mary Lou had seen on television where a child's ear had been grown from scratch on the back of a living mouse. She wondered if the man's lips had been grown under similar circumstances.

The burns were not the kind of thing that could go unremarked on. The first time they had met, the black man had explained to Mary Lou without her asking that he had been in an automobile accident. The car had exploded, burning alive his wife and child. He had barely escaped with his own life, and subsequent surgeries had healed his body if not his heart; he said the memories of that night still haunted him, and the part he played in the death of both his wife and child was something he could not forgive himself for, let alone forget. Drunk, Mary Lou suspected but did not say.

Jasper Goode told her, "We'll leave it here, then take it into the parking lot after lunch." Mary Lou made a point of looking at her watch, and he added, "They work better on a full belly."

"I'm sure they do," Mary Lou answered, hoping her tone conveyed her displeasure.

"She don't look as bad as I thought she would," the black man offered, as if the cross were a ship and not a symbol of Jesus's sacrifice.

"Well, good," she returned, wondering if this meant they would charge less. She doubted it.

As if sensing her thoughts, he added, "She'll still take a while."

"You promised it would be ready for Sunday," Mary Lou reminded him, trying to keep the tremor out of her voice. She didn't think Jasper Goode was the type who went to church on Sundays, and if the decision had been left to Mary Lou, she would have hired Bob Harper instead. Five hundred dollars was a small price to pay to employ someone who was invested in his own salvation.

Jasper stared at her. "I wants to thank you, ma'am, for giving me this job. It's kind of hard to get work for me now, and I appreciate it."

She nodded, slightly taken aback by his admission.

Jasper held her gaze. "You feelin' all right, ma'am?"

"I'll feel better when the cross is fixed," she told him.

His mouth grimaced into what might be a smile. "We'll have it on time," Jasper assured her. He took out a white handkerchief to wipe at his sweating, bald head. He said something Mexican to the crew, and they scampered off, showing more hustle than they had shown thus far on the job.

Mary Lou shifted in the pew again, trying to find a comfortable position. Her office was over the old chapel, which was now the gymnasium, and the air conditioner there left much to be desired. If not for the fact that she could not afford to miss another day of work, she would have just stayed home today.

She let out a heavy sigh, staring at the pulpit. The blank space where the cross had been made the chapel feel hollow, as if the heart had been removed from its chest. It was a mystery how the cross had become damaged. A parishioner had mentioned something about the cross looking "off" one Sunday, and Mary Lou and Pastor Stephen had come in after the service, both staring up until their necks kinked. There had been a definite lilt to the side, but from the ground they had not been able to tell why.

A week later Mary Lou was in the church office stuffing envelopes when Randall, the church custodian, burst in, mumbling something about a sign from God. This was not the first time that Randall, whose own mother admitted that he was slightly touched in the head, had claimed such a vision, but Mary Lou had followed him into the chapel to stretch her legs. They found the cross tilting almost sideways, the thick cables that anchored it to the ceiling vibrating as if under great pressure. As Mary Lou and Randall stood there, a great cracking sound filled the room, followed by a terrible, low moan, as if Jesus Himself was on the cross, His arm being ripped from His body. She could still see it play in her mind in slow motion: the arm of the cross snapping, the cables twisting and bending as the weight shifted. Sometimes at night, she could hear that awful low moan of the wood breaking, and she would begin to sweat uncontrollably, knowing that the breaking cross had something to do with her.

As a girl, her uncle Buell had been what was called a lay minister, which meant he had received no special ordination from Christ yet still chose to teach the Bible. His following had dwindled as Mary Lou got older, but there was always a core group of people who listened to his teachings. They worshipped Buell as they worshipped the Lord Himself.

Every Sunday and Wednesday, the basement of Buell's ranch-style house would be filled with ten to twenty people, all come to hear Buell speak on the Word. His favorite theme was what he called the insidiousness of sin. Sin was a heavy burden, Buell said, and it would eventually break you one way or another. A good man might beat his wife. A good woman might lie to her husband. These were simple ways that sin could break you in two. This split gave easy entry to more sin, more evil, into your heart. It was up to the sinner to seek out Jesus, to ask for redemption, to seek His help in becoming whole again. God never gave a sinner more than he could carry, Buell insisted. That was His gift to man: He would never break you beyond repair. In every aspect of man's life, even at the end of it, there existed God's opportunity for redemption.

"Only Jesus can put you back together once you've been broken by sin," Buell had preached. "And that part of you that is broken becomes all the stronger for it." He called this strengthening the blessing of brokenness. Even on his hospital bed, dying of bone cancer, he had refused treatment, insisting God had broken his bones only to heal them and make Buell stronger. In the end, the morphine had convinced him there were angels in the room. Or maybe not. Buell was known to see angels without the benefit of drugs too.

Mary Lou turned in the pew as she heard footsteps in the foyer. Pastor Stephen entered the chapel, his shirtsleeves rolled up, his hands tucked into his pockets. Stephen Riddle was the exact opposite of her uncle Buell. His sermons were not about working for redemption, but being blessed with it. There was no burden Jesus would not take from you, no problem He would not solve. Stephen's favorite admonition was that it was a sin to worry, whereas Buell's charge at the end of every service was to go home and worry, to pick through your life and find out what you were doing wrong and pray to Jesus that He would help you correct it.

Of course, Buell never lacked volunteers for even the smallest task. Such was the devotion of his flock that when his truck broke down, a mechanic appeared to fix it. When his house needed a new roof, the men of the congregation banded together and installed a new one over the weekend. Stephen Riddle would watch the church crumble to the ground around him before the thought even entered his mind to ask his parishioners to carry their proper load.

"Hot day," Stephen said, then gave her a sideways glance. "You doing okay?"

Mary Lou nodded, feeling a bead of sweat on her upper lip. She suddenly wanted to go home and lie down in bed so badly that she could almost feel the sheets across her body. Her sick days were used up, though. She could not afford to lose the money. While she accepted that Stephen was genuinely concerned about her health, she also knew that he would dock her pay if she left a minute before she was supposed to. After what had happened between them, Mary Lou should have had power over the preacher. She should have been able to exert this power any way she chose. For some unknown reason, she could not.

"How's our project going?" he asked, gesturing to the empty space above the pulpit. "Do you feel good about this contractor?"

She knew what he was getting at. Mary Lou had not been in her office all day. "I thought it best to keep an eye on them."

"You look like you've lost a little weight," he said, offering her a polite smile.

"I have," she said, not pointing out that it was not just some, but a considerable amount. Food did not agree with her lately. Everything she ate sat in her stomach like a piece of coal, waiting to burn her from inside.

Stephen nodded, tucking his chin into his chest as he raised his eyebrows. He did this when there was more to say but he could not find words. The trick was a good one, and it made him seem thoughtful and introspective when the truth was that he was simply incapable of expressing himself. "A man of words," Buell would have said, "though none of them good."

"Well," she said, meaning to move Stephen along, but she could see his lips twisted to the side, his eyes focused on her wrist. The bracelet suddenly felt like an albatross.

He looked up quickly, offering a pained smile. The smile was familiar too. He was a man well versed in gestures that brought him compassion under the guise of giving it.

Mary Lou watched him as he walked over to the cross, laying his hand on it with some sort of reverence. His fingers gently glided along the wood, softer than they had ever been on her. She thought of Anne Riddle, his wife, and hated her with a bright, searing hate that burned her up inside. Anne was serene and beautiful, her hips jutting out into the air, her skin the finest porcelain. She was the perfect preacher's wife: reverent, righteous, reserved.

"Cleaned up nice," Stephen mumbled.

Mary Lou did not tell him that the cross had not yet been cleaned. Instead, she nodded, and tried to smile when he looked up at her.

He asked, "How's Pud doing?"

"Still in school," she answered, her voice as quiet as his.

"You get that roof fixed yet?"

She frowned, thinking about the money it would take to fix her roof. Nothing short of the lottery would bail her out of the hole she found herself in.

"Think we'll get those fliers mailed out today?" he asked, meaning the antiabortion leaflets, the church's bread and butter. Their mailing list was one of the largest in the nation, and people from as far away as Michigan contributed money to the cause.

This was what had brought Mary Lou to the chapel this morning, the thought that she could not stuff one more color copy into one more envelope without wanting to slit her wrists. Her stomach rolled when she thought about the photograph on the fliers, the fetus ripped in two, the head caved in by some sharp, foul instrument, the headline above beseeching, "Why did you let my mommy kill me?"

"Mary Lou?"

She shook her head and tears came to her eyes.

"Mary Lou," Stephen repeated, but she waved him off, the ridiculous charm bracelet jingling against her wrist. "Why are you still wearing that?" he asked, obviously resigned to what her answer would be.

"A memento," she said, sliding the bracelet around her wrist.

"They're supposed to be lucky," he said, glancing back at the cross, stroking the soft wood again.

"Supposedly," she said. The worst news of her life had come on the day she had been given the trinket, and Mary Lou could not help but shiver at the evil that discharged from the thing like poisonous gas.

Stephen stared at his hand on the cross, his displeasure evident. The bracelet, like so many things between them, was a secret. Stephen had told the church he was taking a sabbatical to minister to the poor in the Blue Ridge Mountains when in fact he had joined his brother in Las Vegas for a convention of the Greater West Coast Waste Management Association.

That his brother was a garbage man was not something that Stephen liked to brag about—by different accounts the brother was a neurosurgeon, a banker, a missionary—but Mary Lou had been pleased enough when Stephen had brought back the charm bracelet for her. He'd said that he had used all his blackjack winnings to buy it especially for Mary Lou. The bracelet had been displayed in one of the shop windows at the Venetian, and he had passed by and instantly thought of her. It was only later that she had noticed the flaws: at some point, the bracelet had been broken and inexpertly welded back together; some of the charms had sharp points that tore her clothes. The snake got caught on her sleeve all the time and the tiny cross's Jesus was horrible to witness, His pain so evident in His features that Mary Lou could not stand to look at it.

Despite all of this, she had taken to wearing it at night, and her dreams when she managed to sleep were filled with horrible visions: a bear traversing the darkness in search of human prey; a grown man slit stem to stern; severed hands reaching out as if to strangle her in her sleep. Even when she woke screaming, the skeleton key caught in her hair as if to unlock some horrible secret in her brain, Mary Lou had refused to remove the bracelet.

As if knowing all of this, Stephen suggested, "Maybe you shouldn't wear it."

"Why?" she asked, knowing he would not have an answer. It was a reminder; her own Scarlet Letter.

Stephen stood there uncertain, then finally left her with a slight bow, as if he was conceding this round. She listened as his footsteps receded, first a dull thud against the carpeted aisle, then a sharp clicking on the tiles in the foyer, and he was gone. Stephen was better at exiting than most men.

Brian, Mary Lou's ex-husband, had stuck around about ten years too long. She had known for some time that he was cheating on her, but her uncle Buell's words about a divorced woman still hung heavy on her shoulders. So she had left it to Brian to do the leaving, and Brian had hated her for that, as had their son. Both men had come to see Mary Lou as weak, a punching bag who would take any amount of abuse but still hang in there, waiting for more.

Pud was worse. Not that she thought of her teenage son as "Pud." She had named him William when he was born and insisted most of his life that it not be shortened to anything crude like Willy or Bill. Pud was the name William had given himself two years ago, around the time puberty had hit and he had started listening to rap music and wearing his pants so that the crack of his ass showed when he bent over. She had watched her darling son change into an unknown creature, a pseudo pickaninny with his blond hair tightly braided in cornrows and his clothes hanging off his body like a wet paper bag on a stick. His language changed so that she could not understand a word he said, and he sang along to that awful music, saying "nigga" this and "nigga" that, a word Mary Lou had never used around him and was ashamed to hear coming from his mouth. At the same time, William could not stand black people and went out of his way to make derogatory comments about them, even when Mary Lou had people from the church over.

Though she loved her son, the smile William had given Mary Lou when he told her that from now on he would answer only to "Pud" made her want to slap him for the first time in her life. That mischievous set to his lips as he said the word, as if Mary Lou were an idiot and did not know that "pulling your pud" was slang for male masturbation. She had been a substitute teacher for the first few years of William's life. She had heard worse than *pud* in the teachers' lounge.

Her biggest problem with William was his anger, though she had no idea what he had to be angry about. Brian spoiled him even as he refused to be seen in public with the boy. Anything his son wanted, he got. Two-hundred-dollar tennis shoes and an eighty-dollar skateboard (no helmet) that William had tried once and never again were just a few of the things Brian used to justify paying less child support to Mary Lou. They were constantly arguing over this, with Brian screaming and Mary Lou crying because her anger was such a tight knot inside her that it could only squeeze out tears. Child support was not the only thing Brian was supposed to pay. By court order, he was responsible for half of the upkeep of the house. Still the roof leaked when it rained and there were not enough buckets in the world to catch the water.

No matter how much Mary Lou cleaned, mildew grew on the cabinets in the kitchen, and walking into the house was like walking across a loaf of molded bread. Thank God Pud had his two-hundred-dollar tennis shoes to keep his feet from having to touch the ground.

The sound of hammering came from outside the chapel, and Mary Lou slowly moved to the edge of the pew so that she could stand. The bracelet clunked against the armrest, and she glanced around before grinding the edge of the praying angel into the soft wood until it bit out a small gouge. Cramps seized her belly as she tried to rise, and Mary Lou thought for the first time about going to the doctor. A quick calculation of the remaining money in her checkbook convinced her that was not a possibility, even if she sent William to his father's to eat.

She gritted her teeth as she pushed herself up, groaning from the movement. Sweat dripped down her back, and she tried to think about something cool to counteract the sensation. What came to mind was the church retreat she went on last Christmas, and how her life had been unalterably damaged by what had happened there.

Gatlinburg, Tennessee, was about as close as the South came to having a ski resort, even if they still had to blow fake snow onto the mountains most days just so people could slide down on their skis. Brian had agreed to take William for a week, a miracle in itself, and Mary Lou had managed to get the church to help pay some of the cost in exchange for extra help with the youth group.

She had gone to Gatlinburg with no illusions that she would ski. Mary Lou had never been athletic. She was a large woman who did not embrace the outdoors unless it was on a beach somewhere with a pina colada and a trashy book close by. What she had envisioned for herself was sitting in front of a roaring fire, her feet propped up as she read a romance where the women were strong and the men were worshipful. In the evenings, there would be dinners with various members of the congregation, then some socializing. The event was billed as a religious retreat for singles. As a recent single, Mary Lou qualified for this, but she had not gone with the intention of meeting anyone. There were far too many complications in her life without putting another person in the picture.

Of course, Pastor Stephen Riddle was not a new person in her life, and despite the strictures of their employer-employee relationship, she had long thought of him as a trusted counselor if not a friend. Anne, his wife, was also an acquaintance, and Mary Lou had helped out at birthday parties for their children and even volunteered to clean the house when Anne's father had passed away. That Mary Lou and Stephen had ended up going back to her room the third night of the retreat still surprised her. Ostensibly, they had gone upstairs to talk away from the crowd. Mary Lou knew that her ex-husband had not taken William without strings attached, and that this latest kindness would mean less child support at the end of the month. She had wanted to broach the subject of an advance with the pastor. She had been hoping Stephen would see her plight and volunteer a raise.

When Stephen had moved closer to her, Mary Lou had invited the comfort. When his gentle touching had turned more insistent and she had felt him stiffen against her, Mary Lou had proceeded as if in a fog. Sex with Brian had always been something to endure, and though she had read enough about orgasms in her women's magazines, Mary Lou had considered them much as she considered the recipes and craft suggestions: interesting, but nothing she would ever have time to do. Stephen had not delivered in that area either, but it felt so good to be held, to have the solid weight of him on top of her, to watch his face contort in pleasure, that she had found herself crying out, biting her lip so that she would not scream.

Stephen had mistaken this for ardor, and though he had slinked out the door a few minutes later, making excuses about being in his room in case Anne or one of the children called, the next evening he had knocked at her door again. She had let him in, somewhat thrilled with the wrongness of what they were doing. Mary Lou had never done anything bad. Her life was spent being as good as she could manage for fear of some greater retribution in the afterlife. To her surprise, there was a certain pleasure to be had from breaking a cardinal rule: not just sex, but sex with a married man. Not just a married man, but her pastor.

The ensuing nights, when Stephen had suggested things he wanted to do, positions he wanted to try, she had encouraged him. In fact, she had begged him, the thought that he had never tried these things with Anne making her almost giddy with power. Even as she leaned on her elbows, her hind end high in the air like a dog in heat, she had encouraged him, thinking in some perverse way that she deserved this degradation.

After the retreat, Stephen had pretended nothing had happened, his polite demeanor a slap in her face. Twice she had tried to talk to him, but it was not until he had returned from Las Vegas, holding the charm bracelet in his hand as if he held the world for her, that she got the message. To put a finer point on it, he had told her, "I cannot do this. I am a man of God."

When she had cried, he had held her, then shushed her with his kisses, more gentle than any she had known their few times together. This had made her cry even harder; not for the loss of him but for the loss of the gentleness she could have had. Big, racking sobs took hold, and she had started to hate Anne, because she understood that Stephen's gentleness belonged to Anne and that Mary Lou had been nothing but his whore.

"Ma'am?" A voice interrupted her thoughts.

Mary Lou started, aware that tears were threatening to fall.

"Yes?" she managed, wiping her eyes as she turned to see the black man standing behind her. He was patting the top of his head again with the now not-so-white handkerchief. She could see the Mexicans behind him, waiting for orders.

"We just about ready to start," he said.

She nodded, her hand on the back of the pew, trying to remember what he was talking about. The cross. Of course, the cross.

Mary Lou looked at her watch, as if she had something important scheduled. "How much longer?"

" 'Bout ten minutes, I s'pose." He nodded to the Mexicans. "Take us that long to get 'er set up."

"You're in the north parking lot?" she queried, though she had seen his beat-up old truck and tools set up there and knew they would do as she instructed for fear of being discharged.

"Yes'm," he told her, then again nodded to the men.

They all proceeded down the aisle as if for a wedding, their footsteps slow and deliberate. Mary Lou watched the Mexicans lift the broken cross, which seemed heavier than she had thought, or maybe they were putting on a show. There was much straining and groaning before the thing was high enough to be carried away, and Mary Lou wondered if Jesus had made as much of a commotion carrying the damn thing up the mountain.

" 'Bout ten minutes," Jasper repeated.

After they left, Mary Lou thought about sitting back down, but she knew if she did she would have an even harder time standing up again. Instead, she walked over to the window and leaned against the glass as she watched the men carrying the cross to the back parking lot. It was just as she had thought: they moved much more quickly when they thought she wasn't looking.

There were six sawhorses already set up in an approximate pattern of the cross, and Jasper moved them into position as the cross was lowered onto them. He held the broken right arm in one hand as he did this, pushing the sawhorses with his feet, tugging them with his free hand. The chapel window was higher than the parking lot, and Mary Lou was afforded an aerial view of the proceedings. The cross seemed smaller again now that it was farther away. Distance could do that to things, make them seem smaller. Time could do the same. When Mary Lou thought about Gatlinburg, for instance, it seemed like a smaller event in her life. What had ensued of course loomed larger, because it had yet to come to any sort of conclusion.

Uncle Buell was fond of saying that a woman can run faster with her skirt up than a man can with his pants down, but he had failed to point out that when both of them finally stopped trying to run, it was the woman who could not escape the consequences. Stephen Riddle, Mary Lou was sure, had prayed to the Lord for forgiveness and been granted it. Mary Lou had prayed for redemption and been given a child.

Her periods had always been erratic. Working at the church so closely with Stephen, going to the school twice a week to beg them not to expel William, had taken all of her energy, so that when months had gone by without any blood in the toilet, Mary Lou had not noticed. She was a large woman on top of this, and when her stomach began to swell, she had attributed this to too much fast food and late nights eating chips in front of the television. It might be menopause, she had found herself reasoning. She had even welcomed the Change as one less thing she would have to worry about.

Still, part of her must have known, because when she had finally managed to go to the doctor, she did not go to Dr. Patterson, who had delivered William, but to a doctor in Ormewood, two towns over, who was just setting up his practice.

"Congratulations," the doctor had said when Mary Lou had called for the results. He had then given a long list of instructions on diet and exercise and offered the name of a good midwife as well as the hospital he preferred for the delivery.

Mary Lou had written all this down on a stack of bills by the phone in the church office, all the while praying that no one would walk in. For a panicked few seconds, she had wondered if the phone was tapped, but then realized the church would be too cheap to pay for such a thing. They were more likely to tell Randall to stand at the door and listen. As far as Mary Lou could tell, no one was outside lurking.

The doctor had asked, "Do you have any questions?"

"What about . . ." Mary Lou had begun, her voice lowered, still afraid of an unseen listener. "What about other options?"

Even as she had asked the question, Mary Lou had known exactly what she meant. She had been stuffing envelopes all day, putting the same color photocopy of that twisted child into a crisp white envelope, sticking on a label from their national mailing list, then running it through the postage meter so that the letter would get there as soon as possible.

"Mrs. Riddle," the doctor had said, using the name Mary Lou had given him. "I don't think you understand. You're in your third trimester."

"Yes," she had said, wondering what the problem was.

The doctor had gotten haughty. "Third trimester abortions are illegal in the state of Georgia, Mrs. Riddle." Then he had gone on to tell Mary Lou that he did not think he would have time to see her as a regular patient and suggested someone else across town.

She had kept her hand on the receiver long after putting it down, dumbstruck by the doctor's words. Third trimester abortions were routinely performed all over America. She had over ten thousand pamphlets on her desk talking about cases around the nation where viable fetuses—infants, children, really—had been aborted in the womb, their skulls punctured so they could collapse, their brains sucked out through little vacuum hoses so their parts could be sold to medical researchers. Partial-birth abortions were the scourge of the United States. They were as common as night and day.

After a moment's thought, Mary Lou had locked her office door and sat on the floor behind her desk with the Atlanta phone book. Routinely, the church organized protests where they all piled into the church van and, barring unexpected rain, picketed in front of different abortionaries in Atlanta. They carried signs that said, MURDERERS! and STOP KILLING BABIES! The doctors who worked at the clinics were so ashamed that they could not look at the church members. They kept their heads down, their ears covered as the chanting began. "Save the babies! Kill the doctors!"

Mary Lou had called these places first. When they had all explained to her the same thing that the doctor had earlier said, she had moved on to the Yellow Pages, trying all the gynecologists whose names looked like they might be open to helping her out. She had started with the Jewish doctors, followed by a couple of Polish-sounding ones, then a Hispanic doctor's office where the woman answering the phone barely spoke English yet managed to convey to Mary Lou that not only was what Mary Lou was asking illegal, it was against God's law.

Those names exhausted, Mary Lou had called the obvious places, the clinics with the word *women* in their names, then the "feminist" centers. She had searched the Internet and found numbers for places relatively close by in Tennessee and Alabama, but all of them, down to the last, had told her in no uncertain terms that such a procedure could not be performed. One woman who sounded sympathetic had told her that there were a handful of states that did allow abortions this late in the term, but there had to be clear evidence that the mother's life was in danger.

Mary Lou had considered the phrase, finally coming to the conclusion that her life *was* in danger. She could not continue working at the church as an unwed mother. There was barely enough money to feed William and herself, let alone another child. What's more, babies were always sick, always needing medicine and office visits and God; the thought of it made her feel as if she had swallowed glass. The church was exempt from the law that would have required them to give her health insurance, and the private plan she had looked into years ago was six hundred dollars a month. After paying the mortgage and car insurance so she could drive to work, Mary Lou had barely six hundred dollars left over from her paycheck. The visit to the doctor across town had meant peanut butter and jelly sandwiches for two weeks.

The last phone call she had made to a clinic nearly sent her over the edge. The woman on the other end of the line had actually preached to her, said there were good Christian organizations that would help her through this difficult time. Mary Lou had bitten her tongue to keep from screaming that she was part of that Christian organization and she would be out on the street if they found out.

Instead, she had slammed down the phone, furious. She was not a crack addict, for God's sake. She was not like those women who used abortion for birth control. She wasn't some career-minded whore who did not have time for a child. She loved children. She volunteered at the church nursery the last Sunday of every month. She was a *mother*.

Tears sprang into her eyes, and she found herself putting her wrist to her mouth, sucking it as she had done as a child. The charms on the bracelet chattered against her teeth, and the metallic taste burned her throat. She worked each charm into her mouth, sucking it as if to draw some sort of power. She had always seen the thing as evil, a nasty reminder of her sin, but now she found herself counting off the charms—the locket, the ballet slippers, the lighthouse, the cross—like a rosary.

Mary Lou had been teasing the cross with the tip of her tongue when it had occurred to her that of course these places would refuse to say anything incriminating over the phone. She could be anyone, after all. A state regulator, a detective, a pro-life activist trying to trap them into saying something while the phone call was secretly being recorded. Mary Lou would have to go in and meet them face-to-face. She had no doubt that they would help her then. They would see she was not someone out to trick them but someone who genuinely needed their help.

Stephen had seemed surprised when Mary Lou had asked for a day off. She was given a certain number of sick days every quarter, but at that point in time she had taken no more than a handful of them over the course of her ten years at the church. Still, he had given her a look that said, "Don't make a habit of this."

She could have said something about the affair then, something that would have given her the upper hand, but they both knew she would not do it. The church was all that she had left. It was literally her life. She worked here and worshipped here, and what few remaining friendships she had were through the church. Mary Lou spent more hours in this place than she did in her own home. If the affair got out, it would not be Stephen they blamed. They would all point the finger at her. Even when Brian had left her, cheating on her in such an obvious way that his own mother had called him worthless, people had still blamed Mary Lou. What had she done to make her husband stray? Was she not a good wife? Surely the fault could not lie with Brian. He was a good man who always provided well for his family, right up until the day he left them.

Much the same logic would come to the defense of Stephen. Not only was he a married man with two adorable children, neither of them insisting on being called Pud, he was a man of God, a learned man. Stephen Riddle had attended seminary in Atlanta. He had a doctorate in biblical studies. He was not the type to be hurt by this kind of exposure. Knowing the congregation, Mary Lou suspected they would love him even more for having been through such a trial while still remaining loyal to his family. She could even imagine the sermon he would get out of it. "God tested me, and I failed," he would say, spreading the blame even as he waited for his sins to be washed away.

Regret bit into her every time she thought about the way Stephen had treated her as she stood in his office, asking for what was rightly hers. The groundwork giving him all the power had been laid that very moment, and unsurprisingly he had been a much more skillful engineer. When he had challenged her with a curt "Is that all?" Mary Lou had been unable to do anything but nod. He had then looked down at his desk, at his open Bible, dismissing her with the top of his head.

The clinic in Atlanta was tucked out of the way, but Mary Lou had known how to find it. She had driven there several times, actually, with anywhere from twenty to fifty people, most of them women, holding small coolers of sandwiches and thermoses of coffee, as if they were going on a field trip instead of going to prevent what amounted to murder.

It was murder, after all. There was no way around that. Mary Lou had avoided this basic truth as she drove to Atlanta, a considerable distance. As it had so many times the last few months, her mind had wandered back to her childhood. She had imagined herself sitting in the basement of her uncle Buell's house, listening to the gospel. How simple things had seemed back then, how black and white everything had been. There was nothing that hard work and prayer could not eventually overcome. There was nothing the spirit could not embrace. God never gave you more than you could bear, and even if you broke from the stress, he would build you back and make you stronger. That was his blessing. That was his gift.

Having never been inside the abortion clinic, Mary Lou had been shocked to find how welcoming everyone was. From the outside, the building had seemed gloomy and forbidding, like the death chamber it was. The bars on the windows and the guard at the door certainly lent to this air, as if the women passing through the heavy wooden door were prisoners on death row. Inside, there were cheerful posters of children and animals covering the brightly painted walls. Most surprising were the pamphlets on fertility treatments, adoption, and postnatal care. She had never realized that the clinic was also a gynecological office where women got routine pap smears and received counseling. Most shocking of all, there were pictures of children on a crowded bulletin board by the door, living children delivered by doctors who worked at the clinic.

Looking at the pictures of children, with sudden clarity Mary Lou had realized she could not go through with this. Her stomach had pitched, but not with morning sickness. Instead, what she had felt was fear so intense that her bowels seized as if they had been clamped into a vice.

When the nurse called for "Mrs. Riddle," Mary Lou had bolted out the door, gasping for air as she had walked across the street to her car. Still mindful that she was in Atlanta, Mary Lou had kept her keys in her fist, the sharpest one pointed out in case she was attacked. She was not attacked, but there was a man leaning against her car when she had gotten to it.

He had said, "Good morning, sister," looking her up and down the way a farmer might appraise a cow he was thinking of buying. He was filthy-looking, obviously homeless. His arms were crossed over his chest the way her father's used to be when Mary Lou had done something to displease him.

"Please move," she had said, though there was no threat in her voice. She was exhausted, emotionally spent, and incapable of articulating anything but defeat.

"You come from that place," he had said, indicating the clinic. "I seen you leaving."

"No," she had lied, trying to breathe through her mouth as the wind shifted and she smelled him. "Please move aside or I'll be forced to call the police."

He had given her that look again, the same look she had been getting all of her life: You're worthless. You won't stand up to me because you know you deserve this. William looked at her this way and Brian before him and now Stephen Riddle. She was suddenly fed up and decided then and there that she would not take it from a seedy stranger. Anger had welled up inside her, and without thinking, Mary Lou had lunged at the homeless man, scratching wildly with the key, a startlingly primal yell coming from her mouth as she gouged his face, his neck, his hands, as he held them up in an attempt to protect himself.

The attack was still fresh in her mind as she had driven home to Elawa. She had actually drawn blood. Mary Lou had jumped on the disgusting homeless man with more vengeance than she had ever known, anger washing over her like a flood, eroding her better judgment, leaving nothing in its wake but a loose silt of hatred that would not come clean. Part of her had wanted to kill the man. Most surprising, part of her had been *capable* of killing him. Mary Lou had never even thought it possible to have the strength to defend herself, let alone to be the kind of person someone should have to defend himself against.

When she had looked into the rearview mirror, she had been surprised to see blood on her cheek. This wasn't from the homeless man, she knew. The blood was her own. Mary Lou had scratched herself with the charm bracelet as she drew back the key and aimed for his eyes. Had he not turned away his head in that split second, she would have blinded him. Had he not managed to crawl under the closest car when she had raised her foot to kick him, Mary Lou had no doubt that she would have strangled him with her own hands.

How had that happened? she wondered. What had gotten into her? The poor man had probably wanted nothing more than money, a few dollars for a cup of coffee or whatever rotgut had made him homeless in the first place. What had turned inside her that made Mary Lou Dixon capable of murder?

She had put her wrist to her mouth as she drove, her mind reeling with possibilities. She could taste her blood on the charms, and she had suckled them like a child. There was something bad inside her, something that was turning her into a monster. She had nearly slammed into an eighteen-wheeler in the next lane when she realized what it was. Mary Lou had dropped her hand, shifting the gears and pulling onto the shoulder of the highway to a cacophony of car horns.

The bad thing inside her was Stephen's child. The child was her sin, working against her, trying to break her. The solution was simple: the only way to rid herself of her sin was to dispel the child.

Prayer had come to her like salvation. Around the time William was born, she had lost her connection to God. Being a mother had become the focus of her life, and she had found herself bowing her head only during the difficult times. Chest-rattling coughs from William's room in the middle of the night. High fevers that would not go away. Inexplicable scrapes and bruises. Meningitis at the neighboring preschool.

When Stephen called for silence in the chapel, Mary Lou merely went through the motions, bowing her head and waiting, the possibility of actually convening with God far from her mind as she glanced at her watch, took note of who was wearing what and sitting with whom. Working for the church as she did made everything more about the business than the church, so that when she was sitting in church all she could think was that the upholstery on the deacons' chairs needed mending or that Randall needed to be reminded to dust the baseboard around the stage.

After her sexual encounters with Stephen, even the thought of prayer had seemed blasphemous. Buell had set it in her mind early on that the preacher was the conduit through which God could be reached. Mary Lou could not see Stephen as a conduit. As a matter of fact, whenever she imagined him, all she could see was the time he was behind her, moaning in pleasure, and she had opened her eyes to see what all the excitement was about, only to glimpse her breasts hanging down like the udders of a cow that had not been milked in some time.

Sitting in her car on the highway outside Atlanta, Mary Lou had felt lifted up by the possibility of salvation. She had kept the bracelet in her mouth, nestling the tiny cross on her tongue, praying to God to release her from her sins. As the car shook from passing traffic, she had squeezed her eyes tightly shut and begged Him to break her no more. It had to be possible that God would forgive her without completely ripping her in two. She had prayed for His understanding of her situation, and when prayer failed, she had prayed for the strength to do what she knew she had to do.

With sudden clarity, she had understood what she needed to do. The only way to redeem herself was death. As she had merged back onto the highway, Mary Lou had justified the act, knowing William would be happier living with his father. Brian certainly would be ecstatic to be rid of her, and Stephen was desperately looking for a way to get Mary Lou out of the church office and out of his life. She was to them a constant reminder of their disappointments. She was not a good wife, a good mother, or even a particularly good lover.

What she had prayed for as she drove was wisdom in the act. Her hands had begun to sweat as she had considered driving off one of the many bridges between Atlanta and Elawa, and she had reasoned that ramming her car into another vehicle would have been incredibly selfish.

Over the course of the next few days, she had read up on suicide, considering her options the same way she consulted *Consumer's Digest* back in the fall to see which was the better refrigerator to buy. The best course of action, she had decided, would be to use a gun, but she did not have enough money to buy one, and besides, buying a gun in Elawa was almost as difficult as getting an abortion. They wanted fingerprints. There was a waiting period. There were so many obstacles, as a matter of fact, that Mary Lou had begun to wonder if the people writing all these pamphlets about America going to hell in a handbasket were aware that the things they were warning about were actually harder to do than you'd think.

Pills were an obvious means to her end, but she did not know where to get the right kind and was afraid that if she asked William he would know, maybe even give her some of his own. Even if she did know where to get pills, surely illegal drugs cost a lot of money, and after two doctor's visits—the clinic had demanded payment up front—Mary Lou had none. She had Valium from the time when Brian divorced her, but there were only ten left, hardly enough to accomplish the act. There was no garage to her house or she would have left the car running, letting the exhaust do the trick. Passing away in her sleep seemed like the easiest way out, but perhaps that was why it was the hardest to actually accomplish.

Cutting her wrists seemed like a good idea for about an hour's time, but then she had thought about William finding her, and the blood he would see. It wasn't so much that she had worried he would be emotionally scarred from finding his mother dead in a pool of her own blood, but that he might like it, and that by killing herself in such a way she was creating the next Ted Bundy or Jeffrey Dahmer.

Again Mary Lou had suckled the cross on the bracelet and again she had prayed to God that He would show her how to kill herself. Oddly enough, His sign had come in the form of a flier. Exactly seven days had passed since she had nearly killed the homeless man, and Mary Lou was not yet back to herself. Normally she threw out junk mail, but for some reason she had started reading everything that came through the church's post office box as if her life depended on it.

She had scanned the offers from *Reader's Digest* and American Clearinghouse from start to finish, and entered the youth minister in a sweepstakes for a million-dollar prize (even knowing that should he win the church would never see a penny of it). Then she had come across a bright pink flier folded in on itself. The color should have alerted Mary Lou, but she was beyond alerts since returning from Atlanta. Absently, she opened the folded sheet of paper, her eyes immediately going to the image of an unwound clothes hanger, the tip blackened with little drops of blood around it because of course these pro-abortion organizations could not afford full-color copies like the church could. The headline asked, "Do you want women to go back to back-alley abortions?"

Mary Lou had opened her mouth, the charm dropping out and slapping wetly against her chin. She knew His answer. She knew what had to be done.

The startling part of the whole procedure was the pain. Something had made Mary Lou think that she was beyond pain, but such was the intensity that she had passed out during the middle of it. How long she was out, she had no idea. It was dark outside when she had finally come to, and Mary Lou did not think to look at the clock. Like a splinter, it was more painful taking out the clothes hanger than when she had jammed it in. There was blood, but not as much as Mary Lou had anticipated. It was dark and viscous, not at all like the blood on television and therefore not as real.

She had cramped the whole night but still did not pass the child. What she wanted above all was sleep, and though it had occurred to her that perhaps she had succeeded in killing herself now that God wanted her to live, Mary Lou was fine with this. All she wanted in the world, all she needed in the world, was sleep. She needed peace.

A week had passed, and her sick days were up. If William noticed his mother was unwell, he said nothing. She had tracked his comings and goings by the music being played at full blast in his room. For all she knew, the stereo was on a timer. There was no telling what her son was up to.

She had gone back to the church because she had to, not because she could. There was a lesson in doing things out of duty, she knew, but the first day back had been so difficult that Mary Lou had actually considered her suicide plans again. She had felt an infection burning in her like a smoldering fire. She had not bled enough. She had not seen fingers or toes in the toilet. There should have been something by now, and if there wasn't, that could only mean that it was still up there, still festering inside of her.

What could she do? A physician at the hospital would know instantly what had happened. She could not go to her regular doctor because he was a deacon at the church. The only thing she could think to do was to call his office and tell them she had a sinus infection but did not have time to come in for an appointment. Thankfully, the nurse had called in some antibiotics without asking any more questions. Mary Lou was not certain that the pills were working, though. Antibiotics were tricky. There were certain kinds for certain infections. Was a sinus infection the same as the infection that boiled in her lower regions? Was this slow, rotting sickness the thing that would finally kill her? Had she gone through all of this, dishonored her family, her God, coveted her neighbor, committed mortal sins, all for nothing?

She had longed to pray, to talk to God and ask again for His guidance, but she could not bring her mind to do it. Even when she had taken the bracelet into her mouth as a sacrament, thoughts refused to form. She had contemplated speaking aloud to the Lord, confessing her predicament, but what if someone heard? What if Stephen Riddle overheard her confession and renounced her from the pulpit? What if the entire church found out what she had done and cast her out? She would lose what friends she had and William would be taken away from her. She would have nothing left, nothing, not even a place to worship.

Slowly she had felt herself begin to fade from the life she had known. After years of unsuccessful dieting, she had suddenly lost weight. Food did not appeal. She no longer read, no longer watched television. When the school suspended William, she had hardly had the strength to shrug. When Brian had told her he would not be able to pay his half of the mortgage, she had simply hung up the phone without another word.

"Ma'am?" Jasper called from the doorway, and Mary Lou realized she had let herself begin to fade yet again. She turned away from the window, her fingers going to the charm bracelet as she looked at the black man. He stood at the edge of the chapel, and if he'd had a hat it would have been in his mauled hands. She wondered if he was uncomfortable being in a church. He certainly seemed like it, his toes just at the edge of the carpet, not quite crossing back into the room.

"Coming," she said, clasping the bracelet as she walked toward him. He looked like he might offer her his hand when she reached the foyer, but Mary Lou crossed her arms over her chest, making it clear she did not need help. She could tell from the expression on his contorted face that she did not look well. She had chills despite the heat in the foyer, and the back of her legs felt prickly, like a thousand needles stinging her skin at the same time.

They crossed the parking lot, the heat enveloping them like a blanket. The sun was so intense that it appeared to be black against the blue afternoon sky. Mary Lou kept her eyes on the sawhorses, unable to make out the pattern of the cross. She stumbled, grabbing on to Jasper so she would not fall. His skin was warm under the long sleeves, and she could feel the sinew of his damaged arm, the muscles contracting as he tried to support her. She fell to her knees anyway, her arms flailing out beside her, grasping at the dry air. The pain in her belly was too much now, and she pitched forward, the hot asphalt slapping her face, penetrating her clothes like hellfire.

A racking pain overcame her, as if something was living inside her belly, clawing its way out. She grasped her stomach, screaming in agony, closing her eyes against the black hole that was the sun as her bowels seized and her womb contracted, expelling her sin onto the asphalt. The blood that she had not bled before seeped out between her legs like honey, and she could feel the heavy liquid and tissue dripping down her thighs like great chunks of wet clay.

Mary Lou rolled onto her back and the Mexicans stepped back quickly, as if acid had been poured at their feet. The hand she put over her mouth was covered in her own blood and something else she could not name. The ground was rich with it, a slick black oil. She looked to find the sun in the sky, to stare at the black dot until the image was forever burned into her eyes, but her vision was blocked by the enormous arm of the cross. They had fixed it, a small seam showing where the cross had been rejoined. The point of fracture had been healed like a fresh wound, the scar toughening the wood, making it stronger.

"Holy mother," one of the Mexicans said, and she felt more liquid explode between her legs.

Pain shot through Mary Lou again, a knife cutting from the inside. The throbbing between her legs seized her, and she screamed so loud that her throat ached as if she were being choked. Inch by inch, she felt her flesh ripping apart, being clawed open from the inside.

"Steady," Jasper said, his ugly hands reaching between her legs. She was bared to them all, her dress up above her waist, wet panties around her knees. She could see a figure standing in the window of the chapel. Was it Stephen? Was he watching this, waiting to see what happened? She called out to him, but the figure moved away.

"It's okay," Jasper soothed, his mauled hands inside her now, trying to pull something out. She felt a final rip, then just as suddenly a dull ache replaced the pain, blood flowing freely with the obstruction removed.

"Lord Jesus," the Mexicans prayed, speaking English as if for her benefit. They took off their hats and bowed their heads.

Jasper held up a tiny bundle of legs and arms, all attached to a torso that moved up and down in rapid beats as the child screamed at the top of his lungs. His cries were an accusation, a condemnation to the whore who had brought him into this world.

One of the Mexicans kneeled beside Mary Lou, holding out a dirty towel for the baby. He gently cradled the baby boy in his arms, cooing.

Jasper stayed beside her, rummaging through his tool box. She saw him take out an old, beat-up pocketknife, and he used this to cut through the cord that attached Mary Lou to the child. One of the Mexicans caught the cord, tying it with a piece of twine. Jasper did not bother with the end that was connected to Mary Lou. She could tell from the look in his eyes that there was nothing that could stop the flow. Her spirit was being drawn out from between her legs, and anything that made to slow it down would only be postponing the inevitable.

Jasper's big black hand grasped hers, his lips moving almost imperceptibly. The skin on his face was tighter than she had ever noticed, and the discoloration more prominent than before. Her eyes were again drawn to his unnaturally colored lips as he closed his eyes and began to whisper. She strained to hear what he was saying and was so surprised by his words that for just a moment she forgot the pain. A sudden lightness filled her chest, and she felt the power of Jasper's words flow through her like a cleansing balm. The drumbeat of her blood pounding in her ears began to recede. As she drew breath, she drew in the man's words, holding them in her lungs until they felt full enough to carry her away.

"Lord God," Jasper said through his beautiful pink lips. "Please welcome this woman into Your house. Shine Your light down upon her to lead the way. Help her see Your power and glory."

Mary Lou tried to thank him even as she felt herself slip away. She wanted to let Jasper know that his words had brought her peace. The child continued to scream, and she reached her hand out to him, the gold bracelet on her wrist scraping across the asphalt. The sun caught the chain, illuminating where the link had been broken and mended like new.

"For him," she said. She was broken so the child could be strong.

"For him," Jasper repeated, his bloody hands working the clasp of the bracelet.

"No," she said, but her voice was gone now, the word only spoken in her head.

Jasper removed the bracelet and placed it in the blanket beside the boy, telling Mary Lou, "He'll remember his mother. He'll always have this."

"No," she tried again, then she looked into her son's face and it did not matter. Nothing mattered but the fact that her son had lived. He had fought for his life, challenged the will of his mother to honor the will of God.

Yes, she thought. He would be strong because the bracelet would teach him the lessons that had broken those before him. The many charms would forever tell their stories: the key to vanity, the gluttony of the monkey, the greed of the dollar sign, the envious ballerina, the angry goblin, the lustful tiger, and even the cross, which Mary Lou suddenly understood represented her own indolence.

As her fingers slipped from Jasper Goode's hand, Mary Lou felt herself smile. She looked up at the heavens, at the black sun. The child would be good. Like Jesus, he would wash away her sins. He would be strong where his mother was not. He would realize the gift of her death, that only through Mary Lou's sacrifice could he be born, and born again. He would be strong because of her weakness. One day, he would look at the bracelet and know her story.

One day, he would understand the blessing of brokenness.

BIOGRAPHIES

Karin Slaughter is the *New York Times* and #1 internationally bestselling author of fourteen thrillers, including *Cop Town, Unseen, Criminal, Fallen, Broken, Undone, Fractured, Beyond Reach, Triptych, Faithless,* and the e-original short stories "Snatched," "Busted," and "Go Deep." She is a native of Georgia.

Born in Dublin in 1969 and now living in Canada, **Emma Donoghue** is an award-winning novelist, dramatist, and screenwriter. She is best known for her novel *Room,* which was a finalist for the Man Booker Prize and has sold over two million copies; Donoghue also wrote the film adaptation due out at the end of 2015. Her other books include *Astray, The Sealed Letter, Life Mask,* and *Slammerkin,* as well as her first literary mystery, *Frog Music.*

Peter Robinson's award-winning Inspector Banks novels have been named "a Best Book of the Year" by *Publishers Weekly,* "a Notable Book" by the *New York Times,* and "a Page Turner of the Week" by *People.* Robinson was born and brought up in Yorkshire, and now divides his time between North America and the UK.

Actress and writer **Fidelis Morgan's** TV appearances include *Jeeves and Wooster* and *As Time Goes By.* She appears in Alan Rickman's 2015 film *A Little Chaos.* Her plays *Pamela* and *Hangover Square* won her a Most Promising Playwriting nomination. She has written nineteen books including the groundbreaking *The Female Wits,* biographies of charismatic women from the seventeenth and eighteenth centuries, and six novels including the historical mystery series featuring the countess Ashby de la Zouche. Her latest novel is *The Murder Quadrille.* She was the 2014 Granada Artist-in-Residence at the University of California.

www.fidelismorgan.com

Internationally bestselling author **Lynda La Plante** has created some of the best known crime dramas on television, such as *Trial and Retribution* and *Prime Suspect* in which Helen Mirren played the iconic role of DCI Jane Tennison. Her work has earned her the Dennis Potter Award from BAFTA and the Edgar Allen Poe Writer's Award. Lynda is a member of the Crime Thriller Awards Hall of Fame and is the only layperson to become a fellow of the Forensic Science Society. Lynda was also awarded a CBE in the Queen's Birthday Honors List 2008 for services to Literature, Drama and to Charity. She is currently writing the prequel to *Prime Suspect, Tennison,* which will be published in 2015.

www.lyndalaplante.com

Lee Child is the author of nineteen *New York Times* bestselling Jack Reacher thrillers, ten of which have reached the #1 position. All have been optioned for major motion pictures; the first, *Jack Reacher,* was based on *One Shot.* Foreign rights in the Reacher series have sold in almost 100 territories. A native of England and a former television director, Lee Child lives in New York City.

Mark Billingham is one of the UK's most acclaimed and popular crime writers whose series of novels featuring DI Tom Thorne has twice won him the Crime Novel of the Year award. His stand-alone thriller *In the Dark* was chosen as one of the twelve best books of the year by the *Times,* and his debut novel, *Sleepyhead,* was chosen by the *Sunday Times* as one of the 100 books that had shaped the 2000s.

A television series based on the Thorne novels starred David Morrissey as Tom Thorne and adaptations of both *In the Dark* and *Rush of Blood* are currently in development with the BBC.

Mark Billingham's latest novel is *Time of Death.*

www.markbillingham.com

Denise Mina left school at sixteen and worked as an auxiliary nurse in a geriatric and terminal care home and then as a waitress, and after a sabbatical concentrating on meat-processing factory work she went to night classes and passed exams to get into law school, hoping to make the world a better place. Four years later she left law school, heavy of heart, and misused a PhD grant to write her first novel, *Garnethill,* which won the CWA John Creasy Gold Dagger. *Exile* and *Resolution* completed the trilogy, and *Sanctum*, her first stand-alone novel, followed shortly afterward. She was knackered and tired of changing out of her pajamas and doing her hair every day, so she stayed at home to write *The Field of Blood*, which is the first of a new series and, frankly, proved a bastard to write.

John Harvey is best known as a writer of crime fiction whose work has been translated into more than twenty languages. He is also a dramatist and poet, sometime publisher, and occasional broadcaster. The first of his twelve Charlie Resnick novels, *Lonely Hearts,* was named by the *Times* as one of the 100 Best Crime Novels of the Century. The last century, that is. The recipient of honorary doctorates from the Universities of Nottingham and Hertfordshire, in 2007 he was awarded the British Crime Writers' Association Cartier Diamond Dagger for sustained excellence in crime writing.

www.mellotone.co.uk

Kelley Armstrong is the #1 *New York Times* bestselling author of the Otherworld series, as well as the Darkest Powers and Darkness Rising trilogies for young adults and the Nadia Stafford series. She lives in Ontario, Canada.

Tomas Ross is Holland's bestselling author of crime novels. Three of his novels received the most prestigious Dutch crime award De Gouden Strop (The Golden Noose Award): Bêta (*Beta*) in 1987, *Koerier voor Sarajevo* (*Messenger to Sarajevo*) in 1997, and *De zesde mei* (*The Sixth of May*) in 2003. He is also the writer of the prestigious, award-winning television series *Wij Alexander* (*We, Alexander*). His script *In belang van de staat* (*In the Interest of the State*) won the Golden Calf Award in 1997 for best television screenplay.

John Connolly is the author of *The Wrath of Angels, The Burning Soul, The Book of Lost Things,* and *Bad Men,* among many others. He is a regular contributor to the *Irish Times* and lives in Dublin, Ireland. For more information, see his website at JohnConnollyBooks.com, or follow him on Twitter @JConnollyBooks.

A finalist for both the Edgar and the Anthony Award, **Jane Haddam** is best known for her mysteries featuring Gregor Demarkian. She lives in Litchfield County, Connecticut.

Since her debut in 1997, **Laura Lippman** has been heralded for her thoughtful, timely crime novels set in her beloved hometown of Baltimore. She is the author of twenty works of fiction, including eleven Tess Monaghan mysteries. She lives in Baltimore, New Orleans, and New York City with her family.

Peter Moore Smith lived in Panama, Nebraska, Alaska, North Carolina, New York, New Jersey, and Virginia—all before he was twelve. He then spent eight years in Europe before attending college. His short fiction has appeared in several publications, and his short story "Oblivion, Nebraska" won the 2002 Pushcart Prize. He is also the author of *Raveling* and is currently directing a feature film based on his screenplay *Forgetting the Girl.*

Jerrilyn Farmer is the #1 *Los Angeles Times* bestselling author of the Madeline Bean mystery series, and the winner of numerous mystery writing awards. While her story in *Like a Charm* taps into her dark side, Jerrilyn's latest novel, *Murder at the Academy Awards,* was cowritten with beloved comedienne Joan Rivers. Jerrilyn teaches mystery writing at UCLA Extension's Writers' Program.

Copyright Notices